THE BEST: Tom Clancy

THE BEAR AND THE DRAGON

President Jack Ryan faces a world crisis unlike any he has ever known . . .

"INTOXICATING . . . A JUGGERNAUT."

—*Publishers Weekly* (starred review)

RAINBOW SIX

Clancy's shocking story of international terrorism—closer to reality than any government would care to admit . . .

"GRIPPING . . . BOLT-ACTION MAYHEM."

—*People*

EXECUTIVE ORDERS

Jack Ryan has always been a soldier. Now he's giving the orders.

"AN ENORMOUS, ACTION-PACKED, HEAT-SEEKING MISSILE OF A TOM CLANCY NOVEL."

—*The Seattle Times*

DEBT OF HONOR

It begins with the murder of an American woman in the back streets of Tokyo. It ends in war . . .

"A SHOCKER CLIMAX SO PLAUSIBLE YOU'LL WONDER WHY IT HASN'T YET HAPPENED!"

—*Entertainment Weekly*

continued . . .

THE HUNT FOR RED OCTOBER

The smash bestseller that launched Clancy's career—the incredible search for a Soviet defector and the nuclear submarine he commands . . .

"BREATHLESSLY EXCITING!" —*The Washington Post*

RED STORM RISING

The ultimate scenario for World War III—the final battle for global control . . .

"THE ULTIMATE WAR GAME . . . BRILLIANT!"
—*Newsweek*

PATRIOT GAMES

CIA analyst Jack Ryan stops an assassination—and incurs the wrath of Irish terrorists . . .

"A HIGH PITCH OF EXCITEMENT!"
—*The Wall Street Journal*

THE CARDINAL OF THE KREMLIN

The superpowers race for the ultimate Star Wars missile defense system . . .

"*CARDINAL* EXCITES, ILLUMINATES . . . A REAL PAGE-TURNER!" —*Los Angeles Daily News*

CLEAR AND PRESENT DANGER

The killing of three U.S. officials in Colombia ignites the American government's explosive, and top secret, response . . .

"A CRACKLING GOOD YARN!" —*The Washington Post*

THE SUM OF ALL FEARS

The disappearance of an Israeli nuclear weapon threatens the balance of power in the Middle East—and around the world . . .

"CLANCY AT HIS BEST . . . NOT TO BE MISSED!"
—*The Dallas Morning News*

WITHOUT REMORSE

The Clancy epic fans have been waiting for. His code name is Mr. Clark. And his work for the CIA is brilliant, cold-blooded, and efficient . . . but who is he really?

"HIGHLY ENTERTAINING!" —*The Wall Street Journal*

Tom Clancy's
Op-Center

LINE
OF
CONTROL

Created by
Tom Clancy and Steve Pieczenik

written by
Jeff Rovin

B

BERKLEY BOOKS, NEW YORK

This is a work of fiction. Names, characters, places, and incidents are either the product of the author's imagination or are used fictitiously, and any resemblance to actual persons, living or dead, business establishments, events, or locales is entirely coincidental.

TOM CLANCY'S OP-CENTER: LINE OF CONTROL

A Berkley Book / published by arrangement with
Jack Ryan Limited Partnership and S & R Literary, Inc.

PRINTING HISTORY
Berkley edition / June 2001

All rights reserved.
Copyright © 2001 by Jack Ryan Limited Partnership and
S & R Literary, Inc.
This book, or parts thereof, may not be reproduced in
any form without permission.
For information address: The Berkley Publishing Group,
a division of Penguin Putnam Inc.,
375 Hudson Street, New York, New York 10014.

The Penguin Putnam Inc. World Wide Web site address is
http://www.penguinputnam.com

ISBN: 0-425-18005-0

BERKLEY®
Berkley Books are published by The Berkley Publishing Group,
a division of Penguin Putnam Inc.,
375 Hudson Street, New York, New York 10014.
BERKLEY and the "B" design
are trademarks belonging to Penguin Putnam Inc.

PRINTED IN THE UNITED STATES OF AMERICA

10   9   8   7   6   5   4   3   2

Acknowledgments

We would like to acknowledge the assistance of Martin H. Greenberg, Larry Segriff, Robert Youdelman, Esq., Tom Mallon, Esq., and the wonderful people at Penguin Putnam Inc., including Phyllis Grann, David Shanks, and Tom Colgan. As always, we would like to thank Robert Gottlieb, without whom this book would never have been conceived. But most important, it is for you, our readers, to determine how successful our collective endeavor has been.

—Tom Clancy and Steve Pieczenik

PROLOGUE

Siachin Base 3, Kashmir
Wednesday, 5:42 A.M.

Major Dev Puri could not sleep. He had not yet gotten used to the flimsy cots the Indian army used in the field. Or the thin air in the mountains. Or the quiet. Outside his former barracks in Udhampur there were always the sounds of trucks and automobiles, of soldiers and activity. Here, the quiet reminded him of a hospital. Or a morgue.

Instead, he put on his olive green uniform and red turban. Puri left his tent and walked over to the front-line trenches. There, he looked out as the rich morning sun rose behind him. He watched as a brilliant orange glow crept through the valley and settled slowly across the flat, deserted demilitarized zone. It was the flimsiest of barriers in the most dangerous place on earth.

Here in the Himalayan foothills of Kashmir, human life was always in jeopardy. It was routinely threatened by the extreme weather conditions and rugged terrain. In the warmer, lower elevations it was at risk whenever one failed to spot a lethal king cobra or naja naja, the Indian cobra, hiding in the underbrush. It was endangered whenever one was an instant too late swatting a disease-carrying mosquito or venomous brown widow spider in time. Life was in even greater peril a few miles to the north, on the brutal Siachin Glacier. There was barely enough air to support life on the steep, blinding-white hills. Avalanches and subzero temperatures were a daily danger to foot patrols.

Yet the natural hazards were not what made this the most dangerous spot on the planet. All of those dangers were nothing compared to how humans threatened each other here. Those threats were not dependent on the time of day or the season of the year. They were constant, every minute of every hour of every day for nearly the past sixty years.

Puri stood on an aluminum ladder in a trench with corrugated tin walls. Directly in front of him were five-foot-high sandbags protected by razor wire strung tightly above them from iron posts. To the right, about thirty feet away, was a small sentry post, a wooden shelter erected behind the sandbags. There was hemp netting on top with camouflage greenery overhead. To the right, forty feet away, was another watch post.

One hundred and twenty yards in front of him, due west, was a nearly identical Pakistan trench.

With deliberate slowness, the officer removed a pouch of ghutka, chewable tobacco, from his pants pocket. Sudden moves were discouraged out here where they might be noticed and misinterpreted as reaching for a weapon. He unfolded the packet and pushed a small wad in his cheek. Soldiers were encouraged not to smoke, since a lighted cigarette could give away the position of a scout or patrol.

As Puri chewed the tobacco he watched squadrons of black flies begin their own morning patrol. They were searching for fecal matter left by red squirrels, goatlike markhors, and other herbivores that woke and fed before dawn. It was early winter now. Puri had heard that in the summer the insects were so thick they seemed like clouds of smoke drifting low over the rocks and scrub.

The major wondered if he would be alive to see them. During some weeks thousands of men on both sides were killed. That was inevitable with more than one million fanatic soldiers facing one another across an extremely narrow, two-hundred-mile-long "line of control." Major Puri could see some of those soldiers now, across the sandy stretch between the trenches. Their mouths were covered with black muslin scarves to protect them against the westward-blowing winds. But the eyes in their wind-burned faces blazed with hatred that had been sparked back in the eighth century. That was when Hindus and Muslims first clashed in this region. The ancient farmers and merchants took up arms and fought about trade routes, land and water rights, and ideology. The struggle became even more fierce in 1947 when Great Britain abandoned its empire on the subcontinent. The British gave the rival Hindus and Muslims the nations of India and Pakistan to call their own. That partition also gave India control over the Muslim-dominated region of Kashmir. Since that time the Pakistans have regarded the Indians as an occupying force in Kashmir. Warfare has been almost constant as the two sides struggled over what became the symbolic heart of the conflict.

And I am in the heart of the heart, Puri thought.

Base 3 was a potential flashpoint, the fortified zone nearest both Pakistan and China. It was ironic, the career soldier told himself. This "heart" looked exactly like Dabhoi, the small town where he had grown up at the foot of the Satpura Range in central India. Dabhoi had no real value except to the natives, who were mostly tradesmen, and to those trying to get to the city of Broach on the Bay of Cambay. That was where they could buy fish cheap. It was disturbing how hate rather than cooperation made one place more valuable than another. Instead of trying to expand what they had in common they were trying to destroy what was uncommon.

The officer stared out at the cease-fire zone. Lining the sandbags were orange binoculars mounted on small iron poles. That was the only thing the Indians and Pakistans had ever agreed on: coloring the binoculars so they would not be mistaken for guns. But Puri did not need them here. The brilliant sun was rising behind him. He could clearly see the dark faces of the Pakistans behind their cinderblock barricades. The faces looked just like Indian faces except that they were on the wrong side of the line of control.

Puri made a point of breathing evenly. The line of control was a strip of land so narrow in places that cold breath was visible from sentries on both sides. And being visible, the puffs of breath could tell guards on either side if their counterparts were anxious and breathing rapidly or asleep and breathing slowly. There, a wrong word whispered to a fellow soldier and overheard by the other side could break the fragile truce. A hammer hitting a nail had to be muffled with cloth lest it be mistaken for a gunshot and trigger return rifle fire, then artillery, then nuclear weapons. That exchange could happen so fast that the heavily barricaded bases would be vaporized even before the echoes of the first guns had died in the towering mountain passageways.

Mentally and physically, it was such a trying and unforgiving environment that any officer who successfully completed a one-year tour of duty was automatically eligible for a desk job in a "safe zone" like Calcutta or New Delhi. That was what the forty-one-year-old Puri was working toward. Three months before, he had been transferred from the army's HQ Northern Command where he trained border patrols. Nine more months of running this small base, of "kiting with tripwire," as his predecessor had put it, and he could live comfortably for the rest of his life. Indulge his passion for going out on anthropological digs. He loved learning more about the history of his people. The Indus Valley civilization was over 4,500 years old. Back then the Pkitania and Indian people were one. There was a thousand years of peace. That was before religion came to the region.

Major Puri chewed his tobacco. He smelled the brewed tea coming from the mess tent. It was time for breakfast, after which he would join his men for the morning briefing. He took another moment to savor the morning. It was not that a new day brought new hope. All it meant was that the night had passed without a confrontation.

Puri turned and stepped down the stairs. He did not imagine that there would be very many mornings like this in the weeks ahead. If the rumors from his friends at HQ were true, the powder keg was about to get a new fuse.

A very short, very hot fuse.

ONE

Washington, D.C.
Wednesday, 5:56 A.M.

The air was unseasonably chilly. Thick, charcoal-gray clouds hung low over Andrews Air Force Base. But in spite of the dreary weather Mike Rodgers felt terrific.

The forty-seven-year-old two-star general left his black 1970 Mustang in the officers' parking lot. Stepping briskly, he crossed the neatly manicured lawn to the Op-Center offices. Rodgers's light brown eyes had a sparkle that almost made them appear golden. He was still humming the last tune he had been listening to on the portable CD player. It was Victoria Bundonis's recording of the 1950s David Seville ditty "Witch Doctor." The young singer's low, torchy take on "Oo-ee-oo-ah-ah" was always an invigorating way to start the day. Usually, when he crossed the grass here, he was in a different frame of mind. This early, dew would dampen his polished shoes as they sank into the soft soil. His neatly pressed uniform and his short, graying black hair would ripple in the strong breeze. But Rodgers was usually oblivious to the earth, wind, and water—three of the four ancient elements. He was only aware of the fourth element, fire. That was because it was bottled and capped inside the man himself. He carried it carefully as though it were nitroglycerin. One sudden move and he would blow.

But not today.

There was a young guard standing in a bullet-proof glass booth just inside the door. He saluted smartly as Rodgers entered.

"Good morning, sir," the sentry said.

"Good morning," Rodgers replied. " 'Wolverine.' "

That was Rodgers's personal password for the day. It was left on his GovNet e-mail pager the night before by Op-Center's internal security chief, Jenkin Wynne. If the password did not match what the guard had on his computer Rodgers would not have been allowed to enter.

"Thank you, sir," the guard said and saluted again. He pressed a button and the door clicked open. Rodgers entered.

There was a single elevator directly ahead. As Rodgers walked toward it he wondered how old the airman first class was. Twenty-two? Twenty-three? A few months ago Rodgers would have given his rank, his experiences, everything he owned or knew to be back where this young sentry was. Healthy and sharp, with all his options spread before him. That was after Rodgers had disastrously field-tested the Regional Op-Center. The mobile, hi-tech facility had been seized in the Middle East. Rodgers and his personnel were imprisoned and tortured. Upon the team's release, Senator Barbara Fox and the Congressional Intelligence Oversight Committee rethought the ROC program. The watchdog group felt that having a U.S. intelligence base working openly on foreign soil was provocative rather than a deterrent. Because the ROC had been Rodgers's responsibility he felt as though he'd let Op-Center down. He also felt as though he had blown his last, best chance to get back into the field.

Rodgers was wrong. The United States needed intelligence on the nuclear situation in Kashmir. Specifically, whether Pakistan had deployed warheads deep in the mountains of the region. Indian operatives could not go into the field. If the Pakistanis found them it might trigger the war the United States was hoping to avoid. An American unit would have some wiggle room. Especially if they could prove that they were bringing intelligence about Indian nuclear capabilities to Pakistan, intelligence that a National Security Agency liaison would be giving Rodgers in the town of Srinagar. Of course, the Indian military would not know he had that. It was all a big, dangerous game of three-card monte. All the dealer had to do was remember where all the cards were and never get busted.

Rodgers entered the small, brightly lit elevator and rode it to the basement level.

Op-Center—officially the National Crisis Management Center—was housed in a two-story building located near the Naval Reserve flight line. During the Cold War the nondescript, ivory-colored building was a staging area for crack flight crews. In the event of a nuclear attack their job would have been to evacuate key officials from Washington, D.C. With the fall of the Soviet Union and the downsizing of the air force's NuRRDs—nuclear rapid-response divisions—the building was given to the newly commissioned NCMC.

The upstairs offices were for nonclassified operations such as news monitoring, finance, and human resources. The basement was where Hood, Rodgers, Intelligence Chief Bob Herbert, and the rest of the intelligence-gathering and -processing personnel worked.

Rodgers reached the underground level. He walked through the cubicles in the center to his office. He retrieved his old leather briefcase from under the desk. He packed his laptop and began collecting the diskettes he would need for his journey. The files contained intelligence reports from India and Pakistan, maps of Kashmir, and the names of contacts as well as safe houses throughout the region. As he packed the tools of his trade Rodgers felt almost like he did as a kid growing up in Hartford, Connecticut. Hartford endured fierce winter storms. But they were damp storms that brought packing snow. Before putting on his snow suit Rodgers would get his bucket, rope, spade, and swimming goggles and toss them into his school gym bag. His mother insisted on the goggles. She knew she could not prevent her son from fighting but she did not want him getting hit by a snowball and losing an eye. Once outside, while all the other kids were building snow forts, Rodgers would climb a tree and build a snow tree house on a piece of plywood. No one ever expected that. A rain of snowballs from a thick branch.

After Rodgers had his briefcase packed he would head to the "Gulf cart" parked at the back door. That was what the military had christened the motorized carts that had shuttled officers from meeting to meeting during both Desert Shield and Desert Storm. The Pentagon bought thousands of them just before what turned out to be the last gasp of face-to-face strategy meetings before secure video-conferencing was created. After that, the obsolete carts had been distributed to bases around the country as Christmas presents to senior officers.

The Gulf cart would not have far to travel. A C-130 Hercules was parked just a quarter of a mile away, in the holding area of the airstrip that passed directly behind the NCMC building. In slightly under an hour the hundred-foot-long transport would begin a NATO supply trek that would secretly ferry Rodgers and his Striker unit from Andrews to the Royal Air Force Alconbury station in Great Britain to a NATO base outside Ankara, Turkey. There, the team would be met by an Indian Air Force AN-12 transport, part of the Himalayan Eagles squadron. They would be flown to the high-altitude base at Chushul near the Chinese border and then choppered to Srinagar to meet their contact. It would be a long and difficult journey lasting just over twenty-four hours. And there would be no time to rest when they reached India. The team had to be ready to go as soon as they touched down.

But that was fine with Mike Rodgers. He had been "ready to go" for years. He had never wanted to be second-in-command of anything. During the Spanish-American War, his great-great-grandfather Captain Malachai T. Rodgers went from leading a unit to serving under upstart Lt. Colonel Teddy Roosevelt. As Captain Rodgers wrote to Mrs. Rodgers at the time, "There is nothing better than running things. And there is nothing worse than being a runner-up, even if that happens to be under a gentleman you respect."

Malachai Rodgers was right. The only reason Mike Rodgers had taken the deputy director's position was because he never expected Paul Hood to stay at Op-Center. Rodgers assumed that the former Los Angeles mayor was a politician at heart who had eyes on the Senate or the White House. Rodgers was wrong. The general hit another big bump in the road when Hood resigned from Op-Center to spend more time with his family. Rodgers thought Op-Center would finally be his. But Paul and Sharon Kent Hood weren't able to fix what was wrong with their marriage. They separated and Hood came back to Op-Center. Rodgers went back to being number two.

Rodgers needed to command. A few weeks before, he and Hood had ended a hostage siege at the United Nations. Rodgers had directed that operation. That reminded him of how much he enjoyed risking everything on his ability to outthink and outperform an adversary. Doing it safely from behind a desk just was not the same thing.

Rodgers turned to the open door a moment before Bob Herbert arrived. Op-Center's number three man was always announced by the low purr of his motorized wheelchair.

"Good morning," Herbert said as he swung into view.

"Good morning, Bob," Rodgers replied.

"Mind if I come in?"

"Not at all," Rodgers told him.

Herbert swung the wheelchair into the office. The balding, thirty-nine-year-old intelligence genius had lost the use of his legs in the Beirut embassy bombing in 1983. The terrorist attack had also taken the life of Herbert's beloved wife. Op-Center's computer wizard Matt Stoll had helped design this state-of-the-art wheelchair. It included a computer that folded into the armrest and a small satellite dish that opened from a box attached to the back of the chair.

"I just wanted to wish you good luck," Herbert said.

"Thanks," Rodgers replied.

"Also, Paul asked if you would pop in before you left," Herbet said. "He's on the phone with Senator Fox and didn't want to miss you."

Rodgers glanced at his watch. "The senator is up early. Any particular reason?"

"Not that I know of, though Paul didn't look happy," Herbert said. "Could be more fallout over the UN attack."

If that were true then there was an advantage to being the number two man, Rodgers thought. He did not have to put up with that bullshit. They had absolutely done the right thing at the United Nations. They had saved the hostages and killed the bad guys.

"They're probably going to beat us up until the secretary-general cries uncle," Rodgers said.

"Senator Fox has gotten good at that," Herbert said. "She slaps your back real hard and tells your enemies it's a lashing. Tells your friends it's a pat on the back. Only you know which it is. Anyway, Paul will deal with that," Herbert went on. He extended his hand. "I just wanted to wish you well. That's a remote, hostile region you're heading into."

Rodgers clasped Herbert's hand and grinned. "I know. But I'm a remote, hostile guy. Kashmir and I will get along fine."

Rodgers went to withdraw his hand. Herbert held it.

"There's something else," Herbert said.

"What?" Rodgers asked.

"I can't find out who your contact man is over there," Herbert said.

"We're being met by an officer of the National Security Guard, Captain Prem Nazir," Rodgers replied. "That's not unusual."

"It is for me," Herbert insisted. "A few calls, some promises, a little intel exchange usually gets me what I want. It lets me check up on people, make sure there isn't a double-cross on the other end. Not this time. I can't even get anything on Captain Nazir."

"To tell you the truth, I'm actually relieved that there's tight security for once," Rodgers laughed.

"Tight security is when the opposition doesn't know what is going on," Herbert said. "I get worried when our own people can't tell me exactly what is going on."

"Cannot or will not?" Rodgers asked.

"Cannot," Herbert said.

"Why don't you call Mala Chatterjee," Rodgers suggested. "I bet she would be delighted to help."

"That's not funny," Herbert said.

Chatterjee was the young Indian secretary-general of the United Nations. She was a career pacifist, the most vocal critic of Op-Center and the way they had taken over and resolved the crisis.

"I talked to my people at the CIA and at our embassies in Islamabad and New Delhi," Herbert went on. "They don't know anything about this operation. That's unusual. And the National Security Agency does not exactly have things under control. The plan has not gone through the usual com-sim. Lewis is too busy housecleaning for that."

"I know," Rodgers said.

"The usual com-sim" was a computer simulation that was run on any plan that had been approved for the field. The sponsoring agency typically spent days running the simulations to find holes in the main blueprint and also to give backup options to the agents heading into the field. But the National Security Agency had recently been shaken up by the resignation of their director, Jack Fenwick. That occurred after Hood had identified Fenwick as one of the leaders of a conspiracy to help remove the president from office. His replacement, Hank Lewis, formerly assistant to the president, coordinator of strategic planning, was spending his time removing Fenwick loyalists.

"We'll be okay," Rodgers assured him. "Back in Vietnam my plans were always held together with spit."

"Yeah, but there at least you knew who the enemy was," Herbert pointed out. "All I want you to do is stay in touch. If something seems out of whack I want to be able to let you know."

"I will," Rodgers promised. They would be traveling with the TAC-SAT phone. The secure uplink would allow Striker to call Op-Center from virtually anywhere in the world.

Herbert left and General Rodgers picked up the files and diskettes he wanted to take. The hall outside the door was getting busier as Op-Center's day crew arrived. It was nearly three times the size of the skeletal night crew. Yet Rodgers felt strangely cut off from the activity. It was not just the focused "mission mode" Rodgers went into before leaving the base. It was something else. A guardedness, as if he were already in the field. In and around Washington that was not far from the truth.

Despite Rodgers's assurances, what Herbert said had resonated with him. Herbert was not an alarmist and his concerns did worry Rodgers a little. Not for himself or even his old friend Colonel Brett August. August would be commanding Op-Center's elite Striker unit. Rodgers was worried about the young multiservice members of Striker who would be joining him in Kashmir. Especially the ones with families. That was never far from any commander's mind. Herbert had helped to give it a little extra volume.

But risk came with the uniform and the generous pension. Rodgers would do everything he could to safeguard the personnel and the mission. Because, in the end, there was one inescapable truth about actions taken by men like Mike Rodgers and Brett August.

The goal was worth the risk.

TWO

Srinagar, India
Wednesday, 3:51 P.M.

Five hours after giving a false name to officials at the Foreigners' Regional Registration Office at Srinagar Airport, Ron Friday was walking the streets of what he hoped would be his home for the next year or two. He had checked into a small, cheap inn off Shervani Road. He'd first heard about Binoo's Palace the last time he was here. There was a gaming parlor in the back, which meant that the local police had been paid to keep the place secure. There, Friday would be both anonymous and safe.

The National Security Agency officer was happy to have gotten out of Baku, Azerbaijan. He was happy not only to get out of the former Soviet Republic but to be here, in Srinagar, less than twenty-five miles from the line of control. He had been to the capital of the northern state before and found it invigorating. Distant artillery fire was constant. So were the muted pops of land mines in the hills. During early morning there was the scream of jets and the distinctive whumping sound of their cluster bombs and the louder crashes of their guided missiles.

Fear was also in the air day and night. The ancient resort city was governed and patrolled by Indian Hindu soldiers while commerce was controlled by Kashmiri Muslims. Not a week went by without four or five deaths due to terrorist bombings, shoot-outs, or hostage situations.

Friday loved it. Nothing made each breath sweeter than when you were walking through a minefield.

The forty-seven-year-old Michigan native walked through the largest open-air market in the city. It was located on the eastern end of the town, near hills that had once been fertile grazing areas. That was before the military had appropriated the hills as a staging area for helicopter flights and convoys headed out toward the line of control. A short walk to the north was the Centanr Lake View Hotel, which was where most foreign tourists stayed. It was located near the well-kept waterfront region known collectively as the Mughal Gardens. These gardens, which grow naturally, helped give the region its name Kashmir, which meant "Paradise" in the language of the Mughal settlers.

A cool, light rain was falling, though it did not keep away the regular crowds and foreigners. The market smelled like nowhere else Friday had ever been. It was a combination of musk—from the sheep and damp rattan roofs on the stalls—lavender incense, and diesel fuel. The fuel came from the taxis, minibuses, and scooter-rickshaws that serviced the area. There were women in saris and young students in western clothing. All of them were jockeying for position at the small wooden stands, looking for the freshest fruits or vegetables or baked goods. Merchants whipped small switches at sheep who had been driven from adjacent fields by depleted pasturage or by soldiers practicing their marksmanship. The strays tried to steal carrots or cabbage. Other customers, mostly Arab and Asian businessmen, shopped at a leisurely pace for shawls, papier-mâché trinket boxes, and leather purses. Because Srinagar and the rest of Kashmir were on the list of "no-go zones" at the State Department, British Foreign Office, and other European governments, very few Westerners were here.

A few merchants hawked rugs. There were farmers who had parked their trucks and carts at one end and were carrying baskets with fresh produce or bread to various stands. And there were soldiers. Except in Israel, Friday had never seen a public place where there were nearly as many soldiers as there were civilians. And those were only the obvious ones, the men in uniform. He was sure that there were members of the Special Frontier Force, which was a cocreation of the CIA and India's Research and Analysis Wing, their foreign espionage service. The job of the SFF was to disrupt the flow of matériel and intelligence to and from enemy positions. Friday was equally sure the crowd included members of Pakistan's Special Services Group. A division of the army's Directorate for Inter-Services Intelligence, the group monitored actions behind enemy lines. They also worked with freelance operatives to commit acts of terrorism against the Indian people.

There was nothing like this in Baku, where the markets were quiet and organized and the local population was small and relatively well behaved. Friday liked this better. One had to watch for enemies while trying to feed one's family.

Having a desk at the embassy in Baku had been interesting but not because of the work he was doing for Deputy Ambassador Dorothy Williamson. Friday had spent years working as an attorney for Mara Oil, which was why Williamson had welcomed him to her staff. Officially, he was there to help her draft position papers designed to moderate Azerbaijani claims on Caspian oil. What had really made Friday's tenure exciting was the undercover work he had been doing for Jack Fenwick, the president's former national security advisor.

The broad-shouldered man had been recruited by the NSA while he was still in law school. One of his professors, Vincent Van Heusen, had been an OSS operative during World War II. Professor Van Heusen saw in Friday some of the same qualities he himself had possessed as a young man. Among those was independence. Friday had learned that growing up in the Michigan woods where he went hunting with his father for food—not only with a rifle but with a longbow. After graduating from NYU Friday spent time at the NSA as a trainee. When he went to work for the oil industry a year later he was also working as a spy. In addition to making contacts in Europe, the Middle East, and the Caspian, Friday was given the names of CIA operatives working in those countries. From time to time he was asked to watch them. To spy on the spies, making certain that they were working only for the United States.

Friday finally left the private sector five years ago. He grew bored with working for the oil industry full-time and the NSA part-time. He had also grown frustrated, watching as intelligence operations went to hell overseas. Many of the field agents he met were inexperienced, fearful, or soft. This was especially true in the Third World and throughout Asia. They wanted creature comforts. Not Friday. He wanted to be uncomfortable, hot, cold, hurting, off balance.

Challenged. Alive.

The other problem was that increasingly electronic espionage had replaced hands-on human surveillance. The result was much less efficient mass-intelligence gathering. To Friday that was like getting meat from a slaughterhouse instead of hunting it down. The food didn't taste as good when it was mass-produced. The experience was less satisfying. And over time the hunter grew soft.

Friday had no intention of ever growing soft. When Jack Fenwick had said he wanted to talk to him, Friday was eager to meet. Friday went to see him at the Off the Record bar at the Hay-Adams hotel. It was during the week of the president's inauguration so the bar was jammed and the men were barely noticed. Fenwick recruited Friday to the "Undertaking," as he had called it. An operation to overthrow the president and put a new, more proactive figure in the Oval Office. One of the gravest problems facing America was security from terrorists. Vice President Cotten would have dealt with the problem decisively. He would have informed terrorist nations that if they sponsored attacks on American interests their capital cities would be bombed flat. Removing fear from Americans abroad would have encouraged competitive trade and tourism, which would have helped covert agencies infiltrate nationalist organizations, religious groups, and other extremist bands.

But the plotters had been stopped. The world was once again safe for warlords, anarchists, and international muggers.

Fortunately, the resignations of the vice president, Fenwick, and the other high-profile conspirators were like cauterizing a wound. The administration had its main perpetrators. They stopped the bloodletting and for the time being seemed to turn attention away from others who may have assisted in the plan. Friday's role in setting up the terrorist Harpooner and actually assassinating a CIA spoiler had not been uncovered. In fact, Hank Lewis was trying to get as much intel as possible as fast as possible so he could look ahead, not back. NSA operatives outside Washington were being called upon to visit high-intensity trouble spots and both assist in intelligence operations and report back firsthand. That was why Friday left Baker. Originally he tried to get transferred to Pakistan, but was moved to India by special request of the Indian government. He had spent time here for Mara Oil, helping them evaluate future productivity in this region as well as on the border between the Great Indian Desert in India's Rajasthan Province and the Thar Desert in Pakistan. He knew the land, the Kashmiri language, and the people.

The irony, of course, was that his first assignment was to help a unit from Op-Center execute a mission of vital importance to peace in the region. Op-Center, the group that had stopped the Undertaking from succeeding.

If politics made strange bedfellows then covert actions made even stranger ones. There was one difference between the two groups, however. Diplomacy demanded that politicians bury their differences when they had to. Field agents did not. They nursed their grudges.

Forever.

THREE

Washington, D.C.
Wednesday, 6:32 A.M.

Mike Rodgers strode down the corridor to the office of Paul Hood. His briefcase was packed and he was still humming "Witch Doctor." He felt energized by the impending challenge, by the change of routine, and just by getting out of the windowless office.

Hood's assistant, Stephen "Bugs" Benet, had not yet arrived. Rodgers walked through the small reception area to Hood's office. He knocked on the door and opened it. Op-Center's director was pacing and wearing headphones. He was just finishing up his phone conversation with Senator Fox. Hood motioned the general in. Rodgers made his way to a couch on the far end of the room. He set his briefcase down but did not sit. He would be sitting enough over the next day.

Though Hood was forty-five, nearly the same age as Rodgers, there was something much younger-looking about the man. Maybe it only seemed that way because he smiled a lot and was an optimist. Rodgers was a realist, a term he preferred to pessimist. And realists always seemed older, more mature. As an old friend of Rodgers's, South Carolina Representative Layne Maly, once put it, "No one's blowin' sunshine up my ass so it ain't showin' up between my lips." As far as Rodgers was concerned that pretty much said it all.

Not that Hood himself had a lot to smile about. His marriage had fallen apart and his daughter, Harleigh, was suffering from post-traumatic stress disorder, a result of having been taken hostage at the United Nations. Hood had also taken a bashing in the world press and in the liberal American media for his guns-blazing solution to the UN crisis. It would not surprise Rodgers to learn that Senator Fox was giving Hood an earful for that. The goddamn thing of it was nothing helped our rivals more than when we fought among ourselves. Rodgers could almost hear the cheering from the Japanese, from the Islamic Fundamentalists, and from the Germans, the French, and the rest of the Eurocentric bloc. And we were arguing after saving the lives of their ambassadors.

It was a twisted world. Which was probably why we needed a man like Paul Hood running Op-Center. If it were up to Rodgers he would have taken down a few of the ambassadors on his way out of the UN.

Hood slipped off the headphones and looked at Rodgers. There was a flat look of frustration in his dark hazel eyes. His wavy black hair was uncharacteristically unkempt. He was not smiling.

"How are you doing?" Hood asked Rodgers. "Everything set?"

Rodgers nodded.

"Good," Hood said.

"How are things here?" Rodgers asked.

"Not so good," Hood said. "Senator Fox thinks we've gotten too visible. She wants to do something about that."

"What?" Rodgers asked.

"She wants to scale us back," Hood said. "She's going to propose to the other members of the COIC that they recharter Op-Center as a smaller, more covert organization."

"I smell Kirk Pike's hand in this," Rodgers said.

Pike was the newly appointed head of the Central Intelligence Agency. The ambitious former chief of navy intelligence was extremely well liked on the Hill and had accepted the position with a self-prescribed goal: to consolidate as many of the nation's intelligence needs as possible under one roof.

"I agree that Pike is probably involved, but I think it's more than just him," Hood said. "Fox said that Secretary-General Chatterjee is still grumbling about bringing us before the International Court of Justice. Have us tried for murder and trespassing."

"Smart," Rodgers said. "She'll never get the one but the jurists may give her the other."

"Exactly," Hood said. "That makes her look strong and reaffirms the sovereign status of the United Nations. It also scores points with pacifists and with anti-American governments. Fox apparently thinks this will go away if our charter is revoked and quietly rewritten."

"I see," Rodgers said. "The CIOC acts preemptively to make Chatterjee's action seem bullying and unnecessary."

"Bingo," Hood said.

"Is it going to happen?" Rodgers asked.

"I don't know," Hood admitted. "Fox hasn't discussed this with the other members yet."

"But she wants it to happen," Rodgers said.

Hood nodded.

"Then it will," Rodgers said.

"I'm not ready to concede that," Hood said. "Look, I don't want you to worry about the political stuff. I need you to get this job done in Kashmir. Chatterjee may be secretary-general but she's still Indian. If you score one for her side she'll have a tough time going after us."

"Not if she passes the baton to Pike," Rodgers said.

"Why would she?" Hood asked.

"Back-scratching and access," Rodgers said. "A lot of the intel I have on Kashmir came from the CIA. The Company works very closely with the Indian Intelligence Bureau."

"The domestic surveillance group," Hood said.

"Right," Rodgers said.

Under the Indian Telegraph Act, the Indian Intelligence Bureau has the legal authority to intercept all forms of electronic communication. That includes a lot of faxes and e-mail from Afghanistan and other Islamic states. It was IIB that blew the whistle on Iraq's pharmaceutical drug scam back in 2000. Humanitarian medicines were excluded from the United Nations sanctions. Instead of going to Iraqi hospitals and clinics, however, the medicines were hoarded by the health minister. When shortages pushed up demand the drugs were sold to the black market for hard foreign currency that could be used to buy luxury goods for government officials, bypassing the sanctions.

"The IIB shares the information they collect with the CIA for analysis," Rodgers went on. "If Director Pike helps Chatterjee, the Indians will continue to work exclusively with him."

"Pike can have the trophy if he wants," Hood said. "We still get the intelligence."

"But that isn't all Pike wants," Rodgers said. "People aren't satisfied just winning in Washington. They have to destroy the competition. And if that doesn't work they go after his friends and family."

"Yeah—well, he'll have to get a task force for that one," Hood said quietly. "We Hoods are kind of spread out now."

Rodgers felt like an ass. Paul Hood was not living with his family anymore and his daughter, Harleigh, spent a lot of time in therapy. It was careless to have suggested that they might be at risk.

"Sorry, Paul. I didn't mean that literally," Rodgers said.

"It's all right," Hood replied. "I know what you meant. I don't think Pike will cross that line, though. We've got pretty good muckrakers and a great press liaison. He won't want to take any rivalry public."

Rodgers was not convinced of that. Hood's press liaison was Ann Farris. For the last few days the office was quietly buzzing with the rumor that the divorcée and Paul Hood were having an affair. Ann had been staying late and the two had been spotted leaving Hood's hotel together one morning. Rodgers did not care one way or the other as long as their relationship did not impact the smooth operation of the NCMC.

"Speaking of family, how is Harleigh doing?" Rodgers asked. The general was eager to get off the subject of Pike before leaving for India. The idea of fighting his own people was loathsome to him. Though the men did not socialize very much, Rodgers was close enough to Hood to ask about his family.

"She's struggling with what happened in New York and with me moving out," Hood said. "But she's got a good support system and her brother's being a real trouper."

"Alexander's a good kid. Glad to hear he's stepping up to the plate. What about Sharon?" Rodgers asked.

"She's angry," Hood said. "She has a right to be."

"It will pass," Rodgers said.

"Liz says it may not," Hood replied.

Liz was Liz Gordon, Op-Center's psychologist. Though she was not counseling Harleigh, she was advising Hood.

"Hopefully, the intensity of Sharon's anger will diminish," Hood went on. "I don't think she and I will ever be friends again. But with any luck we'll have a civil relationship."

"You'll get there," Rodgers said. "Hell, that's more than I've ever had with a woman."

Hood thought for a moment then grinned. "That's true, isn't it? Goes all the way back to your friend Biscuit in the fifth grade."

"Yeah," Rodgers replied. "Look, you're a diplomat. I'm a soldier. I'm a prisoner to my scorched earth nature."

Hood's grin became a smile. "I may need to borrow some of that fire for my dealings with Senator Fox."

"Stall her till I get back," Rodgers said. "And just keep an eye on Pike. I'll work on him when I get back."

"It's a deal," Hood said. "Stay safe, okay?"

Rodgers nodded and the men shook hands.

The general felt uneasy as he headed toward the elevator. Rodgers did not like leaving things unresolved—especially when the target was as vulnerable as Hood was. Rodgers could see it in his manner. He had seen it before, in combat. It was a strange calm, almost as if Hood were in denial that pressures were starting to build. But they were. Hood was already distracted by his impending divorce, by Harleigh's condition, and by the day-to-day demands of his position. Rodgers had a feeling that the pressure from Senator Fox would become much more intense after the CIOC met. He would give Bob Herbert a call from the C-130 and ask him to keep an eye on Op-Center's director.

A watcher watching the watcher, Rodgers thought. Op-Center's intelligence chief looking after Op-Center's director, who was tracking Kirk Pike. With all the human drama gusting around him the general almost felt as if it were routine to go into the field to search for nuclear missiles.

But Rodgers got his perspective back quickly. As he walked onto the tarmac he saw the Striker team beginning to assemble beside the Hercules transport. They were in uniform, at ease, their grips and weapons at their feet. Colonel August was reviewing a checklist with Lieutenant Orjuela, his new second-in-command.

Behind him, in the basement of the NCMC, there were careers at risk. Out here men and women were about to buy their way into India using their lives as collateral.

The day that became routine was the day Rodgers vowed to hang up his uniform.

Stepping briskly, proudly, Rodgers made his way toward the shadow of the plane and the sharp, bright salutes of his waiting team.

FOUR

Kargil, Kashmir
Wednesday, 4:11 P.M.

Apu Kumar sat on the old, puffy featherbed that had once been used by his grandmother. He looked out at the four bare walls of his small bedroom. They had not always been bare. There used to be framed pictures of his late wife and his daughter and son-in-law, and a mirror. But their houseguests had removed them. Glass could be used as a weapon.

The bed was tucked in a corner of the room he shared with his twenty-two-year-old granddaughter Nanda. At the moment the young woman was outside cleaning the chicken coop. When she was finished she would shower in the small stall behind the house and then return to the room. She would unfold a small card table, set it beside her grandfather's bed, and pull over a wooden chair. The bedroom door would be kept ajar and their vegetarian meals would be served to them in small wooden bowls. Then Apu and Nanda would listen to the radio, play chess, read, meditate, and pray. They would pray for enlightenment and also for Nanda's mother and father, both of whom died in the roaring hell that was unleashed on Kargil just four years ago. Sometime around ten or eleven they would go to sleep. With any luck Apu would make it through the night. Sudden noises tended to wake him instantly and bring back the planes and the weeks of endless bombing raids.

In the morning, the Kargil-born farmer was permitted to go out and look after his chickens. One of his houseguests always went with him to make sure he did not try to leave. Apu's truck was still parked beside the coop. Even though the Pakistanis had taken the keys Apu could easily splice the ignition wires and drive off. Of course, he would only do that if his granddaughter Nanda were with him. Which was why they were never allowed outside together.

The slender, silver-haired man would feed the chickens, talk to them, and look after any eggs they had left. Then he was taken back to the room. In the late afternoon it was Nanda's turn to go out to do the more difficult work of cleaning the coop. Though Apu could do it, their guests insisted that Nanda go. It helped keep the headstrong young woman tired. When they had enough eggs to bring to market one of their houseguests always went to Srinagar for them. And they always gave the money to Apu. The Pakistanis were not here for financial profit. Though Apu tried hard to eavesdrop, he was still not sure why they were here. They did not do much except talk.

For five months, ever since the five Pakistanis arrived in the middle of the night, the physical life of the sixty-three-year-old farmer had been defined by this routine. Though daily visits to the coop had been the extent of the Kumars' physical life, Apu had retained his wits, his spirit, and most importantly his dignity. He had done that by devoting himself to reading and meditating on his deep Hindu beliefs. He did that for himself and also to show his Islamic captors that his faith and resolve were as powerful as theirs.

Apu reached behind him. He raised his pillow a little higher. It was lumpy with age, having been through three generations of Kumars. A smile played on his grizzled, leathery face. The down had suffered enough. Perhaps the duck would find contentment in another incarnation.

The smile faded quickly. That was sacrilegious. It was something his granddaughter might have said. He should know better. Maybe the months of incarceration were affecting his reason. He looked around.

Nanda slept in a sleeping bag on the other side of the room. There were times when Apu would wake in the small hours of the night and hear her breathing. He enjoyed that. If nothing else their captivity had allowed them to get to know each other better. Even though her nontraditional religious views bothered him, he was glad to know what they were. One could not fight the enemy without knowing his face.

There were two other rooms in the small stone house. The door to the living room was open. The Pakistanis stayed there during the day. At night they moved to the room that used to be his. All save the one who took the watch. One of them was always awake. They had to be. Not just to make sure Apu and Nanda stayed inside the house but to watch for anyone who might approach the farm. Though no one lived close by, Indian army patrols occasionally came through these low-lying hills. When this group of Pakistanis first arrived they had promised their unwilling hosts that they would stay no more than six months. And if Apu and Nanda did what they were told they would not be harmed after that time. Apu was not sure he believed the four men and one woman but he was willing to give them the time they asked for. After all, what choice did he have?

Though he would not mind if the authorities came and shot them dead. As long as he did not cause harm to befall them it would not affect his future in this life or the next. The shame of it was that as people they would all get along fine. But politics and religion had stirred things up. That was the story of this entire region from the time Apu had been a young man. Neighbors were neighbors until outsiders turned them into enemies.

There was one small window in the room but the shutters had been nailed closed. The only light came from a small lamp on the nightstand. The glow illuminated a small, old, leatherbound copy of the Upanishads. Those were the mystical writings of Apu's faith. The Upanishads comprised the final section of the Veda, the Hindu holy scriptures.

Apu turned his mind back to the text. He was reading the earliest of the Upanishads, the sections of verse that addressed the doctrine of Brahman, the universal self or soul. The goal of Hinduism, like other Eastern religions, was nirvana, the eventual freedom from the cycle of rebirth and the pain brought about by one's own actions or karma. This could only be accomplished by following spiritual yoga, which led to a union with God. Apu was determined to pursue that goal, though actually achieving it was a dream. He was also devoted to the study of the post-Vedic Puranas, which address the structure of life in an individual and social sense and also take the reader through the repeating cycle of creation and end of the universe as represented by the divine trinity of Brahma, the creator; Vishnu, the preserver; and Shiva, the destroyer. He had had a hard life, as befitted his farmer caste. But he had to believe that it was just a blink in the cosmic cycle. Otherwise, there would be nothing to work toward, no ultimate end.

Nanda was different. She put more trust in the poet-saints who wrote religious songs and epics. The literature was essential to Hinduism but she responded to the outpourings of men more than the doctrines they were describing. Nanda had always liked heroes who spoke their minds. That had been her mother's nature as well. To say what she believed. To fight. To resist.

That was what had helped cost Apu his daughter and son-in-law. When the Pakistani invaders first arrived, the two sheep farmers made Molotov cocktails for the hastily organized resistance fighters. After two weeks both Savitri and her husband, Manjay, were caught transporting them inside bags of wool. The bags were ignited with the couple bound in the cab of their truck. The next day Apu and Nanda found their bodies in the blackened ruins. To Nanda they were martyrs. To Apu they had been reckless. To Apu's ailing wife, Pad, they were the final blow to a frail body. She died eight days later.

"All human errors are impatience," it was written. If only Savitri and Manjay had asked, Apu would have told them to wait. Time brings balance.

The Indian military eventually pushed most of the Pakistanis out. There was no reason for his children to have acted violently. They hurt others and added that burden to their spiritual inventory.

Tears began to fill his eyes. It was all such a waste. Though, strangely, it made him cherish Nanda all the more.

She was the only part of his wife and daughter that he had left.

There was a sudden commotion in the other room. Apu shut his book and set it on the rickety night table. He slid into his slippers and quietly crossed the wooden floor. He peeked out the door. Four of the Pakistanis were all there. The houseguests were working on something, arms and heads moving over something between them. The backs of three of the men were toward him so he could not see what they were doing. Only the woman was facing him. She was a slender, very swarthy woman with short black hair and a frowning, intense look. The others called her Sharab but Apu did not know if that was her real name.

Sharab waved a gun at him. "Go back!" she ordered.

Apu lingered a moment longer. His houseguests had never done anything like this before that he was aware of. They came and went and they talked. Occasionally they looked at maps. Something was happening. He edged forward a little more. There appeared to be a burlap sack on the floor between the men. One of the men was crouching beside it. He appeared to be working on something inside the bag.

"Get back!" the woman yelled again.

There was a tension in her voice that Apu had never heard before. He did as he was told.

Apu kicked off his slippers and lay back on the bed. As he did he heard the front door open. It was Nanda and presumably the fifth Pakistani. He could tell by how loud the door creaked. The young woman always opened it boldly, as if she wanted to hit whoever might be standing behind it.

Apu smiled. He always looked forward to seeing his granddaughter. Even if she had only been gone an hour or two.

This time, however, things were different. He did not hear her footsteps. Instead he heard quiet talking. Apu held his breath and tried to hear what was being said. But his heart was beating louder than usual and he could not hear. Quietly, he raised himself from the bed and eased toward the door. He leaned closer, careful not to show himself. He listened.

He heard nothing.

Slowly, he nudged the door open. One of the men was there, looking out the window. He was holding his silver handgun and smoking a cigarette. The Pakistani glanced back at Apu.

"Go back in the room," the man said quietly.

"Where is my granddaughter?" Apu asked. He did not like this. Something felt wrong.

"She left with the others," he said.

"Left? Where did they go?" Apu asked.

The man looked back out the window. He drew on his cigarette. "They went to market," he replied.

FIVE

Washington, D.C.
Wednesday, 7:00 A.M.

Colonel Brett August had lost track of the number of times he had ridden in the shaking, cavernous bellies of C-130 transports. But he remembered this much. He had hated each and every one of those damn flights.

This particular Hercules was one of the newer variants, a long-range SAR HC-130H designed for fuel economy. Colonel August had ridden in a number of customized C-130s: the C-130D with ski landing gear during an Arctic training mission, a KC-130R tanker, a C-130F assault transport, and many others. The amazing thing was that not one of those versions offered a comfortable ride. The fuselages were stripped down to lighten the aircraft and give it as much range as possible. That meant there was very little insulation against cold and noise. And the four powerful turboprops were deafening as they fought to lift the massive plane skyward. The vibrations were so strong that the chain around Colonel August's dog tags actually did a dance around his neck.

Comfort was also not in the original design-lexicon. The seats in this particular aircraft were cushioned plastic buckets arranged side by side along the fuselage walls. They had high, thick padded backrests and headrests that were supposed to keep the passenger warm. Theoretically that would work if the air itself did not become so cold. There were no armrests and very little space between the chairs. Duffel bags were stowed under the seats. The guys who designed these were probably like the guys who drew up battle plans. It all looked great on paper.

Not that Colonel August was complaining. He remembered a story his father once told him about his own military days. Sid August was part of the U.S. 101st Airborne Division, which was trapped by the 15th Panzer Grenadier Division shortly before the Battle of the Bulge. The men had only K rations to eat. Invented by an apparently sadistic physiologist named Ancel Benjamin Keys, K rations were flat-tasting compressed biscuits, a sliver of dry meat, sugar cubes, bouillon powder, chewing gum, and compressed chocolate. The chocolate was code-named D ration. Why chocolate needed a code name no one knew but the men suspected the starving Germans would fight harder knowing there was more than just dry meat and cardboardlike biscuits in the enemy foxholes.

The airmen ate the K rations sparingly while lying low. After a few days the air force managed to night-drop several cases of C rations and extra munitions to the soldiers. The C rations contained dinner portions of meat and potatoes. But introducing real food to their systems made the men so sick and flatulent that the noise and smell actually gave their position away to a German patrol. The airmen were forced to fight their way out. The story always made Brett August uneasy with the idea of having too much comfort available to him.

Mike Rodgers was sitting to August's right. August smiled to himself. Rodgers had a big, high-arched nose that had been broken four times playing college basketball. Mike Rodgers did not know any way but forward. They had just taken off and that nose was already hunkered into a briefcase thick with folders. August had flown with Rodgers long enough to know the drill. As soon as the pilot gave the okay to use electronic devices, Rodgers would pull some of those folders out. He would put them on his left knee and place his laptop on the right knee. Then, as Rodgers finished with material, he would pass it to August. About halfway over the Atlantic they would begin to talk openly and candidly about what they had read. That was how they had discussed everything for the forty-plus years they had known each other. More often than not it was unnecessary to say anything. Rodgers and August each knew what the other man was thinking.

Brett August and Mike Rodgers were childhood friends. The boys met in Hartford, Connecticut, when they were six. In addition to sharing a love of baseball they shared a passion for airplanes. On weekends, the two young boys used to bicycle five miles along Route 22 out to Bradley Field. They would just sit on an empty field and watch the planes take off and land. They were old enough to remember when prop planes gave way to the jet planes. Both of them used to go wild whenever one of the new 707s roared overhead. Prop planes had a familiar, reassuring hum. But those new babies—they made a boy's insides rattle. August and Rodgers loved it.

After school each day the boys would do their homework together, each taking alternate math problems or science questions so they could finish faster. Then they would build plastic model airplanes, boats, tanks, and jeeps, taking care that the paint jobs were accurate and that the decals were put in exactly the right place.

When it came time to enlist—kids like the two of them didn't wait to be drafted—Rodgers joined the army and August went into the air force. Both men ended up in Vietnam. While Rodgers did his tours of duty on the ground, August flew reconnaissance missions over North Vietnam. On one flight northwest of Hue, August's plane was shot down. He mourned the loss of his aircraft, which had almost become a part of him. The flier was taken prisoner and spent over a year in a POW camp, finally escaping with another prisoner in 1970. August spent three months making his way to the south before finally being discovered by a patrol of U.S. Marines.

Except for the loss of his aircraft, August was not embittered by his experiences. To the contrary. He was heartened by the courage he had witnessed among American POWs. He returned to the United States, regained his strength, and went back to Vietnam to organize a spy network searching for other American POWs. August remained undercover for a year after the U.S. withdrawal. After he had exhausted his contacts trying to find MIAs, August was shifted to the Philippines. He spent three years training pilots to help President Ferdinand Marcos battle Moro secessionists. After that August worked briefly as an air force liaison with NASA, helping to organize security for spy satellite missions. But there was no flying involved and being with the astronauts now was different from being with the monkey Ham when he was a kid. It was frustrating working with men and women who were actually getting to travel in space. So August moved over to the air force's Special Operations Command, where he stayed ten years before joining Striker.

Rodgers and August had seen one another only intermittently in the post-Vietnam years. But each time they talked or got together it was as if no time had passed. When Rodgers first signed on at Op-Center he had asked August to come aboard as the leader of the Striker force. August turned him down twice. He did not want to spend most of his time on a base, working with young specialists. Lt. Colonel Charlie Squires got the post. After Squires was killed on a mission in Russia, Rodgers came to his old friend again. Two years had passed since Rodgers had first made the offer. But things were different now. The team was shaken by the loss and he needed a commander who could get them back up to speed as fast as possible. This time August could not refuse. It was not only friendship. There were national security issues at stake.

The NCMC had become a vital force in crisis management and Op-Center needed Striker.

The colonel looked toward the back of the plane. He watched the group as they sat silently through the slow, thunderous ascent. The quick-response unit turned out to be more than August had expected. Individually, they were extraordinary. Before joining Striker, Sergeant Chick Grey had specialized in two things. One was HALO operations—high-altitude, low-opening parachute jumps. As his com-

mander at Bragg had put it when recommending Grey for
the post, "the man can fly." Grey had the ability to pull his
ripcord lower and land more accurately than any soldier in
Delta history. He attributed this to having a rare sensitivity
to air currents. Grey believed that also helped with his second
skill—marksmanship. Not only could the sergeant hit whatever he said he could, he had trained himself to go without
blinking for as long as necessary. He'd developed that ability
when he realized that all it took was the blink of an eye to
miss the "keyhole," as he called it. The instant when the
target was in perfect position for a takedown.

August felt a special kinship with Grey because the sergeant was at home in the air. But August was close to all
his personnel. Privates David George, Jason Scott, Terrence
Newmeyer, Walter Pupshaw, Matt Bud, and Sondra De-
Vonne. Medic William Musicant, Corporal Pat Prementine,
and Lieutenant Orjuela. They were more than specialists.
They were a team. And they had more courage, more heart
than any unit August had ever worked with.

Newly promoted Corporal Ishi Honda was another marvel.
The son of a Hawaiian mother and Japanese father, Honda
was an electronics prodigy and the unit's communications
expert. He was never far from the TAC-SAT phone, which
Colonel August and Rodgers used to stay in touch with Op-
Center. The backpack containing the unit was lined with
bullet-proof Kevlar so it would not be damaged in a firefight.
Because it was so loud in the cabin Honda sat with the TAC-
SAT in his lap. He did not want to miss hearing any calls.
When he was in the field, Honda wore a Velcro collar and
headphones of his own creation. They plugged directly into
the pack. When the collar was jacked in, the "beep" was
automatically disengaged; the collar simply vibrated when
there was an incoming call. If Striker were on a surveillance
mission there was no sound to give them away. Moreover,
the collar was wired with small condensor microphones that
allowed Honda to communicate subvocally. He could whisper and his voice would be transferred clearly to whoever
was on the other end.

But Striker was more than just a group of military elite drawn from different services. Lt. Colonel Squires had done an extraordinary job turning them into a smart, disciplined fighting unit. They were certainly the most impressive team August had ever served with.

The plane banked to the south and August's old leather portfolio slid from under his seat. He kicked it back with his heel. The bag contained maps and white papers about Kashmir. The colonel had already reviewed them with his team. He would look at them again in a few minutes. Right now August wanted to do what he did before beginning every mission. He wanted to try and figure out why he was here, why he was going. That was something he had done every day since he was first a prisoner of war: take stock of his motivations for doing what he was doing. That was true whether August was in a Vietcong stockade, getting up in the morning to go to the Striker base, or leaving on a mission. It was not enough to say he was serving his country or pursuing his chosen career. He needed something that would allow him to push himself to better than he did the day before. Otherwise the quality of his work and his life would suffer.

What he had discovered was that he could not find another reason. When he was optimistic, pride and patriotism had been his biggest motivators. On darker days he decided that humans were all territorial carnivores and prisoners of their nature. Combat and survival were a genetic imperative. Yet these could not be the only things that drove us. There had to be something unique to everyone, something that transcended political or professional boundaries.

So what he searched for in these quiet times was the other missing motivation. The key that would make him a better soldier, a better leader, a stronger and better man.

Along the way, of course, he discovered many things, thought many interesting thoughts. And he began to wonder if the journey itself might be the answer. Given that he was heading to one of the birthplaces of Eastern religion, that would be a fitting revelation. Maybe that was all he would find. Unlike the mission, there were no maps to show him the terrain, no aircraft to take him there.

But for now he would keep looking.

SIX

Srinagar, India
Wednesday, 4:22 P.M.

There was a two-and-one-half-hour time difference between Baku and Kashmir. Still on Azerbaijan time, Ron Friday bought several lamb skewers from one of the food merchants. Then he went to a crowded outdoor café and ordered tea to go with his dinner. He would have to eat quickly. There was a dusk-to-dawn curfew for foreigners. It was strictly enforced by soldiers who patrolled the streets wearing body armor and carrying automatic rifles.

Though the rain had stopped, the large umbrellas were still open over the tables. Friday had to duck to make his way through. He shared his table with a pair of Hindu pilgrims who were reading while they drank their tea. The two men were dressed in very long white cotton robes that were tied at the center with a brown belt. It was the wardrobe of holy men from the United Provinces near Nepal, at the foot of the Himalayas. There were heavy-looking satchels at their sides. The men were probably on their way to a religious shrine at Pahalgam, which was located fifty-five miles south of Srinagar. The presence of the satchels suggested that they were planning to spend some time at the shrine. The men did not acknowledge Friday as he sat, though they were not being rude. They did not want to interrupt his tranquillity. One of the men was looking over a copy of the *International Herald Tribune.* That struck Friday as odd, though he did not know why it should. Even holy men needed to keep up with world events. The other man, who was sitting right beside Friday, was reading a volume of poems in both Sanskrit and English. Friday glanced over the man's forearm.

"Vishayairindriyagraamo na thrupthamadhigachathi ajasram pooryamaanoopi samudraha salilairiva," it said in Sanskrit. The English translation read, "The senses can never be satisfied even after the continuous supply of sensory objects, as the ocean can never be filled with a continuous supply of water."

Friday did not dispute that. People who were alive had to drink in everything around them. They consumed experiences and things and turned that fuel into something else. Into something that had their fingerprints on it. If you weren't doing that you were living, but not alive.

While the pilgrims sat at the table they were approached by a Muslim. The man offered low-price shelter at his home if they wished to stay the night. Often, pilgrims had neither the time nor the money to stay at an inn. The men graciously declined, saying they were going to try and catch the next bus and would rest when they reached the shrine. The Muslim said that if they missed this bus or one of the later ones he could arrange for his brother-in-law to drive them to the shrine the next day. He gave them a card with his address handwritten on it. They thanked him for his offer. The man bowed and excused himself. It was all very civil. Contact between the Muslims and Hindus usually was cordial. It was the generals and the politicians who provoked the wars.

Behind Friday two men had stopped for tea. From their conversation he gathered that they were heading to the night shift at a nearby brick factory. To Friday's left three men in the khaki uniforms of the Kashmir police force were standing and watching the crowd. Unlike in the Middle East, bazaars were not typically the scene of terrorist attacks in Kashmir. That was because as many Muslims as Hindus frequently mingled in marketplaces. Hindu-specific sites were usually targeted. Places such as homes of local officials, businesses, police stations, financial institutions, and military bases. Even militaristic, aggressive groups like the Hezb-ul Mujahedeen guerrillas did not typically attack civilian locales, especially during business hours. They did not want to turn the people against them. Their war was with the Hindu leaders and those who supported them.

The two pilgrims quickly finished their tea. Their bus was pulling up three hundred yards to the right. It braked noisily at a small, one-room bus stop at the far western side of the market. The bus was an old green vehicle, but clean. There were iron racks on the roof for luggage. The uniformed driver came out and helped passengers off while a luggage clerk brought a stepladder from inside the bus stop. While he began to unload the bags of riders who were disembarking, ticket-holders began queuing up beside him to board. For the most part the line was extremely orderly. When the two men were finished they both entered the small wooden structure.

The two pilgrims at Ron Friday's table had put away their reading material and picked up their big lumpy bags. With effort, the men threw the satchels over their shoulders and made their way onto the crowded street. Watching them go, Friday wondered what the punishment was for stealing. With customers packed so closely together and focused on getting what they needed, the market would be a pickpocket's heaven. Especially if they were going to get on a bus and leave the area quickly.

Friday continued to sip his tea as he ate the lamb from the wooden skewers. He watched as other pilgrims rushed by. Some of them were dressed in white or black robes, others were wearing Western street clothes. The men and women who were not wearing traditional robes would be permitted to worship at the shrine but not to enter the cave itself. A few people were pulling children behind them. Friday wondered if their hungry expressions were anxiety about getting onto the bus or a physical manifestation of the religious fervor they felt. Probably a little of both.

One of the police officers walked toward the bus stop to make sure the boarding process was orderly. He walked past the police station, which was to his left. It was a two-story wooden structure with white walls and green eaves. The two front windows were barred. Beyond the police station, practically abutting it, was a decades-old Hindu temple. Friday wondered if the local government had built the police station next to a temple in an effort to protect it from terrorists. Friday had been to the temple once before. It was a dvi-bheda—a bidivisional house of worship that honored both Shiva, the god of destruction, and Vishnu, the preserver. The main portal was fronted by the five-story-tall Rajagopuram, the Royal Tower. To the sides were smaller towers over the auxiliary entrances. These white-brick structures were trimmed with green and gold tile and honored the two different gods. The walls were decorated with canopies, roaring lions, humanlike gatekeepers in what appeared to be dancing poses, and other figures. Friday did not know a great deal about the iconography. However, he did recall that the interior of the temple was designed to symbolize a deity at rest. The first room was the crest, followed by the face, the abdomen, the knee, the leg, and the foot. The entire body was important to the Hindus, not just the soul or the heart. Any part of a human being without the other part was incomplete. And an incomplete individual could not manifest the ultimate perfection required by the faith.

However fast they were going, each pilgrim took a moment to turn to it and bow slightly before continuing on. As important as their individual goals were, the Hindus understood that there was something much greater than they were. Other pilgrims were exiting the temple to catch the bus. Still other Hindus, probably local citizens, as well as tourists were moving in and out of the arched portal.

A block past the temple was a movie theater with an old-style marquee. India made more motion pictures than any nation in the world. Friday had seen several of them on videotape, including *Fit to Be a King* and *Flowers and Vermilion.* Friday believed that the dreams of a people—hence, their weaknesses—could be found in the stories, themes, and characters of their most popular films. The Indians were especially drawn to the three-hour-long contemporary action-musicals. These films always starred attractive leads who had no names other than "Hero" and "Heroine." They were Everyman and Everywoman in epic struggles yet there was always music in their hearts. That was how the Indians viewed themselves. Reality was a disturbing inconvenience they did not choose to acknowledge. Like an oftentimes cruel caste system. Friday had a theory about that. He had always believed that castes were an embodiment of the Indians' faith. In society as in the individual there was a head, feet, and all parts in between. All parts were necessary to create a whole.

Friday glanced back at the market proper. Movement continued unabated. If anything it was busier than before as people stopped by before dinner or on their way home from work. Customers on foot and on bicycles made their way to different stalls. Baskets, wheelbarrows, and occasionally truckloads of goods continued to arrive. The markets usually remained open until just after sunset. In Srinagar and its environs, workers tended to be very early risers. They were expected to arrive at the local factories, fields, and shops around seven in the morning.

Friday finished eating and looked over at the bus. The driver had returned and was helping people board. The bus stop employee was back on his stepladder loading bags onto the roof. What was amazing to Friday was that amid all the seeming chaos there was an internal order. Every individual system was functioning perfectly, from the booths to the shoppers, from the police to the bus. Even the supposedly antagonistic religious factions were doing just fine.

A fine drizzle started up again. Friday decided to head over to the bus station. It looked as if there were new construction there and he was curious to see what lay beyond. As Friday followed the last of the pilgrims he watched the bus driver take tickets and help people onboard.

Something was not the same.

It was the driver. He was not a heavyset man but a rather slender one. Maybe he was a new driver. It was possible; they all wore the same jackets. Then he noticed something else. The clerk who was loading bags into the rack was being very careful with them. Friday had not gotten a very good look at the clerk. The exiting passengers had blocked his view. He could not tell if this were the same man.

The bus was still two hundred yards away. The American quickened his pace.

Suddenly the world to Friday's left vanished, swallowed in a flash of bright white light, infernal white heat, and deafening white noise.

SEVEN

Washington, D.C.
Wednesday, 7:10 A.M.

Paul Hood sat alone in his office. Mike Rodgers and
Striker were on their way and nothing else was pressing.
Hood's door was shut and a file labeled "Working OCIS"
was open on his computer. The "working" part of the heading indicated that this was not the original draft but a copy.
The OCIS was a clickable chart of Op-Center's internal
structure. Under each division was a list of the departments
and personnel. Attached to each name was a subfile. These
were logs that were filed each day by every employee. They
outlined the activities of the individual. Only Hood, Rodgers,
and Herbert had access to the files. They were maintained to
allow the Op-Center directors to track and cross-reference
personnel activities with phone records, e-mail lists, and
other logs. If anyone were working at cross-purposes with
the rest of the team—cooperating with another agency or
even another government—this was the first line of security.
The computer automatically flagged any activity that did not
have a log entry ordering or corroborating it.

Right now Paul Hood was not looking for moles. He was
looking for lambs. The sacrificial kind. If Senator Fox and
the Congressional Intelligence Oversight Committee wanted
cutbacks he had to be prepared to make them. The question
was where?

Hood clicked on Bob Herbert's intelligence department.
He scrolled through the names. Could Herbert get by with
just daytime surveillance of e-mail communications in Europe? Not likely. Spies worked around the clock. What about
a single liaison with the CIA and the FBI instead of one for
each? Probably. He would ask Herbert which one he wanted

to lose. Hood moved the cursor to the tech division. What about Matt Stoll? Could he survive without a satellite interface officer or a computer resources upgrade manager? Matt could outsource the work he needed whenever they had to eavesdrop on foreign communications satellites or change hardware or software. It would be inconvenient but it would not be debilitating. He double-clicked on the upgrade manager and the position disappeared.

Hood's heart sped up as he checked the next department. It was the office of the press liaison. Did Op-Center really need someone to issue news releases and organize press conferences? If Senator Fox were afraid that the National Crisis Management Center was too visible, then the press officer and her one assistant should be the first to go.

Hood stared at the computer. Never mind what Senator Fox thought. What did he think?

Hood did not see the list. He saw the face of Ann Farris. After years of flirting the two had finally spent a night together. It was at once the most wonderful and devastating encounter of Hood's life. Wonderful because he and Ann cared about each other, deeply. Devastating because Hood had to acknowledge that a bond existed. It was even stronger than the one he had felt when he encountered his old lover Nancy Jo Bosworth in Germany. Yet he was still married to Sharon. He had his children's well-being to consider, not to mention his own. And he would have to deal with Sharon's feelings if she ever found out. Though Hood loved being close to Ann this was not the time for another relationship.

And what would Ann think? After a rough divorce of her own, Ann Farris was not a very secure woman. She was poised when meeting the press and she was a terrific single mother. But those were what psychologist Liz Gordon had once described at an employee "Job vs. Parenting" seminar as "reactionary qualities." Ann responded to external stimuli with good, natural instincts. Inside, where she had allowed Paul to go, she was a scared little girl. If Hood let her go she would think he was doing it to keep her away. If he kept her she would think he was playing favorites, protecting her.

Personally and professionally it was a no-win situation. And Hood was not even considering how the rest of Op-Center would react. They had to know what was going on between him and Ann. They were a tight-knit office and an intelligence group. This had to be the worst-kept secret on the base.

Hood continued to stare at the screen. He no longer saw Ann Farris's face. He saw only her name. The bottom line was that Hood had to do his job, whatever the consequences. He could not do that if he let personal feelings interfere.

Hood double-clicked the mouse. Not on a name but on an entire two-person department.

A moment later the press division was gone.

EIGHT

Srinagar, India
Wednesday, 4:41 P.M.

Ron Friday felt as though someone had jabbed tuning forks in his ears. His ears and the inside of his skull seemed to be vibrating. There was a high-pitched ringing and he could not hear anything except for the ringing. His eyes were open but he could not tell what he was looking at. The world was a cottony haze, as though a still fog had moved in.

Friday blinked. White powder dropped into his eyes, causing them to burn. He blinked harder then pushed a palm into one eye, then the other. He opened them wide and looked out again. He still was not sure what he was looking at but he realized one thing. He was lying on his belly with his face turned to the side. He put his hands under him and pushed up. White powder fell from his arms, his hair, his sides. He blinked it away. He tasted something chalky and spit. His saliva was like paste. The chalky taste was still there. He spit again.

Friday got his knees under him. His body ached from the fall but his hearing was beginning to return. Or at least the ringing was going away; he did not hear anything else. He looked to his left. For a moment he felt as if he were inside a cloud that was inside a cloud. Then the dust that had been shaken from his body began to settle. He could see what he had been looking at a moment ago, what had made no sense to him.

It was wreckage. Where the temple and the police station had stood there was now a hodgepodge of rubble between jagged walls. Through the mist of the powder he could see the sky.

The ringing continued to subside. As it did, Friday heard moans. He put a hand on his knee, pushed down, and began to rise. His back ached and he was trembling. Then his head grew light and his vision darkened. He settled back down on his knees for a moment. He looked ahead and saw the bus through the hanging dust. He also saw people coming toward him.

Suddenly, behind the people, the area around the bus turned yellow-red. Time seemed to slow as the colors exploded in all directions. It was followed by another loud crack that quickly became a rumble. The bus seemed to jump apart. It looked like a balloon that someone had stepped on—stretched out at both ends and then gone. Most of the pieces flew out, away, or down. Some shards skidded along the ground, moving fast and straight like vermin. Larger chunks such as the seats and tires tumbled away, end over end. The people standing nearest the bus were swallowed whole by the fire. Those who were farther away were thrown left, right, and back like the bigger pieces of the bus.

He continued to watch as a charcoal-gray cloud surged forward. Like lightning, flashes of blood and flame punctuated the rolling darkness.

Friday removed his hands from his ears. He rose slowly. He looked down, checking his legs and torso to make sure he had not been hurt. The body had a way of shutting off pain in cases of extreme trauma. His side and right arm ached where he had hit the asphalt. His eyes were gummy from the dust and he had to keep blinking to clear them. Except for the coating of dust from the blasted temple he appeared to be intact.

Papers from books and offices had been lofted high by the blast. They were just now beginning to return to earth. Many of them were just fragments, most were singed, some were ash. A few of the more delicate pages looked like they had belonged to prayer books. Perhaps they had been part of the Sanskrit text the pilgrim had been studying just minutes before.

The gray cloud reached Friday and engulfed him. Nine or ten feet high, it carried the distinctive, noxious smell of burning rubber. Beneath that smell was a sweeter, less choking odor. The stench of charred human flesh and bone. Friday drew a handkerchief from his pocket and held it over his nose and mouth. Then he turned away from the stinging cloud. Behind him the bazaar was still. People had flung themselves to the ground not knowing what might explode next. They were lying under stalls or behind wheelbarrows and carts. As his ears began to clear Friday could hear sobbing, prayer, and moans.

Friday turned back toward the remains of the temple and the police station. The drizzle was helping to thin the cloud of smoke and douse the few fires that had been ignited. No longer light-headed, he began walking toward the rubble. He just now noticed that the police officers who had been standing outside were dead. The backs of their uniforms were bloodied, peppered with shrapnel. Whatever did this had been a concussive device rather than incendiary.

It was strange. Besides the bus, there appeared to be two blastways, the fanlike spray debris followed from the epi-center of an explosion. One line led from the front of the police station. The other led from deep inside the temple. Friday could not understand why there had been two separate explosions on this site. It was unusual enough for two religious targets to be bombed, a temple and a busload of pilgrims. Why was the police station attacked as well?

Sirens cut through the cottony quiet as police who had been on patrol began to arrive. Other officers, who had been out on foot, began to run toward the toppled buildings. People began to get up and leave the bazaar proper. They did not want to be here if there were more explosions. Only a few people headed toward the rubble to see if they might be able to help pull out any survivors.

Ron Friday was not one of those people.

He started walking back toward the inn where he was staying. He wanted to get in touch with his contacts in India and Washington. Learn if they had any intel on what had just happened.

There was a sound like bowling pins falling. Friday looked back just as one of the surviving back walls of the temple crashed onto the rubble. Thick balls of dust swirled from the new wreckage, causing people to step back. After the blocks stopped tumbling, people started moving forward again. Many of them had dustings of white on their faces and hands, like ghosts.

Friday continued walking. His mind was in overdrive.

A police station. A Hindu temple. A busload of pilgrims. Two religious targets and one secular site. Friday could imagine the temple being brought down by accident, collateral damage from an attack on the police station. A lot of terrorist bomb makers were not skilled enough to measure precise charges. A lot of terrorist bomb makers did not care if they took down half a city. But there were those two blast lines suggesting concurrent explosions. And the bus proved that this was a planned assault against Hindus, not just against Indians. Friday could not remember a time when that had happened. Certainly not on this scale.

Yet if Hindus were the target, why did the terrorists attack the police station as well? By striking two religious sites they were obviously not looking to disguise their intent.

Friday stopped walking.

Or were they? he thought suddenly. What if the attack on the temple and bus were distractions? Maybe something else was happening here.

Explosions drew crowds. What if that were the point? To get people to a place or away from one.

Friday wiped his eyes and continued ahead. He looked around as he walked. People were either hurrying toward the disaster site or away from it. Unlike before there were no eddies within eddies. That was because the choices were simple now. Help or flee. He peered down side streets, into windows. He was looking for people who did not appear to be panicked. Perhaps he would see someone, perhaps he would not. The bag on the bus could have been planted at a previous stop. Explosives could have been set to go off with a timer in a suitcase or backpack well padded to take the bumps of the road. Maybe the passenger who was carrying the luggage got off here, deposited additional explosives in the temple and police station, and walked on. Perhaps the bomber was someone who had been masquerading as a pilgrim or a police officer. Perhaps one of the men Friday had been sitting with or looked at had been involved. Perhaps one or more terrorists had been killed in the blast. Anything was possible.

Friday continued to look around. He was not going to see anyone. In terrorist terms, years had passed. Whoever did this was dead or long gone. And he could not see anyone watching from the street, a room, or a rooftop.

The best way to deal with this now was with intel. Collect data from outside the targets and use it to pinpoint possible perpetrators. Then move in on them. Because this much was clear: Now that Hindu targets had been attacked, unless the guilty parties were found and punished, the situation in Kashmir was going to deteriorate very, very quickly. With nuclear war not just an option but a real possibility.

NINE

Srinagar, India
Wednesday, 4:55 P.M.

Sharab was sitting forward in the passenger's seat of the old flatbed truck. To her left the driver sat with his hands tightly clutching the steering wheel. He was perspiring as he guided them north along Route 1A, the same road that had brought the bus to the bazaar. Between them sat Nanda, her right ankle cuffed to an iron spring under the seat. Two other men were seated in the open deck of the truck, leaning against the bulkhead amid bags of wool. They were huddled under a tarp to protect them from the increasingly heavy rain.

The windshield wipers were batting furiously in front of Sharab's dark eyes and the air vent howled. The young woman was also howling. First she had been screaming orders at her team. Get the truck away from the market and stick to the plan, at least until they had additional information. Now she was screaming questions into her cell phone. The young woman was not screaming to be heard over the noise. She was screaming from frustration.

"Ishaq, did you already place the call?" Sharab demanded.

"Of course I placed the call, just as we always do," the man on the other end informed her.

Sharab punched the padded dashboard with the heel of her left hand. The suddenness of the strike caused Nanda to jump. Sharab struck it again but she did not say a word, did not swear. Blaspheming was a sin.

"Is there a problem?" Ishaq asked.

Sharab did not answer.

"You were very specific about it," Ishaq went on. "You wanted me to call at exactly forty minutes past four. I always do what you say."

"I know," the woman said in a low monotone.

"Something is wrong," the man on the telephone said. "I know that tone of voice. What is it?"

"We'll talk later," the woman replied. "I need to think." Sharab sat back.

"Should I turn on the radio?" the driver asked sheepishly. "Maybe there is news, an explanation."

"No," Sharab told him. "I don't need the radio. I know what the explanation is."

The driver fell silent. Sharab shut her eyes. She was wheezing slightly. The truck's vents had pulled in slightly acrid, smoky air from the bazaar blast. The woman could not tell whether it was the air or the screaming that had made her throat raw. Probably both. She shook her head. The urge to scream was still there, at the top of her throat. She wanted to vent her frustration.

Failure was not the worst of this. What bothered Sharab most was the idea that she and her team had been used. She had been warned about this five years ago when she was still in Pakistan, at the combat school in Sargodha. The Special Services Group agents who trained her said she had to be wary of success. When a cell succeeded over and over it might not be because they were good. It might be because the host was allowing them to succeed so they could be watched and used at some later date.

For years Sharab's group, the Pakistan-financed Free Kashmir Militia, had been striking at select targets throughout the region. The modus operandi for each attack was always the same. They would take over a house, plan their assault, then strike the target. At the moment of each attack whichever cell member had remained behind would telephone a regional police or military headquarters. He would claim credit for the attack on behalf of the Free Kashmir Militia. After that the FKM would move to another home. In the end, the isolated farmers whose homes and lives they briefly borrowed cared more about survival than about politics. Many of them were Muslim anyway. Though they did not want to cooperate and risk arrest, they did not resist the FKM.

Sharab and her people only struck military, police, and government offices, never civilian or religious targets. They did not want to push or alienate the Hindu population of Kashmir or India, turn them into hawkish adversaries. They only wanted to deconstruct the resources and the resolve of the Indian leaders. Force them to go home and leave Kashmir.

That was what they were trying to do in the bazaar. Cripple the police but not harm the merchants. Scare people away and impact the local economy just enough so that farmers and shoppers would fight the inflammatory presence of Indian authorities.

They had been so careful to do just that. Over the past few nights one member of the party would go to the bazaar in Srinagar. He would enter the temple dressed in clerical robes, exit in back, and climb to the roof of the police station. There, he would systematically lift tiles and place plastique beneath them. Because it was in the middle of a night shift, when this section of the city was usually quiet, the police were not as alert as during the day. Besides, terrorist attacks did not typically occur at night. The idea of terrorism was to disrupt routine, to make ordinary people afraid to go out.

This morning, well before dawn, the last explosives were placed on the roof along with a timer. The timer had been set to detonate at exactly twenty minutes to five that afternoon. Sharab and the others returned at four thirty to watch from the side of the road to make sure the explosion went off.

It did. And it punched right through her.

When the first blast occurred Sharab knew something was wrong. The plastique they had put down was not strong enough to do the damage this explosion had done. When the second blast went off she knew they had been set up. Muslims had seemingly attacked a Hindu temple and a busload of pilgrims. The sentiments of nearly one billion people would turn against them and the Pakistan people.

But Muslims had not attacked Hindu targets, Sharab thought bitterly. The FKM had attacked a police station.

Some other group had attacked the religious targets and timed it to coincide with the FKM attack.

She did not believe that a member of the cell had betrayed them. The men in the truck had been with her for years. She knew their families, their friends, their backgrounds. They were people of unshakable faith who would never have done anything to hurt the cause.

What about Apu and Nanda? Back at the house they had never been out of their sight except when they were asleep. Even then the door was always ajar and a guard was always awake. The man and his granddaughter did not own a transmitter or cell phone. The house had been searched. There were no neighbors who could have seen or heard them.

Sharab took a long breath and opened her eyes. For the moment, it did not matter. The question was what to do right now.

The truck sped past black-bearded pilgrims in white tunics and mountain men leading ponies from the marketplace. Distant rice paddies were visible at the misty foot of the Himalayas. Trucks bearing more soldiers sped past them, headed toward the bazaar. Maybe they did not know who was responsible for the attack. Or maybe they did not want to catch them right away. Perhaps whoever had framed them was waiting to see if they linked up with other terrorists in Kashmir before closing in.

If that was the case they were going to be disappointed.

Sharab opened the glove compartment and removed a map of the region. There were seventeen grids on the map, each one numbered and lettered. For the purposes of security the numbers and letters were reversed.

"All right, Ishaq," she said into the phone, "I want you to leave the house now and go to position 5B."

What Sharab really meant was that Ishaq should go to area 2E. The *E* came from the *5* and the *2* from the *B*. Anyone who might be listening to the conversation and who might have obtained a copy of their map would go to the wrong spot. "Can you meet us there at seven o'clock?"

"Yes," he said. "What about the old man?"

"Leave him," she said. She glanced at Nanda. The younger girl's expression was defiant. "Remind him that we have his granddaughter. If the authorities ask him about us he is to say nothing. Tell him if we reach the border safely she will be set free."

Ishaq said he would do that and meet the others later.

Sharab hung up. She folded the cell phone and slipped it in the pocket of her blue windbreaker.

There would be time enough for analysis and regrouping. Only one thing mattered right now.

Getting out of the country before the Indians had live scapegoats to parade before the world.

TEN

Siachin Base 3, Kashmir
Wednesday, 5:42 P.M.

Major Dev Puri hung up the phone. A chill shook him from the shoulders to the small of his back.

Puri was sitting behind the small gunmetal desk in his underground command center. On the wall before him was a detailed map of the region. It was spotted with red flags showing Pakistan emplacements and green flags showing Indian bases. Behind him was a map of India and Pakistan. To his left was a bulletin board with orders, rosters, schedules, and reports tacked to it. To his right was a blank wall with a door.

Affectionately known as "the Pit," the shelter was a twelve-by-fourteen-foot hole cut from hard earth and granite. Warping wood-panel walls backed with thick plastic sheets kept the moisture and dirt out but not the cold. How could it? the major wondered. The earth was always cool, like a grave, and the surrounding mountains prevented direct sunlight from ever hitting the Pit. There were no windows or skylights. The only ventilation came from the open door and a rapidly spinning ceiling fan.

Or at least the semblance of ventilation, Puri thought. It was fakery. Just like everything else about this day.

But the cool command center was not what gave Major Puri a chill. It was what the Special Frontier Force liaison had said over the phone. The man, who was stationed in Kargil, had spoken just one word. However, the significance of that word was profound.

"Proceed," he had said.

Operation Earthworm was a go.

On the one hand, the major had to admire the nerve of the SFF. Puri did not know how high up in the government this plan had traveled or where it had originated. Probably with the SFF. Possibly in the Ministry of External Affairs or the Parliamentary Committee on Defence. Both had oversight powers regarding the activities of nonmilitary intelligence groups. Certainly the SFF would have needed their approval for something this big. But Puri did know that if the truth of this action were ever revealed, the SFF would be scapegoated and the overseers of the plot would be executed.

On the other hand, part of him felt that maybe the people behind this deserved to be punished.

A "vaccination." That was how the SFF liaison officer had characterized Operation Earthworm when he first described it just three days before. They were giving the body of India a small taste of sickness to prevent a larger disease from ever taking hold. When the major was a child, smallpox and polio had been fearful diseases. His sister had survived smallpox and it left her scarred. Back then, *vaccination* was a wonderful word.

This was a corruption. However necessary and justifiable it might be, destroying the bus and temple had been vile, unholy acts.

Major Puri reached for the Marlboros on his desk. He shook a cigarette from the pack and lit it. He inhaled slowly and sat back. This was better than chewing the tobacco. It helped him to think clearly, less emotionally.

Less judgmentally.

Everything was relative, the officer told himself.

Back in the 1940s his parents were pacifists. They had not approved of him becoming a soldier. They would have been happy if he had joined them and other citizens of Haryana in the government's fledgling caste advancement program. The Backward Classes list guaranteed a gift of low-paying government jobs for underprivileged natives of seventeen states. Dev Puri had not wanted that. He had wanted to make it on his own.

And he had.

Puri drew harder on the cigarette. He was suddenly disgusted with his own value judgments. The SFF had obviously viewed this action as a necessary extension of business as usual. Trained jointly by the American CIA and the Indian military's RAW—Research and Analysis Wing—the SFF were masters of finding and spying on foreign agents and terrorists. For the most part, enemy operatives and suspected collaborators were eliminated without fanfare or heavy firepower. Occasionally, through a specially recruited unit, Civilian Network Operatives, the SFF also used foreign agents to send disinformation back to Pakistan. In the case of Sharab and her group, the SFF had spent months planning a more elaborate scheme. They felt it was necessary to frame Pakistan terrorists for the murder of dozens of innocent Hindus. Then, when the Pakistani cell members were captured—as they would be, thanks to the CNO operative who was traveling with them—documents and tools would be "found" on the terrorists. These would show that Sharab and her party had traveled the country planting targeting beacons for nuclear strikes against Indian cities. That would give the Indian military a moral imperative to make a preemptive strike against Pakistan's missile silos.

Major Puri drew on the cigarette again. He looked at his watch. It was nearly time to go.

Over the past ten years more than a quarter of a million Hindus had left the Kashmir Valley to go to other parts of India. With a growing Muslim majority it was increasingly difficult for Indian authorities to secure this region from terrorism. Moreover, Pakistan had recently deployed nuclear weapons and was working to increase its nuclear arsenal as quickly as possible. Puri knew they had to be stopped. Not just to retain Kashmir but to keep hundreds of thousands more refugees from flooding the neighboring Indian provinces.

Maybe the SFF was right. Maybe this was the time and place to stop the Pakistani aggression. Major Puri only wished there had been some other way to trigger the event.

He drew long and hard on the cigarette and then crushed it in the ashtray beside the phone. The tin receptacle was filled with partly smoked cigarettes. They were the residue of three afternoons filled with anxiety, doubt, and the looming pressure of his role in the operation. His aide would have emptied it if a Pakistani artillery shell had not blown his right arm off during a Sunday night game of checkers.

The major rose. It was time for the late afternoon intelligence report from the other outposts on the base. Those were always held in the officers' bunker further along the trench. This meeting would be different in just one respect. Puri would ask the other officers to be prepared to initiate a code yellow nighttime evacuation drill. If the Indian air force planned to "light up" the mountains with nuclear missiles, the front lines would have to be cleared of personnel well in advance of the attack. It would have to be done at night when there was less chance of the Pakistanis noticing. The enemy would also be given a warning, though a much shorter one. There would be no point in striking the sites if the missiles were mobile and Pakistan had time to move them.

Around seven o'clock, after the meeting was finished, the major would eat his dinner, go to sleep, and get up early to start the next phase of the top-secret operation. He was one of the few officers who knew about an American team that was coming to Kashmir to help the Indian military find the missile silos. The Directorate of Air Intelligence, which would be responsible for the strikes, knew generally where the silos were located. But they needed more specific information. Scatter-bombing the Himalaya Mountains was not an efficient use of military resources. And given the depth at which the silos were probably buried, it might be necessary to strike with more than conventional weapons. India needed to know that as well.

Of course, they had not shared this plan with their unwitting partners in this operation.

The United States wanted intelligence on Pakistan's nuclear capacity as much as India did. The Americans needed to know who was helping to arm Islamabad and whether the missiles they had deployed could reach other non-Muslim nations. Both Washington and New Delhi knew that if an American unit were discovered in Kashmir it would cause a diplomatic row but not start a war. Thus, the U.S. government had offered to send over a team that was off the normal military radar. Anonymity was important since Russia, China, and other nations had moles at U.S. military installations. These spies kept an eye on the comings and goings of the U.S. Navy SEALs, the U.S. Army Delta Force 1st Special Forces Operational Detachment, and other elite forces. The information they gathered was used internally and also sold to other nations.

The team that was en route from Washington, the National Crisis Management Center's Striker unit, had experience in mountain silo surveillance going back to a successful operation in the Diamond Mountains of North Korea years before. They were linking up with a NSA operative who had worked with the the Indian government and knew the area they would be searching.

Major Puri had to make certain that as soon as the American squad arrived the search-and-identify mission went smoothly and quickly. The Americans would not be told of the capture of the Pakistani cell. They would not know that a strike was actually in the offing. That information would only be revealed when it was necessary to blunt international condemnation of India's actions. If necessary, the participation of the Striker unit would also be exposed. The United States would have no choice then but to back the Indian strike.

Puri tugged on the hem of his jacket to straighten it. He picked up his turban, placed it squarely on his head, and headed for the door. He was glad of one thing, at least. His name was not attached to the SFF action in any way. As far as any official communiqués were concerned, he had simply been told to help the Americans find the silos.

He was just doing his job.

He was just carrying out orders.

ELEVEN

Washington, D.C.
Wednesday, 8:21 A.M.

"This is not good," Bob Herbert said as he stared at the computer monitor. "This is not good at all."

The intelligence chief had been reviewing the latest satellite images from the mountains bordering Kashmir. Suddenly, a State Department news update flashed across the screen. Herbert clicked on the headline and had just started reading when the desk phone beeped. He glanced with annoyance at the small black console. It was an outside line. Herbert jabbed the button and picked up the receiver. He continued reading.

"Herbert here," he said.

"Bob, this is Hank Lewis," said the caller.

The name was familiar but for some reason Herbert could not place it. Then again, he was not trying very hard. He was concentrating on the news brief. According to the update there had been two powerful explosions in Srinagar. Both of them were directed at Hindu targets. That was going to ratchet up tensions along the line of control. Herbert needed to get more information and brief Paul Hood and General Rodgers as soon as possible.

"I've been meaning to call since I took over at NSA," Lewis said, "but it's been brutal getting up to speed."

Jesus, Herbert thought. That's who Hank Lewis was. Jack Fenwick's replacement at the National Security Agency. Lewis had just signed off on the NSA's participation in the Striker mission. Herbert should have known the name right away. But he forgave himself. He had a mission headed into a hot zone that had just become hotter. His brain was on autopilot.

"You don't have to explain. I know what the workload is like over there," Herbert assured him. "I assume you're calling about the State Department update on Kashmir?"

"I haven't seen that report yet," Lewis admitted. "But I did receive a call from Ron Friday, the man who's supposed to meet your Striker team. He told me what you probably read. That an hour ago there were three powerful bomb blasts in a bazaar in Srinagar."

"Three?" Herbert replied. "The State Department says there were two explosions."

"Mr. Friday was within visual range of ground zero," Lewis informed him. "He said there were simultaneous explosions in both the police station and in the Hindu temple. They were followed by a third blast onboard a bus full of Hindu pilgrims."

Hearing the event described, Herbert flashed back to the embassy bombing in Beirut. The moment of the explosion was not what stayed with him. That was like running a car into a wall, a full-body hit. What he remembered, vividly, was the sickness of coming to beneath the rubble and realizing in a sickening instant exactly what had happened.

"Was your man hurt?" Herbert asked.

"Incredibly, no," Lewis said. "Mr. Friday said the explosions would have been worse except that high-impact concussive devices were employed. That minimized the damage radius."

"He was lucky," Herbert said. HiCon explosives tended to produce a big percussive center, nominal shock waves, and very little collateral damage. "So why is Friday so sure the first two hits were separate blasts? The second one could have been an oil or propane tank exploding. There are often secondary pops in attacks of this kind."

"Mr. Friday was very specific about the explosions being simultaneous, not successive," Lewis replied. "After the attack he also found two very similar but separate debris trails leading from the buildings. That suggests identical devices in different locations."

"Possibly," Herbert said.

An expression from Herbert's childhood came floating back: He who smelt it dealt it. Op-Center's intelligence chief briefly wondered if Friday might have been responsible for the blasts. However, Herbert could not think of a reason for Friday to have done that. And he had not become cynical enough to look for a reason. Not yet, anyway.

"Let's say there were three blasts," Herbert said. "What do your nerve endings tell you about all this?"

"My immediate thought, of course, is that the Pakistans are turning up the heat by attacking religious targets," Lewis replied. "But we don't have enough intel to back that up."

"And if the idea was to hit at the Hindus directly, why would they strike the police station as well?" Herbert asked.

"To cripple their pursuit capabilities, I would imagine," Lewis suggested.

"Maybe," Herbert replied.

Everything Lewis said made sense. Which meant one of two things. Either he was right or the obvious answer was what the perpetrators wanted investigators to believe.

"Your Strikers won't be arriving for another twenty-two hours and change," Lewis said. "I'm going to have Mr. Friday go back to the target area and see what he can learn. Are there any resources you can call on?"

"Yes," Herbert said. "India's Intelligence Bureau and the Defense Ministry helped us to organize the Striker mission. I'll see what they know and get back to you."

"Thanks," Lewis said. "By the way, I'm looking forward to working with you. I've followed your career ever since you went over to Germany to take on those neo-Nazis. I trust men who get out from behind their desk. It means they put job and country before personal security."

"Either that or it means they're crazy," Herbert said. "But thanks. Stay in touch."

Lewis said he would. Herbert hung up.

It was refreshing to talk to someone in the covert community who was actually willing to share information. Intelligence chiefs were notoriously secretive. If they controlled information they could control people and institutions. Herbert refused to play that game. While it was good for job security it was bad for national security. And as Jack Fenwick had demonstrated, a secretive intelligence chief could also control a president.

But though Ron Friday was a seasoned field operative, Herbert was not quite as willing to bet the ranch on his report. Herbert only believed in people he had worked with himself.

Herbert phoned Paul Hood to brief him on the new development. Hood asked to be conferenced on the call to Mike Rodgers whenever that took place. Then Herbert put in a call to the Indian Intelligence Bureau. Sujit Rani, the deputy director of internal activities, told Herbert pretty much what he expected to hear: that the IIB was investigating the explosions but did not have any additional information. The notion that there had been three explosions, not two, was something the IIB had heard and was looking into. That information vindicated Ron Friday somewhat in Herbert's eyes. Herbert's contact at the Defense Ministry told him basically the same thing. Fortunately, there was time before Striker reached India. They would be able to abort the mission if necessary.

Herbert went into the Kashmir files. He wanted to check on other recent terrorist strikes in the region. Maybe he could find clues, a pattern, something that would help to explain this new attack. Something about it did not sit right. If Pakistan were really looking to turn up the heat in Kashmir they probably would have struck at a place that had intense religious meaning, like the shrine at Pahalgam. Not only was that the most revered site in the region but the terrorists would not have had to worry about security. The Hindus trusted completely in their sacred trinity. If it was the will of Vishnu the preserver then they would not be harmed. If they died violently then Shiva the destroyer would avenge them. And if they were worthy, Brahma the creator would reincarnate them.

No. Bob Herbert's gut was telling him that the Hindu temple, the bus, and the police station were struck for some other reason. He just did not know what that reason was.

But he would.

TWELVE

C-130 Cabin
Wednesday, 10:13 A.M.

When he first joined Striker, Corporal Ishi Honda discovered that there was not a lot of downtime on the ground. There was a great deal of drilling, especially for him. Honda had joined the team late, replacing Private Johnny Puckett who had been wounded on the mission to North Korea. It was necessary for Honda, then a twenty-two-year-old private, to get up to speed.

Once he got there Honda never let up. His mother used to tell him he was fated never to rest. She ascribed it to the different halves of his soul. Ishi's maternal grandfather had been a civilian cook at Wheeler Field. He died trying to get home to his family during the Japanese attack on Pearl Harbor. Ishi's paternal grandfather had been a high-ranking officer on the staff of Rear Admiral Takajiro Onishi, chief of staff of the Eleventh Air Fleet. Onishi was the architect of the Japanese attack. Ishi's parents were actors who met and fell in love on a show tour without knowing anything about the other's background. They often debated whether knowing that would have made a difference. His father said it absolutely would not have. With a little shake of her head, her eyes downturned, his mother said it might have made a difference.

Ishi had no answers and maybe that was why he could not stop pushing himself. Part of him believed that if he ever stopped moving he would inevitably look at that question, whether or not a piece of information would have kept him from being born. And he did not want to do that because the question had no answer. Honda did not like problems without solutions.

What he did like was living the life of a Striker. It not only taxed him mentally, it challenged him physically.

From the time he was recruited to join the elite unit there were long daily runs, obstacle courses, hand-to-hand combat, arms practice, survival training, and maneuvers. The field work was always tougher for Honda than for the others. In addition to his survival gear he had to carry the TAC-SAT equipment. There were also tactical and political sessions and language classes. Colonel August had insisted that the Strikers learn at least two languages each in the likely event that those skills would one day be required. At least Honda had an advantage there. Because his father was Japanese, Honda already had a leg up on one of the languages he had been assigned. He selected Mandarin Chinese as the other. Sondra DeVonne had chosen Cantonese as one of her languages. It was fascinating to Honda that the languages shared identical written characters. Yet the spoken languages were entirely different. While he and DeVonne could read the same texts they could not communicate verbally.

Though the time the Strikers spent on the ground was rewarding, Honda had learned that their time in the air was anything but. They rarely took short trips and the long journeys could be extremely dull. That was why he had come up with constructive ways of filling his time.

Wherever they were going, Honda arranged to patch his personal computer into the data files of both Stephen Viens at the National Reconnaissance Office and those of Op-Center's computer chief, Matt Stoll. The NRO was the group that managed most of America's spy satellites. Because Viens was an old college chum of Stoll's, he had been extremely helpful in getting information for Op-Center when more established groups like military intelligence, the CIA, and the NSA were fighting for satellite time. Viens was later accused of forward-funding two billion dollars of NRO money into a variety of black ops projects. He was vindicated with Op-Center's help and recently returned to duty.

Before Striker headed to any territory, Viens set aside satellite time to do all the photographic recon that Colonel August needed. That imaging was considered of primary importance and was sent on the mission in Colonel August's files. Meanwhile, Stoll spent as much time as possible collecting electronic intelligence from the region. Police departments and the military did not share everything they knew, even with allies. In many foreign countries, especially Russia, China, and Israel, American operatives were often watched without their knowledge by foreign operatives. It was up to Op-Center to pick up whatever information they could and protect themselves accordingly. They did this by diverging from the agreed-upon routes and time schedules, using "dispensable" team members to mislead tails, or occasionally subduing whoever was following them. A host nation could not complain if the person they had sent to spy on an ally was later found bound and gagged in a hotel closet.

The ELINT Stoll had gathered was composed of everything from fax messages and e-mail to phone numbers and radio frequencies. Everything that came to or went from official sources or known resistance and opposition forces. These numbers, frequencies, and encryption codes were then run through programs. They were compared with those of known terrorists or foreign agents. If there were any possible "watchdogs or impediments" in the region, as mission planners referred to them, these scans helped to find and identify them. The last thing American intelligence chiefs wanted was to have undercover operatives photographed or their methods observed by foreign governments. Not only could that information be sold to a third party, but the United States never knew which friendly governments might one day be intelligence targets.

"Think Iran," Colonel August reminded them whenever they went on a joint mission with allies.

Honda had brought along a Striker laptop. The computer was equipped with a wireless, high-speed modem to download data Stoll was still collecting. Honda would memorize any relevant data. When Striker reached India, the computer would be left on the transport and returned to the base. Colonel August would keep his laptop to download data. Where they were going, the less Corporal Honda had to carry the happier he would be.

As the new intelligence was dumped into Honda's computer, an audio prompt pinged. It was alerting him to an anomaly that Stoll's program had picked up at Op-Center. Honda accessed the flagged data.

The Bellhop program on the air force's "Sanctity" satellite continually scanned the cell phones and radios that used police bands. Op-Center and the other U.S. intelligence agencies had these numbers for their own communications with foreign offices. It was a simple matter to hack the computers and look for other incoming calls.

The Bellhop had picked up a series of point-to-point calls made on a police-registered cell phone. It was coded "field phone" in the Bellhop lexicon. Most of the calls were placed over a five-month period from Kargil to the district police headquarters in Jammu, coded "home phone." During that time there was only one call to that field phone from the home phone. Stoll's program, which integrated Op-Center intel with NRO data, indicated that the call was placed less than one second before the Kashmir-focused ClusterStar3 satellite recorded an explosion in a bazaar in Srinagar.

"Damn," Honda muttered.

Honda wondered if Colonel August or General Rodgers had been informed about a possible terrorist attack. The fact that a police cell phone made a call to the site an instant before the explosion could be a coincidence. Perhaps someone was phoning a security guard. On the other hand there might be a connection between the two. Honda unbuckled himself from the uncomfortable seat and went forward to inform his commanding officers. He had to walk slowly, carefully, to keep from being bucked against his teammates by the aircraft's movements in the turbulent air.

August and Rodgers were huddled together over the general's laptop when he arrived.

"Excuse me, sirs," Honda said. He had to shout to be heard over the screaming engines.

August looked up. "What have you got, Corporal?"

Honda told the two officers about the explosion. August informed Honda that they were just reading an e-mail from Bob Herbert about the blast. It provided what few details anyone had about the attack. Then Honda informed his superiors about the phone calls. That seemed to grab General Rodgers's interest.

"There were two calls a day for five months, always at the same time," Honda said.

"Like a routine check-in," Rodgers said.

"Exactly, sir," Honda replied. "Except for today. There was just one call and it was made to the field phone. It was placed a moment before the explosion that took out the temple."

Rodgers sat back. "Corporal, would you go through the data file and see if this calling pattern is repeated, probably from field phones with different code numbers? Outgoing calls to one home phone and one or none coming back?"

"Yes, sir," Honda replied.

Honda crouched on the cold, rumbling floor and raised one knee. He put the laptop upon it. He was not sure what the officers were looking for exactly and it was not his place to ask. He input the code number of the home phone and asked for a Bellhop search. Colonel August's hunch was correct. He told them that in addition to this series there were seven weeks of calls from another field phone in Kargil. They were made twice a day at the same times. Before that there were six weeks of calls from another field phone, also two times daily. Thirteen weeks was as far back as these Bellhop records went.

"New Delhi must have had civilian agents tracking a terrorist cell," Rodgers said.

"How do you know that?" August asked. "The calls may just have been field ops reporting in."

"I don't think so," Rodgers told him. "First of all, only one of the calls on Corporal Honda's list was made from the home phone to the field phone."

"That was the one made at the time of the explosion," August said.

"Correct," Rodgers replied. "That would suggest the officers in charge of the recon did not want field phones ringing at inopportune moments."

"I'll buy that," August said.

"There's more than that, though," Rodgers said. "When Pakistan was knocked out of Kargil in 1999, the Indian Special Frontier Force knew that enemy cells would be left behind. They couldn't hunt them down with soldiers. The locals would have known if strangers were moving through a village. And if the locals knew it members of the cell would have known it. So the SFF recruited a shitload of locals to serve in their Civilian Network Operatives unit." The general tapped his laptop. "It's all here in the intelligence overview. But they couldn't give the recruits normal militia radios because, that close to Pakistan, those channels are routinely monitored by ELINT personnel. So the SFF gave their recruits cell phones. The agents call the regional office and complain about break-ins, missing children, stolen livestock, that sort of thing. What they're really doing is using coded messages to keep the SFF informed about suspected terrorist movements and activities."

"All right," August said. "But what makes you think the calls on this list aren't just routine field reports?"

"Because CNO personnel don't make routine field reports," Rodgers said. "They only report when they have something to say. There's less chance of them being overheard that way. I'm willing to bet that there are terrorist strikes to coincide with the termination of each of those series of calls. A target was hit, the cell moved on, the calls stopped being placed."

"Perhaps," August said. "But that doesn't explain the call to the temple right before the blast."

"Actually, it might," Rodgers told him.

"I don't follow," August said.

Rodgers looked up at Honda. "Corporal, would you please get the TAC-SAT?"

"Yes, sir."

Rodgers turned back to August. "I'm going to ask Bob Herbert to check on the dates of terrorist strikes in the region," he said. "I want to see if reports from field phones stopped coming in after terrorist strikes. I also want Bob to look into something else."

"What's that?" August asked.

Honda closed his laptop and stood. He lingered long enough to hear Rodgers's reply.

"I want to know what kind of detonator caps the SFF uses for counterterrorist strikes," the general replied.

"Why?" August asked.

"Because the Mossad, the Iraqi Al Amn al-Khas, Abu Nidal's group, and the Spanish Grapo have all used PDEs on occasion," Rodgers said. "Phone-detonated explosives."

THIRTEEN

Srinagar, Kashmir
Wednesday, 6:59 P.M.

It was nearly dark when Ron Friday returned to the bazaar. Though he was curious to see how the authorities here were handling the investigation he was more interested in what he might be able to find out about the attack. His life might depend on that information.

The rain had stopped and there was a cold wind rolling off the mountains. Friday was glad he had worn a baseball cap and a windbreaker, though the drop in temperature was not the reason he had put them on. Even from his room he could hear helicopters circling the area. When Friday arrived he found that the two police choppers were hovering low, less than two hundred feet up. In addition to looking for survivors, the noise echoing loudly through the square helped to keep onlookers from staying too long. But that was not the only reason the choppers were there. Friday guessed that they were also maintaining a low altitude to photograph the crowd in case the terrorist was still in the area. The cockpits were probably equipped with GRRs—geometric reconstructive recorders. These were digital cameras that could take photographs shot at an angle and reconfigure the geometry so they became accurate frontal images. Interpol and most national security agencies had a "face-print" file consisting of mug shots and police sketches of known and suspected terrorists. Like fingerprints, face-print photographs could be run through a computer and compared to images on file. The computer superimposed the likenesses. If the features were at least a 70 percent match, that was considered sufficient to go after the individual for interrogation.

Friday had worn the baseball cap because he did not want to be face-printed by the chopper. He did not know which governments might have his likeness on file or for what reason. He certainly did not want to give them a picture with which to start a file.

The blast sights had been roped off with red tape. Spotlights on ten-foot-tall tripods had been erected around the perimeters. Physically, the main market area reminded Friday of a gymnasium after a dance. The event was over, the place eerily lifeless, and the residue of activity was everywhere. Only here, instead of punch there were bloodstains. Instead of crepe there were shredded awnings. And instead of empty seats there were abandoned carts. Some of the vendors had taken their carts away, leaving dust-free spots on the ground in the shape of the stall. In the sharp light they resembled the black shadows of trees and people that had been burned on the walls of Hiroshima and Nagasaki by nuclear fire. Other carts had been simply abandoned. Perhaps the owners had not been there when the blast occurred and the hired help did not want to stick around. Maybe some of the sellers had been injured or killed.

Militiamen from the regular army were stationed around the perimeters. They were carrying MP5K submachine guns, very visible in the bright lights. Police were patrolling the square carrying their distinctive .455 Webley revolvers. Apart from discouraging looters—which did not really require exposed firearms—there was only one reason to haul out artillery after a strike. It was a means of restoring wounded pride and reassuring the public that the people in charge were still a potent force. It was all so sadly predictable.

Reporters were allowed to make their news broadcasts or take their pictures and then were asked to leave. An officer explained to a crew from CNN that it would be more difficult to watch for looters if a crowd gathered.

Or maybe they just did not want cameras recording their own thefts, Friday thought. He was willing to bet that many of the goods that had been left behind would be gone by morning.

A few people had come to the marketplace just to stare. Whatever they expected to see—broken bodies, the spectacle of destruction, news being made—it did not appear to fulfill them. Most left looking deflated. Bomb sites, combat zones, and car wrecks often did that to people. They were drawn to it and then repulsed. Maybe they were disappointed by a sudden awareness of their own bloodthirstiness. Some people came with flowers, which they laid on the ground beneath the tape. Others just left behind prayers for dead friends, relatives, or strangers.

At the destroyed police station and temple, building inspectors were moving through surrounding structures to determine whether they had been weakened or damaged in the blasts. Friday recognized them by their white hard hats and palm-sized echometers. These devices emitted either single- or multidirectional sound waves that could be adjusted to the composition of an object, from stone to concrete to wood. If the sound waves encountered anything that was inconsistent with the makeup of the material—which typically meant a breach—an alarm would sound and the officials would examine the site further.

Apart from the engineers there were the usual police recovery units and medical personnel working at all three sites. But Friday was surprised by one thing. Typically, terrorist attacks in India were investigated by the district police and the National Security Guard. The NSG was established in 1986 to act as a counterterrorist force. The so-called Black Cat Commandos handled situations ranging from in-progress hijackings and kidnappings to forensic activities at bomb sites. However, there was not a single black-uniformed NSG operative here. These sites were under the control of the brown-uniformed Special Frontier Force. Friday had never been to any bomb sites in Srinagar. Maybe this was the way responsibility for antiterrorist investigations had been parceled out, with the SFF getting the region nearest the line of control.

Friday was motioned along by one of the police officers. He would not be able to get into the rubble himself. But he could still come up with some sound ideas about how the attack was made. As he walked toward the place where the bus had exploded, Friday used his cell phone to call Samantha Mandor at the NSA's photo archives. He asked her to search the AP, UPI, Reuters, and other digital photograph files for pictures of sites struck by terrorists in Kashmir. He also wanted her to pull together any analysis files that were attached to the photographs. He probably had some of those in his own computer files back in his room. But he wanted information that was incident-specific. Friday told her to phone back the minute she had the photo and text archives.

The American operative neared the roped-off bus site. Unlike the two buildings, where the walls had kept people and objects from the street, the bus debris had been strewn everywhere by the powerful explosion. The bodies had been cleared away but the street was covered with metal, leather, and glass from the bus itself. There were books and cameras that the passengers had been carrying and travel accessories, clothing, and religious icons that had been packed in luggage. Unlike the buildings, this scene was a snapshot of the moment of impact.

Friday's cell phone beeped as he neared the red tape. He stopped walking and took the call.

"Yes?" he said.

"Mr. Friday? It's Samantha Mandor. I have the photographs and information you asked for. Do you want me to send the images somewhere? There are about four dozen color pictures."

"No," Friday said. "When was the last attack in Srinagar?"

"Five months ago," Samantha told him. "It was against a shipment of artillery shells that were en route to the line of control. The attack caused one hell of an explosion."

"Was it a suicide bombing?" he asked.

"No," Samantha said. "There's a microscopic image of liquid crystal display fragments that were found near ground zero. The lab analysis says it was part of a timer. They also said a remote sensor was found in the debris but that it was apparently not detonated."

That was probably part of a backup plan, Friday thought. Professionals often included a line-of-sight device to trigger the explosives in case the timer did not work or if the device were discovered before the timer could activate them. The presence of an LOS receiver meant that at least one of the terrorists was almost certainly in the area when the device exploded.

"What about the personnel at the bomb site?" Friday asked. "What kind of uniforms were they wearing?"

"There were National Security Guard officers as well as local police on the scene," the woman informed him.

"Any members of the Special Frontier Force?" Friday asked.

"None," she said. "There were additional assaults against military targets in Srinagar. They occurred six and seven weeks prior to that attack. National Security Guard officers were present there as well."

"Did anyone claim responsibility for those attacks?" Friday asked.

"According to the data file those two and this one were claimed by the same group," Samantha told him. "The Free Kashmir Militia."

"Thank you," Friday said. He had heard of them. Reportedly, they had the backing of the Pakistan government.

"Will you need anything else?" Samantha asked.

"Not right now," he replied and clicked off.

Friday hooked the cell phone to his belt. He would call his new boss later, when he had something solid to report. He looked around. There were no Black Cat Commandos here. Maybe that was significant, maybe it was not. Their absence might have been a territorial issue. Or maybe the NSG had been unable to stop the terrorists and the problem had been turned over to the SFF. Perhaps a former SFF officer had been named to a high government post. Appointments like that routinely led to reorganizations.

Of course, there was always the possibility that this was not routine. What kind of exceptional circumstances would lead to a department being shut out of an investigation? That would certainly happen if security were an issue. Friday wondered if the NSG might have been compromised by Pakistani operatives. Or maybe the SFF had made it look as though the Black Cats had been penetrated. Because budgets were tighter there was even more interagency rivalry here than there was in the United States.

Friday turned around slowly. There were several two- and three-story-high buildings around the market. However, those would not have been good vantage points for the terrorists. If they had needed to use the remote detonators, the carts with their high banners, awnings, and umbrellas might have blocked the line of sight. If there had been any cooked-food stands in the way smoke might also have obscured their vision. Besides, the terrorists would also have had the problem of renting rooms. There was a danger in leaving a paper trail, like the terrorists who charged the van they used to attack the World Trade Center in New York. And only amateur terrorists paid cash for a room. That was a red flag that usually sent landlords right to the police. Not even the greediest landlord wanted someone who might be a bomb maker living in their building.

Besides, there was no need to hide here. It would have been easy for a terrorist to remain anonymous in this busy marketplace day after day to case the targets, plant the explosives, and watch the site today. But Friday did wonder one thing. Why did the police station and the temple blow up at the same time while the bus did not explode until several seconds later? It was extremely likely that they were related attacks. It could have been that the timers were slightly out-of-synch. Or maybe there was another reason.

Friday continued walking to where the bus had been parked. Traffic had been diverted from Route 1A to other streets. He was able to stand in the broad avenue and look back at the site. This road was the most direct way out of here. It fed any number of roads. Pursuit would have been extremely difficult even if the police knew the individual or kind of vehicle they were looking for. He found the line-of-sight spot that would have been the ideal place to stand in case the timer failed. It was on the curb, near where the bus was parked. It was about four hundred yards from the target, which was near the maximum range for most remote detonators. Obviously, if a terrorist were waiting there for the blast, he would not have wanted the bus to blow up yet. He would have waited until after the temple explosion then moved a safe distance away. The bus explosion would have been scheduled to give him time to get away. Or else he had triggered the blast himself using the same remote he would have used on the temple.

But that still did not tell him why there were two separate explosions for the police station and temple. One large explosion would have brought both structures down.

Friday started back toward the other end of the market. When he got back to his room he would call the NSA. The market attack itself did not bother him. He did not really give a damn who ended up being in charge here. What concerned him were the Black Cats. These people would have access to intelligence about him and Striker once they went into the mountains. If there was even a possibility that the NSG was leaking, he wanted to make sure they were kept out of the circuit.

FOURTEEN

Kargil, Kashmir
Wednesday, 7:00 P.M.

As his motorcycle sped through the foothills of the Himalayas, Ishaq Fazeli wished he had one thing above all. He had left Apu's farm without eating dinner and he was hungry. But he did not want food. He had been driving with his mouth open—a bad habit—and his tongue was dry. But he did not want water. What he wanted most was a helmet.

As the lightweight Royal Endfield Bullet sped through the mountain pass, small, flat rocks spit from under the slender wheels. Whenever the roadway narrowed, as it did now, and Ishaq passed too close to the mountainside, the sharp-edged pebbles came back at him like bullets. He would even settle for a turban if he had the material to make one and the time to stop. Instead, Ishaq adjusted to driving with his face turned slightly to the left. As long as the pebbles did not hit his eyes he would be all right. And if they did he would be philosophical about it. He would still have his left eye. Growing up in the west, near the Khyber Pass, he had learned long ago that the mountains of the subcontinent were not for the weak.

For one thing, even during a short two-hour ride like this, the weather changes quickly. Brutal sunshine can give way to a snow squall within minutes. Sleet can turn to thick fog even quicker. Travelers who are unprepared can freeze or dehydrate or lose their way before reaching safety. Sunshine, wind, precipitation, heat and cold from fissures, caverns, and lofty tors—all rush madly around the immutable peaks, clashing and warring in unpredictable ways. In that respect the mountains reminded Ishaq of the ancient caliphs. They too were towering and imperious, answering only to Allah.

For another thing, the foothills of the Himalayas are extremely difficult to negotiate on foot, let alone on a motorcycle. The mountain range is relatively young and the slopes are still sharp and steep. Here, in Kashmir, the few paths one finds were originally made by the British in 1845 at the onset of the Anglo-Sikh Wars. Queen Victoria's elite mountain forces used the routes, known as "cuts," to flank enemy troops that were encamped in lower elevations. Too narrow for trucks, cars, and artillery, and too precarious for horses and other pack animals, the cuts fell into disuse at the time of the First World War and remained largely untraveled until the Pakistanis rediscovered them in 1947. While the Indians used helicopters to move men and matériel through the region, the Pakistanis preferred these slower, more secretive paths. The cuts peaked at around eight thousand feet, where the temperatures were too low at night and the air too cold to support simple bedroll camps or sustained marches.

Not that the hazards or the discomfort mattered to Ishaq right now. He had a mission to accomplish and a leader to serve. Nothing would get in the way of that. Not precipitous falls, or the hornetlike pebbles that wanted to send him there, or the sudden drop in the temperature.

Fortunately, the motorcycle performed as heroically as its reputation. More than a year before, Ishaq had taken the Royal Endfield Bullet from behind an army barracks. It was a beautiful machine. It was not one of the prized vintage bikes from the 1950s, made when the British company first set up its factory in India. But the machine was standard equipment of local military and police units. As such, it did not attract undue attention. And there were tactical advantages as well. Like all the Royal Endfield Bullets, the distinctive red-and-black motorcycle got exceptional mileage and had a maximum speed of nearly eighty miles an hour. The bike was durable and the 22 bhp engine was relatively quiet. At just under four hundred pounds the bike also caused very little stress on the cliffside portions of the road. And the low noise output was important as he made his way up into the foothills, where loud sounds could cause rock slides.

Ishaq saw small numbers carved in the side of the mountain. They indicated that the elevation was four thousand feet. The Free Kashmir Militiaman was behind schedule. He pushed the bike a little faster. The wind rushed at him, causing his cheeks to flutter. The noise they made sounded almost like the motorcycle engine. By the grace of the Prophet he and the machine had become one. He smiled at the ways of Allah.

Section 2E was near the high midpoint of the cuts. Pakistani troops had spent years mapping this region. When they retreated from Kargil, the troops left a large cache of weapons, explosives, clothes, passports, and medical supplies in a cave at the high point of the sector. Sharab and her team frequently retreated to the spot to replenish their stores.

Ishaq had kept an eye on his watch as he pushed higher into the hills. He did not want to keep Sharab waiting. That was not because their leader was intolerant or impatient but because he wanted to be there for her—whenever, wherever, and for whatever reason she needed him. A political professor with no prior field experience, Sharab's dedication and tactical ingenuity had quickly earned the respect and complete devotion of every member of the team. Ishaq was also a little bit in love with her, although he was careful not to let that show. He did not want her thinking that was the only reason he was with her. She liked to work with patriots, not admirers. Yet Ishaq often wondered if the leaders of the Free Kashmir Militia had asked her to lead this group because she was a woman. When ancient physicians used to cauterize the wounds of warriors it took five or more men to restrain the injured man—or one woman. For love of Sharab or fear of shaming their manhood, there was nothing the men in her cell would refuse to do.

A .38 Smith & Wesson was snug in a holster under his wool sweater. The handgun came to the FKM via the Karachi Airport security police, which had bought nearly one thousand of the weapons from the United States almost thirty years before. The weight of the loaded gun felt good against his ribs. Ishaq's faith taught him that it was only through the

Prophet and Allah that a man became strong. Ishaq believed that, passionately. Prayer and the Koran gave him strength. But there was also something empowering about having a weapon at your side. Religion was a satisfying meal that carried a man through the day. The Smith & Wesson was a snack that got him through the moment.

The road became bumpier due to recent rockfall from a cliff. The outside corners were also more precarious. To make things worse, a cool drizzle began. It nicked his face like windblown sand. But despite all this he pushed the motorcycle even harder. If the rain kept up and had a chance to freeze, the cut would become brutally slick. He also had to watch out for hares and other animals. Hitting one could cause him to skid. Still, he could not slow down. Not if he were going to reach the zone in time. They always met up here after a mission but never with such urgency. First, Sharab usually liked to go back to whatever house or hut or barn they had occupied in order to have a final talk with their host. She wanted to make sure that whoever she left behind understood that they would remain alive only as long as they remained silent. Some of the team members did not agree with her charity, especially when they were Hindus like Apu and his granddaughter. But Sharab did not want to turn the people against her. To her, whether they were Muslim or not, most of these farmers, shepherds, and factory workers were already Pakistani. She did not want to kill innocent countrymen, present or future.

The skies were dark and Ishaq flipped on his headlights. A powerful lamp illuminated the road almost two hundred yards ahead. That was barely enough visibility to allow him to keep moving at his current pace. Curves came up so suddenly that he nearly went off the cut twice. Every now and then he slowed for just a moment to keep from feeling like he could fly. That was a very real delusion at this height and these speeds. He also took that time to glance back. He wanted to make sure he was not being followed. With the hum of the engine echoing off the crags and valleys, the sputtering of his cheeks, and the knocking of the thrown pebbles, Ishaq would not necessarily hear the roar of a pursuing vehicle or helicopter. He had warned Apu to stay in the house and he had cut the telephone line. But still—one never knew how a man would react when a family member was in captivity.

Ishaq saw another roadside marker. He was at forty-five hundred feet now. He did not know exactly how far Sharab and the team would be able to go in the van. They were coming up another cut. Maybe they could get to five thousand feet before the road became too narrow to accommodate the truck. The roads joined a few hundred feet ahead. When he arrived, he would either see their tire treads or else wait for them at the cave. He hoped they were already there. He was anxious to know what had happened, what had gone wrong.

He prayed it was nothing that might keep them from him. If for some reason the others did not show up within twenty-four hours, Ishaq's standing orders were to get to the cave and set up the radio he carried in his small equipment case. Then he was to call the FKM base in Abbottabad, across the border in Pakistan. They would tell him what to do. That meant either he would be advised to wait for replacements or attempt to return home for a debriefing.

If it came to that, Ishaq hoped they would tell him to wait. Going home would mean climbing the mountains to the Siachin Glacier. Or else he would have to attempt to make his way across the line of control. His chances of surviving the trip were not good. FKM command might just as well order him to shoot himself at the cave.

As Ishaq neared the point where the two cuts converged he saw the truck. It was parked in the middle of the road. The flatbed was covered with an earth-tone tarp they carried and the cab was hidden beneath scrub. A smile fought a losing battle against the wind. He was glad they had made it. But that changed when his headlights found the team about two hundred yards ahead. As one they turned and crouched, ready to fire.

"No, it's Ishaq!" he cried. "It's Ishaq!"

They lowered their weapons and continued ahead without waiting for their teammate. Sharab was in front with the girl. Nanda was being urged forward at gunpoint.

That was not like Sharab.

This was bad. This was very, very bad.

FIFTEEN

Washington, D.C.
Wednesday, 10:51 A.M.

Bob Herbert was usually a pretty happy man.

To begin with, Herbert loved his work. He had a good team working beside him. He was able to give Op-Center personnel the kind of heads-up intelligence he and his wife never had in Lebanon. He was also happy with himself. He was not a Washington bureaucrat. He put truthfulness above diplomacy and the well-being of the NCMC above the advancement of Bob Herbert. That meant he could sleep at night. He had the respect of the people who mattered, like Paul Hood and Mike Rodgers.

But Bob Herbert was not happy right now.

Hank Lewis had phoned from the NSA to say that the latest information e-mailed from Ron Friday was being processed by decryption personnel. It would be forwarded to Herbert within minutes. While Herbert waited for the intel he did something he had been meaning to do since the Striker recon mission was okayed by the CIOC. He pulled up Ron Friday's NSA file on his computer. Until now, Herbert and his team had been too busy helping Mike Rodgers and Striker prepare for the mission to do anything else.

Herbert did not like what he saw in Ron Friday's dossier. Or rather, what he did not see there.

As a crisis management center, Op-Center did not keep a full range of military maps and intelligence in what they called their "hot box." The only files that were reviewed and updated on a four-times-daily basis were situations and places where American personnel or interests were directly involved or affected. Kashmir was certainly a crisis zone. But if it exploded, it was not a spot with which Op-Center

would automatically be involved. In fact, that was the reason
Striker had been asked to go into the region and look for
Pakistani nuclear weapons. Pakistani intelligence would not
be expecting them.

Ron Friday was a very late addition to the mission. His
participation had been requested over the weekend by Satya
Shankar, minister of state, Department of Atomic Energy.
Officially, one of Shankar's duties was the sale of nuclear
technology to developing nations. Unofficially, he was responsible for helping the military keep track of nuclear technology within enemy states. Shankar and Friday had worked
together once before, when Shankar was joint secretary, Ex-
ploration, of the Ministry of Petroleum and Natural Gas. Friday had been called in by a European oil concern to assess
legal issues involving drilling in disputed territory between
Great Indian Desert in the Rajasthan Province of India and
the Thar Desert in Pakistan. Shankar had obviously been impressed by the attorney.

Since Op-Center was stuck with Friday, reading his file
had not been a high priority for Herbert. Especially since the
CIOC had already okayed Friday based on his Blue Shield
rating. That meant Ron Friday was cleared to take part in
the most sensitive fieldwork in foreign countries. Red Shield
meant that an agent was trusted by the foreign government.
White Shield meant that he was trusted by his own government, that there was no evidence of double-agent activity.
Yellow Shield meant that he had been revealed to be a
double agent and was being used by his government to put
out disinformation, often without his knowledge or occasionally with his cooperation in exchange for clemency. Blue
Shield meant he was trusted by both nations.

What the Red, White, and Blue rankings really meant was
that no data had ever come up to suggest the agent was
corrupt. That was usually good enough for a project overseer
to rubber-stamp an individual for a mission. Especially an
overseer who was new on the job and overworked, like Hank
Lewis at the National Security Agency. But the Shield system was not infallible. It could simply mean that the agent

had been too careful to be caught. Or that he had someone on the inside who kept his file clean.

Friday's file was extremely skimpy. It contained very few field reports from Azerbaijan, where he had most recently been stationed at the United States embassy in Baku as an aide to Deputy Ambassador Dorothy Williamson. There were zero communications at all from him during the recent crisis in the former Soviet Republic. That was unusual. Herbert had a look at the files of the two CIA operatives who had been stationed at the embassy. They were full of daily reports. Coincidentally, perhaps, both of those men were killed.

Friday's thin file and his apparent silence during the crisis was troubling. One of his superiors at the NSA, Jack Fenwick, was the man who had hired the terrorist known as the Harpooner to precipitate the Caspian Sea confrontation between Azerbaijan, Iran, and Russia. Herbert had not read all the postmortems about the situation. There had not been time. But Friday's silence before and during the showdown led Herbert to wonder: was he really inactive or were his reports made directly to someone who destroyed them?

Jack Fenwick, for example.

If that were true it could mean that Ron Friday had been working with Jack Fenwick and the Harpooner to start a war. Of course, there was always the possibility that Friday had been helping Fenwick without knowing what the NSA chief was up to. But that seemed unlikely. Ron Friday had been an attorney, a top-level oil rights negotiator, and a diplomatic advisor. He did not seem naive. And that scared the hell out of Herbert.

The decrypted NSA e-file arrived and Herbert opened it. The folder contained Friday's observations as well as relevant data about the previous antiterrorist functions of both the National Security Guard and the Special Frontier Force. It did not seem strange to Herbert that SFF had replaced the Black Cats after this latest attack. Maybe the SFF had jurisdiction over strikes against religious sites. Or maybe the government had grown impatient with the ineffectiveness of the Black Cats. There was obviously a terrorist cell roaming

Kashmir. Any security agency that failed to maintain security was not going to have that job for very long.

Either he or Paul Hood could call their partners in Indian intelligence and get an explanation for the change. Herbert's concerns about Ron Friday would not be so easy to dispel.

Herbert entered the numbers 008 on his wheelchair phone. That was Paul Hood's extension. Shortly before Op-Center opened its doors Matt Stoll had hacked the computer system to make sure he got the 007 extension. Herbert had not been happy about Stoll's hacking but Hood had appreciated the man's initiative. As long as Stoll limited his internal sabotage to a one-time hack of the phone directory Hood had decided to overlook it.

The phone beeped once. "Hood here."

"Chief, it's Bob. Got a minute?"

"Sure," Hood said.

"I'll be right there," Herbert said. He typed an address in his computer and hit "enter." "Meanwhile, I'd like you to have a quick look at the e-files I'm sending over. One's a report from the NSA about this morning's attack in Srinagar. Another is Ron Friday's very thin dossier."

"All right," Hood said.

Herbert hung up and wheeled himself down the corridor to Hood's office. As Herbert was en route he got a call from Matt Stoll.

"Make it quick," Herbert said.

"I was just reviewing the latest number grabs from the Bellhop," Stoll told him. "That telephone number we've been watching, the field phone in Srinagar? It's making very strange calls."

"What do you mean?" Herbert said.

"The field phone keeps calling the home phone in Jammu, the police station," Stoll said. "But the calls last for only one second."

"That's it?"

"That's it," Stoll told him. "We read a connect, a one-second gap, then a disconnect."

"Is it happening regularly?" Herbert asked.

"There's been a blip every minute since four P.M. local time, six thirty A.M. our time," Stoll told him.

"That's over four hours," Herbert said. "Short, regular pulses over a long period. Sounds like a tracking beacon."

"It could be that," Stoll agreed, "or it could mean that someone hit the autoredial button by accident. Voice mail answers nonemergency calls at the police station. The field phone may have been programmed to read that as a disconnect so it hangs up and rings the number again."

"That doesn't sound likely," Herbert said. "Is there any way to tell if the field phone is moving?"

"Not directly," Stoll said.

"What about indirectly?" Herbert asked as he reached Paul Hood's office. The door was open and he knocked on the jamb. Hood was studying his computer monitor. He motioned Herbert in.

"If the phone calls are a beacon, then the police in Kashmir are almost certainly following them, probably by ground-based triangulation," Stoll told Herbert. "All of that would be run through their computers. It will take some time but we can try breaking into the system."

"Do it," Herbert said.

"Sure," Stoll said. "But why don't we just call over and ask them what's going on? Aren't they our allies? Aren't we supposed to be running this operation with them?"

"Yes," Herbert replied. "But if there's some way we can accomplish this without them knowing I'd be happier. The police are going to want to know why we're asking. The Black Cats and selected government officials are the only ones who are supposed to know that Striker is coming over."

"I see," Stoll said. "Okay. We'll try hacking them."

"Thanks," Herbert said and hung up as he wheeled into Hood's office. He locked his brakes and shut the door behind him.

"Busy morning?" Hood asked.

"Not until some lunatic decided to set off fireworks in Srinagar," Herbert replied.

Hood nodded. "I haven't finished these files," he said, "but Ron Friday is obviously concerned about us having anything to do with the Black Cats. And you're apparently worried about having anything to do with Ron Friday."

Paul Hood had not spent a lot of time working in the intelligence community and he had a number of weaknesses. However, one of Hood's greatest strengths was that his years in politics and finance had taught him to intuit the concerns of his associates, whatever the topic.

"That's about the size of it," Herbert admitted.

"Tell me about this police line blip," Hood said, still reading.

"The last home phone-to-field phone communication came a moment before the explosion," Herbert said. "But Matt just told me that the regular pulses from field to home started immediately after that. In ELINT we want three things to happen before we posit a possible connection to a terrorist attack: timing, proximity, and probable source. We've got those."

"The probable source being a cell that's apparently been working in Srinagar," Hood said.

"Correct," Herbert said. "I just asked Matt to try and get more intel on the continuing blips."

Hood nodded and continued reading. "The problem you have with Friday is a little dicier."

"Why?" Herbert asked.

"Because he's there at the request of the Indian government," Hood said.

"So is Striker," Herbert pointed out.

"Yes, but they've worked with Friday," Hood said. "They'll give Striker more freedom because they trust Friday."

"There's an irony in there somewhere," Herbert said.

"Look, I see where you're coming from," Hood acknowledged. "Friday worked for Fenwick. Fenwick betrayed his country. But we have to be careful about pushing guilt by association."

"How about guilt by criminal activity?" Herbert said. "Whatever Friday was doing in Baku was removed from his file."

"That's assuming he was working for the NSA," Hood

said. "I just put in a call to Deputy Ambassador Williamson in Baku. Her personal file says that Friday worked as her aide. He was on loan from the NSA to collect intelligence on the oil situation. There's no reason to assume the CIA involved him in the hunt for the Harpooner. And Jack Fenwick was playing with fire. He may not have told Friday what the NSA was really doing in the Caspian."

"Or Fenwick may have sent him there," Herbert pointed out. "Friday's oil credentials made him the perfect inside man."

"You'll need to prove that one," Hood said.

Herbert didn't like that answer. When his gut told him something he listened to it. To him, Hood's habit of being a devil's advocate was one of his big weaknesses. Still, from the perspective of accountability Hood was doing the right thing. That was why Hood was in charge of Op-Center and Herbert was not. They could not go back to the CIOC and tell them they called off the mission or were concerned about Friday's role in it because of Herbert's intuition.

The phone beeped. It was Dorothy Williamson. Hood put the phone on speaker. He was busy typing something on his keyboard as he introduced himself and Herbert. Then he explained that they were involved in a joint operation with Ron Friday. Hood asked if she would mind sharing her impressions of the agent.

"He was very efficient, a good attorney and negotiator, and I was sorry to lose him," she said.

"Did he interact much with the two Company men, the ones who were killed by the Harpooner's man?" Hood asked.

"Mr. Friday spent a great deal of time with Mr. Moore and Mr. Thomas," Williamson replied.

"I see," Hood said.

Herbert felt vindicated. Friday's interaction with the men should have shown up in his reports to the NSA. Now he knew the file had been sanitized.

"For the record, Mr. Hood, I do want to point out one thing," Williamson said. "The Company agents were not killed by one assassin but by two."

That caught Herbert by surprise.

"There were two assassins at the hospital," the deputy ambassador went on. "One of them was killed. The other one got away. The Baku police department is still looking for him."

"I did not know that," Hood said. "Thank you."

Herbert's gut growled a little. The two CIA operatives were killed getting medical attention for a visiting agent who had been poisoned by the Harpooner. Fenwick's plan to start a Caspian war had depended upon killing all three men at the hospital. Fenwick certainly would have asked Friday for information regarding the movements of the CIA operatives. And just as certainly that information would have been deleted from Friday's files. But after the two men were killed, Friday had to have suspected that something was wrong. He should have confided in Williamson or made sure he had a better alibi.

Unless he was a willing part of Fenwick's team.

"Bob Herbert here, Madam Deputy Ambassador," Herbert said. "Can you tell me where Mr. Friday was on the night of the murders?"

"In his apartment, as I recall," Williamson informed him.

"Did Mr. Friday have anything to say after he learned about the killings?" Herbert pressed.

"Not really," she said.

"Was he concerned for his own safety?" Herbert asked.

"He never expressed any worries," she said. "But there was not a lot of time for chat. We were working hard to put down a war."

Hood shot Herbert a glance. The intelligence chief sat back, exasperated, as Hood complimented her on her efforts during the crisis.

That was Paul Hood. Whatever the situation he always had the presence of mind to play the diplomat. Not Herbert. If the Harpooner was killing U.S. agents, he wanted to know why it did not occur to Ms. Williamson to find out why Friday had not been hit.

The deputy ambassador had a few more things to say about Friday, especially praising his quick learning curve on the issues they had to deal with between Azerbaijan and its neighbors. Williamson asked Hood to give him her regards if he spoke with Friday.

Hood said he would and clicked off. He regarded Herbert. "You wouldn't have gotten anywhere hammering her," Hood said.

"How do you know?" Herbert asked.

"While we were talking I looked at her c.v.," Hood said. "Williamson's a political appointee. She ran the spin-doctoring for Senator Thompson during his last Senate campaign."

"Dirty tricks?" Herbert asked disgustedly. "That's the whole of her intelligence experience?"

"Pretty much," Hood said. "With two CIA agents on staff in Baku I guess the president thought he was safe scoring points with the majority whip. More to the point, I'm guessing this whole thing sounds too clean to you."

"Like brass buttons on inspection day."

"I don't know, Bob," Hood said. "It's not just Williamson. Hank Lewis trusted Friday enough to send him to India."

"That doesn't mean anything," Herbert said. "I spoke with Hank Lewis earlier this morning. He's making decisions like a monkey in a space capsule."

Hood made a face. "He's a good man—"

"Maybe, Chief, but that's the way it is," Herbert insisted. "Lewis gets a jolt of electricity and pushes a button. He hasn't had time to think about Ron Friday or anyone else. Look, Hank Lewis and Dorothy Williamson shouldn't be the issues right now—"

"Agreed," Hood said. "All right. Let's assume Ron Friday may not be someone we want on our team. How do we vet him? Jack Fenwick's not going to say anything to anyone."

"Why not?" Herbert asked. "Maybe the rat-bastard will talk in exchange for immunity—"

"The president got what he wanted, the resignations of Fenwick and his coconspirators," Hood said. "He doesn't want a national trial that will question whether he was actually on the edge of a mental breakdown during the crisis, even if it means letting a few underlings remain in the system. Fenwick got off lucky. He's not going to say anything that might change the president's mind."

"That's great," Herbert said. "The guilty go free and the president's psyche doesn't get the examination it may damn well need."

"And the stock market doesn't collapse and the military doesn't lose faith in its commander-in-chief and a rash of Third World despots don't start pushing their own agendas while the nation is distracted," Hood said. "The systems are all too damn interconnected, Bob. Right and wrong don't matter anymore. It's all about equilibrium."

"Is that so?" Herbert said. "Well, mine's a little shaky right now. I don't like risking my team, my friends, to keep some Indian nabob happy."

"We aren't going to," Hood said. "We're going to protect the part of the system we've been given." He looked at his watch. "I don't know if Ron Friday betrayed his country in Baku. Even if he did it doesn't mean he's got a side bet going in India. But we still have about eighteen hours before Striker reaches India. What can we do to get more intel on Friday?"

"I can have my team look into his cell phone records and e-mail," Herbert said, "maybe get security videos from the embassy and see if anything suspicious turns up."

"Do it," Hood said.

"That may not tell us everything," Herbert said.

"We don't need everything," Hood said. "We need probable cause, something other than the possibility that Friday may have helped Fenwick. If we get that then we can go to Senator Fox and the CIOC, tell them we don't want Striker working with someone who was willing to start a war for personal gain."

"All very polite," Herbert grumped. "But we're using kid gloves on a guy who may have been a goddamned traitor."

"No," Hood said. "We're presuming he's innocent until we're sure he's not. You get me the information. I'll take care of delivering the message."

Herbert agreed, reluctantly.

As he wheeled back to his office, the intelligence chief reflected on the fact that the only thing diplomacy ever accomplished was to postpone the inevitable. But Hood was the boss and Herbert would do what he wanted.

For now.

Because, more than loyalty to Paul Hood and Op-Center, more than watching out for his own future, Herbert felt responsible for the security of Striker and the lives of his friends. The day things became so interconnected that Herbert could not do that was the day he became a pretty unhappy man. And then he would have just one more thing to do.

Hang up his spurs.

SIXTEEN

Siachin Base 2E, Kashmir
Wednesday, 9:02 P.M.

Sharab and her group left the camouflaged truck and spent the next two hours making their way to the cliff where the cave was located. Ishaq had raced ahead on his motorcycle. He went as far as he could go and then walked the rest of the way. Upon reaching the cave he collected the small, hooded lanterns they kept there and set them out for the others. The small, yellow lights helped Sharab, Samouel, Ali, and Hassan get Nanda up to the ledge below the site. The Kashmiri hostage did not try to get away but she was obviously not comfortable with the climb. The path leading to this point had been narrow with long, sheer drops. This last leg, though less than fifty feet, was almost vertical.

A fine mist drifted across the rock, hampering visibility as they made their way up. The men proceeded with Nanda between them. Sharab brought up the rear. Her right palm was badly bruised and it ached from when she had struck the dashboard earlier. Sharab rarely lost her temper but it was occasionally necessary. Like the War Steeds of the Koran, who struck fire with their hooves, she had to let her anger out in measured doses. Otherwise it would explode in its own time.

Nanda had to feel her way to the handholds that Sharab and the others had cut in the rock face over a year before. The men helped her as best they could.

Sharab had insisted on bringing the Kashmiri along, though not so they would have a hostage. Men who would blow up their own citizens would not hesitate to shoot one more if it suited them. Sharab had taken Nanda for one reason only. She had questions to ask her.

The other two blasts in the Srinagar marketplace had not been a coincidence. Someone had to have known what Sharab and her group were planning. Maybe it was a pro-Indian extremist group. More likely it was someone in the government, since it would have taken careful planning to coordinate the different explosions. Whoever it was, they had caused the additional explosions so that the Free Kashmir Militia would unwittingly take the blame for attacking Hindus.

It did not surprise Sharab that the Indians would kill their own people to turn the population against the FKM. Some governments build germ-war factories in schools and put military headquarters under hospitals. Others arrest dissidents by the wagonload or test toxins in the air and water of an unsuspecting public. Security of the many typically came before the well-being of the few. What upset Sharab was that the Indians had so effectively counterplotted against her group. The Indians had known where and when the FKM was attacking. They knew that the group always took credit for their attack within moments of the blast. The Indians made it impossible for the cell to continue. Even if the authorities did not know who the cell members were or where they lived, they had undermined the group's credibility. They would no longer be perceived as an anti–New Delhi force. They would be seen as anti-Indian, anti-Hindu.

There was nothing Sharab could do about that now. For the moment she felt safe. If the authorities had known about the cave they would have been waiting here. Once the team was armed and had collected their cold weather gear she would decide whether to stay for the night or push on. Moving through the cold, dark mountains would be dangerous. But giving the Indians a chance to track them down would be just as risky. She could not allow her group to be taken alive or dead. Even possessing their bodies would give the Indian radicals a target with which to rally the mostly moderate population.

Sharab wanted to survive for another reason, also. For the sake of future cells Sharab had to try to figure out how the Indian authorities knew what she and her team had been doing. Someone could have seen them working on the roof of the police station. But that would have led to their arrest and interrogation, not this elaborate plot. She suspected that someone had been watching them for some time. Since virtually none of the FKM's communications were by phone or computer, and no one in Pakistan knew their exact whereabouts, that someone had to have been spying from nearby.

She knew and trusted everyone on her team. Only two other people had been close to the cell: Nanda and her grandfather. Apu would have been too afraid to move against them and Sharab did not see how Nanda could have spoken with anyone else. They were watched virtually all day, every day. Still, somehow, one of them must have betrayed the group.

Ishaq was leaning from the cave about ten feet above. He reached down and helped everyone up in turn. Sharab waited while Ishaq and Ali literally hoisted Nanda inside. The rock was cool and she placed her cheek against it. She shut her eyes. Though the rock felt good, it was not home.

When she was a young girl, Sharab's favorite tale in the Koran involved the seven Sleepers of the Cave. One line in particular came to her each time she visited this place: "We made them sleep in the cave for many years, and then awakened them to find out who could best tell the length of their stay."

Sharab knew that feeling of disorientation. Cut off from all that she loved, separated from all that was familiar, time had lost its meaning. But the woman knew what the Sleepers of the Cave had learned. That the Lord God knew how long they had been at rest. If they trusted in Him they would never be lost.

Sharab had her god and she also had her country. Yet this was not how she had wanted to return to Pakistan. She had always imagined going home victorious rather than running from the enemy.

"Come on!" Samouel called down to her.

Sharab opened her eyes. She continued her climb toward the cave. The moment of peace had passed. She began getting angry again. She pulled herself inside the small cave and stood. The wind wailed around her going into the shallow cave, then whooshed past her as it circled back out. Two lanterns rocked on hooks in the low ceiling. Beneath them were stacked crates of guns, explosives, canned food, clothing, and other gear.

Except for Ishaq, the men were standing along the sides of the cave. Ishaq was reattaching a large tarp to the front of the cave. The outside was painted to resemble the rest of the mountainside. Not only did it help to camouflage the natural cave but it helped keep them warm whenever they were here.

Nanda was near the back of the cave. She was facing Sharab. The ceiling sloped severely and the Kashmiri woman's back was bent slightly so she could remain standing. There was a band of blood staining the ankle of her pants. The cuff must have worn the flesh raw yet Nanda had not complained. The corners of her mouth trembled, her breath came in anxious little puffs, and her arms were folded across her chest. Sharab decided that was probably an attempt to keep warm and not a show of defiance. They were all perspiring from the climb and the cold air had turned their sweat-drenched clothes frigid.

Sharab walked slowly toward her prisoner.

"Innocent people died today," Sharab said. "There will be no retribution, no more killing, but I must know. Did you or your grandfather tell anyone about our activities?"

Nanda said nothing.

"We did not destroy the temple and the bus, you know that," Sharab added. "You've lived with us, you must have heard us making plans. You know we only attack government targets. Whoever attacked the Hindus is your enemy. They must be exposed and brought to justice."

Nanda continued to stand where she was, her arms bundled around her. But there was a change in her posture, in her expression. She had drawn her shoulders back slightly and her eyes and mouth had hardened.

Now she was defiant.

Why? Sharab wondered. Because a Pakistani had dared to suggest that Indians could be enemies to Indians? Nanda

could not be so naive. And if she did not agree, she did not
want to defend her countrymen either.

"Samouel?" Sharab said.

The young bearded man stood. "Yes?"

"Please take care of dinner, including our guest," Sharab
said. "She'll need her strength."

Samouel opened a frost-covered cardboard box that contained military rations. He began passing out the pop-top tins.
Each of the shallow, red, six-by-four-inch containers was
packed with basmati rice, strips of precooked goat meat, and
two cinnamon sticks. A second cardboard box contained cartons of powdered milk. While Samouel handed those to the
men Ali got a jug of water from the back of the cave. He
added it to the powdered milk, pouring in skillful little bursts
that kept the ice that had formed in the jugs from clogging
the neck.

Sharab continued to regard Nanda. "You're coming with
us to Pakistan," Sharab informed her. "Once you're there you
will tell my colleagues what you refuse to tell me."

Nanda still did not respond. That seemed strange to
Sharab. The dark-eyed woman had been talkative enough
during the months at the farm. She had complained about
the intrusion, the restrictions that had been placed on her,
the militaristic leaders of Pakistan, and the terrorist activities
of the FKM. It seemed odd that she would not say anything
now.

Perhaps the woman was just tired from the climb. Yet she
had not said anything in the truck either. It could be that she
was afraid for her life. But she had not tried to get away on
the mountain path or to reach any of the weapons that were
plainly in view.

And then it hit her. The reason Nanda did not want to talk
to them. Sharab stopped a few feet in front of the Kashmiri
woman.

"You're working with them," Sharab said suddenly. "Either you want us to take you to Pakistan or—" She stopped
and called Hassan over. Standing nearly six-foot-five, the
thirty-six-year-old former quarry worker was the largest man
on her team. He had to duck just to stand in the cave.

"Hold her," Sharab ordered.

Now Nanda moved. She tried to get around Sharab. She was apparently trying to reach one of the guns in the box. But Hassan moved behind Nanda. He grabbed her arms right below the shoulders and pinned them together with his massive hands. The Kashmiri woman moaned and tried to wriggle away. But the big man pushed harder. She arched her back and then stopped moving.

Hassan wrestled Nanda over to Sharab. The Pakistani woman felt the pockets of Nanda's jeans and then reached under Nanda's bulky wool sweater. She patted Nanda's sides and back.

She found what she was looking for at once. It was on Nanda's left side, just above her hip. As Nanda renewed her struggles, Sharab pulled up the sweater and exposed the woman's waist.

There was a small leather pouch attached to a narrow elastic band. Inside the pouch was a cellular phone. Sharab removed it and walked closer to one of the hanging lanterns. She examined the palm-sized black phone closely. The liquid crystal display was blank. Though that function had been disengaged the phone itself was working. It vibrated faintly, pulsing for a second and then shutting down for a second. It did that repeatedly. There was also a dark, concave plastic bubble on the top edge. It looked like the eye of a television remote control.

"Ali, Samouel, gather up weapons and supplies," Sharab ordered. "Do it quickly."

The men put down their meals and did as they were told. Hassan continued to hold Nanda. Ishaq watched from the side of the cave. He was waiting for Sharab to tell him what to do.

Sharab regarded Nanda. "This is more than just a cell phone, isn't it? It's a tracking device."

Nanda said nothing. Sharab nodded at Hassan and he squeezed her arms together. She gasped but did not answer. After a moment Sharab motioned for him to relax his grip.

"You could not have spoken to your collaborators without us hearing," Sharab went on. "You must have used the keypad to type information. Now they're probably tracking you to our base. Who are they?"

Nanda did not answer.

Sharab strode toward the woman and slapped her with a hard backhand across the ear. "Who is behind this?" the woman screamed. "The SFF? The military? The world needs to know that we did not do this!"

Nanda refused to say anything.

"Do you have any idea what you've done?" Sharab said, stepping back.

"I do," the Kashmiri woman said at last. "I stopped your people from committing genocide."

"Genocide?"

"Against the Hindu population in Kashmir and the rest of India," Nanda said. "For years we've listened to the promise of extermination on television, shouted outside the mosques."

"You've been listening to the radicals, to Fundamentalist clerics who shout extremist views," Sharab insisted. "All we wanted was freedom for the Muslims in Kashmir."

"By killing—"

"We are at war!" Sharab declared. "But we only strike military or police targets." She held up the cell phone and tapped the top with a finger. "Do you want to talk about extermination? This is a remote sensor, isn't it? We put you close to the site and you used it to trigger explosives left by your partners."

"What I did was an act of love to protect the rest of my people," Nanda replied.

"It was an act of betrayal," Sharab replied. "They moved freely because they knew we would not hurt them. You abused that trust."

Sharab's people took part in these acts primarily in the Middle East where they used their bodies as living bombs. The difference was that Nanda's people had not chosen to make this sacrifice. Nanda and her partners had decided that for them.

But morality and blame did not matter to Sharab right now. Nanda did not have the experience to have originated this plan. Whoever was behind this was coming and undoubtedly they would be well armed. Sharab did not want to be here when they arrived.

She turned to Ishaq. The youngest member of the team was standing beside the cartons eating his goat meat and rice. His lips were pale from the cold and his face was leathery from the pounding the wind had given it during his motor-cycle journey. But his soulful eyes were alert, expectant. Sharab tried not to think about what she was about to tell him. But it had to be done.

She handed Ishaq the cell phone. "I need you to stay here with this," she told him.

The young man stopped chewing.

"You heard what is happening," Sharab went on. "We're leaving but her accomplices must think we're still here."

Ishaq put down the tin and took the phone. The other men stopped moving behind them.

"It's very heavy," Ishaq said softly. "You're right. I think they've added things." He regarded Sharab. "You don't want the Indians to leave here, is that correct?"

"That is correct," Sharab replied quietly. Her voice caught. She continued to look into Ishaq's eyes.

"Then they won't leave," he promised her. "But you had better."

"Thank you," Sharab replied.

The woman turned to help the other men, not because they needed help but because she did not want Ishaq to see her weep. She wanted him to hold on to the image of her being strong. He would need that in order to get through this. Yet the tears came. They had been together every day for two years, both in Pakistan and in Kashmir. He was devoted to her and to the cause. But he did not have the climbing or survival skills the other men had. Without them they would not get across the mountains and the line of control and back to Pakistan.

The remaining members of the team pulled on the heavy coats they kept for extended stays in the cave. They threw automatic weapons over their right shoulders and ropes over their left. They put flashlights and matches in their pockets.

Ali took the backpack he had loaded with food. Hassan grabbed Nanda after Samouel gave him the backpack with pitons, a hammer, extra flashlights, and maps.

Then, in turn, each member of the party hugged Ishaq. He smiled at them with tears in his eyes. Sharab was the last to embrace him.

"I pray that Allah will send to your aid five thousand angels," Sharab whispered to him.

"I would sooner He send them to help you reach home," Ishaq replied. "Then I would be sure that this has not been in vain."

She hugged him even tighter then patted his back, turned, and stepped through the tarp.

SEVENTEEN

Srinagar, Kashmir
Wednesday, 10:00 P.M.

Ron Friday was in his small room when the phone on the rickety night table rang. He opened his eyes and looked at his watch.

Right on time.

The phone was from the 1950s, a heavy black anvil of a thing with a thick brown cord. And it really rang rather than beeped. Friday was sitting on the bed; after sending the encoded message to Hank Lewis, he had turned on the black-and-white TV. An old movie was on. Even with English subtitles Friday had trouble following the plot. The fact that he kept dozing off did not help.

Friday did not answer the phone on the first ring. Or the second. He did not pick up until the tenth ring. That was how he knew the caller was his Black Cat contact. Tenth ring at the tenth hour.

The caller, Captain Prem Nazir, said he would meet Friday outside in fifteen minutes.

Friday pulled on his shoes, grabbed his windbreaker, and headed down the single flight of stairs. There were only twelve rooms at Binoo's Palace, most of them occupied by market workers, women of questionable provenance, and men who rarely emerged from their rooms. Obviously, the police turned a blind eye to more than just the gaming parlor.

The inn did not have much of a lobby. A reception desk was located to the left of the stairs. It was run by Binoo during the day and his sister at night. There was a Persian rug on a hardwood floor with battered sofas on either side. The windows looked out on the dark, narrow street. The smell of the potent, native-grown Juari cigarettes was thick here. The gaming parlor was located in a room behind the counter. A veil of smoke actually hung like a stage scrim behind Binoo's oblivious sister.

The heavyset woman was leaning on the counter. She did not look up from her movie magazine as Friday came down. That was what he loved about this place. No one gave a damn.

The lobby was empty. So was the street. Friday leaned against the wall and waited.

Friday had never met the fifty-three-year-old Captain Nazir. Atomic Energy Minister Shankar knew him and put a lot of trust in him. Friday did not trust anyone, including Shankar. But Captain Nazir's extensive background in espionage, first behind the lines in Pakistan in the 1960s, then with the Indian army, and now with the National Security Guard, suggested that the two men might enjoy a good working relationship.

Unless, that is, there were a problem between the NSG and the Special Frontier Force. That was the first order of business Friday intended to discuss with Nazir, even before they talked about the Striker mission to search for Pakistani nuclear missiles. Friday did not mind going on a sensitive mission for the Black Cats if they did not have the full trust and support of the government. Part of intelligence work was doing things without government approval. But he did mind going out if the Black Cats and the SFF were at war, if one group were looking to embarrass the other. A freeze-out of the NSG at the bomb site did not mean that was the case. But Friday wanted to be sure.

Captain Nazir arrived exactly on schedule. He was strolling in no particular hurry with no apparent destination, and he was smoking a Juari. That was smart. The officer was up from New Delhi but he was not smoking one of the milder brands that was popular in the capital. The local cigarette would help him blend in with the surroundings.

The officer was dressed in a plain gray sweatshirt, khaki slacks, and Nikes. He was about five-foot-seven with short black hair and a scar across his forehead. His skin was smooth and dark. He looked exactly like the photographs Friday had seen.

Ron Friday obviously looked like his photographs as well. Captain Nazir did not bother to introduce himself. They would not say one another's names at all. There were still SFF personnel working in the bazaar. They might have set up electronic surveillance of the area to try to catch the bombers. If so, someone might overhear them.

The officer simply offered Friday his hand and said in a low, rough voice, "Walk with me."

The two men continued in the direction Captain Nazir had been headed, away from the main street, Shervani Road. The narrow side street where the inn was located was little more than an alley. There were dark shops on either side of the road. They sold items that did not usually turn up in the bazaar, like bicycles, men's suits, and small appliances. The street ended in a high brick wall about three hundred yards away.

Nazir drew on the nub of his cigarette. "The minister thinks very highly of you."

"Thanks," Friday said. He looked down and spoke very softly. "Tell me something. What happened today in the marketplace?"

"I'm not sure," Nazir replied.

"Would you tell me if you did?" Friday asked.

"I'm not sure," Nazir admitted.

"Why was the SFF handling the investigation instead of your people?" Friday asked.

Nazir stopped walking. He retrieved a pack of cigarettes from under his sweatshirt and used one to light another. He looked at Friday in the glow of the newly lit cigarette.

"I do not know the answer to that," the officer replied as he continued walking.

"Let me point you in a direction," Friday said. "Does the SFF have special jurisdiction over Srinagar or religious targets?"

"No," Nazir replied.

"But their personnel were on the scene and your people were not," Friday repeated.

"Yes," Nazir said.

This was becoming frustrating. Friday stopped walking. He grabbed Nazir by the arm. The officer did not react.

"Before I head north and risk my life, I need to know if there's a leak in your organization," Friday said.

"Why would you think there is?" Nazir asked.

"Because there was not a single Black Cat Commando at the scene," Friday told him. "Why else would you be shut out of the investigation except for security issues?"

"Humiliation," Nazir suggested. "You have conflicts between your intelligence services. They go to great lengths to undermine one another even though you work toward the same goal."

There was no disputing that, Friday thought. He had killed a CIA agent not long ago.

"The truth is, the SFF has been extremely quiet about their activities of late and we have been quiet about our operations, including this one," Nazir went on. "Both groups have their allies in New Delhi and, eventually, all the intelligence we gather gets shuffled into the system and used."

"Like a slaughterhouse," Friday observed.

"A slaughterhouse," Nazir said. He nodded appreciatively. "I like that. I like it very much."

"I'm glad," Friday replied. "Now tell me something I'm going to like. For example, why we should put ourselves into the hands of an intelligence agency that may be risking our lives to boost their own standing in New Delhi?"

"Is that what you think?" Nazir asked.

"I don't know," Friday replied. "Convince me otherwise."

"Do you know anything about Hinduism?" Nazir asked Friday.

"I'm familiar with the basics," Friday replied. He had no idea what that had to do with anything.

"Do you know that *Hinduism* is not the name we use for our faith. It's something the West invented."

"I didn't know that," Friday admitted.

"We are countless sects and castes, all of which have their own names and very different views of the Veda, the holy text," Nazir said. "The greatest problem we have as a nation is that we carry our factionalism into government. Everyone defends his own unit or department or consulate as if it were his personal faith. We do this without considering how our actions affect the whole. I am guilty of that too. My 'god,' if you will, is the one who can help me get things done. Not necessarily the one who can do the best job for India." He drew on his cigarette. "The tragedy is that the whole is now threatened with destruction and we are still not pulling together. We need more intelligence on Pakistan's nuclear threat. We cannot go and get that information ourselves for fear of triggering the very thing we are trying to avoid—a nuclear exchange. You and your group are the only ones who can help us." Nazir regarded Friday through the twisting smoke of his cigarette. "If you are still willing to undertake this mission I will be the point man for you. I will go as far into the field as I can with maps, clearances, and geographical reconnaissance. The minister and I will make certain that no one interferes with your activities. He does not know the men who are coming from Washington but he has enormous respect for you. He considers you a member of 'his' sect. That is more than simply an honor. It means that in future undertakings of your own you will be able to call on him. To him the members of his team come before anything. But we must secure the intelligence we need to ensure that the team continues. The American force is going in anyway. I am here to make sure that you are still willing to go with them. I hope to be able to report that back to the minister."

Friday did not believe any man who claimed to put the good of the team before his own good. A minister who was running a secret operation with the Black Cats was looking to strengthen his ties to the intelligence community and build his power base. If he could spy on Pakistan today he might spy on the SFF or the prime minister tomorrow.

The fact that a politician might have personal ambition did not bother Friday. He had heard what Captain Nazir was really saying. Minister Shankar wanted Friday to go with Striker to make sure that the Americans were working for

India and not just for Washington. And if Friday did undertake this mission he would have a highly placed ally in the Indian government.

The men reached the brick wall at the end of the street and Nazir lit another cigarette. Then they turned around and started walking back to the inn. Nazir was looking down. He had obviously said what he had come to say. Now it was up to Friday.

"You still haven't convinced me that there isn't a leak in your organization," Friday said. "How do I know we won't go out there and find ourselves ass-deep in Pakistanis?"

"You may," Nazir granted. "That is why we cannot go ourselves. As for leaks, I know everyone in the Black Cats. We have not been betrayed in the past. Beyond that, I cannot give the assurances you ask for." Nazir smiled for the first time. "It is even possible that someone in Washington has leaked this to the Pakistanis. There is always danger in our profession. The only question is whether the rewards are worth the risks. We believe they are, for us—and for you."

That sounded very much like an introductory lecture from a guru at an ashram. But then, Friday should have expected that.

"All right," Friday said. "I'm in—with one condition."

"And that is?"

"I want to know more about today's attack," Friday said. "Something about it is not sitting right."

"Can you tell me exactly what is bothering you?" Nazir asked.

"The fact that the attacker detonated two separate charges to bring down the police station and the temple," Friday said. "There was no reason for that. One large explosion would have accomplished the same thing. And it would have been easier to set."

Nazir nodded. "I've been wondering about that myself. All right. I'll see what I can find out and I will let you know when we are together again—which will be tomorrow around noon. We can meet here and then go to lunch. I will bring the materials I'll be turning over to your team."

"Fair enough," Friday said.

The men reached the inn. Friday regarded the captain.

"One more question," Friday said.

"Of course."

"Why didn't you offer me a cigarette?" Friday asked.

"Because you don't smoke," Nazir replied.

"Did the minister tell you that?"

"No," Nazir told him.

"You checked up on me, then," Friday said. "Asked people I've worked with about my habits and potential weaknesses."

"That's right," Nazir told him.

"So you didn't entirely trust the minister's judgment about bringing me onboard," Friday pointed out.

Nazir smiled again. "I said I knew everyone in the Black Cats. The minister is not one of my commandoes."

"I see," Friday replied. "That was still sloppy. You told me something about yourself, your methods, who you trust. That's something a professional shouldn't do."

"You're right," Nazir replied evenly. "But how do you know I wasn't testing you to see if you'd notice what I did?" The captain offered his hand. "Good night."

"Good night," Friday said. He felt the flush of embarrassment and a trace of doubt as he shook Nazir's hand.

The Black Cat Commando turned then and walked into the night, trailing a thick cloud of smoke behind him.

EIGHTEEN

Alconbury, Great Britain
Wednesday, 7:10 P.M.

Mike Rodgers was looking at files Bob Herbert had e-mailed from Op-Center when the giant C-130 touched down at the Royal Air Force station in Alconbury. Though the slow takeoff had seemed like a strain for the aircraft, the landing was barely noticeable. Maybe that was because the plane shook so much during the trans-Atlantic flight that Rodgers did not realize it had finally touched down. He was very much aware when the engines shut down, however. The plane stopped vibrating but he did not. After over six hours he felt as if there were a small electric current running through his body from sole to scalp. He knew from experience that it would take about thirty to forty minutes for that sensation to stop. Then, of course, Striker would be airbound again and it would start once more. Somewhere in that process was a microcosm of the ups and downs and sensations of life but he was too distracted to look for it right now.

The team left the aircraft but only to stand on the field. They would only be on the ground for an hour or so, long enough for a waiting pair of hydraulic forklifts to off-load several crates of spare parts.

The officers of the RAF referred to Alconbury as the Really American Field. Since the end of World War II it had effectively been a hub of operations for the United States Air Force in Europe. It was a large, modern field with state-of-the-art communications, repair, and munitions facilities. Since every base, every field, every barracks needed a nickname, the Americans here had nicknamed the field "Al." Many of the American servicemen went around humming

the Paul Simon song, "You Can Call Me Al." The Brits did
not really get the eternal American fascination with sobri-
quets for everything from presidents to spacecraft to their
weapons—Honest Abe, Friendship 7, Old Betsy. But Mike
Rodgers understood. It made formidable tools and institutions seem a little less intimidating. And it implied a famil-
iarity, a kinship with the thing or place, a sense that man,
object, and organization were somehow equal.

It was very American.

The members of Striker walked down the cargo bay ramp
and onto the tarmac. Two of the Strikers lit cigarettes and
stood together near an eyewash stand. Other soldiers
stretched, did jumping jacks, or just lay back on the field and
looked up at the blue-black sky. Brett August used one of
the field phones standing off by the warehouse. He was probably calling one of the girls he had in this port. Perhaps he
would bail on the team and visit her on the way back. The
colonel certainly had the personal time coming to him. They
all did.

Mike Rodgers wandered off by himself. He headed toward
the nose of the aircraft. The wind rushed across the wide-
open field, carrying with it the familiar air base smells of
diesel fuel, oil lubricant, and rubber from the friction-heated
tires of aircraft. As the sun went down and the tarmac cooled
and shrunk, the smells seemed to be squeezed out of them.
Whatever airfield in the world Rodgers visited, those three
smells were always present. They made him feel at home.
The cool air and very solid ground felt great.

Rodgers had his hands in his pockets, his eyes on the oil-
stained field. He was thinking about the data Friday had sent
to the NSA and the files Herbert had forwarded to him. He
was also thinking about Ron Friday himself. And the many
Ron Fridays he had worked with over the decades.

Rodgers always had a problem with missions that involved
other governments and other agencies within his own government. Information given to a field operative was not always informative. Sometimes it was wrong, by either
accident, inefficiency, or design. The only way to find out

for sure was to be on the mission. By then, bad information or wrong conclusions drawn from incomplete data could kill you.

The other problem Rodgers had with multigroup missions was authority and accountability. Operatives were like kids in more ways than one. They enjoyed playing outside and they resented having to listen to someone else's "parent." Ron Friday might be a good and responsible man. But first and foremost, Friday had to answer to the head of the NSA and probably to his sponsor in the Indian government. Satisfying their needs, achieving their targets, took priority over helping Rodgers, the mission leader. Ideally, their goals would be exactly the same and there would be no conflict. But that rarely happened. And sometimes it was worse than that. Sometimes operatives or officers were attached to a mission to make sure that it failed, to embarrass a group that might be fighting for the attention of the president or the favor of a world leader or even the same limited funding.

In a situation where a team was already surrounded by adversaries Mike Rodgers did not want to feel as if he could not count on his own personnel. Especially when the lives of the Strikers were at risk.

Of course, Rodgers had never met Ron Friday or the Black Cat officer they were linking up with, Captain Nazir. He would do what he always did: size them up when he met them. He could usually tell right away whether he could or could not trust people.

Right now, though, the thing that troubled Rodgers most had nothing to do with Friday. It had to do with the explosion in Srinagar. In particular, with that last call from the home phone to the field phone.

Other nations routinely used cell phones as part of their intelligence-gathering and espionage efforts. Not just surveillance of the calls but the hardware itself. The electronics did not raise alarms at airport security; most government officials, military personnel, and businesspeople had them; and they already had some of the wiring and microchips that were necessary for saboteurs. Cell phones were also extremely well positioned to kill. It did not take more than a wedge of C-4, packed inside the workings of a cell phone, to blow the side of a target's head off when he answered a call.

But Rodgers recalled one incident in particular, in the former Portuguese colony of Timor, that had parallels to this. He had read about it in an Australian military white paper while he was on Melville Island observing naval maneuvers in the Timor Sea in 1999. The invading Indonesian military had given cell phones to poor East Timorese civilians in what appeared to be a gesture of good will. The civilians were permitted to use the Indonesian military mobile communications service to make calls. The phones were not just phones but two-way radios. Civilians who had access to groups that were intensely loyal to imprisoned leader Xanana Gusmao were inadvertently used as spies to eavesdrop on nationalistic activities. Out of curiosity, Rodgers had asked a colleague in Australia's Department of Defense Strategy and Intelligence if the Indonesians had developed that themselves. He said they had not. The technology had come from Moscow. The Russians were also big suppliers of Indian technology.

What was significant to Rodgers was that the radio function was activated by signals sent from the Indonesian military outpost in Baukau. The signals were sent after calls had indicated that one individual or another was going to be in a strategic location.

Rodgers could not help but wonder if the home phone had somehow signaled the field phone to detonate the secondary blasts. The timing was too uncomfortably close to be coincidence. And the continuation of the signal at such regular intervals suggested that the terrorists were being tracked.

Hell, it did more than suggest that, Rodgers told himself. And the more he thought about it, the more he began to realize that they might have a very nasty developing situation on their hands. The Pentagon's elite think tank, with the innocuous name of the Department of Theoretical Effects, called this process "computing with vaporware." Rodgers had always been good at that, back when the Pentagon still called it "domino thinking."

He had to talk to Herbert about this.

Rodgers called over to Ishi Honda. The communications man was lying on the tarmac with the TAC-SAT beside him. He came running over with the secure phone. Rodgers thanked him then squatted on the field beside the oblong unit and phoned Bob Herbert. He used the earphones so he could hear over the roar of landing and departing jets.

Herbert picked up at once.

"Bob, it's Mike Rodgers," the general said.

"Glad to hear from you. Are you at Al?" Herbert asked.

"Just landed," Rodgers said. "Listen, Bob. I've been thinking about this latest data you sent me. I've got a feeling that the Srinagar bombers have been tagged, maybe by someone on the inside."

"I've got that same feeling," Herbert admitted. "Especially since we've been able to place the calls from field to home before that. They originated at a farm in Kargil. We notified the SFF. They sent over a local constable to check the place out. The farmer refused to say anything and they could not find his granddaughter. Ron and the SFF guy are going over first thing in the morning, see if they can't get more out of him."

"None of this smells right," Rodgers said.

"No, it doesn't," Herbert said. "And there's something else. The farmer's daughter and son-in-law were resistance fighters who died fighting the Pakistani invasion."

"So the farmer certainly had a reason to be part of a conspiracy against the Free Kashmir Militia," Rodgers said.

"In theory, yes," Herbert said. "What we're looking at now is whether there is a conspiracy and whether it could have involved the district police station that was home for the cell phone. Matt Stoll's gotten into their personnel files and my team is looking at the backgrounds of each officer. We want to see if any of them have connections with antiterrorist groups."

"You realize, Bob, that if you find a link between the police and the Pakistani cell, we may have an unprecedented international incident on our hands," Rodgers said.

"I don't follow," Herbert replied. "Just because they might have known about the attack and decided not to prevent it—"

"I think it may have been more than that," Rodgers said. "There were three separate attacks. Only one of them conformed to the established m.o. of the Free Kashmir Militia, the bombing of the police station."

"Wait a minute," Herbert said. "That's a big leap. You're saying the police could have planned this action themselves? That the Indians attacked their own temples—"

"To coincide with the FKM attack, yes," Rodgers said.

"But an operation like that would have to involve more than just the police in Kashmir," Herbert pointed out. "Especially if they're tracking and going to attempt to capture the cell, which is apparently the case."

"I know," Rodgers replied. "Isn't it possible they do have help? From a group that is a little more involved than usual?"

"The SFF," Herbert said.

"Why not? That could be the reason they wanted the bazaar sealed and the Black Cats kept out," Rodgers said.

Herbert thought for a moment. "It's possible," he agreed. "But it's also possible we're getting ahead of ourselves."

"Better than being behind," Rodgers pointed out.

"Touché," Herbert said. "Look. Let's see what Ron Friday and his partner turn up in the morning. I'll bring Paul up to date and let you know when we have anything else."

"Sure," Rodgers said. "But while we're getting ahead of ourselves let's go one step further."

"All right," Herbert said tentatively.

"Striker is going in to Pakistan to look for nukes," Rodgers said. "What if we don't find very many or even none at all? Suppose the Indian government authorized the Srinagar attack just to rouse their population and pick a fight. A fight Pakistan cannot possibly win."

"You think they'll respond with a nuclear strike?" Herbert said.

"Why not?" Rodgers asked.

"The world wouldn't stand for it!" Herbert replied.

"What would the world do?" Rodgers asked. "Go to war against India? Fire missiles on New Delhi? Would they impose sanctions? What kind? To what end? And what would happen when hundreds of thousands of Indians started to starve and die? Bob, we're not talking about Iraq or North Korea. We're talking about one billion people with the fourth largest military in the world. Nearly a billion Hindus who are afraid of becoming the victims of a Muslim holy war."

"Mike, no nation on earth is going to condone a nuclear strike against Pakistan," Herbert said. "Period."

"The question is not condoning," Rodgers said. "The question is how do you respond if it happens. What would we do alone?"

"Alone?"

"More or less," Rodgers said. "I'm betting Moscow and Beijing wouldn't complain too loud, for starters. India nuking Pakistan leaves Moscow free to slam whichever republics they want with a limited nuclear strike. No more long wars in Afghanistan or Chechnya. And China probably wouldn't bitch too loud because it gives them a precedent to move on Taiwan."

"They wouldn't," Herbert said. "It's insane."

"No, it's survival," Rodgers said. "Israel's got a nuclear strike plan ready in case of a united Arab attack. And they'd use it, you know that. What if India has the same kind of plan? And with the same very powerful justification, I might add. Religious persecution."

Herbert said nothing.

"Bob, all I'm saying is that it's like the house that Jack built," Rodgers said. "One little thing leads to another and then another. Maybe it's not those things, but it's nothing good."

"No, it is nothing good," Herbert agreed. "I still think we're overreacting but I'll get back to you as soon as we know anything. Meantime, I have just one suggestion."

"What's that?" Rodgers asked.

"Make sure you sleep on the flight to India," Herbert said. "One way or another you're going to need it."

NINETEEN

Kargil, Kashmir
Thursday, 6:45 A.M.

Ron Friday was annoyed that the call did not come from
Hank Lewis. It came from Captain Nazir. To Friday, that
meant on this leg of the mission Friday was reporting to New
Delhi and not to Washington. That suggested the Black Cats
would be watching him closely. Perhaps the Indian government did not want him talking to the NSA or anyone else
about whatever they might find here. At least, not before they
went on the mission.

They were to go to a chicken farm in the foothills of Kargil. Apparently, an intelligence officer at Op-Center found a
possible link between that location and the bazaar bombing.
Op-Center did not tell Hank Lewis or their Black Cat liaisons
why they thought the farm might be significant or what they
believed that significance to be. All they said was that the
situation in the bazaar was "atypical" and that the terrorists
had to be taken alive. To Friday that translated as, "We aren't
sure the terrorists did this and we need to talk to them."

The pair flew to the farm in a fast, highly maneuverable
Kamov Ka-25 helicopter. Captain Nazir was at the controls.
The compact sky-blue chopper was one of more than two
dozen Ka-25s India bought from Russia when the Soviet Union collapsed and the military began cutting costs. Friday
was not surprised to be riding in a military bird. A black
National Security Guard chopper would stand out. But the
skies here were full of Indian military traffic. Ironically, taking an air force craft was the best way to be invisible on
Pakistani radar.

The men flew north at approximately two hundred feet,
following the increasingly jagged and sloping terrain.

Though their unusually low passage caused some agitation among sheep and horses, and curses from their owners, Nazir explained over the headset that it was necessary. The air currents here were difficult to manage, especially early in the morning. As the sun rose the lower layers of air became heated. They mixed violently with the icy air flowing down from the mountains and created a particularly hazardous navigation zone between five hundred and two thousand feet up. It troubled Friday that a single Pakistani operative with a shoulder-mounted rocket launcher could take out the Ka-25 with no problem. He hoped that whatever information Op-Center had received was not what the intelligence community called a "TM," a "tactical mislead," a lie precipitated by the desire to slow down pursuit by smoking out and eliminating the pursuers.

The two men reached the farmhouse without incident. Before landing, Captain Nazir had buzzed the small barn and then the wood-and-stone farmhouse. An old farmer came out to see what was happening. He seemed surprised as he shielded his eyes to look up at the chopper. Nazir came in lower until he was just above the rooftop.

"What do you think?" Nazir asked. "Is the farmer alone?"

"Most likely," Friday replied. Hostages who had been kept a short while tended to be highly agitated, even panicked. They wanted to get to someone who could protect them. Even if there were other hostages at risk, including close family members, self-preservation was their first, irrepressible instinct. Hostages who had been held a long while were usually just the opposite. They had already bonded with their captors and were very standoffish, frequently antagonistic. The man below them was neither.

Nazir hovered a moment longer and then set down on a nearby field. After the noisy forty-minute flight it was good to hear nothing but the wind. The cool breeze also felt good as they made their way to the farm. Nazir wore a .38 in a holster on his hip. Friday carried a derringer in the right pocket of his windbreaker and a switchblade in the left. The .22 gun did not pack much punch but he could palm it if necessary and easily use it to blind an assailant.

The farmer waited for the men to arrive. Friday made Apu Kumar out to be about sixty-five. He was a small, slope-shouldered man with slits for eyes. His features seemed to have a trace of Mongolian ancestry. That was not uncommon along the Himalayas. Nomads from many Asian races had roamed this region for tens of thousands of years, making it one of the world's truest melting pots. One of the sad ironies of the conflict here was the fact that so many of the combatants had the same blood.

The men stopped a few feet from the farmer. The farmer's dark, suspicious eyes looked them up and down. Beyond the house was the barn. The chickens were still squawking from the flyover.

"Good morning," Nazir said.

The farmer nodded deeply, once.

"Are you Apu Kumar?" Nazir asked.

The farmer nodded again. This time the nod was a little less self-assured and his eyes shifted from Nazir to Friday.

"Does anyone else live here?" Nazir inquired.

"My granddaughter," the farmer replied.

"Anyone else?"

Kumar shook his head.

"Is your granddaughter here now?" Nazir asked.

The farmer shook his head. He shifted a little now. His expression suggested fear for his safety but now his body language said he was also tense, anxious. He was hiding something. Possibly about his granddaughter.

"Where is she?" Nazir pressed.

"Out," Apu replied. "She runs errands."

"I see. Do you mind if we look around?" Nazir asked.

"May I ask what you are looking for?" the farmer asked.

"I don't know," Nazir admitted.

"Well, go ahead," Apu said. "But be careful of my chickens. You've already frightened them once with your machine." He made a disdainful gesture toward the helicopter.

Nazir nodded and turned. Friday hesitated.

"What's wrong?" Nazir asked the American.

Friday continued to look at the farmer. "Your granddaughter is one of them, isn't she?"

Apu did not move. He did not say, "My granddaughter is one of who?" He said nothing. That told Friday a lot.

Friday approached the farmer. Apu started backing away. Friday held up his hands, knuckles out. The derringer was in his right palm where the farmer could not see it. Friday watched both the farmer and the farmhouse door and window behind him. He could not be absolutely certain no was one inside or that Apu would not try to get a gun or ax or some other weapon just inside.

"Mr. Kumar, everything is all right," Friday said slowly, softly. "I'm not going to do anything to you. Nothing at all."

Apu slowed then stopped. Friday stopped as well.

"Good," Friday said. He lowered his hands and put them back in his pockets. The derringer was pointed at Apu. "I want to ask you a question but it's an important one. All right?"

Apu nodded once.

"I need to know if you do not want to talk to us because you and your granddaughter support the terrorists or because they are holding her hostage," Friday said to him.

Apu hesitated.

"Mr. Kumar, people were killed yesterday when a bomb exploded in Srinagar," Captain Nazir said. "Police officers, pilgrims on the way to Pahalgam, and worshipers in a temple. Did your granddaughter have a hand in that or did she not?"

"No!" Apu half-shouted, half-wept. "We do not support them. They forced her to go with them! They left yesterday. I was told to be silent or they said they would kill her. How is she? How is my granddaughter?"

"We don't know," Nazir told him. "But we want to find her and help her. Have they been back here since the explosion?" Nazir asked.

"No," Apu said. "One man stayed behind when the others left. He called and claimed responsibility for an attack. I heard him. But then he left suddenly at around five o'clock."

"Suddenly?" Nazir asked.

"He seemed very upset after talking to someone else on the telephone," Apu told him.

"As if something had gone wrong?" Friday asked. That would certainly confirm what Op-Center was thinking.

"I don't know," Apu said. "He was usually very calm. I even heard him make jokes sometimes. But not then. Maybe something did happen."

"If you came to Srinagar with us, would you be able to tell us what these people look like?" Nazir asked.

Apu nodded.

Friday touched Nazir's arm. "We may not have time for that," the NSA operative said. Whatever is happening seems to be happening very quickly. "Mr. Kumar, were your visitors Pakistani?"

"Yes."

"How many of them were there and how long did they stay with you?" Friday asked.

"There were five and they stayed for five months," Apu told him.

"Did you hear any of their names?" Nazir asked.

"Yes," Apu said. "I heard 'Sharab' but no last names."

"Did they ever leave you alone?" Friday asked.

"Only in our bedroom," Apu told him. "One of them was always on guard outside."

"Did they ever mistreat you?" Friday asked.

Apu shook his head. He was like a prizefighter who kept getting peppered with jabs. But that was how interrogations needed to be conducted. Once the target opened up the interrogator had to keep him open. Friday looked over at the stone barn.

"Who took care of your chickens?" Friday asked.

"I did in the morning and Nanda—that's my granddaughter—she took care of them in the late afternoon," Apu replied.

"The Pakistanis were with you then?" Nazir said.

"Yes."

"How did your eggs get to market?" Friday asked.

"The Pakistanis took them," Apu replied.

That would explain how the terrorists had cased their target in Srinagar without being noticed. But it did not explain the field phone signal that came from here.

"Do you or your granddaughter own a cellular telephone, Mr. Kumar?" Friday asked.

Apu shook his head.

"What did she do in her free time?" Friday pressed.

"She read and she wrote poetry."

"Did she always write poetry?" Friday asked.

Apu said she did not. Friday sensed that he was on to something.

"Do you have any of the poetry?" Friday asked.

"In the room," Apu told him. "She used to recite it to herself while she worked."

Friday was definitely on to something. He and Captain Nazir exchanged glances. They asked to see the poems.

Apu took them inside. Friday was alert as they walked into the two-bedroom house. There was no one inside or anywhere to hide. There was hardly any furniture, just a few chairs and a table. The place smelled of ash and musk. The ash was from the wood-burning stove on which they also did their cooking. The musk, Friday suspected, was from their guests.

Apu led them to the bedroom. He took a stack of papers from the drawer in the nightstand. He handed them to Captain Nazir. The poems were short and written in pencil. They were about everything from flowers to clouds to rain. Nazir read the earliest.

```
It rained five days and flowers grew.
And they stayed fresh and new.
In my cart I kept a few
To sell to all of you.
```

"Not very profound," Nazir said.

Friday did not comment. He was not so sure of that.

The captain flipped through the others. The structure seemed to be the same in all of the poems, a "Mary Had a Little Lamb" cadence.

"Go back to the first," Friday said.

Nazir flipped back to the top sheet.

"Mr. Kumar, you said Nanda recited these poems while she worked?" Friday asked.

"Yes."

"Is she a political activist?"

"She is an outspoken patriot who was devoted to her parents," Apu said. "My daughter and son-in-law were killed resisting the Pakistanis."

"There it is," Friday said.

"I don't follow," Captain Nazir said.

Friday asked Apu to stay in the bedroom. He led Nazir back outside.

"Captain, there were five Pakistanis," Friday told him. "The woman mentions the number five in the first line of the first poem. The Pakistanis stayed here—she mentions that word too. She says something about her cart going to market. The Pakistanis sold the eggs for her. Suppose someone got her a cell phone. Suppose the line was open and monitored twenty-four/seven. You said the poems don't seem very profound. I disagree."

"She could have emphasized words that gave information to someone," Nazir said.

"Right," Friday said. "Doesn't the SFF maintain a group of volunteers from the general population? Civilian Network Operatives?"

"Yes."

"How does that system work?" Friday asked.

"Operatives are recruited in sensitive regions or businesses and visited on a regular basis, either at their place of employment or at home," Captain Nazir said. "They report unusual activities or provide other information they may have collected."

"What if an operative were to miss an appointment?" Friday asked. "What if Nanda failed to show up at the marketplace?"

Nazir nodded. "I see what you mean," he said. "The SFF would come looking for her."

"Exactly," Friday said. "Suppose at some point this woman, Nanda, had been recruited by the SFF. Maybe when the Pakistanis held Kargil, maybe after. If someone showed up with her cart in the bazaar, her SFF contact would have known that something was wrong. They might have arranged to drop a field phone off in the barn where she was sure to find it."

"Yes, it's starting to come together," Nazir said. "The SFF sponsors the woman. She feeds them information about the cell and they decide to let the terrorists make their attack on the police station. At the same time the SFF enlarges the scope of that attack so the Pakistanis will take the blame for striking at religious targets. The SFF also seals off the site to clean up any evidence that might connect them to the other two explosions."

"But the job isn't finished," Friday said. "The terrorists realize they've been set up and are probably trying to get to Pakistan. They take Nanda with them in case they need a hostage."

"More likely a witness," Nazir pointed out. "The terrorists claimed responsibility for the explosion, probably before they knew the full extent of the damage. Nanda knows they were not responsible for the temple bombing. They need her to say that."

"Good point," Friday said. "Meanwhile, if she still has her cell phone with her, she may be signaling the SFF, telling them where to find them."

Nazir was silent for a moment. "If that is true, they probably haven't caught up with the terrorists yet," he said. "I would have heard about it. Which means we've got to get to them first. If the SFF executes the terrorists before they can be heard it will turn nearly one billion Hindus against Pakistan. There will be a war and it will be an all-out war, a holy war, with flame from the nostrils of Shiva."

"Shiva—the destroyer," Friday said. "A nuclear war."

"Provoked by the SFF and its radical allies in the cabinet and the military before Pakistan is equipped to respond," Nazir said.

Friday started running toward the Kamov. "I'm going to get in touch with Op-Center and see if they know more than they're telling," he said. "You'd better grab Mr. Kumar and bring him to the chopper. We may need someone to help convince Nanda she's on the wrong side of this thing."

As Friday hurried across the field he realized one thing more. Something that gave him a little satisfaction, a little boost.

Captain Nazir was not as smart as he had pretended to be back at the inn.

TWENTY

Washington, D.C.
Wednesday, 8:17 P.M.

For most of its history, the shadowy National Reconnaissance Office was the least known of all the government agencies. The spur for the formation of the NRO was the downing of Gary Powers's U-2 spy plane over the Soviet Union in May of that year. President Eisenhower ordered Defense Secretary Thomas Gates to head a panel to look into the application of satellites to undertake photographic reconnaissance. That would minimize the likelihood that the United States would suffer another humiliation like the Powers affair.

From the start there was furious debate between the White House, the air force, the Department of Defense, and the CIA over who should be responsible for administering the agency. By the time the NRO was established on August 25, 1960, it was agreed that the air force would provide the launch capabilities for spy satellites, the Department of Defense would develop technology for spying from space, and the CIA would handle the interpretation of intelligence. Unfortunately, there were conflicts almost from the start. At stake were not just budgeting and manpower issues but the intelligence needs of the different military and civilian agencies. During the next five years relationships between the Pentagon and the CIA became so strained that they were actually sabotaging one another's access to data from the nascent network of satellites. In 1965, the secretary of defense stepped in with a proposal that time and resources would be directed by a three-person executive committee. The EXCOM was composed of the director of the CIA, the assistant secretary of defense, and the president's science advisor. The EXCOM reported to the secretary of defense, though he could not overrule decisions made by the EXCOM. The new arrangement relieved some of the fighting for satellite time though it did nothing to ease the fierce rivalry between the various groups for what was being called "intelligence product." Eventually, the NRO had to be given more and more autonomy to determine the distribution of resources.

For most of its history NRO operations were spread across the United States. Management coordination was handled in the Air Force Office of Space Systems in the Pentagon. Technology issues were conducted from the Air Force Space and Missile Systems Center at Los Angeles Air Force Base in California. Intelligence studies were conducted from the CIA Office of Development and Engineering in Reston, Virginia. Orbital control of NRO spacecraft was initially handled by technicians at the Onizuka Air Force Base in Sunnyvale, California, and then moved to the Falcon Air Force Station in Colorado. Signals intelligence other than photographic reconnaissance was handled by the National Guard at the Defense Support Program Aerospace Data Facility at Buckley Air National Guard Base in Aurora, Colorado. The U.S. Navy's NRO activities were centered primarily on technology upgrades and enhancement of existing hardware and software. These duties were shared by two competing naval groups: the Space and Naval Warfare Systems Command in Crystal City, Virginia, and SPAWAR's Space Technology Directorate Division, SPAWAR-40, located at the Naval Research Laboratory across the Potomac River in the highly secure Building A59.

Though the NRO proved invaluable in bringing data back to earth, the management of the NRO itself became a nightmare of convolution and in-fighting. Though the government did not officially acknowledge the existence of the organization, its denials were a joke among the Washington press corps. No one would explain why so many people were obviously struggling with such rancor to control something that did not exist.

That changed in 1990 with the construction of a permanent NRO facility in Fairfax, Virginia. Yet even while the NRO's existence was finally acknowledged, few people had firsthand knowledge about its day-to-day operations and the full breadth of its activities.

Photographic reconnaissance operations director Stephen Viens was one of those men.

The consolidation of NRO activities under one roof did not end the competition for satellite time. But Viens was loyal to his college friend Matt Stoll. And he would do anything for Paul Hood, who stood by him during some difficult CIOC hearings about the NRO's black ops work. As a result, no group, military or civilian, got priority over Op-Center.

Bob Herbert had telephoned at four P.M. What he needed from Viens was visual surveillance of a specific site in the Himalayas. Viens had to wait two hours before he could free up the navy's Asian OmniCom satellite, which was in a geosynchronous orbit over the Indian Ocean. Even though the navy was using it, Viens told them he had an LAD—life-and-death—situation and needed it at once. Typically, the OmniCom listened to sonar signals from Russian and Chinese submarines and backed them up with visual reconnaissance when the vessels surfaced. That allowed the navy to study displacement and hull features and even to get a look down the hatch when it was opened. The satellite image was sharp to within thirteen inches from the target and refreshed every .8 seconds. If the angle were right the OmniCom could get in close enough to lip-read.

Working at the OmniCom station in the level four basement of the NRO, it was relatively easy for Viens and his small team to use the repositioned satellite to ride the field phone signal to its source. They pinpointed it to a site above the foothills at 8,112 feet. When Viens and his group had repositioned the satellite to look down on the site, dawn was just breaking in Kashmir. The rising sun cleared the mountains to the east and struck an isolated structure. It resembled a slender travertine stalagmite more than it did a mountain peak. Whatever it was, something remarkable was happening on its face.

There were over a dozen figures in white parkas on the eastern side of the peak. They were armed with what looked like automatic weapons. Some were climbing up the peak, others were rappelling down. They were all converging on a small mouth located near the base of the tor.

Viens quickly refined the location of the audio signal. It was not coming from the people on the cliff but from a stationary target. Probably from an individual or individuals inside the cave.

Viens immediately phoned Bob Herbert and redirected the signal to Op-Center.

TWENTY-ONE

Siachin Base 2E, Kashmir
Thursday, 7:01 A.M.

There is nothing like sunrise in the Himalayas.

The higher altitude and thinner, cleaner atmosphere allow a purer light to get through. Ishaq did not know how else to describe it. A photographer in Islamabad once told him that the atmosphere acted like a prism. The lower to the ground you were, the thicker the air blanket was and the more the sunlight was bent to the red. Ishaq was not a scientist. He did not know if that were true.

All the Pakistani knew was that the light up here was like he imagined the eye of Allah to be. It was white, warm, and intense. He wondered if the story of the mountain coming to Mohammad had originated in a peak like this one. For as the sun edged higher above the foothills below and the shadows shortened, the crags actually appeared to move. And as they moved their snow-covered sides glowed brighter and brighter. It was almost as though enlightenment were spreading throughout the land. Perhaps this was what the tale of the Prophet signified. The light of Allah and his Prophet was stronger than anything on this earth. And opening one's heart and mind to them made us as strong and eternal.

That was a comforting thought to Ishaq. If this were to be his last dawn at least he would die satisfied and closer to God. In fact, as he looked back over his life he had just one regret: that he might have to die here and now. He had wanted to be with his comrades when they returned to their homeland. But they had intentionally selected for their armory a cave that had no other direct line of sight nearby. It would have been difficult for anyone to spot the small outpost or to watch them while they were here.

Ishaq had stayed up all night preparing. Then he had watched the sun rise as he ate breakfast. He had not wanted to sleep. There would be time enough for that. Now, as he sat in the dark in the back of the cave, Ishaq heard scraping noises outside.

Sharab was right. They had been tracked here.

The Indians had been quiet at first. Now they were no longer taking pains to conceal their approach. They were probably wearing crampons and they sounded like mice outside a wall, scratching their way in. The sounds grew from a few scrapes along the rear and sides of the cave to constant noise and motion. From the shifting location of the sounds he could tell that the Indians were already within range of the mouth of the cave. They would probably lob teargas before charging in. If the cell had been here there would have been no escape.

Ishaq decided that this would be a good time to put on his gas mask. He slipped the Iranian-made unit on, tightened the straps over his head, and snapped the mouthpiece in place. His breath was coming in little bursts. He was anxious, but not because of what was going to happen. He was worried because he hoped he had done everything right. The Pakistani looked at the wooden crates lined with plastic. He had gathered them nearby, like wives in a harem, ready for a final embrace. It had been a simple process to attach detonators to individual explosives, leave them on the top of the crates, and make sure the receivers were facing him. But he had not been able to examine all of the explosives. They had been stored up here for nearly two years. Though it was dry and cold and dampness should not be a problem, dynamite was temperamental. The sticks they had used in Srinagar had been showing signs of caking. Moisture had gotten inside.

Still, everything should be all right. Ishaq had rigged seven bundles of dynamite with C-4 and remote triggers. All he needed was for one of the bundles to blow. He pulled off his heavy gloves and took the detonator in his right hand. He leaned back against the stone wall.

Ishaq's legs were spread straight out in front of him and his backside was cold. The folded canvas he was sitting on was a bad insulator. Not that it mattered. He would not be sitting on it much longer.

The scraping stopped. He watched the tarp through the greenish tint of his facemask. Curtains of sunlight hung along the side walls of the cave. They shifted and undulated as the wind pushed against the tarp. The covering itself rattled against the hooks that held it in place.

Suddenly, the tarp dropped. Particles of ice that had collected on the outside flew, glistening in the sunlight. The shimmering beads died as two large, cylindrical canisters were lobbed in. They clanked on the cave floor and rolled toward Ishaq. They were already hissing and jetting thick clouds of smoke into the air and across the ground. Some of the gas unfurled sideways, and some of it was sprayed in his direction.

The Pakistani sat there, waiting calmly. The rolling green gas was still about fifteen meters away. The view to the nearest of the detonators remained unobstructed. He had a few more moments.

He began to pray.

Ishaq listened for the scraping to resume. After a moment it did, moving rapidly toward the front of the cave. He watched as the clouds of gas began to billow and roll aside as though people were moving through it. The gas had nearly reached the explosives.

It was time.

The Muslim continued his silent prayer as he pressed the blue "engage" button. A light on top of the small controller came on. Ishaq quickly pressed the red "detonate" button below it.

For a blessed moment the sun shined all around Ishaq and he felt as if he had been embraced by Allah.

TWENTY-TWO

Washington, D.C.
Wednesday, 9:36 P.M.

"What the hell just happened, Stephen?" Bob Herbert asked.

Op-Center's intelligence chief had pulled his wheelchair deep under the desk. He was leaning over the speakerphone as he watched the OmniCom image on his computer. What he had said was not so much a question as an observation. Herbert knew exactly what had happened.

"The side of the mountain just exploded," Viens said over the phone.

"It didn't just explode, it evaporated," Herbert pointed out. "That blast had to have been the equivalent of a thousand pounds of TNT."

"At least," Viens agreed.

Herbert was glad there was no sound with the image. Even just seeing the massive, unexpected explosion wakened his sensory memories. Tension and grief washed over him as he was reminded of the Beirut embassy bombing.

"What do you think, Bob? Was it set off by a sensor or motion detector?" Viens asked.

"I doubt it," Herbert said. "There are a lot of avalanches in that part of the world. They could have triggered the explosion prematurely."

"I didn't think of that," Viens admitted.

Herbert forced himself to focus on the present, not the past. Op-Center's intelligence chief reloaded the pictures the satellite had sent moments before the blast. He asked the computer to enhance the images of the soldiers one at a time.

"It looked to me like the climbers tossed gas inside," Herbert said. "They obviously believed that someone might be waiting for them."

"They were right," Viens said.

"The question is how many people were in there?" Herbert said. "Were the people who used that cave expecting the climbers? Or were they caught by surprise and decided they did not want to be captured alive?"

An image of the first soldier filled Herbert's monitor. There was a clear shot of the man's right arm. On top, just below the shoulder of the white camouflage snowsuit, was a circular red patch with a solid black insignia. The silhouette showed a horse running along the tail of a comet. That was the insignia of the Special Frontier Force.

"Well, one thing's dead for sure," Viens said.

"What's that?" Herbert asked.

"Matt Stoll just phoned to say he's not picking up the cell phone signal anymore," Viens told Herbert. "He wanted to see if we'd lost it too. I just checked. We have."

Herbert was still looking at the monitor. He saved the magnified image of the shoulder patch. "I wonder if the cell led the commandos there to throw them off the trail," he said.

"Possibly," Viens said. "Do we have any idea which way the Indian commandos would have come?"

"From the south," Herbert replied. "How long would it take you to start searching through the mountains north of the site?"

"It will take about a half hour to move the satellite," Viens said. "First, though, I want to make sure we're not wasting our time. If anyone left the cave they would have had to go up before they could go down again. I want to get the OmniCom in for a closer look."

"Footprints in the snow?" Herbert said as the secure phone on his wheelchair beeped.

"Exactly," Viens replied.

"Go for it. I'll wait," Herbert told him as he backed away from the desk so he could reach the phone. He snapped up the receiver. "Herbert."

"Bob, it's Hank Lewis," said the caller. "I've got Ron Friday on the line. He says it's important. I'd like to conference him in."

"Go ahead," Herbert said. He had been wondering what Friday would find at the farmhouse. He was hoping it did not confirm their fears of police or government involvement in the Srinagar market attack. The implications were too grim to contemplate.

"Go ahead, Ron," Lewis said. "I have Director of Intelligence Bob Herbert on the line with us."

"Good," Friday said. "Mr. Herbert, I'm at the Kumar farmhouse in Kargil with my Black Cat liaison. I need to know what other intel you have on the farmer and his granddaughter."

"What have you found out there?" Herbert asked.

"What?" Friday said.

"What did you find at the farm?" Herbert asked.

"What is this, 'I show you mine and you show me yours?' " Friday angrily demanded.

"No," Herbert said. "It's a field report. Tell me what you've got."

"I've got my ass on the front frigging line and you're sitting on your ass safe in Washington!" Friday said. "I need information!"

"I'm on my ass because my legs don't work anymore," Herbert responded calmly. "I lost them because too many people trusted the wrong people. Mr. Friday, I've got an entire team headed toward your position and they may be at considerable risk. You're a piece in my puzzle, a field op for me. You tell me what you have and then I'll tell you what you need to know."

Friday said nothing. Herbert hoped he was considering exactly how to word his apology.

After a few moments Friday broke the silence. "I'm waiting for that information, Mr. Herbert," he said.

That caught Herbert off guard. Okay. They were playing hardball with a hand grenade. He could do that.

"Mr. Lewis," Herbert said, "please thank your field operative for reconnoitering the farmhouse. Inform him we will get our information directly from the Black Cat Commandos and that our joint operation is ended."

"You bureaucratic asshole—!" Friday snapped.

"Friday, Mr. Herbert has the authority to terminate this alliance," Lewis said. "And frankly, you're not giving me a reason to fight for it."

"We need each other out here!" Friday said. "We may be looking at an international catastrophe!"

"That's the first useful insight you've given me," Herbert said. "Would you care to continue?"

Friday swore. "I don't have time for a pissing contest, Herbert. I'll straighten you out later. We've learned that a Pakistani cell, part of the Free Kashmir Militia, stayed at the farm of Apu Kumar for about five months. The farmer's granddaughter, Nanda, is the only child of a couple who died fighting the Pakistanis. The girl wrote poetry the whole time the cell was here. It appears to have contained coded elements reporting on the cell's activities. She used to recite her poems aloud while she took care of the chickens. We suspect members of the Special Frontier Force heard what she was saying, probably by cell phone. She was with them when the bazaar attack in Srinagar took place and we believe the SFF was behind the temple bombing. We also believe that she is still with them, and might have the cell phone to signal SFF."

"She was signaling the SFF," Herbert replied.

"What happened?" Friday asked.

It was time to give Friday a little information, a little trust. "The Indian pursuit team was just taken out by a powerful explosion in the Himalayas," Herbert informed him.

"How do you know that?" Lewis asked.

"We've got ELINT resources in the region," Herbert said.

Herbert used the vague electronics intelligence reference because he did not want Lewis to know that he had satellite coverage of the region. The new NSA head might start pushing the NRO for off-the-books satellite time of his own.

"How many men were killed?" Lewis asked.

"About thirteen or fourteen," Herbert replied. "They were closing in on what appeared to be an outpost about eight thousand feet up in the mountains. The men, the outpost, and the side of the mountain are all gone."

"Were you able to ID the commandos?" Friday asked. "Were they wearing uniforms?"

"They were SFF," Herbert replied.

"I knew it," Friday said triumphantly. "What about the cell?"

"We don't know," Herbert admitted. "We're trying to find out if they got away."

Herbert looked at the computer monitor. Stephen Viens had just finished zooming in slowly on the northern side of the cliff. The resolution was three meters, sufficient to show footprints. The angle of the sun was still low. That would help by casting shadows off the side walls of any prints. Viens began panning the flattest, widest areas of the slopes. Those were the sections where people were likely to be walking in the darkness.

"If the cell did get away the SFF is not going to give up," Friday continued. "There's a possibility the SFF set them up to take the fall for the temple bombings in Srinagar."

"Do you have proof of that?" Herbert asked. He was interested that Friday had come to the same conclusion as he and General Rodgers.

"No," Friday admitted. "But the Black Cats would normally have handled the investigation and they were cut out of it by the SFF. They also obviously knew about the cell."

"That doesn't mean they were involved in the destruction of the temple," Herbert said. "The Free Kashmir Militia are known terrorists. According to Indian radio they already took credit for the bombing—"

"Whoever made that call may not have known the extent of the attack," Friday said.

"That could be," Herbert agreed. "I'm still not ready to declare them innocent. Maybe someone in the group betrayed them and rigged the extra explosions. But let's assume for the moment you're right, that the SFF organized the bombing to advance an agenda. What is that agenda?"

"My Black Cat partner believes it's a holy war," Friday said. "Possibly a nuclear holy war."

"A preemptive strike," Hank Lewis said.

Again, Herbert was encouraged by the fact that Ron Friday and the Indian Black Cat officer reached the same conclusions that he and Rodgers had. It meant there might be some truth to their concerns. But he was also discouraged for the same reason.

"We think the SFF forces used gas against the Pakistani stronghold," Herbert said. "Which would mean they wanted to try and capture them alive."

"A perp walk and confessions," Friday said.

"Probably. But I've got to believe the main reason the cell is running is not to save their own lives," Herbert said. "Even if they get back to Pakistan no one in India is going to take their word that they're innocent."

"They need the girl," Friday said.

"Exactly," Herbert said. "If she worked with the SFF to stage the attack, they need to get a complete public statement from her. One that doesn't look or sound like it's a forced confession."

"I'm missing something here," Lewis said. "If we suspect that this is going on, why don't we just confront the SFF or someone in the Indian government? Get them involved."

"Because we don't know who may already be involved in this operation and how high up it goes," Herbert said. "Talking to New Delhi may just accelerate the process."

"Accelerate it?" Lewis said. "How much faster can it possibly go?"

"In a crisis like this days can become hours if you're not careful," Herbert said. "We don't want to panic the people in charge. If we're right, the SFF will still try to capture the cell."

"Or at least Nanda," Friday said. "Maybe she's the one they're really after. Think about a teary-eyed Hindu woman going on television and telling the public how the FKM plotted to blow up the temple, not caring how many Hindu men, women, and children they killed."

"Good point," Herbert said. "What about the girl's grandfather? If the cell is alive and we can find them before the

SFF does, do you think he'd be willing to talk to her? To convince her to tell the public what she knows?"

"I'll make sure he's willing to talk to her," Friday said.

As they spoke the satellite camera stopped on what looked like it might be several footprints. Viens began zooming in.

"What are you thinking of doing, Bob?" Hank Lewis asked.

"We've already got two men on the ground and a field force on the way," Herbert said. "If I can get Paul to sign off on it, I'm going to ask General Rodgers to try and intercept the cell."

"And do what?" Lewis demanded. "Help avowed terrorists make it home safely?"

"Why not?" Friday said. "That might win us allies in the Muslim world. We can use them."

"America doesn't 'win' allies in the Muslim world. If we're lucky we earn their forbearance," Herbert said.

"A smart man knows how to work that too," Friday said.

"Maybe you'll get to show us how it's done," Herbert replied.

"Maybe," Friday replied.

The intelligence chief had worked with hundreds of field ops over the years. He had been one himself. They were a tough, thorny, independent breed. But this man was more than that. Herbert could hear it in his voice, the edge to his words and the confidence of his statements. Usually, men who sounded like Friday were what spy leaders called HOWs—hungry old wolves. Working on their own year after year they began to feel invisible to the host government and beyond the reach of their own government. They'd been out in the cold so long that they tended to bite anyone who came near them.

But Friday had not spent a lot of time on his own. He had come from an embassy post. That suggested something else to Herbert: an I-spy. The espionage game's equivalent of a bad cop, someone who was in this for themselves. Whatever Striker ended up doing in the field, if it involved Ron Friday Herbert would tell Mike Rodgers to watch him very, very closely.

"Bob?" Viens said on the speakerphone. "You still there?"

"I'm here," Herbert said. He told Lewis and Friday to hold the line.

"Are you looking at the monitor?" Viens asked.

"I am," Herbert said.

"You see that?" Viens asked.

"I do," Herbert replied.

There were footprints. And they were made during the previous night. The sun had not had a chance to melt and refreeze them. The cell had definitely left the cave and was heading north, toward Pakistan. Unfortunately, they could not tell from the jumble of footprints how many people were in the party.

"Good work, Stephen," Herbert said. He archived the image with the rest of them. "Have you got time to follow them?"

"I can track them for a bit but that won't tell you much," Viens said. "I looked at one of the overviews. We're going to lose the trail behind the peak about a quarter of a kilometer to the northwest. After that all we've got is a shitload of mountain to examine."

"I see," Herbert said. "Well, at least let's make sure they went as far as the turn. And see if we can get a better idea of how many people there were and maybe what they were carrying."

"I'm guessing they weren't carrying much," Viens said. "Three inches or so of snow cover, two inches of print. They look about the right depth for an average hundred-and-sixty-pound individual. Besides, I can't imagine they'd be carrying much more than ropes and pitons trekking through that region."

"You're probably right," Herbert said.

"But I'll see if we can't get a head count for the group," Viens said.

"Thanks, Stephen," Herbert said.

"Anytime," Viens replied.

Herbert clicked off the speakerphone and got back on with Hank Lewis and Ron Friday. "Gentlemen, we've definitely got the cell heading north," he said. "I suggest we table the political debate and concentrate on managing the crisis. I'll have a talk with Paul. See if he wants to get involved with this or whether we should abort the Striker mission altogether and turn the problem over to the State Department. Hank, I suggest you and Mr. Friday talk this over and see what you want your own involvement to be. Whether we stick to the original mission or work out a new one, it could get ugly out there."

"We'll also have to talk about what to tell the president and the CIOC," Lewis said.

"I have a suggestion about that," Herbert told him. "If you tag Mr. Friday as a loan-out to Striker as of right now, the NSA doesn't have to be involved in making that decision."

"That's a negative," Lewis told him. "I'm new on the job, Bob, but I'm not a novice. You let me know what Paul's thinking is and I'll make the call on our end."

"Fair enough," Herbert said. He smiled. He respected a man who did not pass the buck. Especially a buck this big.

"Ron," Lewis said, "I'd like you to talk to the farmer and to Captain Nazir. See if they're with you on a possible search-and-capture. I agree with Bob. Mr. Kumar can be very useful if we're able to locate his granddaughter."

"I'll do it," Friday said.

"Good," Herbert said. "Hank, you and I will talk after I've discussed this with Paul and General Rodgers. Mr. Friday— thank you for your help."

Friday said nothing.

Herbert hung up. He swore at the very thought of Ron Friday and then put him from his mind—for now. There were larger issues to deal with.

He made an appointment to see Paul Hood at once.

TWENTY-THREE

Kargil, Kashmir
Thursday, 7:43 A.M.

Before leaving the helicopter Ron Friday opened a compartment between the seats. He found an old backup book of charts in there. The chopper's flight plan was dictated by computer-generated maps. These animated landscapes and grid overlays were presented on a monitor located above the primary flight display screen between the pilot and copilot stations. A keypad beneath the monitor was used to punch in coordinates. Friday tore out the maps he wanted and shoved them in the pocket of his windbreaker.

As he headed back to the farm, Friday punched the air. He unleashed a flurry of strong, angry uppercuts that did not just hit the imaginary chin of Bob Herbert. The punches went through his new nemesis as he struck at the sky. Who the hell did Bob Herbert think he was? The man had been wounded in the line of duty. That entitled him to disability compensation, not respect.

The pismire, Friday thought. Bob Herbert was just a wage-slave drone in the hive.

Friday finished his flurry of blows. His heart was ramming his chest, his arms perspiring. Breathing heavily, he flexed his fingers as he stalked across the rocky, uneven terrain.

It's all right, Friday told himself. He was here, at the heart of the action, in control of his destiny. Bob Herbert was back in Washington barking orders. Orders that could easily be ignored since Lewis had not allowed him to be seconded to Op-Center. Friday put the self-pitying bureaucrat from his mind and concentrated on the work at hand.

Captain Nazir had gone inside with Apu Kumar. The Black Cat officer was looking around the house while Kumar sat quietly on the tattered couch. Both men turned as Friday entered.

"What did they say?" Nazir asked.

"The Pakistani cell is alive and well and apparently moving north through the Himalayas," Friday told Nazir. "Op-Center and the NSA are considering a joint mission to try and apprehend the cell along with Mr. Kumar's granddaughter. They want to keep them all out of the hands of the SFF. Would the Black Cat Commandos and their allies in the government have a problem with an American-run search-and-recover mission?"

"Does your government believe there is a chance for a nuclear exchange?" Nazir asked.

"If they didn't think so, they would not even be considering a covert action," Friday replied. "It looks like your friends from the Special Frontier Force wanted that cell bad enough. Our ELINT resources caught a squad of them chasing the Pakistanis through the mountains."

"Where is the SFF squad?" Nazir asked.

"Waiting in line for reincarnation," Friday replied.

"Excuse me?"

"From what I gathered the commandos were caught by a Pakistani suicide bomber," Friday told him.

"I see," Nazir said. He thought for a moment. "The SFF presence supports what we were thinking, that they set this up."

"It sure looks that way," Friday said.

"Then yes," Nazir said. "The Black Cat Commandos would help you in any way we can."

"Good," Friday said. He walked over to Kumar. "We're going to need your help, too," he told the farmer. "Your granddaughter was apparently working for the SFF. Her testimony is the key to war and peace. If we catch up to them she must be made to tell the truth."

Apu Kumar rolled a slumped shoulder. "She is an honest girl. She would not lie."

"She's also a patriot, isn't she?" Friday asked.

"Of course," Apu agreed.

"Patriotism has a way of dulling the senses," Friday told him. "That's why soldiers sometimes throw themselves on hand grenades. If your granddaughter helped the SFF frame the Pakistanis for the destruction of a Hindu temple, she has to tell that to the Indian people."

Apu seemed surprised and gravely concerned. "Do you think that is what she's done?" he asked.

"We do," Friday told him.

"Poor Nanda," Apu said.

"We're not just talking about Nanda," Captain Nazir said. "If she does not tell what she knows then millions of people may die."

Apu rose. "Nanda could not have known what she was doing. She would never have agreed to such an outcome. But I will help you," he said. "What do you want me to do?"

"For now, get some warm clothes together and wait," Friday said. "If you have extra gloves and long johns, bring them too."

Apu said he would and then hurried to the bedroom. Friday walked over to a small table and pulled the maps from his pocket.

"Captain?" he said. It was a command, not a question.

"Yes?" Nazir replied.

"We need to make plans," Friday said.

"Flight plans?" Nazir said, noticing the charts.

"Yes," Friday replied.

But that was just the start. Whatever the mission and however it turned out, Friday would be in good stead with the Black Cat Commandos and his own friends and advocates in the Indian government. He was sure Hank Lewis would allow him to remain here when this was all over. And then Ron Friday would be free to nurture his ties to the nuclear and oil industries. That was where the nation's future lay.

That was where his own future lay.

TWENTY-FOUR

Siachin Base 3, Kashmir
Thursday, 9:16 A.M.

The call from Commander San Hussain did not surprise Major Dev Puri. Ever since he was informed of the top-secret plan to use the Pakistani cell, the major had been expecting to hear from the Special Frontier Force director at about this time. However, what Commander Hussain had to say was a complete surprise. Major Puri sat in his bunker for several moments after hanging up. For weeks, he had been expecting to play an important part in this operation: the quick and quiet evacuation of the line of control.

But Puri had not anticipated playing this role. The role that was supposed to have been played by the SFF's MEAN—Mountain Elite Attack Nation. That was the name of the original resistance force that worked to overthrow British imperial rule on the subcontinent.

The most important role.

Puri reached into a tin box on the desk. He plucked out a wad of chewing tobacco and placed it beside his gum. He began to chew slowly. Puri had been expecting to hear that the Pakistani cell had been captured in their mountain headquarters. After that, Puri's units were supposed to begin preparing for retreat. The preparations were supposed to be made quietly and unhurriedly, without the use of cell phones or radios. As much as possible should be done underground in the shelters and low in the trenches. The Pakistanis would notice nothing unusual going on. Devi's four hundred soldiers were supposed to be finished by eleven A.M. but they were not to move out until they received word directly from Hussain.

Instead, Commander Hussain had called with a much different project. Major Puri was to take half the four hundred soldiers in his command and move south, into the mountains. They were to carry full survival packs and dress in thermal camouflage clothes. Hussain wanted them to proceed in a wide sweep formation toward the Siachin Glacier, closing in as the glacier narrowed and they neared the summit. "Wide sweep" meant that the militia would consist of a line of men who came no closer than eyesight. That meant the force could be stretched across approximately two miles. Since radio channels might be monitored, Hussain wanted them to communicate using field signals. Those were a standardized series of gestures developed by MEAN in the 1930s. The Indian army adopted them in 1947. The signals told them little more than to advance, retreat, wait, proceed, slow down, speed up, and attack. Directions for attacks were indicated by finger signals: the index finger was north, middle finger south, ring finger west, and pinky east. The thumb was the indication to "go." Those hand signals were usually enough. The commands were issued by noncommissioned officers stationed in the center of each platoon. They could be overruled by the company lieutenants and by Puri himself, who would be leading the operation from the center of the wide sweep. In the event of an emergency, the men had radios they could use.

Puri picked up the phone. He ordered his aide to assemble his lieutenants in the briefing room. The major said he would be there in five minutes. He wanted top-level security for the meeting: no phones or radios present, no laptop computers, no notepads.

Puri chewed his tobacco a moment more before rising. Hussain had told him that the Pakistani cell had evaded capture and was thought to be heading to Pakistan. Four other bases along the line of control were activating units in an effort to intercept the terrorists. Each of the base leaders had been given the same order: to take the cell, dead or alive.

That option did not include their lone hostage, an Indian woman from Kashmir. Commander Hussain said that the SFF did not expect the woman to survive her ordeal. He did not say that she had been mistreated. His tone said something else altogether.

He wanted her not to survive.

Major Puri turned toward the door and left the shelter. The morning light was cold and hazy. He had checked the weather report earlier. It was snowing up in the mountains. That always produced haze here in the lower elevations. Nothing was clear, not even the walls of the trench itself.

Nor his own vision.

Major Puri had not expected to play that part either. The role of assassin. As he headed for the meeting it struck him as odd that a single life should matter. What he did here would contribute to the deaths of millions of people in just a day or two. What did one more mean?

Was he upset because she was Indian? No. Indians would die in the conflagration as well. Was he upset because she was a woman? No. Women would certainly die.

He was upset because he would probably be there when she died. He might even be the one to execute the commander's order.

He would have to look into her eyes. He would be watching the woman as she realized that she was about to die.

In 1984, when India was rocked by intercaste violence, Prime Minister Indira Gandhi ordered a series of attacks on armed Sikh separatists in Amritsar. Over a thousand people were killed. Those deaths were unfortunate, the inevitable result of armed conflict. Several months later, Mrs. Gandhi was assassinated by Sikhs who were members of her own bodyguard. Her murder was a cold-blooded act and a tragedy.

It had a face.

Major Puri knew that this had to be done. But he also knew that he wished someone else would do it. Soldiering was a career he could leave behind. The job of combatant was temporary. But once he killed, even in the name of patriotism, that act would stay with him for the rest of his life.

And the next.

TWENTY-FIVE

Washington, D.C.
Wednesday, 11:45 P.M.

Paul Hood was glad when Bob Herbert came to see him.

Hood had shut his office door, opened a box of Wheat Thins, and worked on the Op-Center budget cuts for the better part of the evening. He had left word with Bugs Benet that he was not to be disturbed unless it were urgent. Hood did not feel like end-of-the-day chitchat. He did not want to have to put on a public face. He wanted to hide, to lose himself in a project—any project.

Most of all Hood did not feel like going home. Or what passed for home these days, an undistinguished fifth-floor suite at the Days Inn on Mercedes Boulevard. Hood had a feeling that it would be a long time, if ever, before he regarded anything but the Hood house in Chevy Chase, Maryland, as home. But he and his wife, Sharon, were separated and his presence at the house created strife for her. She said he was a reminder of their failed marriage, of facing a future without a companion. Their two children did not need that tension, especially Harleigh. Hood had spent time with Harleigh and her younger brother, Alexander, over the weekend. They did things that Washingtonians rarely did: they toured the monuments. Hood had also arranged for them to get a personal tour of the Pentagon. Alexander was impressed by all the saluting that went on. It made him feel important not to have to do it. He also liked the kick-ass intensity of all the guards.

Harleigh said she enjoyed the outing but that was pretty much all she said. Hood did not know whether it was post-traumatic stress, the separation, or both that were on her mind. Psychologist Liz Gordon had advised him not to talk about any of that unless Harleigh brought it up. His job was to be upbeat and supportive. That was difficult without any input from Harleigh. But he did the best he could.

For Harleigh.

What he had been neglecting in all of this were his needs. Home was the biggest and most immediate hole. The hotel room did not have the familiar creaking and pipe sounds and outside noises he had come to know. There was no oil burner clicking on and off. The hotel room smelled unfamiliar, shared, transient. The water pressure was weaker, the soap and shampoo small and impersonal. The nighttime lighting on the ceiling was different. Even the coffeemaker didn't pop and burble the same as the one at home. He missed the comfort of the familiar. He hated the changes.

Especially the biggest one. The huge hole he had dug for himself with Ann Farris, Op-Center's thirty-four-year-old press liaison. She had pursued him virtually from the day she arrived. He had found the pursuit both flattering and uncomfortable. Flattering because Paul Hood and his wife had not been connecting for years. Uncomfortable because Ann Farris was not subtle. Whatever poker face Ann put on during press briefings she did not wear around Hood. Maybe it was a question of balance, of yin and yang, of being passive in public and aggressive in private. Regardless, her open attention was a distraction for Hood and for the people closest to him, like Mike Rodgers and Bob Herbert.

So of course Hood made the desperate mistake of actually making love to Ann. That had ratcheted up the tension level by making her feel closer and him feel even guiltier. He did not want to make love to her again. At least, not until he was divorced. Ann said she understood but she still took it as a personal rejection. It had affected their working relationship. Now she was cool to him in private and hot with the press in public.

How had Paul Hood gone from someone who reached the top of several professions at a relatively young age to someone who had messed up his own life and the lives of those around him? How the hell had that happened?

Ann was really the one that Hood did not want to see tonight. But he could not tell Bugs to keep only her out. Even if she did figure out that was what Hood was doing he did not want to insult her directly.

Ironically, the work Hood was doing involved cutting Ann and her entire division.

Hood was not surprised that Herbert was working this late. The intelligence chief preferred work to socializing. It was not politically correct but it was pure Herbert: he said that it was more of a challenge trying to get inside a spy's head than into a woman's pants. The rewards were also greater, Herbert insisted. The spy ended up dead, in prison, or incapacitated. It was a lesson Hood should have learned from his friend.

Hood was glad when Herbert came to see him. He needed a crisis to deal with, one that was not of his own making. The briefing that Bob Herbert gave Hood was not the low-intensity distraction he had been hoping for. However, the prospect of nuclear war between India and Pakistan did chase all other thoughts from Hood's mind.

Herbert brought Hood up to speed on the conversations he'd had with Mike Rodgers and Ron Friday. When Herbert was finished, Hood felt energized. His own problems had not gone away. But part of him, at least, was out of hiding. The part that had a responsibility to others.

"This is a sticky one," Hood said.

"Yeah," Herbert agreed. "What's your gut say?"

"It says to take this situation to the president and drop it square in his lap," Hood replied.

Herbert regarded Hood for a moment. "There's a 'but' in your voice," Herbert said.

"Actually, there are three 'buts' in my voice," Hood told him. "First, we're only guessing about what's going on. They're educated guesses, but we still don't have proof. Second, let's assume your intel is right. That there is a plot to start a war. If we tell the president, the president will tell State. Once you tell State, the world will know about it through leaks, moles, or electronic surveillance. That could scare the perpetrators off—or it could accelerate whatever timetable they have."

"I agree," Herbert said. "The SFF and their allies would have insecurity issues instead of security issues. Typical when you're keeping information from your own countrymen."

"Exactly," Hood said.

"All right. So what's the third 'but'?" Herbert asked.

"The fact that we may prove a nuclear attack plan is in place," Hood said. "If the United States exposes it we may actually give it impetus."

"I don't understand," Herbert said.

"In terms of military support and intelligence assistance, India has always leaned toward Russia," Hood said. "An entire generation of Indians considers the United States the opposition. Suppose we expose a patriotic plan. Do you think that will cause the Indians to kill it?"

"If it involves a nuclear exchange, yes," Herbert said. "Russia would come down on our side. So would China."

"I don't know if I agree," Hood said. "Russia is facing an Islamic threat along several of its borders. Op-Center just defused a crisis where the Russians were scared about Iran's access to Caspian oil. Moscow fought the mujahedin in Afghanistan. They're afraid of aggressive fifth-column activities in their own cities, in allied republics. We can't be sure they would back a Muslim nation against their old friend India. As for China, they're looking for allies in a move against Taiwan. Suppose India provided them with that, a kind of quid pro quo."

Herbert shook his head slowly. "Paul, I've been in this game a long time. I've seen videos of Saddam using gas and gunships against his own people. I've been to a Chinese execution where five men were shot in the head because they expressed dissenting political beliefs. But I can't believe that sane individuals would make a deal about nuclear strikes that will kill millions of people."

"Why not?" Hood asked.

"Because a nuclear exchange raises the bar for all of human conflict," Herbert insisted. "It says that anything goes. No one gains by that."

"Fair enough," Hood said.

"I still believe that we may have a radical group of Indian officials who may want to nuke Pakistan," Herbert said.

"Then valid or not, all three of my concerns point to the same thing," Hood said.

"We need more intel before we go to the president," Herbert said.

"Right," Hood said. "Is there any way of getting that electronically or from sources in the government?"

"There might be, if we had the time," Herbert said. "But we've got the Pakistani cell on the run in the mountains and the dead SFF commandos behind them. The Indians are not going to wait."

"Has anything been on DD-1 yet?" Hood asked. DD-1 National was the flagship station of Doordarshan, the Indian national television network. The broadcaster was also closely affiliated with Prasar Bharati, All India Radio, which was run and maintained by the Ministry of Information and Broadcasting.

"One of Matt's people is taping the newscasts," Herbert replied. "He's going to give me an assessment of how riled up people are and at what rate the media are adding to the whipping-up process."

"Can we go in and bust up their satellite?" Hood asked.

Herbert grinned. "They use five," he said. "INSAT-2E, 2DT, 2B, PAS-4, and ThaiCom. We can scramble them all if we have to."

"Good," Hood said. He regarded Herbert. "You're pushing for Striker to go in and grab the Pakistanis, aren't you?"

"Hell," Herbert said, "I don't want to just drop Mike and his people into the Himalayas—"

"I know that," Hood assured him.

"But I don't know if we have any other options, Paul," Herbert continued. "Whatever we think of what the Pakistanis have done, they have to get out to tell what they did not do."

"What would we do if Striker weren't headed toward the region?" Hood asked.

Herbert thought for a moment then shrugged. "What we did in Korea, Russia, and Spain," Herbert said. "We'd send 'em."

Hood nodded thoughtfully. "We probably would," he agreed. "Have you run this past Mike?"

"Not in so many words," Herbert said. "But I did tell him to sleep on the flight from Alconbury to Chushul. Just in case."

"How long is that leg of the trip?" Hood asked.

Herbert looked at his watch. "They've got another six hours or so to go," he said. "Four and change with a good tailwind and if we don't keep them on the ground in Turkey for more than a few minutes."

Hood clicked on the Op-Center personnel roster. He opened the file. "Matt is still here," he said, looking at the log-in time.

"He's going over the surveillance photos with Stephen Viens," Herbert said. "He hasn't left his desk since this started."

"He should," Hood said. "We'll need him to work on any ELINT that we need in the region."

"I'll have Gloria Gold spot him for a while," Herbert said.

Gold was the nighttime director of technical affairs. She was qualified to run tech operations though she did not have the same background in analysis that Stoll had.

"We also better get Lowell and Liz Gordon in on this," Hood said. Lowell Coffey was Op-Center's international legal expert. "We need to be up on Pakistani and Indian law in case they get caught. Psych profiles of the Pakistanis would also help. Did we get a detailed jurisdictional map of the region for Striker's missile search?"

"No," Herbert said. "That was going to be pretty tightly localized in Pakistani territory."

"We'll definitely need that, then," Hood said. "We're screwed if Striker stumbles into Chinese spheres of influence and gets caught."

"If Al George doesn't have those maps in archives I'll get them from State," Herbert said. "I've got a friend there who can keep his mouth shut."

"You've got friends everywhere." Hood grinned. It felt good to be part of a team that included people like Bob Herbert. People who were professional and thorough and there to support the team and its leader. It also felt good to smile. "What about Viens? How many satellites are there in the region?"

"Three," Herbert said.

"Will he be able to hold on to them?" Hood asked.

"That shouldn't be a problem," Herbert told Hood. "No one else is asking for intel from that region right now. Viens also has his entire team on rotation, so the satellite monitoring stations will always be manned. They can run three separate recons at once."

"Good," Hood said. He continued to look at the computer screen. There were other people he could call on if needed. Right now, though, he thought it was best to keep the number of people involved to a minimum. He would call Hank Lewis at the NSA and recommend that he do the same. He hoped that the new appointee would be content to let Op-Center run this as a "silent operation"—one in which the chain of command stopped short of involving the president.

Herbert left to get his personnel set up and to obtain the map. Hood called Coffey and tore him away from *Politically Incorrect.* Since Coffey's home phone line was not secure, Hood could not tell him what the late-night meeting was about. All he said was that the title of the TV show pretty well summed it up. Coffey said he would be there as soon as possible.

Hood thanked Coffey. He fished a few more Wheat Thins from the box and sat back. There was still a lot to do before he would authorize this mission. For one thing, Stephen Viens had to find the cell. Without that information they had nothing. Then Hood and Herbert would have to decide whether to land Striker as planned and then chopper them near the cell or try to jump them in. Parachuting would be extremely dangerous in the mountains due to the cold, wind, and visibility. Perhaps they could get Ron Friday out there first to plant flares. But landing would also present a problem since Striker was expected in Srinagar for an entirely different mission. It might be difficult to break away from their hosts as quickly as Op-Center needed them to.

Besides, Hood thought, the fewer people who came into contact with Striker the better it would be for security. Lowell or Herbert could come up with a reason for them to have parachuted in. The Indian air force would have to go along with that or face the mission being scrubbed.

Hood thought about Rodgers and his team. He was proud to be working with them too. Regardless of how this unfolded it would be brutally difficult for Striker if they went forward. Thinking about it did not make Hood's own problems seem less immediate or important. Relativity never worked like that. Harleigh was traumatized by what had happened at the United Nations. Knowing that other people had lost their lives there did not make it any easier to deal with her condition.

But it did do one thing. It reminded Hood what courage was. He would not forget that in the hours and days ahead.

TWENTY-SIX

Washington, D.C.
Thursday, 1:12 A.M.

"We may have something!" Stephen Viens declared.

Gloria Gold was leaning forward in her chair. The excitement in Stephen Viens's voice came through clearly on the computer audio link. He was right. After methodically scanning the terrain for hours the cameras had detected a promising image.

"Hold on," Viens said. "Bernardo is switching us to infrared. The changeover will take about three minutes."

"I'm holding," said Gloria Gold. "Nice work," she added.

"Hold the back-patting," Viens said. "It still could be just a row of rocks or a herd of mountain goats."

"That would be a flock of mountain goats," the fifty-seven-year-old woman pointed out.

"Excuse me?" Viens said.

"Herds are domesticated animals," she said. "Flocks live in the wild."

"I see. Once a professor, always a professor," Viens teased. "But who will have the last laugh if we find out it's goats being led around by a Sherpa with a crook?"

Gloria smiled. "You will."

"Maybe we should bet on it," Viens said. "Your microcam against my lapel pin."

"No go," Gloria said.

"Why not?" Viens asked. "Mine has the range."

"And mine has the substance," she replied.

The NRO recon expert had once showed her the MIT lapel pin he had customized. It contained a dot-sized microphone made of molecules that resonated one against the other. It could broadcast sound to his computer audio recorder up to two hundred miles away. Her microcam was better than that. It broadcast million-pixel images to her computer from up to ten miles away. It was better and it was much more useful.

"Okay," Viens said. "Then let's bet dinner? The loser cooks? It's a fitting deal. Infrared image, microwave meals—"

"I'm a lousy cook," said Gloria.

"I'm not."

"Thanks, but no," said the thrice-divorced woman. For some reason Viens had always had a crush on her. She liked him too but he was young enough to be her son. "We'll make it a gentleperson's bet," she said. "If you found the Pakistanis, we both win."

Viens sighed. "A diplomat's deal. I accept, but under protest."

Tall, slender Gloria Gold smiled and leaned back in her chair. She was sitting at her glass-topped desk in Op-Center's technical sector. The lights of her office were off. The only glow came from the twenty-one-inch computer monitor. The halls were silent. She took a swig from the bottle of Evian water she kept on the floor. After knocking over a bottle and shorting her computer the night after she first came to work here, Gloria had learned not to keep anything liquid on her desk. Luckily her boss, Assistant Director Curt Hardaway— "the Night Commander," as they called him—admitted that he had once done that as well. Whether he had done that or not it was a nice thing to say.

The levity about the bet had been welcome. She had only been at this an hour but Viens had been working all day. And the elements in the image-feed from the NRO did look very promising. They were at five-meter resolution, meaning that anything down to five meters long was visible. The computer's simultaneous PAP—photographic analysis profile— had identified what it thought could be human shadows. Distorted by the terrain and angle of the sun, they were coming from under an intervening ledge. Infrared would ascertain whether the shadows were being generated by living things or rock formations. The fact that the shadows had shifted between two images did not tell them much. That could simply be an illusion of the moving sun.

The Op-Center veteran watched and waited. The quiet of night shift made the delay somehow seem longer.

The tech-sec was a row of three offices set farthest from the busy front-end of the executive level. The stations were so thoroughly linked by computer, webcam, and wireless technology that the occupants wondered why they did not just tear down the walls and shout to each other, just to make human contact now and then. But Matt Stoll had always been against that. That was probably because Matt did things in private he did not want the rest of the world to know about. But Gloria Gold knew his dark secret. She had spied on him one night using her digital microcam hidden on the door handle of his minirefrigerator.

Four or five times a day, Matt Stoll washed down a pair of Twinkies with Gatorade.

That helped to explain the boundless energy and increasing girth of Op-Center's favorite egghead. It also explained the occasional yellowish stains on his shirt. He chugged the Gatorade straight from the bottle. Even now, while Stoll was supposed to be resting on his sofa, he was probably reading the latest issue of *NuTech* or playing a hand-held video game. Unlike his former classmate Viens, Matt Stoll, with his sugar and Gatorade rush, defined the word *wired*.

Gloria's mind was back on the screen as the feed from the National Reconnaissance Office was refreshed. The mostly white image was now the color of fire. There were a series of yellow-white atmospheric distortions radiating from hot red objects along the bottom of the monitor.

"Looking good," Viens said. "Whatever is making the shadows is definitely alive."

"Definitely," Gloria said. They watched as the image refreshed again. The red spot got even hotter as it moved out from under the ledge. The bloblike shape was vaguely human.

"Shit!" Viens said. "Bernardo, go back to natural light."

"That's no mountain goat," Gloria said.

"I'm betting it isn't a Sherpa either," Viens added.

Gloria continued to watch as the satellite switched oculars. This changeover seemed to take much longer than the last.

The delay was not in the mechanical switch itself but in the optics diagnostics the satellite ran each time it changed lenses. It was important to make certain the focus and alignment were correct. Wrong data—off-center imaging, improper focus, a misplaced decimal point in resolution—was as useless as no data.

The image came on-screen in visible light. There was a field of white with the gray ledge slashing diagonally across the screen. Gloria could see a figure standing half beneath it. The figure was not a goat or a Sherpa. It was a woman. Behind her was what looked like the head of another person.

"I think we've got them!" Viens said excitedly.

"Sure looks like it," Gloria agreed as she reached for the phone. "I'll let Bob Herbert know."

Bob Herbert was there before the next image appeared.

The image that clearly showed five people making their way along the narrow ledge.

TWENTY-SEVEN

Kargil, Kashmir
Thursday, 12:01 P.M.

Ron Friday liked to be prepared.

If he were going into a building he liked to have at least two exit strategies. If he were going into a country he always had his eye on the next place he would go to out of choice or necessity. If he had a mission in mind he always checked on the availability of the equipment, clearances, and allies he might need. For him, there was no such thing as downtime.

After talking with Bob Herbert, Friday realized that it might be necessary for him and Captain Nazir to move into the mountains. He knew that the helicopter was good for travel at heights up to twelve thousand feet and temperatures down to twelve degrees Fahrenheit. They had enough fuel left for a seven-hundred-mile flight. That meant they could go into the mountains about four hundred miles and still get back. Of course, there was also the problem of having to set the chopper down at too high an altitude and having liquid-bearing components freeze. Depending on where they had to fly, it could be a long and unpleasant walk back.

Friday removed the detachable phone and kept it with him. Then he checked the gear they had onboard. There was basic climbing equipment but no cold-weather clothing. That might not be a problem, however. He had gone through Apu Kumar's things. There were some heavy coats. There were hats and gloves so those would not be a problem. His biggest concern was oxygen. If he and Captain Nazir had to do a lot of climbing at higher altitudes exhaustion would be a factor.

Perhaps Striker was bringing some of that gear with them. Friday would not know that or the location of the target area itself until he talked to Bob Herbert or Hank Lewis.

In the meantime, Friday reviewed maps with Captain Nazir to familiarize himself with the region. Apu was with them in the small kitchen area of his farmhouse, adding what first-hand knowledge he had of the region. He used to climb the foothills when he was younger.

Friday plotted a course from the Srinagar bazaar to the explosion in the mountains. He also mapped a route from the farm to the Himalayan blast site. There had been more than enough time for both the cell and the man from this farm to have reached the mountain site before the detonation. The question was where they would move from there. The cell only had to cover roughly twenty miles to go from the mountains to the Pakistani border. But they were a mountainous twenty miles that included both the line of control and the brutal Siachin Glacier. Reaching up to some eighteen thousand feet, the glacier would be difficult to climb under the best of circumstances. Tired and presumably pursued from the ground and possibly the air, the Pakistanis would need a miracle to get across.

The helicopter phone beeped while Friday was looking at topographic charts of the region. Nazir answered. It was Bob Herbert and Hank Lewis. He passed the phone to Friday.

"We've found the cell," Herbert said.

"Where are they?" Friday asked eagerly. He bent over the charts that were spread on the table. "I have seven to ten tactical pilotage charts each of the Muzaffarabad border region, the Srinagar border region, and the area from Srinagar to Kargil."

"They're in the Srinagar border region," Herbert said. "Just outside of Jaudar."

"What are the coordinates?" Friday asked as he went to that set and began flipping through the charts, looking for the village.

"Ron, we want you to go at once to thirty-four degrees, thirty minutes north, seventy-five degrees east," Lewis said.

"That's Jaudar," Friday said, looking at the map. "Is that where the cell is? In the village?"

"No," Lewis said. "That's where you'll rendezvous with Striker."

Friday stood up. "Gentlemen, I have a chopper here. I can be there in under an hour. Striker won't be landing for at least four hours. I might be able to get to the cell by then."

"So would your partner," Lewis reminded him.

"And?" Friday pressed.

"We haven't finished our security check on the Black Cat," Lewis said. "We can't take the risk that he'll turn the Pakistanis over to his people."

"That won't happen," Friday assured the new NSA chief. "I'll make sure of it."

"You can't guarantee that," Lewis said. "We also agree that Mr. Kumar should go with you and we can't be certain of his actions either. Mr. Herbert and I have discussed this and we're in agreement. You will meet Striker in Jaudar. They will have up-to-the-minute coordinates of the cell and the resources to get you and your companions into the mountains. If anything changes, we'll let you know."

"We're wasting time," Friday protested. "I could probably be in and out by the time Striker arrives."

"I admire your enthusiasm," Herbert said. "But the leader of the cell is cagey. They've been moving in shadows and beneath overhangs wherever possible. We don't know for certain what weapons they're carrying. They may have a rocket launcher. If you come after them in an Indian chopper they will probably shoot you down."

"If you tell us where they are we can circle wide and intercept them," Friday pointed out.

"There's also a chance that a Pakistani aircraft might try to slip in and rescue the cell," Herbert said. "We don't want to precipitate a firefight with an Indian aircraft. That could give the Indians even more ammunition to launch a major offensive."

Friday squeezed the phone. He wished he could strangle the deskbound bureaucrat. He did not understand field personnel. None of them did. The best field ops did not like sitting still. And the best of the best were able to improvise their way in and out of most things. Friday could do this. More than that, he wanted it. If he could grab the cell and bring them home he would have a chance to get in with their

Pakistani controllers. Having strong ties to New Delhi, Islamabad, and Washington would be invaluable to an operative in this region.

"Are we on the same page?" Herbert asked.

Friday looked down at the map. "Yes," he said. And as he looked he remembered something that Herbert had told him about the explosion. It had occurred at approximately eight thousand feet. That would put the cell on the southwest side of the range. Everything north of that, up through the glacier and the line of control, was at a higher elevation. Friday's grip relaxed. To hell with desk jockeys in general and Bob Herbert in particular.

"We'll brief you again when we have Striker's precise ETA and location," Herbert said. "Do you have any questions?"

"No," Friday replied calmly.

"Is there anything you wanted to add, Hank?" Herbert asked.

Lewis said there was nothing else. The NSA head thanked Friday and the men hung up. Friday returned the phone to its cradle.

"What is it?" Captain Nazir asked.

"What we've been waiting for," Friday said.

"They found the cell?" Nazir asked.

Friday nodded.

"And my granddaughter?" Apu asked.

"She's with them," Friday said. He did not know if she was or not, of course. But he wanted Apu with them. The farmer had harbored the enemy cell. If they needed to forestall any action by India, Apu's confession would play very well on Pakistani TV.

Friday looked at the map. Herbert had told him that the cell was sticking to the mountain ledges. That meant that if the chopper started following the line of the range at eight thousand feet and flew up one side and then down the other they were sure to encounter the cell. Friday glanced down at the inset conic projection and smiled. The round-trip was less than two hundred miles.

He would have them. And he would have that do-nothing Herbert.

"Come on," Friday said to Nazir.

"Where are we going?" the officer asked.

"To catch a terrorist cell," Friday replied.

TWENTY-EIGHT

Washington, D.C.
Thursday, 4:02 A.M.

Paul Hood's office was just a few steps away from Op-Center's high-security conference room. Known as the Tank, the conference room was surrounded by walls of electronic waves that generated static for anyone trying to listen in with bugs or external dishes.

Hood entered after everyone was already there. The heavy door was operated by a button at the side of the large oval conference table. Hood pushed it when he sat down at the head of the table.

The small room was lit by fluorescent lights hung in banks over the conference table. On the wall across from Hood's chair the countdown clock was dark. When they had a crisis and a deadline, the clock flashed its ever-changing array of digital numbers.

The walls, floor, door, and ceiling of the Tank were all covered with sound-absorbing Acoustix. The mottled gray-and-black strips were each three inches wide and overlapped one another to make sure there were no gaps. Beneath them were two layers of cork, a foot of concrete, and then another layer of Acoustix. In the midst of the concrete, on all six sides of the room, was a pair of wire grids that generated vacillating audio waves. Electronically, nothing left the room without being utterly distorted. If any listening device did somehow manage to pick up a conversation from inside, the randomness of the changing modulation made reassembling the conversations impossible.

"Thank you all for coming," Hood said. He turned down the brightness on the computer monitor that was set in the table and began bringing up the files from his office. At the same time, Bugs Benet was busy raising Colonel August on the TAC-SAT. In order to make sure Striker stayed in the loop, August and Rodgers were taking turns sleeping en route to Turkey.

"No problem," Lowell Coffey said. He had been pouring water from a pitcher into a coffee machine on a table in the far corner. The percolator began to bubble and pop. "The roads were empty. I managed to sleep on the way. Anybody think to get doughnuts?"

"That was your job," Herbert pointed out. "You were the only one who wasn't here." He maneuvered his wheelchair into his place at Hood's right.

"I've got mid rats in my office if you're hungry," said Liz Gordon as she settled in to Hood's left.

"No, thanks." Coffey shuddered as he sat across from Hood. "I'll stick to the coffee."

"You've got official military midnight rations?" Herbert asked.

"A three-course packet," Liz said. "Dried apricots and pineapple, jerky, and cookies. A friend of mine at Langley gave them to me. I think you've worked with her. Captain McIver?"

"We worked on some black ops stuff together," Herbert said. He smiled. "Man, mid rats. I haven't had them in years. They always hit the spot in the wee small hours."

"That's because you were tired and not selective," said the admittedly dilettantish Coffey.

Hood's data finished loading a moment before Bugs Benet called. Hood sent the files to the other computer stations around the table. Liz and Coffey scanned the files as Hood's assistant informed him that he had Colonel Brett August ready to be patched through from the C-130 Hercules. Hood put the telephone on speaker and looked across the table.

"We're ready to go," Hood said to the others.

Everyone came to attention quickly.

"Colonel August, can you hear me?" Hood asked.

"As clear as if you were in the cabin with us, sir," the Striker commander replied.

"Good," Hood replied. "Bob, you've been talking to New Delhi. Would you please bring everyone up to speed?"

Herbert looked at his wheelchair computer monitor. "Twenty-one hours ago there was an attack on a market in Srinagar, Kashmir," Herbert said. He spoke loud enough for the speakerphone to pick up his voice. "A police station, a Hindu temple, and a busload of Hindu pilgrims were destroyed. With intel from the NRO and from your NSA contact who happened to be on-site, we have reason to believe that the attack on the station was the work of the Free Kashmir Militia, a militant organization based in Pakistan. However, we suspect that the attacks against the Hindu sites may have been organized by India itself. We believe that elements in the Special Frontier Force, the cabinet, and the military may be trying to win public support for a quick, decisive nuclear strike against Pakistan."

No one moved. The only sounds were the hum of the forced air coming through the overhead vents and the crackling of the coffee machine as it finished brewing.

"What about the Pakistani terrorists?" Coffey asked.

"At this moment the cell is desperately trying to cross the Himalayan foothills—we believe to Pakistan," Herbert replied. "They have a prisoner. She's an Indian woman who apparently coordinated SFF actions to make the attack on the Hindu sites look like the work of the Pakistani Muslims. It is imperative that they reach Pakistan and that their hostage be made to tell what she knows."

"To defuse the outraged Indian populace that will otherwise be screaming for Pakistani blood," Liz said.

"Correct," Herbert said. "So far, the first attempt to capture the Pakistanis failed. SFF commandos were sent into the mountains. They were all killed. We do not know what other pursuit options are being considered or whether the cell has contacted Pakistan. We don't know what rescue efforts Islamabad may be attempting to mount."

"They'd probably be chopper HAP searches," August said.

"Explain," Hood said.

"Hunt and peck," August told him. "The cell would not risk sending a radio beacon to Pakistan or suggesting a rendezvous point. That would be too easy for an Indian listening post at the line of control to pick off. Pakistan doesn't have the satellite resources to spot the cell so they would have to fly in and crisscross suspected routes of egress. And they'd use helicopters instead of jets, to stay below Indian radar."

"Good 'gets,' " Herbert said.

"Paul, there's something that's bothering me," Coffey said. "Do we know for certain that the NSA operative was an observer and not a participant? This action may have been planned a couple of weeks ago, timed to draw attention from their attempted coup in Washington."

Coffey had a point. The former head of the NSA, Jack Fenwick, had been working to replace President of the United States Michael Lawrence with the more militant Vice President Cotten. It was conceivable that Fenwick may have helped to orchestrate this crisis as a distraction from the anticipated resignation of President Lawrence.

"We believe that Friday is clean, though right now we have him quarantined with an Indian officer," Hood replied. "I suspect that if Friday were involved with this he would be trying to get out of the region and keep us out as well."

"Which could also mean he is involved," Liz pointed out.

"In what way?" Hood asked.

"If you're suggesting, as I think you are, that Striker try to help the cell get home, it would be in Mr. Friday's interest to stay close to them and make sure they do not succeed."

"That could work both ways," Herbert said. "If Striker goes in after the cell we can also keep an eye on Friday."

"I want to emphasize here that we have not yet made a final determination on the mission, Colonel," Hood said. "But if we do try to help the Pakistanis the key to success is a timely intervention. Bob, you've been in contact with HQ Central Air Command."

"Yes," Herbert said. "We're dealing directly with Air Chief Marshal Chowdhury and his senior aide. I told the ACM that we may want to change the way we insert Striker."

"You're thinking about an airdrop," August said.

"Correct," replied Herbert. "I asked the ACM for jump gear. He said it will definitely be on the Himalayan Eagles squadron AN-12. But I did not tell him what we may be asking you to do in the region. The good news is, whatever you do will be well shielded. The Indian military continues to be ultrasecretive about your involvement. The SFF and the other people behind the Srinagar attacks do not even know that Striker is en route to the region."

"What about the Indian officer who is with Mr. Friday?" Colonel August asked. "Are we sure we can trust him?"

"Well, nothing is guaranteed," Herbert said. "But according to Friday, Captain Nazir is not looking forward to the prospect of a nuclear attack. Especially when he and Friday are headed toward Pakistan."

"I was just thinking about that," August said. "Do you think you can include lead-lined long johns in the Indian requisition form?"

"Just get behind Mike," Herbert said. "Nothing gets past that sumbitch. Not even high-intensity rads."

There was anxious chuckling about that. The laughter was a good tension breaker.

"We've got Friday and Nazir en route by chopper to a town called Jaudar," Herbert said.

"I know where that is," Colonel August said. "It's southeast of the region we were supposed to be investigating."

"If we decide to move forward with a search and rescue, you'll be hooking up in the mountains north of there," Herbert said. "That's where we've pinpointed the cell."

"Colonel August, if we decide to go ahead with this mission you'll have to jump your people into the Himalayas near the Siachin Glacier, link up with the cell, and get them through the line of control," Hood said. "This is an extremely high-risk operation. I need an honest answer. Is Striker up for it?"

"The stakes are also high," August said. "We have to be up for it."

"Good man," Herbert muttered. "Damn good man."

"People, one thing I have to point out is that the Indians are not going to be your only potential enemies," Liz said. "You also have to worry about the psychological state of the Pakistani cell. They're under extreme physical and psychological duress. They may not believe that you're allies. The nature of people in this situation is to trust no one outside the group."

"Those are very good points and we'll have to talk about them," Hood told her.

"There's something else we'll have to talk about, Paul," Coffey said. "According to your file, the Free Kashmir Militia has acknowledged its involvement with at least part of this attack and with all of the previous attacks in Kashmir. Striker will be helping self-professed terrorists. To say that leaves us vulnerable legally is an understatement."

"That's absolute horseshit," Herbert said. "The guys who blew my wife up are still hanging out in a rat hole in Syria somewhere. Terrorists of warring nations don't get extradited. And the guys who help terrorists don't even get their names in the papers."

"That only happens to guerrillas who are sponsored by terrorist nations," Coffey replied. "The United States has a different form and level of accountability. Even if Striker succeeds in getting the cell to Pakistan, India will be within its rights to demand the extradition of everyone who had a hand in the attack on the bazaar, on the SFF commandos, and in the escape. If New Delhi can't get the FKM they will go after Striker."

"Lowell, India doesn't have any kind of moral high ground here," Herbert said. "They're planning a goddamn nuclear strike!"

"No, a rogue element in the government is apparently planning that," Coffey said. "The lawful Indian government will have to disown them and prosecute them as well."

The attorney rose angrily and got himself a cup of coffee. He was a little calmer as he sat back down and took a sip. Hood was silent. He looked at Herbert. The intelligence chief did not like Lowell Coffey and his disgust with legal technicalities was well known. Unfortunately, Hood could not afford to ignore what the attorney had just said.

"Gentlemen?" August said.

"Go ahead, Colonel," Hood said.

"We are talking about a possible nuclear conflagration here," August said. "The normal rules do not seem to apply. I'll poll the team if you'd like, but I'm willing to bet they say the same thing I'm about to. Given the stakes, the downside is worth risking."

Hood was about to thank him but the words snagged in his throat. Bob Herbert did not have that problem.

"God bless you, Colonel August," Herbert said loudly as he glared across the table at Coffey.

"Thank you, Bob," August said. "Mr. Coffey? If it's any help, Striker can always pull a Lone Ranger on the Pakistanis."

"Meaning what, Colonel?" Coffey asked.

"We can drop them off then ride into the sunset before they can even thank or ID us," August said.

Herbert smiled. Hood did, too, but inside. His face was frozen by the weight of the decision he would have to make.

"We'll get back to you later on all of this," Hood said. "Colonel, I want to thank you."

"For what? Doing my job?"

"For your enthusiasm and courage," Hood said. "They raise the bar for all of us."

"Thank you, sir," August said.

"Get some rest," Hood said. He clicked off the phone and looked across the table. "Bob, I want you to make sure we've got someone at the NRO watching the Pakistani border. If a chopper does come looking for the cell we have to be able to give Striker advance warning. I don't want them to be mistaken for a hostile force and cut down."

Herbert nodded.

"Lowell, find me some legal grounds for doing this," Hood went on.

The attorney shook his head. "There isn't anything," Coffey said. "At least, nothing that will hold up in an international court."

"I don't need anything that will work in court," Hood said. "I need a reason to keep Striker from being extradited if it comes to that."

"Like claiming they were on a mission of mercy," Coffey said.

"Yeah," Herbert interjected. "I'll bet we can find some UN peacekeeping status bullshit that would qualify."

"Without informing the United Nations?" Coffey said.

"You know, Lowell, Bob may have something," Hood said. "The secretary-general has emergency trusteeship powers that allow her to declare a region 'at risk' in the event of an apparent and overwhelming military threat. That gives her the right to send a Security Council team to the region to investigate."

"I'm missing how that helps us," Coffey said.

"The team does not have to consist of sitting Security Council personnel," Hood said. "Just agents of Security Council nations."

"Maybe," Coffey said. "But no one will accept the presence of a team consisting solely of Americans."

"It won't," Hood said. "India's a member of the Security Council. And there are Indians out there."

"Captain Nazir and Nanda Kumar," Herbert said. "Her own countrymen."

"Exactly," Hood replied. "Even if she's a hostile observer, at least she's present."

"Yeah. Since when does the Security Council agree on anything?" Liz pointed out.

"We may have to bring Secretary-General Chatterjee in on this once Striker is on the ground," Hood said. "Then we'll tell her what we know."

"And what if she refuses to invoke her trusteeship powers?" Coffey asked.

"She won't," Hood said.

"How can you be sure?" Coffey asked.

"Because we still have a press department," Hood said. "And while we do, I'll make sure that every paper on earth knows that Secretary-General Chatterjee did nothing while India prepared to launch nuclear missiles at Pakistan. We'll see whose blood the world wants then. Hers or Striker's."

I wouldn't bet the farm on that plan," Coffey warned.

Give me an option," Hood countered.

Coffey and Herbert agreed to have a look at the United Nations charter and brief Hood. Hood agreed to hold off contacting Chatterjee. Herbert left to follow up on the intel reports. Only Liz stayed behind with Hood. Her hands were folded on the table and she was staring hard at them.

"Problem, Liz?" Hood asked.

She looked at him. "You've had some run-ins with Mala Chatterjee."

"True," Hood said. "But forcing her hand or embarrassing her is not on the agenda. I'm only interested in protecting Striker."

"That isn't where I was going with this," she said. "You fought with Chatterjee, you fought with Sharon, and you've shut Ann Farris out." Her expression softened. "She told me about what happened between you."

"Okay," Hood said with a trace of annoyance. "What's your point?"

"I know what you think about psychobabble, Paul, but I want you to make sure you keep all of this on an issues level," Liz said. "You're under a lot of pressure from women. Don't let that frustration get transferred from one woman to another to another."

Hood rose. "I won't. I promise."

"I want to believe that," Liz said. She smiled. "But right now you're pissed at me, too."

Hood stood there. Liz was right. His back was ramrod straight, his mouth was a tight line, and his fingers were curled into fists. He let his shoulders relax. He opened his hands. He looked down.

"Paul, it's my job to watch the people here and point out possible problem spots," Liz said. "That's all I'm doing. I'm not judging you. But you have been under a lot of pressure since the UN situation. You're also tired. All I'm trying to do is keep you the fair, even-handed guy I just saw working things out between Bob Herbert and Lowell Coffey."

Hood smiled slightly. "Thanks, Liz. I don't believe the secretary-general was in danger, but I appreciate the heads-up."

Liz gave him a reassuring pat on the arm and left the room. Hood looked across the room at the crisis clock.

It was still blank. But inside, his own clock was ticking. And the mainspring was wound every bit as tight as Liz had said.

Even so, he reminded himself that he was safe in Washington while Mike Rodgers and Striker were heading into a region where their actions could save or doom millions of lives—including their own.

Next to that, whatever pressure he was feeling was nothing.

Nothing at all.

TWENTY-NINE

New Delhi, India
Thursday, 2:06 P.M.

Sixty-nine-year-old Minister of Defense John Kabir sat in his white-walled office. The two corridors of the Ministry of Defence offices were part of the cabinet complex housed in the eighty-year-old Parliament House Estate at 36 Gurdwara Rakabganj Road in New Delhi. Outside a wall-length bank of open windows the bright afternoon sun shone down on the extensive lawns, small artificial ponds, and decorative stone fountains. The sounds of traffic were barely audible beyond the high, ornamental red sandstone wall that enclosed the sprawling complex. On the right side of the grounds Kabir could just see the edge of one of the two houses of Parliament, the Lok Sabha, the House of the People. On the other side of this ministry annex was the Rajya Sabha, the Council of States. Unlike the representatives in the Lok Sabha, which were elected by the people, the members of the Rajya Sabha were either chosen by the president or selected by the legislative assemblies of the nation's states.

Minister Kabir loved his nation and its government. But he no longer had patience for it. The system had lost its way.

The white-haired official had just finished reading a secure e-mail dispatch from Major Dev Puri on his army's movements into the mountains. Puri and his people were frontline veterans. They would succeed where the SFF commandos had failed.

Kabir deleted the computer file then sat there reflecting on the crossroads to which he had brought his nation. It would be either the triumph or the downfall of his long career. It was a career that began with his rise through the military to captain by the age of thirty-seven. However, Kabir was frus-

trated by the weak social and military programs of Prime
Minister Indira Gandhi. He was particularly upset when India
defeated Pakistan in the 1971 war and failed to absolutely
solidify their hold on Kashmir by creating a demilitarized
zone beyond the line of control. He drew up a plan calling
for a "zone of security." He wanted to use the villages on
the Pakistani side for routine artillery, gunship, and bombing
practice. He wanted to keep them unoccupied. What was the
purpose of winning a war if the victor could not maintain
security along its borders?

Not only was his plan rejected, but Captain Kabir was
reprimanded by the minister of defence. Kabir resigned and
wrote a book, *What Ails the Irresolute Nation,* which became
a controversial best-seller. It was followed by *A Plan for Our
Secure Future.* Within three months of the publication of the
second book he was asked to become general secretary of
the Samyukta Socialist Party. Within three years he was
chairman of the national Socialist Party. At the same time
he was appointed president of the All India Truckers' Fed-
eration. He led a strike in 1974 that crippled the highways
and even railroad crossings, where trucks "broke down."
That helped to trigger the establishment of Prime Minister
Gandhi's "Emergency" in June 1975. That declaration enabled her to suspend civil liberties and incarcerate her foes.
Kabir was arrested and held in prison for over a year. That
did not stop him from campaigning for reform from his jail
cell. Supported by union members and by Russian-backed
socialist groups, Kabir was pardoned. The Russians in particularly liked Kabir's advocacy of a stronger border presence
against China. Kabir drew on his widespread grassroots support to have himself named deputy minister of industry. He
used that post to strengthen his support among the working
castes while restoring his ties to the military. That led to his
appointment as minister of Kashmir affairs and his member-
ship on the Committee on External Affairs. That was where
he became good friends with Dilip Sahani. Sahani was the
officer in charge of the Special Frontier Force in Kashmir.
The men discovered they had the same concerns regarding

the threat posed by both Islamic Fundamentalists and the nuclear research being conducted by Pakistan.

Two years ago, high-ranking officers and government officials who respected Kabir's Zone of Security plan got together and pressed the prime minister to name him minister of defence. Kabir asked the national commander of the SFF to come and work for him and then arranged for Dilip Sahani to take over that post. Together, the men plotted in secret. New Delhi was content to build its own nuclear arsenal as a deterrent and collect intelligence to assess the across-the-border threat. Kabir and Sahani were not. They wanted to make certain that Islamabad never had the opportunity to mount the very real threat of a jihad of mass destruction. With the unwitting help of the FKM cell and a young member of the SFF's Civilian Network Operatives, they were on the verge of realizing their dream. If the field commandos had succeeded in their efforts to capture and destroy the FKM, the goal would be just days if not hours away. Now they had to wait.

Major Puri would not fail them. He would close in on the terrorist cell and then kill them in a firefight. The CNO operative who was with them would tell the story as she saw it from the inside. Even if she died in the fight, she would reveal to Major Puri with her dying breath how the FKM attacked the temple and the bus. How the lives of those Hindus were the first sacrifices of the new jihad. The people of India would believe her because in their hearts they knew she was telling the truth. Her grieving grandfather would back up everything that she said. And then the Indian government would respond.

Of course, the president and prime minister would attack Pakistan as they usually did. With words. That was how nuclear powers were supposed to act. If they replied with weapons the results would be unthinkable. Or so the common wisdom went.

What the rest of the world did not realize was that Pakistan's leaders were willing to endure annihilation. They would sacrifice their nation if it meant the utter destruction of India and the Hindu people. Islam would still have tens of millions of adherents. Their faith would survive. And the dead of Pakistan would live on in Paradise.

Kabir was not going to give Pakistan the chance to attack India. He was, however, perfectly willing to send them to Paradise. He intended to do that with a preemptive strike.

The team that was in charge of the Underground Nuclear Command Center was loyal to Minister Kabir. The key personnel had been carefully selected from among the military and SFF ranks. They would respond to dual commands issued by Minister Kabir and Commander Sahani. When those orders came, nothing on earth could turn them back.

Kabir's plan was to hit Pakistan before they had fully deployed their nuclear arsenal. He would use a total of seventy-nine Indian SRBMs. The short-range ballistic missiles each had a range of eight hundred kilometers. They constituted one-half of India's nuclear arsenal and were housed in silos located just behind the line of control. Eleven of those would hit Islamabad alone, removing it from the map and killing nearly 20 percent of the nation's 130 million people. In the days and weeks to come, radiation from the explosions would kill another 40 million Pakistanis. The rest of the SRBMs would strike at Pakistani military facilities. That included seven suspected silo locations in the Himalayas. Maybe the American team coming into the country would have found them. Maybe they would not. Regardless, their presence would be a powerful public relations tool for Kabir. It would show the world that India had reason to fear Pakistan's nuclear proliferation. The deaths of the Americans would be unfortunate but unavoidable.

Minister Kabir brought the remaining targets up on his computer. In addition to the mountains, SRBMs would be launched at each of Pakistan's air bases. Ten Pakistan Air Force bases were operational full-time. These were the "major operational bases" PAF Sargodha, PAF Mianwali, PAF Kamra, PAF Rafiqui, PAF Masroor, PAF Faisal, PAF Chaklala, PAF Risalpur, PAF Peshawar, and PAF Samungli. They would all be hit with two missiles each. Then there were eleven "forward operational bases" that became fully operational only during wartime. All of these would be struck as well. They were PAF Sukkur, PAF Shahbaz, PAF Multan, PAF Vihari, PAF Risalewala, PAF Lahore, PAF Nawabshah, PAF Mirpur Khas, PAF Murid, PAF Pasni, and PAF Talhar. Finally, there were the nine satellite bases used for emergency landings: PAF Rahim Yar Khan, PAF Chander, PAF Bhagtanwala, PAF Chuk Jhumra, PAF Ormara, PAF Rajanpur, PAF Sindhri, PAF Gwadar, and PAF Kohat. These were little more than landing strips without personnel to man them. Still, they would all be razed. With luck, the PAF would not be able to launch a single missile or bomber. Even if Pakistan did manage to land a few nuclear blows, India could absorb the loss. The leaders would have been moved to the underground bunkers. They would manage the brief conflagration and recovery from the UNCC.

When it was all over, Kabir would take the blame or praise for what happened. But however the world responded, Kabir was certain of one thing.

He will have done the right thing.

THIRTY

Ankara, Turkey
Thursday, 11:47 A.M.

The Indian air force AN-12 transport is a cousin of the world's largest aircraft, the Russian Antonov AN-225 Mriya. The AN-12 is half the size of that six-engine brute. A long-range transport, it is also one-third smaller than the C-130 that had brought Striker as far as Ankara. With the cargo section in the rear and an enclosed, insulated passenger cabin toward the front, the IAF aircraft is also much quieter. For that Mike Rodgers was grateful.

Rodgers had caught five solid hours of sleep on the final leg of the C-130 flight. He did that with the help of wax earplugs he carried expressly for that purpose. Still, the small downclick in sound and vibration was welcome. Especially when Corporal Ishi Honda left his seat in the rear of the small, cramped crew compartment. He ducked as he made his way through the single narrow aisle that ran through the center of the cabin. The team's grips, cold-weather gear, and parachutes were strapped in bulging mesh nets on the ceiling over the aisle.

The communications expert handed the TAC-SAT to General Rodgers. "It's Mr. Herbert," Honda said.

Colonel August was sitting beside Rodgers in the forward-facing seats. The men exchanged glances.

"Thank you," Rodgers said to Honda.

The corporal returned to his seat. Rodgers picked up the receiver.

"There are parachutes onboard, Bob," Rodgers said. "For us?"

"Paul's given the go-ahead for an expedited search-and-recover of the cell," Herbert said.

"Expedited" was spy-speak for "illegal." It meant that an operation was being rushed before anyone could learn about it and block it. It also meant something else. They were probably going to be jumping into the Himalayas. Rodgers knew what that meant.

"We have the target spotted," Herbert went on. "Viens is following them through the mountains. They're at approximately nine thousand feet and heading northwest toward the line of control. They're currently located thirty-two miles due north of the village of Jaudar."

Rodgers removed one of the three "playbooks" from under the seat. It was a fat black spiral-bound notebook containing all the maps of the regions. He found the town and moved his finger up. He turned to the previous page where the map was continued. Instead of just brown mountains there was a big dagger-shaped slash of white pointing to the lower left.

"That puts them on direct course for the Siachin Glacier," Rodgers said.

"That's how our people read it," Herbert said. "They can't be carrying a lot of artillery. It would make sense for them to head somewhere the elements might help them. Cold, blizzards, avalanches, crevasses—it's a fortress or stealth environment if they need it."

"Assuming it doesn't kill them," Rodgers pointed out.

"Trying to go through any lower would definitely kill them," Herbert replied. "The NSA intercepted a SIG-INT report from a Russian satellite listening in on the line of control. Several divisions have apparently moved out and are headed toward the glacier."

"Estimated time of encounter?" Rodgers asked.

"We don't have one," Herbert said. "We don't know if the divisions are airborne, motorized, or on foot. We'll see what else comes through the Russian satellite."

"Can General Orlov help us with this?" Rodgers asked.

Sergei Orlov was head of the Russian Op-Center based in St. Petersburg. General Orlov and Hood had a close personal and professional relationship. Striker leader Lt. Colonel Charles Squires died during a previous joint undertaking, helping to prevent a coup in Russia.

"I asked Paul about that," Herbert said. "He doesn't want to involve them. Russian technology helps drive the Indian war machine. Indian payoffs drive Russian generals. Orlov won't be able to guarantee that anyone he contacts will maintain the highest-level security status."

"I'm not convinced we can guarantee HLS status from the NSA," Rodgers replied.

"I'm with you on that," Herbert said. "I'm not sure Hank Lewis patched up all the holes Jack Fenwick drilled over there. That's why I'm giving information to Ron Friday on a need-to-know basis. He's moving up to Jaudar with a Black Cat officer and the grandfather of the CNO informant who's traveling with the cell."

"Good move," Rodgers said.

"We're also trying to get regular weather updates from the Himalayan Eagles," Herbert said. "But that could all change before you arrive. By the way, how are your new hosts treating you?"

"Fine," Rodgers said. "They gave us rations, the gear is all here, and we're on schedule."

"All right," Herbert said. "I'll give you the drop coordinates at H-hour minus fifteen."

"Confirmed," Rodgers said.

The general looked at his watch. They had three hours to go. That left them just enough time to pass out the gear, check it out, suit up, and review the maps with the team.

"I'll check back in when I have more intel for you," Herbert said. "Is there anything else you need?"

"I can't think of anything, Bob," Rodgers said.

There was a short silence. Mike Rodgers knew what was coming. He had heard the change in Herbert's voice during that last question. It had gone from determined to wistfulness.

"Mike, I know I don't have to tell you that this is a shitty assignment," Herbert said.

"No, you don't," Rodgers agreed. He was flipping through the magnified views of the region of the drop. Never mind the terrain itself. The wind-flow charts were savage. The currents tore through the mountains at fifty to sixty-one miles an hour. Those were gale-force winds.

"But I do have to point out that you aren't a part of Striker," Herbert went on. "You're a senior officer of the NCMC."

"Cut to the chase," Rodgers told him. "Is Paul going to order me to stay behind?"

"I haven't discussed this with him," Herbert said. "What's the point? You've disobeyed his orders before."

"I have," Rodgers said. "Kept Tokyo from getting nuked, if I remember correctly at my advanced age."

"You did do that," Herbert said. "But I was thinking that it might help if we had someone on-site to liaise with the Indian government."

"Send one of the guys the FBI tucked into the embassy," Rodgers said. "I know they're there and so do the Indians."

"I don't think so," Herbert replied.

"Look, I'll be happy to talk to whatever officials I have to from the field," Rodgers said. The general leaned forward. He huddled low over the microphone. "Bob, you know damn well what we're facing here. I've been looking at the charts. When we drop into the mountains the wind alone is going to hammer us. We stand a good chance of losing people just getting onto the ground."

"I know," Herbert said.

"Hell, if they didn't need to fly the plane I'd bring the Indian crew down with me. Let them help save their own country," Rodgers continued. "So don't even try to tell me that I shouldn't do what we're asking Striker to do. Especially not with what's at stake."

"Mike, I wasn't thinking about Striker or the rest of the world," Herbert replied. "I was thinking about an old friend with football-damaged, forty-seven-year-old knees. A friend who could hurt Striker more than help them if he got injured on an ice-landing."

"If that happens I'll order them to leave me where I land," Rodgers assured him.

"They won't."

"They will," Rodgers said. "We'll have to do that with anyone who's hurt." He hung up the receiver and motioned for Corporal Honda to come back and reclaim the TAC-SAT. Then he rose.

"I'll be right back," Rodgers said to August.

"Is there anything we need to do?" August asked.

Rodgers looked down at him. August was in an uncomfortable spot. Rodgers was one of the colonel's oldest and closest friends. He was also a superior officer. That was one of the reasons August had turned down this job when it was first offered to him. It was often difficult for the colonel to find a proper balance between those two relationships. This was one of those times. August also knew what was at risk for his friend and the team.

"I'll let you know in a few minutes," Rodgers said as he walked toward the cockpit.

Walked on rickety knees that were ready to kick some ass.

THIRTY-ONE

Jaudar, Kashmir
Thursday, 3:33 P.M.

The problem with flying an LAHR—low-altitude helicopter reconnaissance—in a region like the Himalayas is that there is no room for error.

From the pilot's perspective, keeping the aircraft steady is practically impossible. The aircraft shakes along the x- and y-axes, the horizontal and vertical, with occasional bumps in the diagonal. Keeping the chopper within visual range of the target area is also problematic. It's often necessary for the pilot to move suddenly and over considerable distances to get around violent air pockets, clouds that blow in and impede the view, or snow and ice squalls. Just keeping the bird aloft is the best that can be hoped for. Whatever intel the observer can grab is considered a gift, not a guarantee.

Wearing sunglasses to cut down on the glare, and a helmet headset to communicate with Captain Nazir in the noisy cabin, Ron Friday alternately peered through the front and side windows of the cockpit. The American operative cradled an MP5K in his lap. If they spotted the terrorists there might be a gunfight. Hopefully, a few bursts in the air from the submachine gun would get them to stop shooting and listen. If not, he was prepared to back off and snipe one or two of them with the 1ASL in the gun rack behind him. If Captain Nazir could keep the chopper steady, the large sharpshooter rifle had greater range than the small arms the terrorists were probably carrying. With a few of them wounded, the others might be more inclined to let Friday land and approach them. Especially if he promised to airlift them to medical assistance in Pakistan.

Apu was seated on a fold-down chair in the spacious cargo area. It wasn't so much a chair as a hinged plastic square with a down cushion on top. The farmer was leaning forward, peering through a hatchway that separated the cargo section from the cockpit. Apu wore an anxious look as he gazed out through the window. Friday was good at reading people's expressions. He was not just concerned about finding his granddaughter. There was a sense of despair in his eyes, in the sad downturn of his mouth. Perhaps Apu had been in the mountains as a young man. He had had some idea what was beyond the foothills. But Apu had certainly never gone this far, never this high. He had never gazed down at the barren peaks. He had never heard the constant roar of the wind over powerful 671 kW rotors, or felt that wind batter an aircraft, or experienced the cold that blasted through the canvas-lined metal walls. The farmer knew that unless they found Nanda the chances were not good that she would survive.

The chopper continued toward the line of control without any of the occupants spotting the terrorists. Friday was not overly concerned. They still had the southward trip along the other side of the range to go.

Suddenly, something happened that Friday was not expecting. He heard a voice in his helmet. A voice that did not belong to Captain Nazir.

"Negative zone three," said the very faint, crackling voice. "Repeat: negative zone three." A moment later the voice was gone.

Friday made sure the headset switch on the communications panel was set on "internal" rather than "external." That meant they were communicating only with the cockpit instead of an outside receiver.

"Who is that?" Friday asked.

Nazir shook his head slowly. "It's not control tower communication." The wheel was shaking violently. He did not want to release his two-handed grip. "Do you see that yellow button below the com-panel?" he asked.

"Yes," Friday said.

"That's the nosedome antenna," Nazir said. "Push it once then push on the external signal again."

Friday did. As soon as the button was depressed the voices began to come in more clearly. Other zones were checking in. There was also a blip on the small green directional map. The signal was coming from the northwest. Friday switched back to internal communications.

"We'd better check it out," Friday said.

"It cannot be a Pakistani search party," Nazir said. "They would not communicate on this frequency."

"I know," Friday replied. "The line of control isn't far from here. I'm worried that it could be an Indian unit moving in."

"A sweep coming down through different zones," Nazir said. "That would be a standard search-and-rescue maneuver. Should we do a flyover?"

"Why?" Friday asked.

"They may have intelligence on the cell's location that we do not," Nazir said. "The direction they are headed may tell us something."

"No," Friday said. He continued to look out the window. "I don't want to waste the time or fuel."

"What do we do if they contact us?" Nazir asked. "Radar at the line of control may pick us up as we near the end of the range. They may ask us to help with the search."

"We'll tell them we're on routine reconnaissance and were about to turn back to Kargil," Friday said.

Apu stuck his small, strong hand through the opening. He tapped Friday on the shoulder. "Is everything all right?" he yelled.

Friday nodded. Just then, about one hundred feet below, he saw snow billowing from under an overhang.

"Hold!" Friday barked at Nazir.

The helicopter slowed and hovered. Ron Friday leaned toward the side. The puffs of snow were concentrated in a small area and inching toward the north. They could be caused by an animal picking its way across the cliff or they could be the result of a wind funnel. It was impossible to tell because of the overhang. The sun was behind the top of the peak and unable to throw shadows behind or in front of the region.

"Do you see that?" Friday asked.

Nazir nodded.

"Take her down and away slowly," Friday said.

The chopper simultaneously began to descend and angle away from the cliff. As the target peak filled less and less of the window, the vastness of the range loomed behind it. The layers upon layers of brownish-purple mountains were a spectacular sight. Snow covered the peaks and Friday could actually see it falling on some of the nearer mountains, off-white sheets like stage scrims. The sun cut a rainbow through one of the storm centers. It was a massive arc, more brilliant than any Friday had ever seen. Though Friday did not have time to enjoy the view, it made him feel for a moment like a god.

They dropped nearly one hundred feet. As they did, three people came into view. They were slightly more than two hundred feet away. The three were walking close together. Each one was wearing dark, heavy clothing and carrying a backpack and weapon. They did not stop or look over at the helicopter until the rotor wash stirred the snow on the ledge beneath their feet. Given the parka tops they were wearing and the low rumble of the wind, Friday was not surprised they did not hear the chopper.

"Is Nanda there?" Apu asked.

Friday could not tell who the three people were. He was disappointed to see that only three of them had gotten this far. Unless—

"Take us back up and head north!" he shouted.

Captain Nazir pulled the U-shaped wheel toward him and the chopper rose. As it did, the tail rotor and starboard side of the cargo area were struck by short, hard blows. Friday could not hear them but he could feel the craft shudder. He could also see the thin shafts of white daylight appear suddenly in the bottom half of the cargo bay.

"What is it?" Nazir yelled.

"They think we are the enemy!" Apu shouted.

"It's a setup!" Friday snarled. "They broke into two groups!"

The chopper wobbled and Friday could hear the portside tail rotor clanging. The weapon fire from the stern had obviously damaged the blades. If they had not pulled up when they did the chopper would probably be plunging tail first into the rocky, mist-shrouded valleys below. As it was, Captain Nazir was having trouble keeping the Ka-25 steady and moving forward, much less gaining altitude. A moment later the chopper stopped climbing altogether.

"I'm losing her!" Nazir said. "And we're leaking fuel."

Friday looked at the gauge and swore. They had already off-loaded whatever gear they were carrying in the back. The only thing left was the fixed-winch. There was no extra weight they could push out. There probably was not time to get rid of it in any case.

Friday looked out the window as the chopper began to shudder violently. The rainbow vanished as the sun's angle changed. He no longer felt like a god but like a grade-A sucker. Of all the damn tricks to fall for. A freaking sleight of hand, a sucker punch. The operative studies the unthreatening team while a backup unit, either hidden or on another side, tears you a new exit.

"You're going to have to set us down anywhere you can!" Friday said urgently.

"I'm looking for a spot," Nazir said. "I don't see one."

A sudden fist of wind turned them nearly forty-five degrees so they were facing the cliff. A second burst of gunfire, this time from the group in front, tore at the undercarriage. The chopper lurched and dropped. They were at the top of a valley. Friday could not see what was below them because of a thick mist. But he did not want to go down there. He did not want to lose the cell and he did not want to be here when the nukes went off.

"I've got to go down while we still have power for a controlled landing," Nazir said.

"Not yet," Friday said. He unbuckled his seatbelt. "Apu, back up."

"What are you going to do?" Nazir asked.

"I'm going to crawl into the back," Friday said. "Do you have forward and aft mobility?"

"Limited," he said. "One of the tail rotors is still working."

"All right," Friday said. "If you can turn the stern toward the peak, Apu and I might be able to use the winch line to rappel to one of the ledges."

"In this wind?" Nazir exclaimed. "You'll be blown off!"

"The wind is blowing southeast, toward the cliff." Friday said. "That should help us."

"It could also smash you into the rocks—"

"We'll have to risk that!" Friday told Nazir. "I've got to reach the cell and tell them about the soldiers ahead."

"Even if you can get to the ledge, they'll gun you down," Nazir said.

"I'll send the old man out first," Friday said. "Nanda may recognize her grandfather's coat. Or they may see us as potential hostages. In any case, that might get them to hold their fire." Friday pulled out his switchblade and cut out the seatbelt. When the strap was free, Friday detached the radio and handed it to Apu. "With luck I'll be able to raise Striker. I'll tell them where we are and approximately where you set down. Striker will help us get to Pakistan and the Himalayan patrol can come and get you. You can tell them you were running independent recon but didn't find the cell."

Nazir did not look convinced. But there was no time to debate the plan and he did as Ron Friday asked. With his feet braced against the floor, his hands tight around the controls, Nazir carefully turned the chopper around and began edging it toward the cliff. As he did, Friday disconnected the communications jack but kept his helmet on. Then he swung through the hatchway between the seats.

"What is happening?" Apu asked. His flesh was paler than usual. Unlike the heated cockpit the cargo bay was damn cold.

"We're bailing," Friday said as he used the seatbelt to create a bandolierlike harness for Apu.

"I don't understand," Apu said.

"Just hang on," Friday said as he fastened the belt in front and then led the farmer to the winch. It was difficult to stand in the bumping cargo bay so they crawled to the rear of the hold. The line was quarter-inch-diameter nylon wound around an aluminum spool. They remained on their knees as Friday unfastened the hook end from the eyelet on the floor.

"You're going to go out first," Friday said as he ran the line through the harness he had created.

"Go out?" Apu said.

"Yes. To your granddaughter," Friday told him. The American tugged on the line. It seemed secure. Then he motioned Apu back until the farmer was crouching on the hatch. "It's going to be a rough ride," Friday warned him. "Just grab the line, huddle down, and hold on until they get you."

"Wait!" Apu said. "How do you know that they will?"

"I don't, but I'll pray for you!" Friday said as he reached for the long lever that controlled the floor hatch. He pulled it. There was a jolt as the hatch began to open. Quickly, he grabbed the remote control that operated the winch. The line began unspooling as frigid air slipped over the doorway and slammed into the hold. "Tell them I'm coming next!" Friday shouted as Apu slid back.

Apu grabbed the line as Friday had said, hugging it to him as he slipped from the hold. With his free hand, Friday held the line himself and edged toward the open hatch. The wind was like a block of ice, solid and biting. He turned his helmet partway into the gale and watched through squinting eyes. As he expected, the wind lofted Apu up and out. It was a surreal vision, a man being hoisted like a kite. The chopper was about twenty-five feet from the cliff. It was listing to the starboard, where the rear rotor was out, and being buffeted up and down by the wind. But Nazir was able to hold it in place as Apu was swept toward the ledge. As Friday had hoped, the forward group went to retrieve him as the rear guard kept their weapons on the helicopter. The closer he got to the cliff, the more Apu was banged around by the wind as crosscurrents whipped down and across the rock face. But one of the cell members was able to grab him, while another cell member held on to his comrade. When everyone was safe, the cell member removed the winch line. Friday reeled it back in. He watched as the farmer spoke with the others. One of the cell members raised and crossed his arms to the group in the rear. They did not fire at the chopper.

When the line came back in, Friday quickly ran it through the handle of the radio then strung it under his armpits and around his waist. He kept the radio against his belly and lay on his back. He wanted to go out feet first to protect the radio. He crab-walked down the open hatch, then pressed the button to send the winch line back out. He grabbed the line, straightened his legs, and began to slide down. The brutally cold air tore along his pants legs. It felt as if his skin were being peeled back. And then, a moment later, he was suddenly on a rocket sled. Because he was not onboard to control it, the line was going out faster than before and the wind was pushing even faster. The cliff came up so fast that he barely had time to meet it with his feet. Friday hit hard with his soles. He felt the smack all the way to the top of his skull. He bounced back then felt a sickening yank, then a drop, as the chopper lurched behind him.

"Shit!" he cried. He felt as if he had been slammed in the chest with a log. The line grew steel-taut as the chopper began to drop.

Hands reached for him from the ledge. The wind kept him buoyed. Someone held the radio while someone else tried to undo the line.

Suddenly, someone in front of him raised an AK-47 and fired a burst above his head. The nylon line snapped and the wind bumped Friday forward. More hands grabbed his jacket and pulled him onto the ledge. Because the wind was still battering him he did not feel as if he were on solid ground. He lay there for a moment as he sucked air into his wounded lungs. He was facing the valley and he watched as the helicopter descended in a slow, lazy spiral.

Then, a moment later, it stopped spiraling. The chopper fell tail first, straight and purposeful, like a metal shuttlecock. It picked up speed as it descended, finally vanishing into the low-lying clouds.

A moment later he heard a bang that echoed hollow through the valley. It was accompanied by a burst of orange-red that seemed to spread through the clouds like dye.

However, Ron Friday did not have time to contemplate the death of Captain Nazir. The hands that had saved him hoisted him up and put him against the wall of the cliff.

A woman put a gun under his chin and forced him to look at her. Her face was frostbitten and her eyes manic. Ice clung to the hair that showed beneath her hood.

"Who are you?" she demanded, screaming to be heard over the wind.

"I'm Ron Friday with American intelligence," he shouted back. "Are you the FKM leader?"

"I am!" she replied.

"Good," he said. "You're the one I'm looking for. You and Nanda. Is she with you?"

"Why?" she shouted.

Friday replied, "Because she may be the only one who can stop the nuclear destruction of your country."

THIRTY-TWO

Washington, D.C.
Thursday, 6:25 A.M.

"What the hell just happened?" Bob Herbert asked Viens.

Op-Center's intelligence chief was sitting at his desk in his darkened office. He had been watching the computer monitor with half-shut eyes until the image suddenly woke him up. He immediately hit autodial on his telephone and raised Stephen Viens at the NRO.

"It looks like a chopper went down," Viens said.

"Chopper," Herbert said. It was more a question than a statement.

"You were dozing," Viens said.

"Yes, I had my eyes closed," Herbert said. "What happened?"

"All we saw was the tail end of a chopper approach the cliff and lower a line with two men on it," Viens told him. "It looks like the cell took the men in and the chopper went down. We did not have a wide enough viewing area to be certain of that."

"Friday had a copter," Herbert said. "Could it have been him?"

"We don't know who was on the end of the line," Viens replied. "One of them looked like he might have been carrying a radio. It was an electronic box of some kind. It did not look like U.S. intelligence issue."

"I'll call you back," Herbert said.

"Bob?" Viens said. "If that was an Indian air force chopper they're going to know where it went down. Even if it wasn't, the explosion is going to register on their satellite monitors or seismic equipment."

"I know," Herbert said. The intelligence head put Stephen Viens on hold and called Hank Lewis's office. The NSA officer was not in yet. Herbert tried Lewis's cell phone but the voice mail picked up. He was either on that line or out of range. Herbert swore. He finally tried Lewis at home. He caught Lewis in the middle of shaving.

Herbert told the NSA chief what had happened and asked if he knew for certain whether Ron Friday was in Jaudar.

"I assume so," Lewis said. "I haven't spoken with him since our conference call."

"Do you have any way of reaching him?" Herbert asked.

"Only if he's in the helicopter," Lewis said.

"What about his cell phone?" Herbert pressed.

"We haven't tried that," Lewis said. "But on the move, in the mountains, it may be difficult."

"True," Herbert agreed. "And the radio?"

"We used a NATO frequency to contact him, but I don't have that info at home," Lewis said.

"Well, we can backtrack and raise him," Herbert said. "Thanks. I'll let you know when we have him."

Herbert ended the call and glanced at the computer clock. It was six thirty. Kevin Custer, Op-Center's director of electronic communications, would be in his office by now. Herbert called over.

Custer was a thirty-two-year-old MIT graduate and a distant relative of General George Armstrong Custer through the general's brother Nevin. Military service was expected in the Custer family and Kevin had spent two years in the army before taking a job at the CIA. He had been there three years when he was snatched up by Bob Herbert. Custer was the most chronically optimistic, upbeat, can-do person Herbert had ever met.

Custer told Herbert that he would get the information for him if he would hold the line. It wasn't even, "I'll get it and call you back." It was, "Don't go away. I'll have it in a second." And he did.

"Let's see," Custer said. "NSA log has the call coming through with input 101.763, PL 123.0 Hz, 855 inversion scrambling. I can contact the source of the call if you like."

"Put it through," Herbert said.

A moment later Herbert heard a beep.

"I'll get off now," Custer said. "Let me know if there's anything else."

"Actually, there is," Herbert said. "Would you ring Paul Hood and patch this call through?"

Custer said he would. The radio beeped again. Then a third time. Then a fourth.

"Bob, what is it?" Hood asked when he got on. He sounded groggy. He had probably been napping too.

"Viens and I just watched the Pakistani cell haul two people in from what looked like a downed chopper," Herbert said. The radio beeped a fifth time. "We're trying to ascertain if one of them was Ron Friday."

"I thought he was going to Jaudar," Hood said.

"Exactly," Herbert replied.

The radio beeped two more times before someone answered. It definitely was not Ron Friday.

"Yes?" said a woman's voice.

"This is 855 base," Herbert said, using the coded identification number. "Who is this?"

"Someone who has your radio and its operator," the woman replied. "I just saved him from death. But the reprieve may only be temporary."

The woman's accent definitely belonged to that region. Herbert would be able to place it better were it not for the screaming wind behind her. The woman was also smart. She had said only that she saved Friday's life. There was no reference to the rest of the cell or the other man they were holding. She had given Herbert as little information as possible.

Herbert hit the mute button. "Paul—I say we talk to her," he said quickly, urgently. "We need to let her know that Striker is on the way."

"This channel isn't secure, is it?" Hood asked.

"No," Herbert admitted.

"Friday will probably tell her that."

"He got there in an Indian chopper. They may not believe him," Herbert said. "Let me give her the overview."

"Be careful, Bob," Hood warned. "I don't want you telling her who we are, exactly."

Herbert killed the mute. "Listen to me," he said. "We are with American intelligence. The man you have works with us."

"He told me that his last name is Friday," the woman said. "What is his first name?"

"Ron," Herbert replied.

"All right," the woman said. "What do you want with us?"

"We want to get you home alive," Herbert said. He weighed his next words with care in case anyone was listening. "We know what happened in Srinagar. We know what your group did and did not do."

He did not have to say more. She would know the rest. There was a short silence.

"Why do you want to help us?" the woman finally asked.

"Because we believe there will be extreme retaliation," Herbert informed her. "Not against you but against your nation."

"Does your person Friday know about this?" she asked.

"He knows about that and more," Herbert informed the woman. "And he is not alone."

"Yes," the woman said. "We rescued an old farmer—"

"That is not what I mean," Herbert said.

There was another brief silence. Herbert could imagine the woman scanning the skies for other choppers.

"I see," said the woman. "I will talk to him. American intelligence, I do not know if I can take this radio with me," the woman went on. "If there is anything else I need to know, tell me now."

Herbert thought for a moment. "There is one more thing," he informed her. He spoke clearly and strongly so she would not miss a word. "We are helping you because inaction would result in unprecedented human disaster. I have no respect for terrorists."

"American intelligence," she said, using that as if it were Herbert's name. "I have lost nothing. If the world respected us before now, there would be no need for terrorism."

With that, the line went dead.

THIRTY-THREE

Mt. Kanzalwan
Thursday, 4:16 P.M.

Sharab could barely feel her fingers as she put the receiver
back inside the radio. Despite the heavy gloves and the constant movement, the cold was beyond anything she had ever
experienced. Her hands were numb when they were still, like
dead weight. They burned when she moved them and blood
was forced to circulate. It was the same with her feet. Her
eyes were wind-blasted dry. Each blink of her icy lashes was
agony.

But the worst pain was still the one inside. It had been
strongest in those moments when the powerful winds slowed
and the overhanging rock receded and the sun burned
through the murderous cold. When survival was not a
moment-to-moment concern and she had time to think.

Sharab had let herself be outsmarted by Indian security
forces. She had let her nation, her people, and her fellow
patriots down. That failure had cost brave Ishaq his life. And
it had brought her and her small loyal militia to this preci-
pice, to this flight. Her failure had made it unlikely that they
would escape these mountains and tell the world the truth,
that India and not Pakistan had been responsible for attacking
the Hindu sites.

And yet, as it said in the Koran, "the wrongdoers shall
never prosper." Perhaps Allah forgave her. It seemed as
though He was looking out for her when this man dropped
from the sky. Sharab did not like or trust Americans. They
made war on Muslims around the world and they had tra-
ditionally curried favor with New Delhi instead of Islamabad.
But she would not question the will of God. It would be
ironic if this man were to provide them with salvation.

Ron Friday was still lying on his stomach. To the right, Nanda was huddled with her grandfather. Sharab would deal with them in a moment. She told Samouel to help pick the American up. Together, they pushed him back under the ledge, against the wall. It was even colder here because the sun was not on them. But there was less chance of them slipping off the ledge. Until Sharab heard what this man had to say, she did not want him falling to his death.

The man groaned as she pinned her forearm against his shoulder to help him stand.

"All right," Sharab said to him. "Tell me what you know."

"What I know?" Friday said. Puffy white breath and gasps of pain emerged from his mouth with each syllable. "To start with, you shot down our ticket out of here."

"You should not have come unannounced in an Indian helicopter," Sharab replied. "That was stupid."

"Unavoidable," Friday protested loudly.

The exclamation was followed by a painful wince. Sharab had to lean into the man to keep him from doubling over. She wondered if he had broken some ribs in the hard landing. But that was all right. Pain could be useful. It would keep him alert and moving.

"Never mind now," Friday said. "The main thing is that the Indian SFF set you up. They set Nanda up. She helped them blow up the temple and the bus. According to our intelligence, the SFF thought that would help solidify the Indian people behind the military. Nanda probably did not know that the Indian military intends to respond to the attack with a nuclear strike."

"For destroying the temple?" Sharab said. She was stunned.

"Yes," Friday said. "We believe certain militants will tell the populace that it's the first shot of an Islamic jihad against the Hindu people. Moderate government ministers and military officials may have no choice but to go along."

"You said you have intelligence," Sharab said. "What intelligence? American?"

"American and Indian," Friday said. "The pilot who brought me here was a Black Cat Commando. He had special information about SFF activities. Our people in Washington arrived at the same conclusion independently. That's why they're diverting the American strike force from their original mission."

"Which was?"

"To help the Indian military scout for possible Pakistani nuclear emplacements," Friday replied.

"They came to help India and now I'm supposed to trust them?" Sharab declared.

"You may not have a choice," Friday said. "There's something else. While we were searching for you we saw a force of Indian soldiers headed this way. They're moving in a wide sweep down from the line of control. You'll never get through them."

"I expected that after we killed their commandos in the mountains," Sharab said. "How many are there?"

"I could only see about one hundred soldiers," Friday told her. "There may be more."

"How many American soldiers are there and how will they find us?" Sharab asked.

"There are about a dozen elite soldiers and they've been watching you by satellite," Friday said.

"They can see us now?" Sharab asked.

Friday nodded.

"Then why did you have to search for us?" the woman pressed.

"Because they didn't want to tell me where you were," Friday said. "I'm with a different agency. There's mistrust, rivalry."

"Stupidity," she snarled. She shook her head. "Less than twenty soldiers against one hundred. When will the Americans be here?"

"Very soon," Friday said.

"How are they arriving?"

"By Indian transport, Himalayan Eagles squadron," Friday replied.

Sharab thought for a moment. Militarily, the American unit would not be much assistance. However, there might be another way that she could use them. "Can you contact the American unit?" she asked Friday.

"Through Washington, yes," he replied.

"Good. Samouel?"

"Yes, Sharab?" said the big man.

"I want you to wait here with Nanda," Sharab said. "I will lead the others down to the valley. A half hour after we leave you continue along the route we planned."

"Yes, Sharab," he replied.

Sharab turned to go over to where Nanda and Apu were speaking.

"Wait!" Friday said. "We're already outnumbered. Why do you want to split up?"

"If we contact the Americans by radio we can make sure the Indian ground troops also pick up the message," Sharab said. "That will draw them to us."

"What makes you think they'll be taking prisoners?" Friday asked.

"It does not matter, as long as we hold them there as long as we can," Sharab said. "It will leave the path clear for Samouel's group to get through. You said yourself that Nanda is the key to stopping the nuclear attack. She must reach Pakistan. Her people will listen to her confession, her testimony."

"How do you know she won't betray you?" Friday asked.

"Because I know something you don't," Sharab said. "The missiles your team is looking for? They are already in place. Dozens of them. They are in the mountains, pointed at New Delhi, Calcutta, Bombay. A strike against Pakistan will turn the entire subcontinent into a wasteland."

"Let me tell my superiors," Friday said. "They will warn the Indians not to strike—"

"Warn them how?" Sharab asked. "I have no proof! I don't know where the missiles are and my government won't reveal that information. I only know that missiles have been deployed. We staged attacks to distract the Indian military when elements were being moved into place." The woman took a breath, calmed herself. If she grew angry and began to perspire the sweat would freeze. "Unless Nanda wishes to see her nation ravaged, she will have to cooperate with us. But that means getting her to Pakistan without the Indians killing her!"

"All right," Friday agreed. "But I'm going with her. She'll need protection. She'll also need international credibility. I was a witness to the blasts. I can make certain that officials from our embassy support her claims."

"How do I know you won't kill her?" Sharab cried. The winds had picked up and she had to shout to be heard over them. "You arrived in an Indian helicopter. How do I know you didn't want to take us back to Kargil? I only have your promises and a radio communication that could have come from anyone! These do not make you an ally!"

"I could have shot at you from the helicopter!" Friday yelled. "That makes me not your enemy."

Sharab had to admit that the American had a point. Still, she was not ready to believe him entirely. Not yet.

"You're wasting what little time we have," the man went on. "Unless you plan on killing me, I'm going with Nanda."

Sharab continued to hold Friday against the wall. His hot breath warmed her nose as she looked at him. His eyes were tearing from the cold but that was the only life in them. Sharab could not find anything else there. Not truth, not conviction, not selflessness. But she also did not see fear or hostility. And at the moment, that would have to be good enough.

"Samouel will run the operation," Sharab told Friday.

Friday nodded vigorously. Sharab released him. Samouel held Friday up until he was sure the American had his feet under him.

"Wait here," Sharab said, then turned.

With her back to the cliff wall Sharab edged toward Nanda. The Indian woman was crouched in a small fissure with her grandfather. She rose when Sharab arrived. She was wearing a heavy scarf across her face. Only her eyes were visible.

Sharab told Nanda that she would be traveling in one group, with Samoeul, the American, and her grandfather.

"Why are you doing that?" Nanda asked.

When Sharab finished telling her everything Friday had said, she saw doubt and concern in Nanda's eyes. Perhaps the Indian woman did not know what the SFF and members of the military had been doing.

Unfortunately, Nanda's reaction told Sharab what she needed to know.

That the American's story could be true.

Nuclear war could indeed be just hours away.

THIRTY-FOUR

Washington, D.C.
Thursday, 6:51 A.M.

Paul Hood was not surprised that Bob Herbert had been blunt with the woman on the radio. Herbert's wife had been killed by Islamic terrorists. Working with the Pakistani cell had to be ripping him apart.

But what Herbert had told the woman, that he opposed her and her profession, was also a smart and responsible alliance tactic. Strangers tend to be suspicious of indulgence and flattery. But tell someone that you don't like them and are only working with them out of necessity and they tend to trust whatever information you give them.

"You okay, Bob?" Hood asked.

"Sure," he replied. "She got in a good one, though."

"So did you."

"She never felt it," Herbert said. "Zealots have skin like a tank. But it's all right," he went on. "I'm a big boy. I know how this works."

"Sometimes it just strikes a little close to the heart," Hood said.

"Yes, it does," Herbert agreed.

Hood had been through situations like this before with Herbert. The intelligence chief just had to work through it.

"We'll talk more about this later, Bob," Hood said. "Right now, I've got to brief the president. He'll need to know what we're planning."

The intelligence chief was silent for a moment. "I guess that's also bothering me, though. Whether we should really be doing this."

"What?" Hood asked. "Letting Striker go in?"

"Yeah."

"Give me an option," Hood said.

"Dump the problem in the president's lap," Herbert said. "Let him slug it out with the Indian government."

"He won't do that without proof," Hood said. "I'll tell him what our concerns are and what we're going to do about it. I know what he's going to say. He will okay having Striker on the ground for on-site intel, especially since the Indian government has authorized their being there. He's going to give us his blessings to go that far. The rest will be Mike's call."

Herbert was silent.

"But you're still uneasy," Hood said.

"Yeah," Herbert told him. "Let's just go over our command tent options again."

"All right," Hood said patiently.

"We've decided that the Indian government is probably out of the loop on this nuclear option," Herbert said. "So unless we get that Kargil woman, Nanda, in front of a TV camera to explain this was an inside job we have no proof to offer the president or the Indian people."

"That's it," Hood said. "We've also got Indian troops moving in to cut Nanda and the Pakistanis down."

"We assume," Herbert said.

"We have to assume it's search and destroy," Hood pointed out. "The SFF gains nothing by capturing the Pakistanis and letting the truth come out. We need to give the cell a chance to get home."

"God help us," Herbert said.

"Bob, there's a bigger picture than aiding terrorists," Hood said. "You know that."

"I know," Herbert said. "I just don't like it."

"The time it would take us to move this through diplomatic channels could cost the Pakistanis their lives," Hood said.

"And going ahead with this operation can cost Striker their lives," Herbert said.

"That's been true every time they've gone into the field," Hood reminded Herbert. "If Mike or Colonel August has any doubts about this action they can call it off at any time."

"They won't," Herbert assured him. "Not with what's at stake."

"That's probably true," Hood agreed.

"And not with the balls Mike's got," Herbert went on.

"It's more than that," Hood said. "He knows his people. Did he ever run that quote past you, the one from the duke of Wellington?"

"I don't think so," Herbert said.

"I was watching Striker drill one morning and I asked Mike how he could tell when he had pushed his people as far as they could go," Hood said. "He told me that Wellington had a simple way to determine when he had created the best fighting unit possible. 'I don't know what effect these men will have upon the enemy,' Wellington wrote, 'but, by God, they terrify me.' Mike said that when he felt his people were tough enough to scare him, that was when he stopped."

"Paul, I don't need to be reminded that Striker is the best," Herbert said. "But I'm worried about the jump into the Himalayas. I'm worried about the odds and having to trust terrorists. I'm worried about having no backup for them and, worse than that, no exit strategy."

"I'm worried about all that too," Hood replied. "I'm also aware that we have no other options."

The intelligence chief was quiet for a moment. The silence was uncomfortable. Hood felt as if Herbert were judging him.

Herbert must have felt that too. "I know we're doing what we have to do," he said. "It doesn't mean I have to like it." Herbert's voice was no longer angry or searching. It was resigned.

Herbert said that he would call the NRO to get the exact location of the cell and then give Striker a final update before H-hour. Hood thanked him and hung up.

Op-Center's director rubbed his eyes. Herbert had his personal demons but so did Hood.

Unlike the intelligence chief, Hood had never put his life on the line. He had been a mayor and a financial officer before taking this job. He had sent Striker into danger before but never into an armed conflict. To do that seemed cavalier, hypocritical, cowardly.

But, as Hood had told Herbert, it was also necessary. Paul Hood's personal issues could not affect his professional decisions. He had to be dispassionate. He owed the president and the nation that much.

Hood stopped rubbing his eyes. He was tired inside and out. It did not help that when this was over he had to deal with the closing of the press office. Fortunately, he would be able to minimize his contact with Ann Farris until then. Because this was a military action Hood would instruct her to institute a total press blackout on any Op-Center activities until noon. She would have to shut down the phones and computers. No press department staff would be permitted to answer their cell phones. Queries to the automated main number would go unreturned. As for Hood, he would go into the Tank with Bob Herbert, Liz Gordon, and Lowell Coffey until the crisis had passed.

Then Hood would give Ann Farris the bad news along with his complete attention.

He owed her that much.

THIRTY-FIVE

The Great Himalaya Range
Thursday, 4:19 P.M.

The parachutes were zero-porosity mixed-fabric PF 3000s "Merits." They had been selected for the Indian military in this region because they gave jumpers maximum control over their descent. If there were a sudden current in any direction the fabric would retain its shape and buoyancy. The canopies themselves were slightly elliptical with a tapered wing. That shape provided for the softest landings. First used militarily by the French air force, the Merits also provided the safest jump for novice parachutists.

The parachutes were stowed in slender Atom Millennium containers. They had classic plastic handle ripcords and narrow chest straps along with lightweight Cordura fabric exteriors. The thin straps and light weight would be relatively unrestrictive if Striker were forced to engage the enemy or the elements before doffing the backpacks. There was also an instant-collapse system operated by a rubber pull-string. That would allow the chute to be deflated immediately upon landing in the event of strong ground winds.

Rodgers and his team had unpacked and repacked the parachutes. They examined the fabric as well as the shroud lines and ring attachments. With elements of the Indian military apparently working at cross-purposes, Rodgers wanted to make certain the equipment had not been sabotaged.

Suited in the white Nomex winter gear they had brought with them, the Strikers were huddled next to the hatch before lining up. The team members were crouched to keep their balance in the bumping aircraft. In addition to their parachutes, each commando wore a hip holster with a Browning 9mm high-power Mark 2 pistol, a Kevlar bullet-proof vest, leather gloves, and climbing boots. The vests had side pockets for flashlights, flares, hand grenades, additional pistol magazines, and maps. Before jumping into the subzero environment the commandos would don the Leyland and Birmingham respirator masks they carried. These full-face masks included large, shatterproof, tinted eyepieces for wide visibility. Medic William Musicant had the added burden of a medical belt. This remarkably compact unit, devised by the Navy SEALs for use in Desert Storm, allowed him to treat a wide range of both fall- and combat-related injuries.

Rodgers reviewed photographs of the terrain with Striker. Viens had transmitted these images from the NRO computer directly to the Striker laptop. Rodgers had printed out two copies to pass around. The general had also printed out a second set of photographs that had just come in.

The team was going into what was referred to as a "high-contrast" terrain. That meant the landing would be problematic. The target area was a large, flat ledge approximately seventy meters by ninety meters. It was the only relatively large horizontal site in the region. The drawbacks were several large outcroppings of rock as well as steep drops on the northern and western sides. Sheer cliffs bounded the area on the south and east. Colonel August was also concerned about the winds. He pointed to the color photograph.

"Depending upon the strength of the winds in the area, this concave southeastern wall could create powerful outdraft," he said. "That could keep us from landing in the target zone."

"Unfortunately, the cell is moving along very narrow ledges," Rodgers said. "That's the only area where we can intercept them."

"Why do we have to catch them in the mountains?" Ishi Honda asked. In addition to his parachute the young corporal was carrying the TAC-SAT in a pouch on his chest.

Rodgers showed them the second photograph Viens had sent. It showed a line of dark shapes moving across a dreary terrain of wheat-colored scrub and patches of snow.

"These are Indian soldiers moving toward the target area," Rodgers said. "The NRO and Bob Herbert both put them at less than five miles from contact. There are up to two hundred of them, though we can't be sure. They obtained these pictures by hacking a Chinese satellite that watches the line of control. We can't pull back for a wider view."

"Which means that if we can't smuggle the cell through we will have to repel a much larger force," August told the group.

"For various reasons negotiation is not an option," Rodgers added. "We have to get past them one way or the other."

The general looked at the faces of his troops. With the exception of the medic, all of these soldiers had been in battle. Most of them had killed. They had shed the blood of others, usually at a distance. They had seen the blood of their teammates, which typically fanned their rage and made the blood of the enemy invisible. They had also faced superior odds. Rodgers was confident that they would give this effort everything they had.

Rodgers listened as Colonel August talked about the strategy they would employ upon landing. Typically, they would go behind enemy lines carrying mines. Two or three operatives would form a subgroup. They would go ahead and plant the mines along the team's route to protect them from enemies. They would also throw out substances such as powdered onion or raw meat to confuse and mislead attack dogs. They did not see dogs in the photographs and hoped that the animals were not part of the army units.

Since there were apparently four members of the cell, plus Friday and the two Indians, August had decided to go forward in an ABBA formation. There would be a Striker in front and behind each group of two Pakistanis. That would enable Striker to control the rate of progress and to watch the personnel they were escorting. Neither Herbert nor Rodgers expected any resistance from the cell, From everything they had been told, both groups wanted the same thing. To reach Pakistan alive. As for the Indian force, the American team was prepared to move at nightfall, wage a guerrilla campaign, or simply dig in, wait them out, and execute an end run when possible. They would do whatever it took to survive.

Striker had drilled for this maneuver high in the Rockies. They called it their red, white, and blue exercise. During the course of two hours their fingers had gone from red to white to blue. At least they knew what they would be facing. Once they reached the ground they would know how to pace themselves. The only uncertainty was what might happen on the way down. That was still what concerned Rodgers the most. They were approximately ten thousand feet up. That was not as long as most high-altitude, low-opening jumps. Those operations typically began at thirty-two-thousand feet. The HALO teams would go out with oxygen-heavy breathing apparatus to keep from suffering hypoxemia. They would also use barometric triggers to activate their chutes at an altitude of roughly two thousand feet above the target. They did that in case the jumper suffered one of two possible ailments. The first was barometric trauma, the result of air being trapped in the intestines, ears, and sinuses and causing them to expand painfully. The other was stress-induced hyperventilation, common in combat situations. Especially when jumpers could be aloft for as long as seventy or eighty minutes. That gave them a lot of alone-time to think, particularly about missing the target. At an average drift rate of ten feet for every hundred feet of fall, that was a concern for every jumper. Breathing bottled oxygen at a rapid pace due to stress could cause a lowering of blood carbon dioxide and result in unconsciousness.

Though neither of those would be a problem at this lower height, it was two thousand feet higher than they had practiced in the Rocky Mountains. And even there, then-Striker Bass Moore had broken his left leg.

Lean Sergeant Chick Grey was chewing gum, unflustered as always. There was a bit more iron determination and aggression in the eyes of waspish privates David George, Jason Scott, and Terrence Newmeyer. Corporal Pat Prementine and Private Matt Bud were popping gloved knuckles and shifting in place, as full of rough-and-tumble energy as always. And the excitable Private Walter Pupshaw looked as if he wanted to tear off someone's head and spit down the windpipe. That

was normal for Striker's resident wild man. The other team
members were calm with the exception of Sondra DeVonne
and the green medic, William Musicant. Both Strikers
seemed a little anxious. Musicant had limited combat experience and Sondra still blamed herself for events that led to
the death of Lt. Colonel Charlie Squires. She had spent many
months being counseled by Liz Gordon. But she had gone
on other assignments with the team since then. While the
young African-American woman was not as relaxed or go-
get-'em as the others, Rodgers was certain he could count
on her. She would not be here otherwise.

When they were ready, Rodgers picked up the phone beside the hatch. The copilot informed him that the plane would
reach the target in less than five minutes. August lined up
his team and stood at their head. After everyone had jumped,
Rodgers would follow.

Since the aircraft was not typically used for jumping, there
was no chute line or lights to indicate that they had reached
the drop zone. August and Pupshaw opened the hatch while
Rodgers remained on the phone with the cockpit. The air
that surged in was like nothing the general had ever felt. It
was a fist of ice, punching them back and then holding them
there. Rodgers was glad they had the masks and breathing
apparatus. Otherwise they would not be able to draw a breath
from the unyielding wall of wind. As it was, August and
Pupshaw were knocked away from the opening. The colonel
and the burly private had to be helped back into position by
the next Strikers in line.

Rodgers moved sternward along the fuselage, away from
the hatch. The howl of the wind was deafening, bordering
on painful. It would be impossible to hear the command to
jump. The general went back three meters, as far as the
phone cord would reach. He used his free hand to cover the
left ear of his hood. He pressed down hard. That was the
only way he could hear the copilot. Meanwhile, August motioned for each Striker to determine individual jump times
by using the "blackout" system. That was the method employed for secret nighttime jumps. It meant putting the right
hand on the shoulder of the jumper in front of them. When

the shoulder moved out from under someone's hand it was time for that person to go.

The wind pressed the Strikers' white uniforms toward the front of the plane. The soldiers looked like action figures to Rodgers. Every crease and fold seemed molded in place like plastic. The soldiers were leaning forward slightly to let the wind slide around them, though not so much as to allow it to batter the person behind them.

Seconds moved at a glacial pace. Then the word came that they were less than a half mile from their target. Then a quarter mile. Then an eighth of a mile.

Rodgers looked at the Strikers one more time. If they knew how difficult this jump was going to be they were not showing it. The team was still outwardly game and disciplined. He was beyond proud of the unit. Rodgers did not believe in prayer, though he hoped that even if some of the Strikers missed the target they would all survive.

August glanced at Rodgers and gave him a thumbs-up. Obviously the colonel could see the small plateau. That was good. It meant there was no snowfall in the drop zone. They would not be jumping directly over it but to the northwest. The copilot had calculated that the wind was blowing to the southeast at an average of sixty-three miles an hour. They would have to compensate so the wind would carry them toward rather than away from the target.

They passed over the plateau. August held up both thumbs. He had spotted the cell. Rodgers nodded.

A moment later Rodgers got the word from the cockpit. "Go!"

Rodgers motioned to August. As the team started moving through the hatch Rodgers shifted to the back of the line. The copilot emerged from the cockpit. He literally had to hug the port-side wall to get past the hatch before cutting to the starboard side to shut it.

Rodgers hoped he made it. The last thing the general saw before jumping was the small-built Indian flyboy tying a cargo strap to his waist before even attempting to crawl toward the sliding door.

Rodgers held his legs together and pressed his arms straight along his sides as he hit the icy mountain air. That gave him a knife-edged dive to get him away from the plane so he would not be sucked into the engine. He immediately reconfigured himself into an aerofoil position. He arched his body to allow the air to flow along his underside. At the same time he thrust his arms back and dipped his head to increase his rate of descent.

The general was now looking almost straight down. Almost at once he knew he was in trouble.

They all were.

THIRTY-SIX

The Great Himalaya Range
Thursday, 4:42 P.M.

At 4:31, Major Dev Puri's spotter, Corporal Sivagi Saigal, saw something that concerned him. He reported it to Major Puri. The officer was deeply troubled by what he heard.

Prior to leaving, he had been assured by the office of Minister of Defense John Kabir that reconnaissance flights in the region had been suspended. Neither Kabir nor Puri wanted independent witnesses or photographic evidence of what they expected to transpire in the mountains: the capture and execution of the Pakistani terrorists and their prisoner from Kargil.

The flyover of the Himalayan Eagle AN-12 transport was not only unexpected, it was unprecedented. The transport was over a dozen miles from the secure flight lanes protected by Indian artillery. As the spotter continued to watch the plane, Puri used the secure field phone to radio Minister Kabir's office. The major asked the minister's first deputy what the aircraft was doing there. Neither Kabir nor any of his aides had any idea. The minister himself got on the line. He suspected that the flyover was an independent air force action designed to locate and then help capture the Pakistani cell. He could not, however, explain why that mission would be undertaken by a transport. Kabir told Puri to keep the channel open while he accessed the transport's flight plan.

As he waited, Puri did not believe that the presence of a recon flight would complicate matters. Even if the cell were spotted, his unit would probably reach them first. Puri and his men would explain how the cell resisted capture and had to be neutralized. No one would dispute their story.

Kabir came back on in less than a minute. The minister was not happy. The AN-12 had gone to Ankara and had been scheduled to fly directly to Chushul. Obviously the aircraft had been diverted. The transport's manifest had also been changed to include parachutes in its gear.

A few moments later, Puri understood why.

"Jumpers!" he said into the radio.

"Where?" Kabir demanded.

"They're about one mile distant," the spotter told Puri. "They're using Eagle chutes," he said when the shrouds began to open, "but they are not in uniform."

Puri reported the information to Kabir.

"The Eagles must have spotted the cell," the minister said.

"Very possibly," Major Puri replied. "But they're not wearing Eagle mountain gear."

"They might have picked up an outside team in Ankara," Kabir replied. "We may have been compromised."

"What do we do?" Puri asked.

"Protect the mission," Kabir replied.

"Understood," Puri replied.

The major signed off and told his unit commanders to move their personnel forward. They were all to converge on the site where the parachutists were descending. Puri's orders were direct and simple.

The troops were to fire at will.

THIRTY-SEVEN

The Great Himalaya Range
Thursday, 4:46 P.M.

Ever since they competed on the baseball diamond back in elementary school, Colonel Brett August always knew that he would rise above his longtime friend Mike Rodgers. August just never expected it would happen quite this way and in a place like this.

Striker's delicately ribbed, white-and-red parachutes opened in quick succession. Each commando was jerked upward as the canopies broke their rapid descent. Some of the Strikers were hoisted higher than the others, depending on the air currents they caught. The wind was running like ribbons among them. Separate streams had been sent upward by the many peaks and ledges below. Though Mike Rodgers had been the last man out of the aircraft the general was in the middle of the group when the canopies had fully unfurled. Brett August ended up being the man on top.

Unfortunately, the view from that height was not what Colonel August had expected.

Almost at once, visibility proved to be a challenge. When the parachute tugged Colonel August up, perspiration from his eyebrows was flung onto the tops of his eyepieces. The sweat froze there. That was a high-altitude problem neither he nor General Rodgers had anticipated when they planned the jump. August assumed that frost was hampering the other Strikers as well. But that was not their greatest problem.

Shortly after jumping, Colonel August had seen the line of Indian soldiers converging in their direction. They were clearly visible, black dots moving rapidly on the nearly white background. He was sure that Rodgers and the others could see them too.

The Strikers knew enough to defend the perimeter once they landed. With the stakes as high as they were the Americans would not surrender. What concerned August was what might happen before they landed. Striker was out of range of ordinary gunfire. But the Indian soldiers had probably left the line of control well prepared. They were expecting to fight an enemy that might be positioned hundreds of meters away, on high ledges or remote cliffs. The Indian infantrymen would be armed accordingly.

There was no way for the colonel to communicate with the other members of the team. He hoped that they saw the potential threat and were prepared for action when they landed.

Assuming they did land.

As the seconds passed the descent proved more brutal than August had expected.

Seen from the belly of a relatively warm aircraft, the mountains had been awe-inspiring. Brown, white, and pale blue, the peaks glided slowly by like a caravan of great, lumbering beasts. But seen from beneath a bucking parachute shroud those same mountains rose and swelled like breaching sea giants, frightening in their size and rapid approach. The formations practically doubled in size every few seconds. Then there was the deafening sound. The mountains bellowed at the intruders, roaring with mighty winds that they snatched from the sky and redirected with ease. August did not just hear every blast of air, he felt it. The wind rose from the peaks two thousand feet below and rumbled past him. The gales kicked the shroud up and back, to the north or east, to the south or west, constantly spinning the parachute around. The only way to maintain his bearings was to try and keep his eyes on the target whichever way he was twisted. He hoped the winds would abate at the lower altitudes so that he and the other Strikers could guide their chutes to a landing. Hopefully, the peaks would shield them from the Indian soldiers long enough to touch down and regroup.

The mountains rushed toward them relentlessly. The lower the Strikers went the faster the sharp-edged peaks came toward them. The colors sharpened as the team penetrated the thin haze. The swaying of the chutes seemed to intensify as the details of the peaks became sharper. That was an illusion but the speed with which the crags were approaching was not. Three of the soldiers around him were on-course and had a good chance of reaching the plateau. The others would have to do some careful maneuvering to make it. Two were in danger of missing the mountain altogether and continuing into the valley below. August could not tell which Strikers were in danger since the winds had lifted some of the chutes more than others and thrown them out of jump order. Whoever they were they would have to contact the rest of the team by radio and link up as soon as possible.

As they neared to within one thousand feet of the target, August heard a faint popping sound under the screaming wind. His back was facing the Indian infantry so he could not be certain the sound came from them.

A moment later August was sure.

The air around them filled with black-and-white cloudbursts. They were flak rockets used against low-flying aircraft. The shells were fired from shoulder-mounted launchers like the Blowpipe, the standard one-man portable system of the Indian army. They fired metal pellets in all directions around them. Within a range of twenty-five meters, the fifty-seven shots in each shell hit with the force of .38-caliber bullets.

August had never been so helpless in his life. He watched as the first shell popped among the parachutists. It was followed moments later by another, then by one more. The canopies obscured his view of the Strikers themselves. But he saw how close the bursts came. There was no way his people were not being peppered with the hollow steel shells.

It did not occur to August that the shrapnel could take him down. Or that he could miss the plateau.

He forgot the cold and the wind and even the mission.

All that mattered was the well-being of his team. And there was nothing he could do to ensure their safety right now. August's eyes had darted from canopy to canopy as the rockets burst around them. Five of the lowest shrouds were heavily perforated within seconds. They folded into their own centers and dropped straight down. A moment later the chutes turned up, like inverted umbrellas, as the Strikers below dragged them through free fall.

Two parachutes in the middle of the group were also damaged. They dropped with their cargo onto another two canopies directly below. The shrouds became tangled in the swirling winds. The lines knit and the jumpers spun with increasing speed toward the valley below.

Even if the soldiers themselves had not been hit by shrapnel there was no way for them to survive the fall. August screamed in frustration. His cry merged with the wailing wind and filled the sky above him.

The attack left just himself and three Strikers still aloft. August did not know who they were. He did not know if they had been struck or if they were even alive. At least now they were below the line of the intervening mountains. They were safe from additional ground fire.

There was a fourth burst. It exploded white-and-black above and in front of August. He felt two punches, one in the chest and another in his left arm. He looked down at his chest. There was dull pain but no blood. Perhaps the vest had protected him. Or perhaps the colonel was bleeding underneath the fabric. He did not feel anything after the initial hit and his heart rate seemed the same. Both good signs. In his heart he was too sick over the Strikers he had just lost to care. But he knew he had to care. He had to survive to complete this mission. Not just for his country and the millions of lives in the balance, but for the soldiers and friends whose lives had just been sacrificed.

There were only a few hundred feet to the plateau. He watched as two of the Strikers landed there. The third missed by several meters, despite the efforts of one of the commandos to grab him. August used the guidelines to maneuver toward the cliff wall. He was descending rapidly but he would still rather hit the peak than miss the ledge.

August's left arm began to sting but he kept his attention on the cliff. He had dropped below the mountaintops. The tors were no longer hazards. They were once again towering, stationary peaks that surrounded and protected him from Indian fire. The enemy now was the valley on two sides of the plateau and the outcroppings of rock that could snap his back if he hit one. The updraft from the cliff slowed August, allowing him to guide the parachute down. He decided to stick close to the steep cliff and literally follow it down, thus avoiding the sharp outcroppings toward the center. Every time the wind would brush him toward the valley he would swing himself against the rock wall. The air rushing up the cliff gave him extra buoyancy. August hit the plateau hard and immediately jettisoned the chute. The shroud crumpled and scooted across the ledge, catching on a three-meter-tall boulder and just hanging there.

Before examining himself for injuries, Brett August stripped off his mask and mouthpiece. The air was thin but breathable. August looked across the plateau for the other Strikers. Medic William Musicant and Corporal Ishi Honda were the two who had made it. Both men were near the edge of the plateau. Musicant was on his knees beside the radio operator. The medic had removed the compact medical belt he wore. Honda was not moving.

The colonel got to his feet and made his way over. As he did he felt his chest under his vest. It was dry. The pellet had not gone through the garment. His arm was bleeding but the freezing air had slowed the flow considerably. He ignored the wound for now. Try as he might he could not clear his mind of the other Strikers. Sondra DeVonne. Walter Pupshaw. Mike. The others.

He concentrated on the Strikers who were just a few meters away. And he forced himself to think about what was next. He still had his weapons and he had his assignment. He had to link up with the Pakistani cell.

As August reached the men he did not have to ask how Honda was. The radio operator was panting hard as blood pumped from beneath his vest. The medic was trying to clean two small, raw wounds on Honda's left side. August could not see Honda's dark eyes behind his tinted eyepieces. The frost had evaporated and misted them over.

"Is there anything I can do?" August asked Musicant.

"Yeah," the medic said urgently. "There's a portable intravenous kit in compartment seven and a vial of atropine sulfate in twelve. Get them. Also the plasma in eight. He's got two more holes in his back. I've got to get him plugged and stabilized."

The colonel removed the items. He began setting up the IV. From triage classes he remembered that the atropine sulfate was used to diminish secretions, including blood loss. That would help stabilize the patient if there were internal bleeding.

"Is your arm all right, sir?" Musicant asked.

"Sure," August said. "Who was that you tried to reach at the ledge?"

"General Rodgers," the medic replied.

August perked. "Was the general wounded?"

"He appeared to be okay," Musicant replied. "He was reaching out, trying to get over a few feet more. The goddamn current grabbed his chute. I couldn't get to him."

Then it was possible that Rodgers had survived. August would try and contact him by point-to-point radio.

"After the IV is ready you'd better try and get in touch with those Indian soldiers," Musicant suggested. "If I can stabilize Ishi we'll need to get him to a hospital."

August finished setting up the small IV tripod beside Honda. Then he uncapped the needle. He would use Honda's radio to contact Op-Center and brief them. He would give Herbert their position and ask him to relay a call for medical assistance. But that was all he would do. He and Musicant could not wait here, however. They still had a mission to complete.

When the IV setup was finished August reached for Honda's TAC-SAT. Musicant had already removed the pack and set it aside. The reinforced backpack had taken some hits along one side but the telephone itself appeared to be undamaged. August wondered if Honda had taken pains to protect it, even at the cost of his own life.

Just then, Corporal Honda began to convulse.

"Shit!" Musicant said.

August watched as the radio operator coughed. Flecks of blood spattered his cheek.

"Ishi, hang on," Musicant yelled. "You can do it. Give me another minute, that's all I'm asking."

Honda stopped panting and coughing. His entire body relaxed.

"Take off his vest!" Musicant yelled. Then the medic grabbed for his medical belt and reached into one of the pockets. He withdrew a hypodermic and a vial of epinephrine.

Colonel August began unfastening Honda's vest. As he bent over the stricken soldier he noticed a stream of red seeping out from between the noncom's spread legs. Honda had to have been losing blood at an incredibly fast pace for it to pool that far down.

August watched as the blood crept to below Honda's knees. When the colonel pulled the vest away he found the front underside to be sticky with blood. The pellets from the Indian projectiles had gone up the corporal's torso through his lower back and emerged through his chest. Honda must have been near ground zero of one of the blasts.

Musicant knelt beside Ishi Honda. The medic spread his knees wide so he was steady beside the patient. Then he pulled aside Honda's bloody shirt and injected the stimulant directly into Honda's heart. August held the radio operator's hand. It was cold and still. Blood continued to pool on the ledge. Musicant leaned back on his heels and waited. Honda did not respond. His face was ashen from more than just the cold. The colonel and the medic watched for a moment longer.

"I'm sorry," Musicant said softly to the dead man.

"He was a good soldier and a brave ally," August said.

"Amen," Musicant replied.

August realized how tightly he was holding Honda's hand. He gently released it. August had lost friends in Vietnam. The emotional territory was bitterly familiar. But he had never lost nearly an entire squad before. For August, that loss was all there in the still, young face before him.

Musicant rose and had a look at August's arm. August was surprised how warm the last few minutes had left him. Now that the drama had ended his heart was slowing and blood flow was severely reduced. The cold would set in quickly. They had to move out soon.

While Musicant cleaned and bandaged the wound the colonel turned to the TAC-SAT. He entered his personal access code and the unit came on. Then he entered Bob Herbert's number. As August waited to be connected he removed the radio from his equipment vest.

He placed another call.

One that he prayed would be received.

THIRTY-EIGHT

Washington, D.C.
Thursday, 7:24 A.M.

"Have we heard anything yet?" Paul Hood asked as he swung into Bob Herbert's office.

The intelligence chief was drinking coffee and looking at his computer monitor. "No, and the NRO hasn't seen them yet either," Herbert said. "Still just the Pakistanis."

Hood looked at his watch. "They should be down by now. Has the transport landed yet?"

"No," Herbert replied. "The pilot radioed the tower in Chushul. He said that the cargo had been delivered but nothing more."

"I don't expect they stuck around to verify that our guys touched down," Hood said.

"Probably not," Herbert agreed. "That close to the Pakistani border I'm guessing the plane just turned south and ran."

"Hell, why not," Hood said. "We're only trying to stop their country from being involved in a nuclear war."

"You're stealing my cynicism," Herbert pointed out. "Anyway, they probably don't know what's at stake."

As Herbert was speaking the phone beeped. It was the secure line. He put it on speaker.

"Herbert here."

"Bob, it's August," said the caller. It was difficult to hear him.

"Colonel, you've got a lot of wind there," Herbert said. "You'll have to speak up."

"Bob, we've had a major setback here," August said loudly and slowly. "Indian troops from the LOC peppered us with flak on the way down. Most of our personnel were neutralized. Musicant and I are the only ones on the plateau.

Rodgers missed but he may have reached the valley. We don't know if he's hurt. I'm trying to reach him by radio."

"Say again," Herbert asked. "Two safe, one MIA, rest dead."

"That's correct," August told him.

The intelligence chief looked up at Hood, who was still standing in the doorway. Herbert's face looked drawn. He muttered something in a taut, dry whisper. Hood could not make out what Herbert was saying. Perhaps it was not meant to be heard.

But Hood had heard what August said.

"Colonel, are you all right?" Hood asked.

"Mr. Musicant and I are fine, sir," August replied. "I'm sorry we let you down."

"You didn't," Hood assured him. "We knew this wasn't going to be an easy one."

August's words were still working their way into Hood's sleep-deprived brain. He was struggling for some kind of perspective. Those lives could not simply have ended. So many of them had only just begun. Sondra DeVonne, Ishi Honda, Pat Prementine, Walter Pupshaw, Terrence Newmeyer, and the rest. Hood's mind flashed on their faces. Dossier photos gave way to memories of drilling sessions he had watched, memorial services, barbecues, tackle football games. It was not the same as the death of one man. Hood had been able to focus on the specifics of losing Charlie Squires or Bass Moore. He had concentrated on helping their families get through the ordeal. The scope of this tragedy and of the personal loss was both overwhelming and numbing.

"What's your assessment, Colonel?" Hood asked. His voice sounded strong, confident. It had to for August's sake.

"We'd still like to try and intercept the cell," August went on. "Two extra guns may help them punch through somewhere along the line."

"We're behind you on that," Hood said.

"But there are a lot of infantrymen headed our way," August went on. "Can you contact the Pakistanis and let them know what happened?"

"We'll try," Hood said. "The Pakistani leader has Friday's phone. She is not the most cooperative person we've dealt with."

"Does she know we're coming?" August asked.

"Affirmative," Hood told him.

"Has there been any arrangement with her?" August asked.

The colonel was asking who would be calling the shots once they linked up. "The cell commander and I did not have that conversation," Hood told him. "Use your own initiative."

"Thank you," August said. "One more thing, sir. We're looking at darkness and some heavy winds and cold coming in. I hope you have a contingency plan in place."

"We were just working on that," Hood lied. "But we're still counting on you and Corporal Musicant to pull this one through."

"We'll do our best," August assured him.

"I know that. We also need you two to stay safe," Hood said.

August said he would. He also said he would inform Op-Center if he managed to raise Mike Rodgers. Then he signed off. Hood disengaged the speakerphone. There was a long moment of silence.

"You all right?" Hood asked Herbert.

Herbert shook his head slowly. "We had thirteen people out there," he said flatly.

"I know," Hood said.

"Kids, mostly."

"This was my call," Hood reminded the intelligence chief. "I gave the operation the go-ahead."

"I backed you up," Herbert replied. "Hell, we had no choice. But this is a price they should not have had to pay."

Hood agreed but to say so seemed pathetic somehow. They were crisis management professionals. Sometimes the only barrier between control and chaos was a human shield. As iron-willed as that barricade could be, it was still just sinew and bone.

Hood moved behind the desk. He looked down at the computer. Logic aside, he still felt hollow. Hood and the others had known going in that there were risks involved with this mission. What galled him was that an attack from allied ground forces was not supposed to be one of those risks. No one imagined that the Indian military would shoot at personnel jumping from one of their own aircraft, suspended from the parachutes clearly identified as those belonging to the Indian air force. This phase of the operation was only supposed to pit trained professionals against severe elements. There was going to be a chance for most if not all the Strikers to survive. How did it go so wrong?

"Colonel August was right about us needing a backup plan," Herbert said. "We went off the playbook. We've got to get to work and give him—"

"Hold on," Hood said. "Something's not right."

"Excuse me?" Herbert replied.

"Look at this satellite image," Hood said.

Herbert did.

"The terrorist cell is still moving beneath the overhanging ledges, just as they've done since sunup," Hood said. "But they've also got a little elbow room now. They have these shadows to move in." Hood pointed at the jagged areas of blackness on the monitor. "See how the shadows are lengthening as the sun sets behind the Himalayas?"

"I see," Herbert said. "But I don't get your point."

"Look at the direction of the shadows relative to the sun," Hood told him. "The cell is moving in a westerly direction. Not northwesterly. That's different from before."

Herbert stared for a moment. "You're right," he said. "Why the hell would they be doing that?"

"Maybe there's a shortcut?" Hood suggested. "A secret path through the glacier?"

Herbert brought up the detailed photographic overviews from NASA's Defense Mapping Agency. These photographic maps were marked with coordinates and were used to target satellites. Herbert asked the computer to mark the area that Viens was studying now. Hood leaned over Herbert's wheelchair and looked closely at the monitor as a faint red cursor began to pulse on the region the cell was crossing.

"There's no shortcut," Herbert said. "What the hell are they doing? They're actually taking a longer route to the line of control."

"Will August still intercept them?" Hood asked.

"Yes," Herbert said. The intelligence chief pointed to a region slightly north of where the cell was. "Brett came down here. He's heading southeast. He'll just be meeting them a lot sooner than we expected." Herbert studied the map. "But this still doesn't make sense. This route isn't going to take the Pakistanis through more accessible terrain. It's farther from the LOC, it's not at a lower altitude, and it doesn't look easier to negotiate."

"Maybe they've got a weapons cache or another hideout along the way," Hood suggested.

"Possibly," Herbert said. He went back to the live NRO image. "But they were relatively close to the border where they were. Why would they want to give the Indians more time to catch them?"

The interagency phone line beeped. Herbert punched it on speakerphone. "Yes?" Herbert said.

"Bob, it's Viens," said the caller. "It's getting dark in the target area. The light is now down enough for us to switch to heat-scan without being blinded. We'll be able to track the cell easier."

"Go ahead," Herbert said. He hit the mute button on the phone.

Herbert and Hood continued to look at the overhead map. Hood was studying the area at the foot of the plateau.

"Bob, if we move the satellite will we be able to look into this valley?" Hood asked, pointing at a grid marked "77."

"I don't know," Herbert told him. He glanced over at his boss. "Paul, I want to find Mike too. But we only have the one satellite in the region. Do we want to tie it up looking for him?"

"Mike could have lost or damaged his radio in the fall," Hood said. "If he's alive there might be something he can do for Brett. We need every resource we can get over there."

"Even if they're two thousand vertical miles and God knows how many as-the-crow-flies miles away?" Herbert asked.

"We don't know for certain where Mike is," Hood pointed out. "We need to find out."

Before the intelligence chief could consider what Paul Hood had said, Viens came back on the line.

"Bob, are you looking at the new satellite photos?" Viens asked.

Herbert killed the mute function. "No," he replied and immediately jumped back to the feed from the OmniCom. "Is there a problem?"

"Maybe," Viens said. "Even when the cell was under the ledge we always caught a glimpse of a head or arm so we knew we still had them. What do you see now?"

Herbert and Hood both leaned closer to the monitor as the image formed. The picture looked psychedelic, like something from the sixties. Hot, red shadows were spilling out along a field of green-colored rocks and snow.

The shadows of only three people.

"What the hell's going on there?" Herbert asked.

"I don't know," Viens admitted. "Some of the terrorists could have been lost along the way."

"It's also possible they turned on Friday and the Indian officer," Herbert thought aloud. "Maybe there were casualties. We should try and get them on the radio."

"No," Hood said. "Contact August and let him know there are three individuals ahead. Tell him they may be hostile and that he is to use discretion whether to shadow rather than engage. Stephen, can you get me a look at grid 77 on file map OP-1017.63?"

"I'll bring that map up, see if it's in the OmniCom's focal range," Viens replied. "It'll only take a minute."

"Thank you," Hood said.

Herbert shook his head. "What reason would the cell have for attacking Friday?" he asked.

"Maybe it was Friday who turned against the cell," Hood said. Then he straightened. "Wait a minute," he said. "It could be possible that none of the above happened."

"What do you mean?" Herbert asked.

"Ron Friday must have told the cell that the Indian soldiers were coming toward them," Hood said.

"Right," Herbert said.

"The Pakistanis could not know there was a threat until Friday joined them," Hood went on. "They did not know that getting Nanda to Pakistan was the only way they might be able to stop a nuclear exchange. What would you do with that knowledge, especially if you were also told that an American strike force was coming to link up with you?" Hood said. "If you were smart and bold and probably a little desperate you would try something unexpected."

"Like splitting your forces and using one group to draw the Indian soldiers away," Herbert said.

"Right. Which means that the other four people may be somewhere else, probably holding to the original course," Hood said.

"If that's true, it means we don't want August and Musicant linking up with the splinter group, since they're probably going to want to draw fire from the Indians," Herbert said.

"Correct. Bob, let August know what we're thinking," Hood said. He leaned back over the computer and returned to the NASA map. "Stephen, I need to see into that valley."

"I've got your map up now," Viens said. "I'm looking to see if the coordinates are in the OmniCom computer."

Meanwhile, Herbert punched in Striker's TAC-SAT number. "Paul, you can't be thinking what I think you are," Herbert said.

"I'm sure I am," Hood informed him.

"Assuming he's all right, you don't even know if you can talk to him," Herbert said.

"One thing at a time," Hood said.

"I can do it!" Viens shouted. "I'm sending up the order now. No guarantees about cloud cover and visibility, Paul, but I'll have you in the valley in ninety seconds."

"Thank you," Hood said.

"What are we looking for?" Viens asked.

"A parachute," Hood said. "One that may have Mike Rodgers on the end of it."

THIRTY-NINE

The Mangala Valley
Thursday, 5:30 P.M.

During the Strikers' descent, the AN-12 had made a quick turn to the south. A powerful downdraft from the fast-departing transport had driven Mike Rodgers toward the center of the parachutists. As a result, he was protected from the main thrust of the flak attack. But Rodgers had heard the explosions. He had seen the results as his teammates fell around him. By the time the general had guided himself toward the target, only he and one other striker were still aloft. Despite the heroic efforts of one of the strikers on the ledge, Rodgers had failed to reach the plateau. He had struck his shins and then his right hip and torso on the ledge. Fortunately, his equipment vest took the brunt of the chest hit. But Rodgers was dropping too fast and was not able to hold on. He was also unable to see what happened to the last aloft teammate. At least that chute was on the correct side of the plateau. If he or she were able to disengage from the chute it would probably be all right.

As the rock target disappeared from view, Rodgers studied the terrain immediately below. He had not given up trying to join the others and looked for a ledge he could reach. Unfortunately, Rodgers could not stay as close to the mountain as he would have liked. There were so many rough outcroppings that he ran the risk of snagging and ripping the parachute. Reluctantly, he made the decision to ride the chute to the valley.

While Rodgers descended, he looked for signs of other parachutes below. He had seen the Strikers fall and did not think any of them could have survived the plunge. If he were able to land near them he could be certain. Rodgers refused

to think about the soldiers who were almost certainly lost.
There would be time to grieve later. All that mattered now
was the mission and Rodgers had to find a way of getting
back into it.

The currents diminished the lower Rodgers dropped. As
he descended into the valley the shroud stopped its side-to-
side swaying. The officer hung as straight as a plumb line,
protected by the mountains from the fierce winds that raced
through the outer range. He floated down through the wispy
clouds.

Rodgers glanced at his large, luminous watch. He had been
aloft for nearly fifty minutes. He was at a low enough altitude
to remove his breathing apparatus and goggles. He strapped
them to his belt. The water vapor in the clouds condensed
on Rodgers's exposed face. It cooled the hot perspiration on
his forehead and cheeks, invigorating him. Below him the
clouds began to thin. He could see the terrain rushing up.

This was not going to be easy.

Technically, the formation below was a valley. It was an
elongated lowland between two mountain ranges. A shallow,
fast-running river cut through the center. To Mike Rodgers,
however, the small, barren formation was just a rocky de-
pression in the rugged foothills. The sloping, sharp-edged
terrain made a soft landing impossible and a safe landing
problematic at best. At least the air was calm. He could work
the chute to try to avoid the most precarious spots.

As he dropped under the last level of clouds he saw the
first of the Striker parachutes. It was bunched like an orchid
in the middle of the river. The Striker was apparently below
it. A moment later Rodgers saw the other chutes. Two of
them were tangled together at the foot of one of the mountains. The Strikers were sprawled beside them. Their cold-
weather outfits were smeared with blood. He saw the fourth
Striker beyond and above them. The canopy was caught on
a small outcropping about thirty feet up. Sondra DeVonne
was suspended close beneath it. She was rocking gently at
the end of the shroud lines.

Don't think about this now, Rodgers warned himself. He
had to look ahead, at the cause for which these soldiers had

sacrificed their lives. Otherwise there would be many more casualties.

Further beyond, to the south, he saw smoke curling up from behind a turn in the valley. Something had either exploded or crashed there. He did not think it was the AN-12. If the aircraft had been hit, the Strikers probably would have heard and certainly would have seen it go down. He glanced briefly to the north. He could see the foot of the glacier ahead. That was why this valley was so damned cold. The glacier had probably cracked this place from the mountains eons ago.

The ground was coming up quickly. As much as he did not want to hit the slopes, Rodgers did not want to land in the water. With the sun setting, his suit would freeze in a matter of minutes. He also did not want to hit one of the ragged slopes bordering the river. That was a good way to rip his cold-weather uniform or break some bones. Unfortunately, the cliffs tapered so sharply toward the river there was not much of a bank to land on.

That left him one other option. It was one that Rodgers did not want to take. But the choices in war were never easy. The general made his decision and forced it to go down.

Rodgers guided himself toward the downed parachute that had blossomed in the lake. The fabric straddled the shore on the eastern side. There were glints of ice around the edges still in the water. The shroud looked as though it would be stiff enough to take his fall without dumping him into the river. Hopefully, Rodgers would be able to stay on his feet and jump to the narrow shore before the canopy folded altogether.

With just seconds to impact, Rodgers positioned himself over the chute. On one side he could see an arm lying underwater. The flesh was blue-white. Rodgers did not want to land on the Striker's body. He kept his eyes on the other side of the canopy.

The target site loomed larger and larger. Its rapid approach created the distinct sensation that gravity had really grabbed Rodgers. Now he felt as if he were falling, not floating.

Rodgers landed lightly on the canopy. The rigid fabric gave in the middle where he landed, but the fringes remained flat. Rodgers managed to remain on his feet. He immediately popped his chute and let it blow away. He turned to the side nearest the shore. It took just over a second for the canopy to sink enough for water to begin flowing over the sides. By that time Rodgers had stridden several steps and leaped over the water to solid ground. The foot of the brownish-white granite cliff was less than four feet away. Rodgers walked toward it so that he could see further along the valley.

Landing on the shroud had caused it to drift slightly down-river. As Rodgers looked back he saw a body lying facedown underwater. The dead Striker's clothing was bloated by the water. The shroud lines were the only things moving.

Rodgers did not move him. He did not have time. He reached into his equipment vest and opened a flap to retrieve his radio.

At least, what was left of it.

Mike Rodgers looked at the unit in his gloved hand. The faceplate was shattered. Yellow and green wires were sticking up from the cracked plastic. Several shards of black casing along with broken chips were rattling in the bottom of the radio. The unit must have been damaged when Rodgers's right side collided with the ledge.

Rodgers glanced at the dead striker's equipment vest. The radio pouch was underwater. Even if he took off his uniform to keep it dry and retrieved the radio, it was not likely to work. He looked downriver at the tangled parachutes of the other two Strikers. The partly inflated canopies were rolling back and forth in the brisk wind. The bodies beyond were on the narrow, rocky stretch of dry land on his side of the river. Rodgers jogged toward them. His right side and his leg hurt but he refused to let that slow him down.

Private Terry Newmeyer and Corporal Pat Prementine lay inert at the other end of the chutes. Newmeyer was on his right side. Rodgers gently rolled him to his back. His uniform and cheek were soaked with thick, nearly frozen blood. Like his body, Newmeyer's radio was crushed. It looked as if it had caught a piece of shrapnel. The general gave the dead man's shoulder a gentle pat then moved over to Prementine. The corporal was sprawled on his back. One eye was shut, the other was half-open. Prementine's left arm was lying across his chest, the right was twisted beneath him. But his radio seemed intact. Removing it from the pouch, Rodgers turned toward the valley wall. As he walked toward the cliff, the general switched the radio on. The red light on the top right corner glowed. At least something else in this goddamn valley was still alive, Rodgers thought bitterly.

The general raised the radio to his lips. He pressed "speak."

And he hoped the Indian army was not monitoring this frequency.

FORTY

The Great Himalaya Range
Thursday, 5:41 P.M.

Brett August and William Musicant had begun moving southward along the plateau. A fierce, cold wind was blowing toward them as the air cooled and the thermal currents stopped rising. The men had to put their goggles back on to keep their eyes from tearing as they worked their way toward the ledge some four hundred meters ahead. According to the NRO, that was the northern artery of the same ledge the Pakistani cell was traveling on.

The colonel halted when the TAC-SAT beeped. He crouched and picked up the receiver. It was Bob Herbert. The intelligence chief instructed the men to wait where they were.

"What's going on?" August asked.

"There's a chance the cell may have divided," Herbert informed him. "The group that's coming toward you may be bait to draw the Indian soldiers to the northwest."

"That would make sense," August said.

"Yes, but we don't want you to be caught in the middle of that," Herbert said. "There's also a chance that there may have been a struggle of some kind. We just don't know. We want you to proceed to a forward point that you can defend and then wait there."

"Understood," August said. The point where the plateau narrowed would be ideal for that.

"Paul has asked Stephen Viens to have a look around the area northeast of the plateau," Herbert went on. "We have reason to believe the rest of the cell may be headed that way."

"That's where Mike went down," August said.

"I know," Herbert said. "Paul's thinking is if we can locate Mike he can help us find the branch cell—"

A firm, low, intermittent beep began to sound in a pocket of August's equipment vest.

"Bob, hold on!" August interrupted. "I've got an incoming point-to-point radio transmission."

"Careful, Brett," Herbert said.

The colonel set the phone down. He plucked his radio from the equipment vest and punched it on. He would not let himself hope that it was a Striker. More likely it was someone who'd found one of the radios or an Indian army communications officer cutting into their frequency.

"Atom," August said. That was the code name he had selected. It was derived from the first initial of his last name. The Strikers used code names when they were uncertain about the origin of a call. If any of them were taken prisoner and forced to communicate they would use a backup code name based on the initial of their first name.

"Atom, it's Reptile," the caller said.

August did not feel the wind or the cold. The world that had felt so dead suddenly had a faint pulse.

"Are you okay?" August asked.

"Yeah," Rodgers replied. "But I'm the only one. You?"

"Midnight and I are fine," he replied. As he was speaking, August pulled the area map from a vest pocket. These were specially marked with coded grids. He laid it on the ground and stepped on one end while he held the other. "Do you have your map?" August asked.

"Getting it now," Rodgers said. "I'm at 37–49."

"Three-seven-four-nine," August repeated. "I copy that. Are you secure at that location?"

"I seem to be," Rodgers replied.

"Very good," August said. "I'm going to relay that information home. We may have new instructions."

"Understood," Rodgers said.

Colonel August set the radio on the map and picked up the TAC-SAT receiver. As he did he gave Musicant a thumbs-up. The medic smiled tightly. But at least it was a smile.

"Bob, it was Mike," August said. "He's safe in the valley, about three miles from the foot of the glacier."

"Thank you, Lord," Herbert said. "Other survivors?"

"Negative," August told him.

"I see. All right, Colonel," Herbert said. "Set up your perimeter, hang tight, and tell Mike to do the same. I'll pass the update to Paul."

"Bob, keep in mind that there is some very rough terrain out here and it's going to get dark and cold pretty fast," August said. "If we're going to send Mike on any search-and-recon missions, he's only got another forty minutes or so of visibility."

"I'm aware of the situation," Herbert said. "Tell him to get a good look at the landscape. We'll get back to you ASAP."

August hung up the TAC-SAT and briefed Rodgers. The general was his usual stoic self.

"I'll be okay down here," Rodgers replied. "If I have to move north it's a pretty straight shot to the glacier. I'll just follow the river."

"Good. Is your suit intact?" August asked.

"Yes," Rodgers replied. "There's only one thing I need. It's probably the same thing you need."

"What's that?" August asked.

Rodgers replied, "To find whoever sold us out and make them regret it."

FORTY-ONE

Washington, D.C.
Thursday, 8:30 A.M.

Paul Hood was on the phone with Senator Barbara Fox when the interoffice line beeped.

Now that the mission was beyond the point of recall, and politics would not get in the way of international security, Hood briefed the senator on the status of Striker and its mission. Several years before, the senator had lost her own teenage daughter in a brutal murder in Paris. Hood had expected her to respond with compassion and to give her support to the personnel who were still in the field.

She did not. The senator was furious.

"Op-Center took too much responsibility in this operation," the woman charged. "The other intelligence agencies should have been involved to a much greater extent."

"Senator, I told the CIOC that we have a crisis requiring immediate attention," Hood said. "I said we were involving the NRO and the NSA to the extent that time and on-site manpower permitted. You did not object to our handling of this at that time."

"You did not outline the specifics of the danger," she replied, "only the gravity of the threat."

"We did not know the specifics until we were in the middle of this," Hood pointed out.

"Which is exactly my point," she replied. "You sent resources into this situation without adequate intelligence. And I mean that in every sense of the word, Mr. Hood."

The interoffice line beeped again.

"Do you want me to pull the remaining assets out?" Hood asked the senator. Hell, he thought. If she was going to criticize his judgment he might as well leave the rest of the mission in her hands.

"Is there another way of resolving the crisis?" she asked.

"Not that we've come up with," Hood replied.

"Then unfortunately we are married to the scenario you've mapped out," the senator said.

Of course, Hood thought. It was now a no-lose situation for the politician. If it worked she would grab the credit for involving the CIOC at this juncture, for saving the lives of the rest of the Strikers as well as countless Indians and Pakistanis. If the mission failed Hood would take the full hit. This was not the first crisis the two had been through together. But it was the first one of this magnitude and with this high a price tag. Hood was disappointed that she was looking for a scapegoat instead of a solution.

Or maybe he was the one looking for someone to blame, he thought. What if the senator was right? What if he had fast-tracked this operation simply because Striker was en route and it seemed relatively risk-free at the onset? Maybe Hood should have pulled the plug when he learned how risky the jump itself would be. Maybe he had let himself become a prisoner to the ticking clock he feared instead of the things he knew for certain.

The interoffice line beeped a third time.

Years before, Chad Malcolm, the retiring mayor of Los Angeles, gave Hood some of the best advice he had ever received. Malcolm had said that what any good leader did was take information in, process it, and still react with his gut. "Just like the human body," the mayor had said. "Goes in through the top and out through the bottom. Any other way just isn't natural."

Senator Fox informed Hood that the CIOC would take up this "fiasco" in an emergency session. Hood did not have anything else to say. He clicked the senator off and took the call.

"Yes?" Hood said.

"Paul, we've got him," Herbert said. "Brett spoke with Mike."

"Is he okay?" Hood asked.

"He's fine," Herbert replied. "He landed in the valley at the foot of the plateau."

"Bob, thank you." Hood wanted to shout or weep or possibly both. He settled for a deep sigh and a grateful smile.

"While I was waiting for you to pick up the phone I called Viens," Herbert told him. "Instead of searching for Mike I've got him looking to see if the cell broke off. The way I read my map, there's a point between where Ron Friday joined the cell and where Colonel August is now that would have been perfect for the Pakistani group to split. If one team headed straight toward Pakistan, they would have had a relatively short distance of about nine or ten miles to cross. The two barriers they would face there were the line of control and the Siachin Glacier. But if Indian soldiers have been moved from the LOC to this new forward line, that would leave the border relatively clear."

"Which makes the glacier the big impediment," Hood said.

"Right. But that makes stamina instead of greater numbers the big obstacle," Herbert pointed out. "Under the circumstances, that's the challenge I'd choose to face."

"I agree," Hood said.

"The good news is, Mike is at the foot of the glacier," Herbert went on. "If we find a second group of Pakistanis, he has a good shot at intercepting them."

Hood brought up the map on his computer. He studied it for a moment. "Who's in touch with Mike?"

"Brett is," Herbert said.

"Bob, we're going to have to have Mike move out of the valley now," Hood said.

"Whoa," Herbert said. "You want him on the glacier before we know for sure that the Pakistanis are even there?"

"We don't have a choice," Hood replied.

"We do," Herbert protested. "First, we find the cell. Second, if they exist, we see which way they're going. If they're coming toward the valley, and we've sent him up the glacier, we'd be committing him to some pretty unfriendly terrain for nothing."

"I'm looking at the relief map of the region," Hood said. "They have to take the glacier. The valley route adds another twelve miles or so to the trek."

"Twelve relatively flat, easy miles," Herbert added. "Listen to me, Paul. That glacier is over eighteen thousand feet high."

"I see that."

"The cell was seven thousand, three hundred feet up in the mountains when Friday caught up with them," Herbert went on. "They would have to be out of their minds to go up when they could go down to a valley that's just two thousand feet above sea level."

"Certainly the Indian army would assume that," Hood said.

"Maybe," Herbert said.

"No, they'd have to," Hood insisted. "Think about it. If your manpower were depleted at the LOC would you reinforce the valley exit or the glacier? Especially if you thought the cell was moving in another direction altogether?"

"I just think it's premature to send Mike up there," Herbert said. "Especially if he just ends up walking back down with the cell. What we need to do is have Viens find the cell and see which way they're going. Then we can decide."

"If Viens finds them and if there's time to get Mike up there," Hood said. "The satellite has a lot of terrain to cover."

"Then here's an alternate plan," Herbert said angrily. "Why don't we just have August hold an AK-47 on the group that's heading his way and make them tell him what their plans are?"

"Would you trust what they tell you?" Hood asked.

That obviously caught Herbert by surprise. He was silent.

"Think about it logically, Bob," Hood continued. "If the cell divided they won't want to run into a sizable Indian force. That means taking the glacier route, which is where they would need Mike's help the most. If he doesn't start out now there's a chance he may not catch them."

" 'If,' " Herbert said. " 'Would.' 'May.' There's a lot of conjecture there, Paul. An awful lot."

"Yeah," Hood agreed. "And Barbara Fox just ripped me a new one for letting this mission out of the gate without sufficient intel. Maybe I did. Nuclear war is pretty serious stuff. But right now the goal is very clear. The key person isn't Mike, it's that girl from Kargil. And the mission is to get her safely to Pakistan. If there is a second group of Pakistanis and they go over the glacier, we can't afford to have Mike stuck in the valley or racing to catch them. He's our strongest, maybe our only asset. We need him in play."

"All right, Paul," Herbert said. "It's your call. I'll have Brett relay your orders to Mike."

"Thank you," Hood said.

"But I'm not with you on this one," Herbert added sharply. "My gut isn't telling me much because it can't. It's tied in a big goddamn knot. But my brain is telling me that before we send Mike up that glacier we need more time and intel to properly assess the situation."

Herbert hung up.

Slowly, Paul Hood replaced the receiver. Then he turned to his computer and diminished the map of the Himalayas. He switched programs to receive the direct feed from the NRO.

The OmniCom was just completing its retargeting and a barren, brown-and-white image began to fill the screen. Hood watched through tired eyes as the pixels filled in. Right now he wished that he were there, in the field with Mike Rodgers. The general had an organization solidly behind him, people praying for him, honor and pride at the end of the day, whichever way events took him.

But no sooner did Paul Hood stumble onto that thought than two others bumped it aside. First, that he had no right to be thinking about himself. Not after the sacrifice Striker had made or the risks Mike Rodgers, Brett August, and the others were taking.

Second, that he had to finish the operation he had started. And there was only one way to do that.

With resolve greater than that of the people who had started it.

FORTY-TWO

The Great Himalaya Range
Thursday, 6:42 P.M.

Brett August had become a soldier for two very different reasons.

One was to help keep his country strong. When August was in the sixth grade he read about countries like England and Italy that had lost wars. The young New Englander could not imagine how he would feel saying the Pledge of Allegiance each morning, knowing that the United States had ever been defeated or was under the heel of a conquering nation.

The other reason Brett August became a soldier was that he loved adventure. As a kid he grew up on cowboy and war shows on television, and comic books like *GI War Tales* and *4-Star Battle Tales*. His favorite activities were to build snow forts in the winter and tree forts in the summer. The latter were carefully woven together from the limbs shorn from poplar trees in the backyard. He and Mike Rodgers took turns being Colonel Thaddeus Gearhart at Fort Russell or William Barrett Travis at the Alamo, respectively. Rodgers liked the idea of acting a young officer dying dramatically as he battled vastly superior numbers.

The reality of everything August had anticipated was different from the way he had always imagined them.

The greatest threats against the United States were not from forces outside our borders but from those within. He had seen that when he returned from captivity in Vietnam. There were no honors awaiting him. There was condemnation from many of August's old acquaintances for having fought in an immoral war. There was condemnation from some corners of the military because August wanted to go back and finish the job he had started. They wanted to bomb the Cong into submission. The melting pot of America had become the melting point. People fighting rather than learning from their differences.

As for adventure, there was valor but little drama or glory in slaughter and captivity. Death was not big and flamboyant, it was ugly and lonely. The dying did not pause to salute the proud flag of Colorado or Texas but screamed about his wound or cried for a loved one a world away. Fear for himself and his friends made it impossible for August ever to feel anything but unadorned gratification whenever his patrol returned to base.

At the moment, August was driven by just one force: the battle-seasoned resolve of a professional soldier. Even his survival instinct was not that strong. Most of his unit were dead. Living with that loss was going to be difficult. He wondered, unhappily, if that was why William Barrett Travis had reportedly charged the Mexican army single-handedly at the onset of the battle for the Alamo. Not due to courage but to spare himself the pain of having to watch his command fall.

August decided this was not the time to think of hopeless charges. He needed to be in the here-and-now and he needed to win.

Poised behind a jagged-edged boulder twice his size, August watched the narrow, curving ledge just ahead. His visibility was only about fifty yards due to the sharp turn in the ledge. Soon darkness would be a problem. The sun was nearly down and he would have to put on his night-vision goggles. He wanted to wait in order to save the batteries. They might be forced to fight the Indian skirmish line before night's end.

Musicant was behind an even larger boulder. It was situated twenty-odd yards to August's left. Between them the Strikers could set up a crossfire between the end of the ledge and the plateau. No one would be able to get through without identifying themselves and being disarmed, if necessary.

To August's right was the TAC-SAT. He had switched the phone from audio to visual signal in order to maintain a position of silent-standing. The visual signal was on dim. If it shined, the light would not be seen from the other side of the boulder.

A steady wind blew from behind the men. It raised fine particles of ice from the plateau and swept them from the peaks. The icy mist rose in sharp arcs and wide circles, flying high enough to glimmer in the last light of the sun before dropping back to the dark stone. August was glad to see the airborne eddies. They would limit the visibility of anyone coming along the ledge.

August was crouched against the cold stone when the TAC-SAT flashed. He snatched the receiver without taking his eyes from the ledge.

"Yes!" he shouted. He had to press a hand against his hood to shut his open ear.

"Brett, it's Bob. Anything?"

"Not yet," August replied. "What about with you?"

"We need you to radio Mike," Herbert said. "We think a splinter cell might be headed toward the Siachin Glacier. Viens is looking for them. In the meantime, Paul wants Mike to head up there."

"That's a helluva trek," August said.

"Tell me about it," Herbert replied. "If there is a separate group, Paul's afraid Mike will miss them unless he leaves now. Tell Mike that if Viens spots them we'll pass along their location."

"Very good," August replied. "And if this cell knows anything I'll let you and Mike know."

"Fine," Herbert said. "I've tried to raise them on the radio but they're not answering. Listen, Brett. If Mike doesn't think he can do this I want to hear about it."

"Do you really think Mike Rodgers would turn down an assignment?" August asked.

"Never," Herbert said. "That's why I need you to listen between the lines. If there's a problem, tell me."

"Sure," August said.

August hung up and slipped the radio from the belt. Mike had the best "poker voice" in the United States armed forces. The only way August might find out if he had a problem with a mission was to ask him outright. Even then, Rodgers might not give him an answer.

Rodgers answered and August gave him Hood's instructions.

"Thank you," Rodgers replied. "I'm on it."

"Mike, is it doable without more gear? Herbert wants to know."

"If I don't answer the radio again, it wasn't," the general replied.

"Don't be an ass-pain," August warned.

"If you can feel your ass you're doing a lot better than I am," Rodgers replied.

"Point, Rodgers," August told him. "Stay in touch."

"You, too," Rodgers replied.

August switched the radio to vibrate rather than beep. Then he slipped it back into his belt. He was still watching the ledge. The wind had grown stronger over the past few minutes. The ice crystals were no longer blowing in gentle patterns. They were charging past the boulder in sharp diagonal sheets. The fine particles struck the cliff and bounced off hard at a right angle. They created the illusion of a scrim hanging in front of the ledge.

Suddenly, a dark shape appeared behind the driving ice. It was blacker than the surrounding amber-black of sunset. It did not appear to be holding a weapon, though it was too dark to be certain.

August motioned to Musicant, who nodded that he saw it.

For the colonel the rest of the world, the future, and philosophy vanished. He had only one concern.

Surviving the moment.

FORTY-THREE

The Great Himalaya Range
Thursday, 6:57 P.M.

Sharab had lost all sense of time. She knew that they had
been walking for hours but she had no idea how many. The
woman's thighs burned from the struggle of the upward and
then downward trek, and her feet were blistered front and
back. Every step generated hot, abrasive pain. Sharab did not
know how much longer she could continue. Certainly getting
down to where she believed the Indian army was situated
would be virtually impossible. She would have to find some
way of slowing the enemy down from up here.

The men behind her were not faring any better. They had
discarded their flashlights and heavier shoulder-mounted
weapons. They had also left behind all but a few of the explosives they planned to use to attract the attention of the
Indian soldiers. They'd eaten the food so they would not
have to carry it. The water had frozen in their canteens and
they had left those behind as well. When they were thirsty
they simply broke off the icicles they found in small hollows.
All they carried were a rifle with a pocketful of shells as well
as a handgun apiece and two extra clips. If there were an
army coming toward them, Sharab knew she would not be
able to overcome them. All she could hope to do now was
draw them off and delay them long enough to give the American, Nanda, and the others a chance to get to Pakistan.

Surviving was also increasingly unlikely. If the Indians did
not kill them the elements would.

Sharab even had some question now whether they would
even find this elusive Indian army. They had heard some kind
of artillery fire earlier. She wondered if the elite American
unit had landed and engaged the enemy. She hoped not. The

last thing she wanted was to send the Indians back to the line of control. That would only cause the military to bring in reinforcements. On the other hand, if any of the Americans had managed to land, that was good. They could certainly use the help fighting the Indians.

Unfortunately, Sharab could not find out what had happened. The radio she had used to communicate with Washington had become such a burden that she had left it behind.

Particles of wind-blown ice coated her wool hood and clung there. The cold had already numbed her scalp and frozen her sweat-soaked hair. The weight of the hood was such that it kept her head bent forward. That was good. It protected her eyes and cheeks from the sting of the ice pellets.

Sharab was feeling her way along the cliff and also using it for support. Ali was behind her, holding the hem of her parka. Every now and then she felt a tug as he halted or stumbled. Hassan was behind Ali. Sharab knew he was still there because she could hear him praying.

As the ledge widened, Sharab heard another sound. At first it sounded like a sudden, sharp quickening of the wind. But then she heard it again, louder. It was not the wind. Someone was shouting.

Sharab stopped and raised her eyes. She shielded them with her hand and peered ahead.

The young woman saw a cottage-sized boulder with something large moving behind the right side. Sharab could not make out what it was. She replayed the howl in her mind. Asian black bears and deer did not live this high. Perhaps it was a wild pig or goat.

It could also be a man.

It howled again. Sharab pulled off her hood and turned her right ear toward the boulder. She also removed her glove, tucked it in her left pocket, and drew the handgun from her right pocket.

"Who are you?" the figure shouted.

Sharab backed away. "Who wants to know?" she shouted back. The woman was surprised at the effort it took to yell. It actually caused her heart to race. Her voice sounded flat in the close, cold air.

"We are with the man who joined you before," the other man said. "Where is he?"

"Which man?" Sharab asked. "There were two." The man was speaking in English with an American-sounding accent. That was encouraging.

"We only know about one of them," the speaker said.

"What was his name?"

The man hesitated. Obviously, someone was going to have to make the first move to prove who they were. It was not going to be Sharab.

"Friday," the man said.

Sharab stepped forward again very tentatively. "He is not with us!"

"What happened to him?"

"He left," she replied. "Let's talk face-to-face."

"Come closer with your hands raised," the American said.

The speaker did not step from behind the boulder. It was the woman's turn to trust him.

Sharab protected her eyes again and tried to look past the boulder. She saw a second, smaller boulder off to the right but no sign of any other men. There could not be that many soldiers behind the two rocks. But the two boulders would provide good cover for a crossfire.

Sharab told Hassan and Ali to stay where they were. They nodded. Both men had drawn their weapons and were huddled close to the rock. Ali had moved out slightly to provide her some backup.

"If anything happens to me, fight your way out of this," she added. "You must keep the Indian army occupied."

The men nodded again.

The speaker was a few hundred yards away. Sharab did not put her gun away. She raised her hands shoulder-high and began moving toward the nearest boulder. It was difficult to see because of the blowing ice and she had to turn her face toward the side. Her scarf had fallen away and was whipping behind her. The ice particles lashed her flesh. Her cheek felt as if it were on fire. Sharab finally had to lower her left arm to protect it. There was no mountainside to lean against so her sore feet were taking all of her weight. She shambled from side to side to keep from putting all of her weight straight down. At least the terrain was level. That made it easier on her leg muscles.

Her eyes tearing from wind and pain, Sharab staggered the last few yards to the boulder. She fell against it and her knees just shivered and unlocked. She began to slide down the side. Strong, gloved hands reached around and helped to hold her up. She was still holding the gun. But even if Sharab had wanted to defend herself, her finger was too cold to pull the trigger.

A man in white winter gear pulled her behind the boulder. He sat her down and used his body to protect her from the wind. He bent close to her ear.

"Are you the leader?" he asked.

"First tell me who you are," Sharab said. She was barely able to say the words. Her lips were trembling.

"I am Colonel August of the U.S. Striker team," he said.

"I am the leader of these FKM fighters," Sharab replied weakly. She squinted across the dark plateau. She saw another man crouched there.

"That's Mr. Musicant, my medic," August said. "If any of your people need attention, I'll send him over."

"I think we're all right, except for the cold," the woman said. "Fingers, feet, mouth."

The man leaned nearer. He exhaled hotly on her lips. It felt good. He did it again.

"How many men have you?" Sharab asked.

"Three," he replied.

She fired him a look. "Just three?"

He nodded.

"The sounds we heard—?" she asked.

"Indian ground fire," he said. "It took out most of my team. Where is Mr. Friday?"

"We split the group," Sharab told him. "He is with the other half. They went in another direction."

"Over the glacier?" the colonel asked.

Sharab nodded.

"Is that how they're getting back to Pakistan?" August pressed.

The woman did not answer immediately. She looked up into his face. He was wearing goggles and she could not see his eyes. His mouth was straight, unemotional. His skin was pale but rough. He was definitely an American and he had seen some hardship.

"What will you do with the information?" she asked him.

"The third survivor of our drop landed in the valley," August replied. "He'll try and link up with your teammates."

"I see," she said. "Yes. The others are going to try and stay on the glacier until they are home."

"Do you have any way of contacting them?" August asked.

She shook her head.

"And what were you trying to do?" he asked. "Draw the Indian soldiers away from the other group, toward the northwest?"

"Yes," Sharab said. "We're carrying explosives. We thought we could attract their attention, maybe cause some rock slides."

"That won't be necessary," August informed her. "The Indian force is heading toward us. It'll be pretty tough for them to get up here so we'll be able to keep them busy while they bring in choppers from the LOC." August reached for his radio. "Do you and your men need food or water?"

"Food would be nice," she admitted.

August left the radio in his belt. He opened a vest pocket and removed several sticks of jerky. "Give some to your teammates and ask them to join us," he said as he handed her the flat, wrapped servings. "We should set up a defensive perimeter on this plateau. The Indians saw us come down here. I'm pretty sure that if we wait they'll come to us. That will give us a chance to rest, especially if they wait until morning to come after us."

"All right," Sharab said.

She started to stand. August helped her up. As he did, she looked up at him. "I'm sorry about your people."

"Thank you," he replied.

"But be consoled," she said. "Their death in the service of our people will earn them a place in Paradise. 'The steadfast who do good works, forgiveness and a rich reward await them,' " Sharab assured him.

The American smiled tightly. He left the woman supporting herself against the rock while he retrieved his radio.

Sharab winced as she put weight back on her swollen feet. She began hobbling back toward the ledge. But at least now she knew one thing that she did not know a few minutes ago.

The pain would end very soon.

FORTY-FOUR

Washington, D.C.
Thursday, 10:30 A.M.

It had been a grueling ninety minutes for Paul Hood. But then, suffering was relative, he told himself. He was in no physical danger. His children were safe. That helped him to keep his situation in perspective.

After his disagreement with Bob Herbert, Paul Hood had asked Liz Gordon, Lowell Coffey, Ann Farris, and political liaison Ron Plummer to come to his office. Hood had wanted to tell them what had happened to Striker. He also needed to mobilize them at once. Liz would have to put together grief counselors for Op-Center personnel as well as family members of the fallen Strikers. Coffey would have to be prepared to deal with any legal ramifications that might arise from recovering the bodies. And for the first time in years Ann would have to do nothing. As far as domestic officials and foreign governments were concerned, Op-Center would stand by the original mission profile. The team had been sent into Kashmir at the request of the Indian government to search for nuclear missile sites. Striker had been shot accidentally by Indian soldiers who were looking for the Pakistani terrorists. If Ann owed anyone at one of the major news outlets any favors she could tell them what Op-Center was saying to government officials. That, and nothing more. Ann was thoroughly professional and supportive. If she suspected there was anything wrong between her and Hood she did not show it.

Only the president had been told the truth. Lawrence and Hood had spoken briefly before the others had come to Hood's office. The president seemed neither shaken nor pleased by what Hood told him. Lawrence said only that he supported the plan from this point forward. The president's "no comment" did not surprise Hood. It would give him the room to praise or lambaste the NCMC at the end of the day, depending upon how things went.

President Lawrence did suggest, however, that the Pakistani ambassador to Washington be told the truth at once. He did not want Islamabad or Ambassador Simathna issuing statements about America's anti-Muslim activities or pro-India bias. If Mike were to show up with the cell after that it would taint the validity of the operation. It would seem as if America had forced Nanda to lie to repair bridges with Pakistan and the Muslim world.

Hood gave that job to Ron Plummer. He also wanted Plummer to stay with the ambassador, ostensibly to brief him on all the latest developments. In fact, Hood wanted to make certain the truth did not leak out prematurely. He was afraid that India might respond with a massive strike in the region. Since the terrorists were still on the run, and still being blamed for all the bombings, New Delhi would have the moral high road and world opinion on their side.

As the meeting was ending Hood received a call from Bob Herbert.

"I just spoke with Brett August and I've got some good news," Herbert informed him. "He's linked up with the cell."

Hood motioned for Ron Plummer not to leave and to shut the door. The small, slender political liaison closed the door behind Lowell Coffey. Plummer remained standing.

"Thank God for that," Hood said. "Bob, Ron's in here with me. I'm putting you on speakerphone."

"Okay," Herbert said. "Anyway, we were right," he went on. "The Pakistanis did spin off another group. Nanda Kumar and her grandfather are part of it, along with Ron Friday and one Pakistani. And you were correct, Paul. They're headed across the Siachin Glacier."

"Did Brett talk to Mike?" Hood asked.

"Not yet," Herbert replied. "They've got electrostatic interference from an ice storm on the plateau. Brett says the ice comes in waves. He's going to keep trying for a window."

Hood suddenly felt very guilty about his warm office and fully functional telephone.

"Paul, I have a suggestion," Herbert said. "I think we should ask the Pakistanis for help in extracting the teams. After all, it's their butts we're hauling out of the fire."

"We can't do that," Plummer told him.

"Why not?" Herbert asked.

"If the situation is as tense as Paul's described, an incursion by the Pakistani air force would only make it worse. It would give the Indian military more incentive to attack."

"At least then it would be a conventional fight," Herbert said.

"Not necessarily," Plummer said, "especially if there are Pakistani silos somewhere in the mountains. Also, we'd be giving Pakistan foreknowledge of a possible nuclear strike. That might encourage Islamabad to hit first."

"A jihad," Hood said.

"The clerics might call it that," Plummer said. "For the generals it would simply be a responsible tactical maneuver. The situation is hair-trigger enough without throwing more partisan armies into the fray."

"What about the United States sending additional forces into the mountains?" Hood suggested.

"That's not going to happen," Herbert said gravely. "Even if the Joint Chiefs and the president okayed a strike force out of Turkey or the Middle East, it would take hours for them to get there."

"There's one thing I'm missing here," Plummer said. "Why do we need a military response? Can't we let India know what their Special Frontier Force unit did? I'm sure that very few government officials knew about the plot to frame the terrorists."

"I'm sure it was a very tight conspiracy," Hood agreed. "The problem is we have no idea who was in it."

"Someone is obviously tapped into the Op-Center–New Delhi pipeline," Herbert said. "How else could they have known about Striker's mission? Anyway, before the bombing the moderate Indians might have done something. But Kev Custer has been monitoring the TV and radio broadcasts over there. There's a fast-growing grassroots movement in support of the militants."

"Meaning that moderates may be afraid to speak out," Hood said.

"Exactly," Herbert said.

"What about the United Nations secretary-general?" Plummer said. "You know her, Paul. Forget the bad blood between you. She's Indian. She'll have a very good reason to get out the facts about the attack."

"Mala Chatterjee?" Herbert said. "She's so soft on terrorism her speeches turn even bleeding hearts into a lynch mob. She flapped her lips while hostages were being assassinated in the Security Council."

"Chatterjee has far too many enemies of her own," Hood agreed. "At this point her involvement would only make things worse."

"I'll say it again, Paul. Maybe the Russians would be willing to help rein India in," Herbert said. "They want to be seen as serious peacemakers."

"Possibly," Hood said. "But even if we went to them, wouldn't time be a problem?"

"Time and recent history," Plummer said. "Pakistan has very close ties with Afghanistan. There are still a lot of Russian leaders who would like to see both countries pounded flat."

"But a continued stalemate between India and Pakistan means a continued weapons buildup," Herbert said. "Money talks. New Delhi would still have to buy weapons and matériel from Moscow."

"True, but then there's the point that Paul raised," Plummer said. "The same debate that we're having would keep the Kremlin busy for days if not longer. We don't have that kind of time."

"Well, Ron, I'm kind of running dry and getting a little frustrated," Herbert snapped.

"And I'm just doing the devil's advocate thing, Bob," Plummer replied defensively. "We can run some of these proposals up the flagpole in Moscow and at the Pentagon, but I don't see any of them getting the kind of support we need."

"Unfortunately, that's the problem with crisis management instead of crisis prevention," Hood said sadly. "Once you're in it there are not a lot of options."

"I count exactly one," Herbert said.

The intelligence chief was right, of course. With all the resources the United States had at its disposal, there was only one asset standing between India, Pakistan, and a possible nuclear exchange. One asset currently out of touch, under-equipped, and on his own.

General Mike Rodgers.

FORTY-FIVE

The Siachin Glacier
Thursday, 9:11 P.M.

During the flight from Washington, Mike Rodgers had read a number of white papers on the Siachin Glacier. The most interesting was written by a Pakistani intelligence officer.

Dubbed "the world's highest battleground" by both the Indian and the Pakistani press, the Siachin Glacier has no strategic value. Long claimed by Pakistan, the glacier reaches nearly eighteen thousand feet in height, the temperatures drop below minus thirty-five degrees Celsius, and the near-constant blizzards and lack of oxygen make the region "subhuman," as one Indian report put it. No one lives there and no one crosses it on foot.

The glacier became a war zone in 1984 when Indian intelligence officers began showing up in the region. Their thinking, apparently, was to force Pakistan to assign human resources to the region, thus making them unavailable for war in habitable Kashmir and along the line of control. However, Pakistan discovered the presence of the Indian reconnaissance teams early in the process thanks to a mountaineering advertisement that appeared in an Indian magazine. The full-page ad showed recent photographs of the region without naming it. The text offered experienced climbers excellent compensation and the adventure of a lifetime to help lead tours through "uncharted territories." Pakistani counterespionage operatives began tracking and capturing the Indian recon teams. The conflict escalated and soon the region was drawing resources from both sides of the dispute. Nearly twenty years later, thousands of troops and aircraft from both sides were assigned to patrol the massive formation.

If they were out there now, Rodgers could neither see nor hear them. He had been in many isolated places during his long military career but he had never experienced anything like this. Standing at the foot of the glacier he was not just alone, surrounded by mountain and ice, but he could only see as far as his flashlight let him. And he was unable to get anything but static on his radio. He shined the light up the sloping white ice. The foot of the glacier reminded him of a lion's paw. There were long, large lumps of dirty white ice about ten feet high with crevasses between them. They led to a gently sloping area that rose higher and higher into the darkness. The formation made him feel fragile and insignificant. The glacier had probably looked exactly like this when the first humans were tossing sticks and berries at each other from trees in the valley.

Suddenly, Rodgers's radio beeped. He grabbed it quickly. "Yes?"

"The target is up there," said the caller.

The transmission was broken and the voice was barely recognizable. But Rodgers had no doubt that it was Brett August. The colonel did not know how long he would be able to transmit. So he got right to the heart of the communication without wasting words.

"Copy that," Rodgers said.

"Team of four," August said. "Girl and grandfather, Friday, and one cell member."

"I copy," Rodgers said again. "I'm at the foot of the zone. Should I go up now?"

"If you wait till sunup you may miss them," August said. "I'm sorry."

"Don't be," Rodgers said.

"Will try and keep enemy busy," August went on. His voice began to break up. "Storming here—cell exhausted. Ammo low."

"Then bail out," Rodgers said. "I'll be okay."

August's response was lost in static.

"I've got a good head start," Rodgers went on. He was shouting each syllable, hoping he would be heard. "Even if they enter the valley now they won't catch up to me. I'm ordering you to pull back. Do you read? Pull back!"

There was no response. Just a loud, frustrating crackle.

Rodgers turned down the volume and kept the channel open for another few moments. Then he shut the radio off to conserve the batteries and slipped the unit back in his belt.

Rodgers hoped that August would not try to stick this one out. Going back down the mountain might not be an option for August and the others. But finding a cave and building a fire would be a better use of their energies than hanging on to a slope and trying to draw the Indian army toward them. Unfortunately, Rodgers knew the colonel too well. August would probably regard retreat as abandonment of a friend as well as a strategic position. Neither of those was acceptable to August.

The plateau was also the place where the Strikers had died. That made it sacred ground to August. There was no way he would simply turn and walk away from it. Rodgers understood that because he felt the same way. It made no sense to fight for geography without strategic value. But once blood had been spilled there, one fought for the memory of fallen comrades. It validated the original sacrifice in a way that only combat soldiers could understand.

Rodgers took a moment to walk along the bottom of the glacier. It did not seem to matter where he started. He had to pull himself up one of the "toes" and start walking.

There were collapsible steel bipoint ice crampons in his vest. Rodgers removed them and slipped them over his rigid boots. The two-pronged claws on the bottoms would allow for a surer grip on the ice.

He strapped them on and removed the pitons from another pocket. He would hold them in his fists and use them to assist his climb. He would not take the time to hammer them in unless he had to.

Before he left, Rodgers secured the flashlight in his left-hand shoulder strap. There were powerful cadmium batteries in the specially made lights. The bulb itself was a low-intensity scatter-beam in front of a highly polished mirror. They would definitely last through the night. As he rested the toe of his left boot on the "toe" of the glacier, he took one last look up the mountain of ice.

"I'm going to beat you," he muttered. "I'm going to get up there and finish the job my team started."

Rodgers's eyes continued up through the darkness. He saw the stars, which were dimly visible through the wispy clouds. Time seemed to vanish and Rodgers suddenly felt as if he were every warrior who had ever undertaken a journey, from the Vikings to the present. And as he jabbed the base of one crampon into the ice and reached up with a piton, Mike Rodgers no longer saw stars. He saw the eyes of those warriors looking down on him.

And among them the eyes of the Strikers looking after him.

FORTY-SIX

Washington, D.C.
Thursday, 12:00 P.M.

The embassy of the Islamic Republic of Pakistan is located in a small, high-gated estate on Massachusetts Avenue in northwest D.C.

Ron Plummer drove his Saab to the gate, where a voice on the other end of the intercom buzzed him through. He headed up the curving concrete driveway to a second security checkpoint at the back of the mansion.

Plummer pulled up to the white double doors and was greeted by a security guard. The man was dressed in a black business suit. He wore sunglasses, a headset, and a bullet-proof vest under his white shirt. He carried a handgun in a shoulder holster. The man checked Plummer's ID then directed him to a visitor's spot in the small lot. The guard waited while Plummer parked.

As he hurried back to the mansion, Ron Plummer ran a hand through his untamed, thinning brown hair and adjusted his thick, black-framed glasses. The thirty-nine-year-old former CIA intelligence analyst for Western Europe was not just feeling the pressure of his own part in this drama. The political and economics officer was also aware of how many things had to go right or the Indian subcontinent would explode.

The National Crisis Management Center had not had a lot of dealings with the Pakistani embassy. The only reason the ambassador, Dr. Ismail Simathna, personally knew them was because of Paul Hood and Mike Rodgers. After the men had ended the hostage stalemate at the United Nations, Simathna asked them to visit the embassy. Plummer was invited to join them. The ambassador claimed to be paying his respects to

a brave and brilliant American intelligence unit. Among the
many lives they had saved were those of the Pakistani ambassador to the United Nations and his wife. But Hood and
Plummer both suspected that Simathna simply wanted to
meet the men who had embarrassed the Indian secretary-
general. That feeling was reinforced when the visit received
considerable coverage in the Islamabad media. Hood was
glad, then, that Plummer had come along. Op-Center's PEO
gave the appearance of substance to a meeting that was conceived to make a statement about India's ineffective contri-
bution to world peace.

The security officer turned Plummer over to the ambassador's executive secretary. The young man smiled pleas-
antly and led Plummer to Simathna's office. The
white-haired ambassador came out from behind his glass-
topped desk. He was wearing a brown suit and a muted yellow tie. The sixty-three-year-old ambassador had been a
frontline soldier and bore a scar on both cheeks where a
bullet had passed through his jaw. He had also been an intelligence expert and a professor of politics and political so-
ciology at Quaid-E-Azam University in Islamabad before
being tapped to represent his nation in Washington, D.C. He
greeted Op-Center's political officer warmly.

Plummer had not told Ambassador Simathna why he
needed to see him, only that it was urgent.

The men sat in modern armchairs on the window side of
the office. The thick bullet-proof glass muted their voices.
As Plummer spoke he sounded almost conspiratorial.

The ambassador's lean face was serious but unemotional
as Plummer spoke. He leaned forward, listening quietly, as
Plummer told him about the Striker operation from concep-
tion to present, and Hood's fears about the actions of India's
SFF. When Plummer was finished, the ambassador sat back.

"I am disappointed that you did not come to me for intelligence on the nuclear situation in Kashmir," the ambassador
said.

"We did not want to impose on your friendship," Plummer
replied. "It means a great deal to us."

"That was thoughtful of you," he replied with a little smile. "But you have come to me now."

"Yes," Plummer replied. "For your advice, your confidence, your patience, and most of all your trust. We believe we have a good chance to keep this under control but the hours ahead will be extremely difficult."

"One could describe nuclear brinkmanship in those terms," the ambassador said softly. "Your Strikers were quite brave, going into the mountains the way they did. And the surviving members give me hope. Nations are not monolithic, not even India and Pakistan. When people care enough about one another great things can be accomplished."

"Paul Hood and I share your optimism," Plummer said.

"Even at this moment?"

"Especially at this moment," Plummer replied.

Throughout the exchange Plummer had watched the ambassador's dark eyes. Simathna's mind was elsewhere. Plummer feared that the ambassador was thinking of alerting his government.

The ambassador rose. "Mr. Plummer, would you excuse me for a few minutes?"

Plummer also stood. "Mr. Ambassador, one more thing."

"Yes?"

"I don't wish to push you, sir, but I want to make certain I've made the situation clear," Plummer said. "It is vital that your government take no action until our people in the field have had a chance to extract the Indian operative."

"You have made that quite clear," the ambassador replied.

"There is the very real danger that even a leaked word could turn this into a self-fulfilling nightmare," Plummer added.

"I agree," Simathna assured him. The tall Pakistani smiled slightly and started toward the door.

"Mr. Ambassador, please tell me what you're going to do," Plummer implored. The American was going to feel very foolish if Simathna were going to get an aspirin or visit the lavatory. But Plummer had to know.

"I am going to do something that will require your assistance," Simathna replied.

"Anything," Plummer said. "What can I do?"

The ambassador opened the door and looked back. "You must give me something that you just requested of me."

"Of course," Plummer told him. "Name it." While the PEO waited he replayed the conversation in his mind on fast-forward, trying to remember what the hell he had asked the ambassador for.

"I need your trust," Simathna said.

"You have it, sir. That's why I came here," Plummer insisted. "What I need to know is if we're on the same tactical page."

"We are," Simathna replied. "However, I have access to footnotes that you do not."

With that, the Pakistani ambassador left his office and quietly shut the door behind him.

FORTY-SEVEN

The Siachin Glacier
Thursday, 10:57 P.M.

Ron Friday's anger kept him from freezing.

The NSA operative was not angry when he started this leg of the mission. He had been optimistic. He had effectively taken charge of the mission from Sharab. Even if the woman survived her encounter with the Indian army, Friday would be the one who led the cell into Pakistan. The triumph would be his. And the journey appeared feasible, at least according to the Indian military reconnaissance maps he had taken from the helicopter. The line of control did not appear to be heavily guarded at the Bellpora Pass. The region was extremely wide and open and easy to monitor from the air. Captain Nazir had told Friday that anyone passing through the jagged, icy region risked being spotted and picked off. So Friday and his group would have to remain alert. If the cell was still in the pass during a flyover, they would find a place to hide until it was finished.

However, Friday became less enthusiastic about the operation as the hours passed. He was accustomed to working alone. That had always given him a psychological advantage. Not having to worry about or rely on someone else enabled him to make fast tactical turns, both mentally and physically. It had been the same with his romantic relationships. They were paid for by the hour. That made them easy, to the point, and, most importantly, over.

Samouel was holding up well enough. He was in the lead. The Pakistani was deftly poking the ground with a long stick he had picked up, making sure there were no pockets of thin ice. Friday was directly behind him. There were two unlit torches tucked under his right arm. They were made with sturdy branches the men had picked up before the tree line ended. They were capped by tightly wound strangler vines. The thick vines glowed rather than burned. Friday had stuffed very dry ryegrass between the vines to serve as primers. The torches would only be used in an emergency. Friday had five matches in his pocket and he did not want to waste them.

Nanda and her grandfather were at the rear of the line. Nanda herself was doing all right. She was a slight woman and she lost body heat quickly. But she had a fighting spirit and would have kept up the pace if not for Apu. The elderly farmer was simply exhausted. If not for his granddaughter the Indian probably would have lain down and died.

As darkness had descended over the ice and the temperature had fallen, Friday had become increasingly disgusted with the Kumars. He had no tolerance for Apu's infirmity. And Nanda's devotion frustrated him. She had a responsibility to end the crisis she had helped cause. Every minute they spent nursing Apu across the glacier slowed their progress and drained the energies of Nanda, Friday, and the other man.

The farmer's life just did not matter that much.

Friday had taken a last look around before night finally engulfed them. The group was on a flat, barren expanse. To the right, about a half mile distant, the blue-white glacier rose thousands of feet nearly straight up. The surface appeared to be rough and jagged, as though a mountain-sized section had been ripped away. To the left the terrain was much smoother, probably worn down by ages of rain and runoff from the mountains. It sloped downward into what looked like a distant valley. Friday could not be certain because a mist was rising from the lower, warmer levels of the glacier.

Not that it mattered. Pakistan was ahead, due north. And unless Ron Friday did something to speed up this group's progress they would not get there in time, if at all.

Friday took out his small flashlight and handed it to Samouel. The batteries would probably not last until sunrise.

Friday told the Pakistani to get a good look at the terrain and then shut the light off until he absolutely needed it again. Then the American dropped to the left side of the loose formation. The air was still and the night was quiet. The glacier was protecting them from the fierce mountain winds. Friday waited for Nanda and her grandfather to catch up. Then he fell in beside the woman. She was holding Apu's hand close to her waist and walking slightly ahead of him. With each step Nanda stopped and literally gave her grandfather a firm but gentle tug across the ice. She was breathing heavily and Apu was bent deeply at the waist.

"We're not going to make it at this rate," Friday said.

"We'll make it," she replied.

"Not in time," Friday insisted. He did not know that for a fact. But saying it emphatically would make it sound true to Nanda.

Nanda did not respond.

"If either side drops a nuclear missile anywhere in the mountains, this glacier will become a freshwater lake," Friday pointed out. "Let me leave Samouel with your grandfather. You come with me. When we reach Pakistan we can send help."

"Leave my grandfather with one of the men who held us captive?" she said. "I can't trust a man like that."

"Circumstances have changed," Friday said. "Samouel wants to save his people. That means protecting your grandfather."

The young woman continued to help her grandfather along. Friday could not see her expression in the dark. But he could hear the farmer's feet drag along the ice. Just the sound had an enraging quality.

"Nanda, I need your cooperation on this," Friday pressed.

"I am cooperating," she replied evenly.

"You don't understand," Friday said. "We have no idea what's happening in the outside world. We need to get you across the line of control as quickly as possible."

Nanda stopped. She told her grandfather to rest for a moment. The farmer gratefully lowered himself to his knees while the woman took Friday aside. The American told Samouel to keep moving. Friday would find him by the bursts from the flashlight.

"If we leave the terrorist and my grandfather here, no one will come back," Nanda said. "I know this border region. There will be a great deal of tension on both sides of the glacier. No one will want to make any unnecessary or provocative military moves. Samouel will leave without him."

"We'll send a civilian helicopter back here," Friday said. "The American embassy can arrange it quickly."

"They'll be dead by then," Nanda told him. "My grandfather is pushing himself as it is. If I leave he'll give up."

"Nanda, if you don't leave, two nations may cease to exist," Friday pointed out. "You played a key role in this. You have to set it right."

The young woman was silent. Friday could not see her in the blackness but he could hear her breathing. It had slowed somewhat. Nanda was thinking. She was softening.

She was going to agree.

"All right," she said. "I'll do what you ask but only if you stay and help my grandfather."

That caught Friday by surprise. "Why?"

"You know how to survive out here," Nanda replied. She placed her hand on the unlit torches for emphasis. "I think I saw a valley to the west. You will be able to get him down there in the dark, find shelter, warmth, and water. Promise me you'll take care of him and I'll go ahead with Samouel."

The perspiration on the American's face was beginning to freeze. It was a strange feeling, like candle wax hardening. The insides of his thighs were badly chafed and his lungs hurt from the cold air they had been breathing. The longer he stood here the more aware he became of how vulnerable they were. It would be easy to stand still a moment too long and die.

Friday set the two torches down and removed the glove from his right hand. He scratched the frozen sweat from his cheeks and forehead. Then he slipped his hand into his coat pocket. Nanda was Friday's trophy. He had no intention of staying behind or being dictated to.

He removed the pistol from his pocket. Nanda could not see it or know what he was going to do. If he put a bullet in the farmer's head Nanda would have no choice but to press on, even if only to bring Friday to justice. Friday, of course, would argue that Apu was distraught about holding the others back. He had tried to reach the gun to end his own life. There was a fight. It went off.

Friday hesitated. He considered the possibility that a shot might attract the attention of the Indian soldiers from the line of control. But he realized that the many peaks and winding ice valleys would make the sound impossible to pinpoint. And those ice peaks were far enough away so that a shot would probably not bring loose sections crashing down. Especially if the blast were muffled by the parka of the dead man.

Friday walked around Nanda. "All right," he said with finality. "I will take care of your grandfather."

FORTY-EIGHT

Washington, D.C.
Thursday, 1:28 P.M.

Ron Plummer was not a patient man. And that had been a great help to him throughout his career.

Intelligence officers and government liaisons could not afford patience. They had to have restless minds and curious imaginations. Otherwise they could not motivate their people or themselves to look past the obvious or accept impasses. However, they also needed to possess control. The ability to appear calm even when they were not.

Ordinarily, Ron Plummer was also a calm man. At the moment his self-control was being tested. Not by the crisis but by the one thing a former intelligence operative hated most.

Ignorance.

It had been nearly forty-five minutes since Ambassador Simathna left the office. Plummer had sat for a few minutes, paced slowly, sat some more, then stood and walked in circles around the large office. He looked at the bookcases filled with histories and biographies. Most were in English, some were in Urdu. The wood-paneled walls were decorated with plaques, citations, and photographs of the ambassador with various world leaders. There was even one of Simathna with United Nations Secretary-General Chatterjee. Neither of them was smiling. The PEO hoped that was not an omen. He stopped in front of a framed document that hung near the ambassador's desk. It was signed in 1906 by Aga Khan III, an Indian Muslim. The paper was an articulate statement of objectives for the All-India Muslim League, an organization that the sultan's son had founded to oversee the establishment of a Muslim state in the region. Plummer wondered if that was the last time Indian and Muslim interests had coincided.

Plummer saw his own reflection in the UV glass. The image was translucent, which was fitting. A political liaison had to have enough substance to know what he stood for but enough flexibility to consider the needs of others. He also had to have the skill to intermediate between the different parties. Even good, sensible, well-intentioned men like Hood and Simathna could disagree strongly.

Plummer glanced at his watch. Paul Hood would be waiting for an update. But Plummer did not want to call Op-Center. For one thing, the political liaison had nothing to report. For another, the embassy was certainly wired with eavesdropping devices. The office and phones were surely bugged. And any number Plummer punched into his cell phone would be picked up by electronic pulse interceptors. These devices were about the size and shape of a pocket watch. They were designed to recognize and record only cell phone pulses. Thereafter, whenever that number was used within the listening range of the embassy's antennae, Pakistani intelligence—or whomever Islamabad sold the data to—could hack and listen in on the call. It was one thing when cell phone users accidentally intercepted someone else's conversation. It was different when those calls were routinely monitored.

Plummer considered what Ambassador Simathna might be up to. Plummer decided on three possibilities. He certainly would have reported the intelligence to the chief executive of the republic, General Abdul Qureshi. Either Islamabad or the embassy might then draft a press release condemning New Delhi for their duplicity. The Indians would vehemently deny the charges, of course. That would rally the people around their respective leaders and ratchet tensions even higher. Especially at Op-Center, which would surely be cited by Islamabad for having provided them with the information.

The second possibility was that there would be no press release. Not yet. Instead, Qureshi and the generals of Pakistan's National Security Council would plan a swift, merciless nuclear strike against India. They would attempt to destroy as many missile installations as possible before releasing the intelligence Op-Center had provided. That would drag the United States into the conflict as a de facto ally of Pakistan.

Hood and Plummer had known that those were both possibilities. They simply hoped that reason would triumph. On the whole, Ambassador Simathna was a reasonable man.

That allowed Plummer to hold out hope for a third possibility, what he called "the one-eighty." It was an option the experts never considered, a development that popped up one hundred and eighty degrees from where the common wisdom had staked its tent. It was the Allies invading Normandy beach instead of Calais during World War II, it was Harry Truman beating Thomas Dewey for the presidency in 1948.

Simathna's parting words, about there being a footnote that only he could access, gave Plummer hope for a one-eighty.

The door opened while Plummer was reading the ninety-year-old paper signed by Khan.

"I often stand where you are and gaze at that document," the ambassador declared as he entered the room. "It reminds me of the dream for which I am an honored caretaker."

The Pakistani shut the heavy door and walked toward his desk. The ambassador seemed to be a little more distracted than before. That could be a good thing or a bad thing for Plummer. Either diplomacy had triumphed and Islamabad would give Mike Rodgers time to try to finish the mission. That meant the ambassador would be the hero or the scapegoat. Or else the children of Aga Khan III were about to write a new Muslim League document. One that would be blasted into the history books by plutonium 239.

Simathna walked quickly behind his desk. He gestured toward a chair on the other side. Plummer sat after the ambassador did. Simathna then turned a telephone toward the American political liaison.

"Would you please call Mr. Hood and ask him to connect you to General Rodgers," Simathna said. "I must speak with them both."

Plummer sat forward in the armchair. "What are you going to tell them?" he asked.

"I spoke with General Qureshi and the members of the National Security Council," the ambassador told him. "There was deep concern but no panic. Preparations are quietly being made to activate defense systems and policies already in place. If what you say about the Indian woman is true, we believe the situation need not escalate."

"How can Op-Center help?" Plummer pressed.

Ambassador Simathna told Plummer what the Pakistani leaders had discussed. Their plan was more than a one-eighty. It was an option that Plummer never could have thought of.

Plummer also realized that the plan carried an enormous risk. The Pakistanis could be looking for an ally in the war against India. If the ambassador were misleading Plummer about their intent, the Pakistani proposal would put the United States at the epicenter of the conflagration.

Literally.

Fortunately or unfortunately, all Ron Plummer had to do was make the call.

Paul Hood was the one who had to make the decision.

FORTY-NINE

Washington, D.C.
Thursday, 1:36 P.M.

Paul Hood was stealing a slice of pizza from his assistant's desk when the call came from Ron Plummer. Hood asked Bugs to have Bob Herbert join him. Then he hurried back to his desk to take the call.

"What have you got?" Hood said as he picked up. He heard the slight reverberation sound that indicated he was on speaker. Hood engaged his own speaker option.

"Paul, I'm here with Ambassador Simathna," Plummer said. "He has a proposal."

"Good afternoon, Mr. Ambassador," Hood said. "Tell me how we can help you."

Herbert wheeled in then and shut the door behind him.

"First, Director Hood, I want to offer my condolences on the tragic loss of your Striker unit, and my government's appreciation for what they were attempting to accomplish," Simathna said.

"Thank you," Hood replied. The ambassador sounded a little too compassionate. He had obviously figured out that the team had not been in the region to help stop Indian aggression.

Herbert was a little more blunt. The intelligence chief made an up-and-down motion with his fist.

"Second, my government has a plan that may assist General Rodgers and his personnel," Simathna went on. "As I have already explained to Mr. Plummer, it will require an understanding with your government that details of the operation must remain confidential."

"I am not in a position to speak for the government, only my small corner of it," Hood said. "If you tell me your idea

I will immediately confer with people who are in a position to offer those assurances."

Paul Hood was dying inside. Vital seconds and quite possibly lives were slipping away while he and Ambassador Simathna postured. But this was how the dance was done.

"The plan we propose is that your group proceed to a nuclear missile site that our military has erected in the glacier," Simathna said. "It is a remotely operated site with video cameras monitoring the interior. The Indian woman can make her broadcast from inside the silo."

Hood stared at Bob Herbert. Mike Rodgers was being invited to visit one of the silos Striker had originally been sent to find. The irony of the proposal was almost painful. What was difficult to process, however, was the dangers inherent in the plan.

"Mr. Ambassador, would you excuse me a minute?" Hood asked.

"Given the situation I would not take much longer than that," Simathna replied.

"I understand, sir, but I need to confer with one of my associates," Hood replied.

"Of course," Simathna said.

Hood punched the mute button. "What do your instincts tell you, Bob? Are they using us?"

"Man, I just don't know," Herbert admitted. "My gut says that the team needs to get to the nearest, warmest refuge as soon as possible. The more I looked at photographs of the glacier the more I started thinking they'll never be able to cross it without more gear and supplies than they're carrying. And the weather reports for the region suck. It's going to be around ten below zero before midnight. But I have to tell you, of all the places they could go, a Pakistani nuclear silo would be my absolute last choice."

"I agree with all of that," Hood replied. "The problem is we also have to get Nanda Kumar on-camera as fast as possible."

"Nanda, yes," Herbert said. "The problem is Mike and Ron Friday. If the Pakistanis get them on video there's no telling what bullshit story Islamabad might concoct. They could kill the audio, release the video to the news media, and say that Mike and Friday are there as technical advisors. How's that going to play in India, Russia, China, and God knows where else? An American general and intelligence officer working closely with Pakistani nuclear missiles?"

"They'd say we were in on the Pakistani operation from the start," Hood said. "I'm just not seeing any other viable options."

Herbert shook his head. "Nothing's jumping out at me either."

"Then let's move this along and just watch our step," Hood told him. "The first thing we have to do is try to get Brett on the line. Let's see if he can even contact Mike."

"I'm on it," Herbert said.

"I'll get the coordinates of the missile silo from Simathna," Hood told him. "Then I'll call Hank Lewis, Senator Fox, and the president and let them know what we want to do."

"You won't get support from Fox or the president," Herbert said.

"I know, but I don't think they'll shut the operation down," Hood replied. "We're already in this too deep. If Mike and Friday cross the line of control with the Pakistani cell, Islamabad will say the United States was helping them escape. That would be nearly as damaging."

Herbert agreed. He turned and wheeled himself into a corner of the office and punched the TAC-SAT number into his wheelchair phone.

Meanwhile, Paul Hood got back on the line with Ambassador Simathna. Hood turned off the speakerphone so his conversation would not interfere with Herbert's call.

"Mr. Ambassador?" Hood said.

"I am here," Simathna replied.

"Thank you for holding, sir," Hood said. "We agree that your proposal should be pursued."

" 'Pursued,' " the ambassador replied. "Does that mean you are also considering other courses of action?"

"Not at the moment," Hood said.

"But you might," the ambassador pressed.

"It's possible," Hood agreed. "Right now we're not even certain we can contact General Rodgers, let alone get him to the silo. We also don't know the condition of his party."

"I appreciate your uncertainty but you must understand my concern," the ambassador said. "We do not wish to give out the location of our defensive silo unless your officer is going to use it."

The conversation was becoming an exercise in hedging, not cooperation. Hood needed to change that, especially if he were going to trust Mike Rodgers's fate to this man.

"I do understand, Mr. Ambassador," Hood said.

Suddenly, Herbert turned. He shook his head.

"Hold on, Mr. Ambassador," Hood said urgently. He jabbed the mute button. "What is it, Bob?"

"Brett can't raise Mike," Herbert told him.

Hood swore.

"All he gets on the radio is heavy static," Herbert went on. "Sharab tells him the winds won't cut out for another five or six hours."

"That doesn't help us," Hood said.

Hood thought for a moment. They had thousands of satellites in the air and outposts throughout the region. There had to be some way to get a message to Mike Rodgers.

Or someone with him, Hood thought suddenly.

"Bob, we may be able to do something," Hood said. "Tell Brett we'll get back to him in a few minutes. Then put in a call to Hank Lewis."

"Will do," Herbert said.

Hood deactivated the mute. "Mr. Ambassador, can you stay on the line?"

"The security of my nation is at risk," Simathna said.

"Is that a 'yes,' sir?" Hood pressed. He did not have time for speeches.

"It was an emphatic yes, Mr. Hood."

"Is Mr. Plummer still with you?" Hood asked.

"I'm here, Paul," Plummer said.

"Good. I may need your help," Hood said.

"I understand," Plummer replied.

"I'm putting you on speaker so you can both be a part of what's going on," Hood said.

The ambassador thanked him.

Simathna sounded sincere. Hood hoped he was. Because if Simathna did anything to jeopardize Rodgers or the mission, Hood would know about it immediately.

Ron Plummer would make sure of that.

FIFTY

The Siachin Glacier
Thursday, 11:40 P.M.

It was the last thing Ron Friday expected to feel.

As he neared the kneeling body of Apu Kumar, Friday felt the cell phone begin to vibrate in his vest pocket. It could only be a call from someone at the National Security Agency. But the signal absolutely should not be able to reach him out here. Not with the mountains surrounding the glacier, the distance from the radio towers in Kashmir, and the ice storms that whipped around the peaks in the dark. The friction of the ice particles produced electrostatic charges that made even point-to-point radio communications difficult.

Yet the phone line was definitely active. Absurdly so, as if he were riding the Metro in Washington instead of standing on a glacier in the middle of the Himalayas. Friday stopped and let the gun slip back into his pocket. He reached inside his coat, withdrew the phone, and hit the talk button.

"Yes?" Friday said.

"Is this Ron Friday?" the caller asked in a clear, loud voice.

"Who wants to know?" Friday asked incredulously.

"Colonel Brett August of Striker," said the caller.

"Striker?" Friday said. "Where are you? When did you land?"

"I'm with Sharab in the mountains overlooking your position," August said. "I'm calling on our TAC-SAT. Director Lewis gave us your number and the call code 1272000."

That was the correct ID number for the NSA director in coded communications. Still, Friday was suspicious.

"How many of you are there?"

"Only three of us," August informed him.

"Three? What happened?" Friday asked.

"We were caught in fire from the Indian army," August told him. "Is General Rodgers with you?"

"No," Friday replied.

"It's important that you watch for him and link up," August said.

"Where is he?" Friday asked.

"The general reached the Mangala Valley and is headed east," August said. "Satellite recon gave him your general position."

"The valley," Friday said. His eyes drifted to where Samouel was moving through the darkness. "That's just ahead."

"Good. When you link up you are to proceed to these coordinates on the pilot's map you're carrying," August went on.

"Hold on while I get it," Friday said.

The American crouched and set the phone on the ice. He pulled the map and a pen from his pocket. Friday tried to read the map by the green glow of the cell phone but that was not possible. He was forced to light one of his torches. The sudden brightness caused him to wince. He tried jamming the branch into the glacier but the surface was too solid. Apu reached over and held it for him. Friday remained crouching with the map spread before him.

"I'm set," Friday said as his eyes adjusted to the light.

"Go to seventeen-point-three degrees north, twenty-one-point-three degrees east," August told him.

Friday looked at the coordinates. He saw absolutely nothing on the map but ice.

"What's there?" Friday asked.

"I don't know," August told him.

"Excuse me?"

"I don't know," August repeated.

"Then who does?" Friday demanded.

"I don't know that either," August admitted. "I'm just relaying orders from our superiors at Op-Center and the NSA."

"Well, I don't go on blind missions," Friday complained as he continued to study the map. "And I see that following the coordinates you gave me will take us away from the line of control."

"Look," August said. "You know what's at stake in the region. So does Washington. They wouldn't ask you to go if it weren't important. Now I'm sitting up here with my forces depleted and the Indian army at my feet. I've got to deal with that. Either I or William Musicant will call back in two hours with more information. That's about how long it should take you to reach the coordinates from the mouth of the valley."

"Assuming we go," Friday said.

"I assume you'll follow orders the same way my Strikers did," the colonel said. "August out."

The line went dead. Friday shut his phone off and put it away. Arrogant son of a bitch.

Nanda's voice rose from the darkness. "What is it?" she asked.

Friday continued to squat where he was. The heat of the torch was melting the ice beside him but the warmth felt good. The woman obviously had not seen what he was about to do before the telephone vibrated.

"The know-it-alls in Washington have a new plan for us but they won't tell us what it is," Friday said. "They want us to go to a spot on the map and wait for instructions."

Nanda walked over. "What spot?" she asked.

Friday showed her.

"The middle of the glacier," she said.

"Do you know what might be out there?" Friday asked.

"No," she replied.

"I don't like it," Friday said. "I don't even know if that was Colonel August on the line. The Indian army might have captured him, made him give them the code number."

"They didn't," a voice said from the darkness.

Friday and Nanda both started. The American grabbed the torch and held it to his left. That was the direction from which the voice had come.

A man was walking toward them. He was dressed in a white high altitude jumpsuit and U.S. Army equipment vest, and he was carrying a flashlight. Samouel was trailing slightly behind him. Friday shifted the torch to his left hand. He slipped his right hand back into the pocket with the gun. He rose.

"I'm General Mike Rodgers of Striker," said the new arrival. "I assume you're Friday and Ms. Kumar."

"Yes," the woman replied.

Friday was not happy to have company. First, he wanted to be sure the man was who he claimed to be. Friday studied the man as he approached. He did not appear to be Indian. Also, his cheeks and the area around his eyes were wind-blasted red and raw. He looked like he could be someone who walked a long way to get here.

"How do you know that it was actually August who called me?" Friday demanded.

"Colonel August spent several years as a guest of the North Vietnamese," Rodgers said. "He didn't tell them anything they wanted to know. Nothing's changed. Why did he contact you?"

"Washington wants us to go to a point northeast of here, away from the line of control," Friday replied. "But they didn't tell us why."

"Of course not," Rodgers said. "If we're captured by the enemy we can't tell them where we're headed." He removed his radio and tried it. There was only static. "How did Colonel August contact you?"

"TAC-SAT to cell phone," Friday replied.

"Clever," Rodgers said. "Is he holding up all right?"

Friday nodded. As long as August kept the Indians off their trail, he did not care how the pack animal was holding up.

Rodgers walked over to Apu and offered him a hand. Water had begun to pool around the Indian's feet.

"I suggest we start walking before we freeze here," Rodgers said.

"That's it, then?" Friday said. "You've decided that we should go deeper into the glacier?"

"No. Washington decided that," Rodgers replied. He helped Apu to his feet but his eyes remained on Friday.

"Even though we don't know where we're going," Friday repeated.

"Especially because of that," Rodgers said. "If they want to keep the target a secret it must be important."

Friday did not disagree. He simply did not trust the people in Washington to do what was best for him. On top of that, Friday loathed Rodgers. He had never liked military people. They were pack animals who expected everyone else to obey the pack leader's commands and conform to the pack agenda, even if that meant dying for the pack. Standing up to captors instead of cooperating for the good of all. That was not his way. It was the reason he worked alone. One man could always find a way to survive, to prosper.

Nanda and Samouel both moved to where Rodgers was standing with Apu. If the Indian woman had decided to continue on to the line of control, Friday would have gone with her. But if she was joining Rodgers, Friday had no choice but to go along with them.

For now.

Friday extinguished the torch by touching it to the melted ice. The water would freeze in seconds and he could knock the ice off if they needed the torch again.

The group continued its trek across the ice with Samouel in the lead and Rodgers and Nanda helping Apu. Friday kept his right hand in his pocket, on the gun. If at any point he did not like how things were going he would put them back on their original course.

With or without General Rodgers.

FIFTY-ONE

The Himachal Peaks
Thursday, 11:41 P.M.

It had been an arduous day for Major Dev Puri and the two hundred men of his elite frontline regiment. This was supposed to be a straightforward sweep of the foothills of the Great Himalaya Range. Instead, it had become a forced march sparked by surprising intelligence reports, unexpected enemies, evolving strategies, and constantly changing objectives.

The most recent shift was the riskiest. It carried the danger of drawing the attention of Pakistani border forces. Because of Puri's mission, it would be much easier for the enemy to cross the line of control at Base 3.

The Indian soldiers had been marching virtually without rest since they left the trenches. The terrain was merely rugged to start. Then the higher elevations brought cold and walls of wind. The successful attack on the paratroopers had given the force a much-needed morale boost as they continued to search for the Pakistani cell. But darkness and sleet had battered them as they ascended. Now they were looking at a climb that was going to tax their energies to the limit. Then there was the unknown factor: the strength and exact location of the enemy. It was not the way Major Puri liked to run a campaign.

Nearly eight hours before, the Indian soldiers had begun closing ranks at the base of the Gompa Tower in the Himachal cluster of peaks. The latest intelligence Puri had received was that American soldiers were jumping in to help the terrorists get through the line of control to Pakistan. That was where the parachutists had been headed. The Pakistani cell was almost certainly there as well. There was no way forward except through the Indian soldiers. The Pakistanis were undoubtedly exhausted and relatively underarmed now that the Americans had been stopped. Still, Major Puri did not underestimate them. He never took an enemy for granted when they had the high ground. The plan he and his lieutenants had worked out was to have twenty-five men ascend the peak while the rest covered them from the ground with high-powered rifles and telescopic sights. Twenty-five more would be ready to ascend as backup if needed. One or another of the teams was bound to take the cell. One or another of the teams was also likely to take casualties. Unfortunately, Defense Minister Kabir did not want to wait for the Pakistanis to come down. Now that Americans had been killed there would be hard questions from Washington and New Delhi about what had happened to the paratroopers. The minister was doing his best to stall air reconnaissance from moving in to locate and collect the American remains. He had already informed the prime minister that Major Puri's team was in the region and would pinpoint them for the Himalayan Eagles. What Kabir feared was that air reconnaissance might locate the Pakistanis as well as the paratroopers. The defense minister did not want the cell to be taken alive.

Using night glasses and shielded flashlights, the Indian troops had been deploying their climbing gear. They had detected faint heat signatures above and knew the enemy was up there waiting. Unfortunately, flyovers would not help them now. The fierce ice storms above made visibility and navigation difficult. And blind scatter-bombing of the region was not guaranteed to stop the cell. There were caves they could hide in. Besides, there were very holy, anchoritic religious sects and cliff-dwelling tribes living in the foothills and in some of the higher caves. The last thing either side wanted was to collaterally destroy the homes or temples of these neutral peoples. That would force them or their international supporters into political or military activism.

The Indian soldiers were nearly halfway into the preparations to scale the cliff when Major Puri received a surprising radio communiqué. Earlier in the day a helicopter on routine patrol had reported what looked like the wreckage of

an aircraft in the Mangala Valley. However, there was no
room for the chopper to descend and search for possible survivors. Major Puri had dispatched a four-soldier unit to investigate. Two hours before, the men had reported the
discovery of a downed helicopter. It looked like a Ka-25.
But the aircraft was so badly burned they could not be certain. Puri called the Base 3 communications center. They
checked with the air ministry. There were no choppers on
special assignment in the region.

Because the chopper went down in the narrow valley, rescue personnel would not be dispatched until the following
day. A parachute drop at night was too risky and, in any
case, there were no survivors.

An hour later, Puri's group found the remains of ten American paratroopers. Major Puri relayed that information to the
defense minister. The minister said he would sit on that information until after the cell had been taken. He had already
come up with a scenario in which, regrettably, Puri's soldiers
had mistaken the Americans for Pakistanis and had shot the
team down.

What surprised the Indian reconnaissance team was what
they discovered on the body of one of the Americans. The
soldier, a black woman, was hanging from a ledge by her
parachute. There was a point-to-point radio in her equipment
belt. Occasionally, the red "contact" light flashed. Someone
in the communications link was trying to contact her or
someone else in the link. That meant not all the soldiers had
been killed. Unfortunately, the Indian soldiers could not confirm that. All they got on the radio was static.

Puri expected that he would find those soldiers in the cliffs
above, with the Pakistanis. But the Mangala Valley unit had
employed infrared glasses in a scan of the region. They had
come up with a different scenario.

"We're detecting a very strong heat source several miles
to the northeast," Sergeant Baliah, the leader of the reconnaissance unit, had reported. "There is a singular heat source
on the glacier."

"It could be some of the native people," Puri said.

Several groups of mountain dwellers lived in the upper foothills of the ranges that surrounded the glacier. They often hunted at night after small game and the larger gazelles had returned to their dens and warrens. They also used the darkness to set traps for predators that hunted in the early morning. The Tarari did not eat the wolves and foxes but used their fur for clothing. The traps also kept the animals from becoming so numerous that they depopulated the region of prey.

"It's a little far west for them," Baliah remarked. "The heat signature is also less than we would get from a string of torches. I'm wondering if it might be some of the Americans. If their equipment was damaged in the jump, they might have built a campfire."

"How far is 'several miles'?" Puri asked.

"Approximately four," Baliah responded. "What I don't understand is why the Americans would have left the valley. The weather is much more temperate there. They could not have failed to see the ice."

"The survivors might have found the wreckage of the helicopter and anticipated a recon team. They moved on," Puri suggested.

"But then why would they have left the radio?" the sergeant wondered aloud. "They could easily have gotten it down. Then no one would know there were survivors."

"Maybe we were meant to find it," Puri said. "That way they could feed us miscommunications." Yet even as the major said that, he knew it did not make sense. The Americans could not have known that a reconnaissance unit was en route to the site.

Puri began to consider likely scenarios. The helicopter was probably in the valley to support the clandestine American operation. Perhaps it was there to extract the soldiers when their mission was completed. That was why there was no immediate flight profile. Perhaps the Americans were only supposed to link up with the Pakistanis and see them as far as the border.

And then it hit him. Maybe that was still the objective.

"Sergeant, can you make your way to that heat source double-time?" Major Puri asked.

"Of course," Baliah replied. "What do you think is going on, sir?"

"I'm not sure," Major Puri told him. "It's possible that some of the Americans survived the drop and joined the Pakistani cell on our plateau. But other paratroopers may have been blown clear of the valley."

"And you think the two may be trying to stay in touch point-to-point in order to find each other?" Sergeant Baliah asked.

"That's possible," Puri replied.

The major looked up at the plateau his men were getting ready to climb. The peak was dark but he could see the outline by the way it blocked the clouds above. Except for the presence of the American paratroopers he did not know for certain that the cell was up there. What if they were not? What if the American drop had been a feint? The shortest way to Pakistan from this region was across the Siachin Glacier, Base 3 sector.

Right through his command.

"Sergeant, pursue the Siachin element," Puri decided. "I'm going to request immediate air support in that region."

"At night?"

"At night," Puri said. "Captain Anand knows the region. He can get a gunship to the target. I want you there in case an enemy is present and he digs in where the rockets can't get him."

"We're on our way, sir," the sergeant replied. "We'll have a report in two hours or so."

"That should be about the time the chopper arrives," Puri said. "Good luck, Sergeant."

Baliah thanked him and clicked off.

The major walked over to his communications officer and asked him to put in a call to the base. Puri would brief Captain Anand and get the air reconnaissance underway. Puri would make certain that the operation be as low-key as possible. Anand was to take just one chopper into the field and there would be no unnecessary communications with the base. Even if the Pakistanis could not interpret the coded messages, a sudden increase in radio traffic might alert them that something was going on.

While the major waited for Captain Anand he told the lieutenant in charge of the ascent to finish the preparations but to put the operation itself on hold. They could afford to wait two hours more before risking the climb. The Pakistanis on the plateau were not going anywhere.

If there really were Pakistanis on the ledge.

FIFTY-TWO

The Siachin Glacier
Friday, 12:00 A.M.

When Mike Rodgers was in boot camp, his drill instructor had told him something that he absolutely did not believe.

The DI's name was Glen "the Hammer" Sheehy. And the Hammer said that when an opponent was punched during an attack, the odds were good that he would not feel it.

"The body ignores a nonlethal assault," the Hammer told them. "Whatever juices we've got pour in like reserves, numbing the pain of a punch or a stab or even a gunshot and empowering the need to strike back."

Rodgers did not believe that until the first time he was in a hand-to-hand combat situation in Vietnam. U.S. and Vietcong recon units literally stumbled upon each other during a patrol north of Bo Duc near the Cambodian border. Rodgers had suffered a knife wound high in the left arm. But he was not aware of it until after the battle. One of his friends had been shot in the butt and kept going. When the unit returned to camp and the medics had put the survivors back together, one of Rodgers's buddies gave him a black bandanna with a slogan written in red grease pencil. It said, "It only hurts when I stop fighting."

It was true. Moreover, there was no time to hurt. Not with more lives depending upon you.

The reality of losing the Strikers was with Rodgers every moment. But the pain had not yet sunk in. He was too busy staying fixed on the goal that had brought them here.

Rodgers was leg-weary as his group made its way across some of the starkest landscape Rodgers had ever encountered. The ice was glass-smooth and difficult to navigate. Nanda and Samouel slipped with increasing regularity.

Rodgers was glad he still had his crampons, heavy though they were. Rodgers continued to help Apu Kumar along. The farmer's left arm was slung across Rodgers's neck and they were on a gradual incline. Apu's feet had to be dragged more than they moved. Rodgers suspected the only thing that kept the elderly man moving at all was a desire to see his grand-daughter reach safety. The American officer would have helped the farmer regardless, but he was touched by that thought.

That was not a sentiment Ron Friday seemed to share.

Friday had stayed several paces behind Rodgers, Apu, and Nanda. Samouel continued to hold the point position, turning the flashlight on at regular intervals. At just under an hour into the trek, Friday stepped beside Rodgers. He was panting, his breath coming in wispy white bursts.

"You realize you're risking the rest of this mission by dragging him along," Friday said.

Though the NSA operative spoke softly, his voice carried in the still, cold air. Rodgers was certain that Nanda had heard.

"I don't see it that way," Rodgers replied.

"The delay is exponential," Friday continued. "The longer it takes the weaker we become, slowing us down even more."

"Then you go ahead," Rodgers said.

"I will," he said. "With Nanda. Across the border."

"No," she said emphatically.

"I don't know why you're both so willing to trust those bastards in Washington," Friday went on. "We're at our clos-est approach to the border. It's just about twenty or thirty minutes north of here. Troops have probably been pulled out to man the incursion line."

"Some," Rodgers agreed. "Not all."

"Enough," Friday replied. "Heading there makes more sense than going another hour northeast to God-knows-where."

"Not to the guys we report to," Rodgers reminded him.

"They're not here," Friday shot back. "They don't have on-site intelligence. They aren't in our shoes."

"They're not field personnel," Rodgers pointed out. "This is one of the things we trained for."

"Blind, stupid loyalty?" Friday asked. "Was that also part of your training, General?"

"No. Trust," Rodgers replied. "I respect the judgment of the men I work with."

"Maybe that's why you ended up with a valley full of dead soldiers," Friday said.

Mike Rodgers let the remark go. He had to. He did not have the time or extra energy to break Friday's jaw.

Friday continued to pace Rodgers. The NSA agent shook his head. "How many disasters have to bite a military guy in the ass before he takes independent action?" he asked. "Hell, Herbert isn't even a superior officer. You're taking orders from a civilian."

"And you're pushing it," Rodgers said.

"Let me ask you something," Friday went on. "If you knew you could cross the line of control and get Nanda to a place where she could broadcast her story, would you disobey your instructions?"

"No," Rodgers replied.

"Why?"

"Because there may be a component to this we're not aware of," Rodgers replied.

"Like what?" Friday asked.

"A 'for instance'?" Rodgers said. "You flew out here with an Indian officer instead of waiting for us to join the cell, against instructions. Well, you hate taking orders. Maybe you were being headstrong. Or maybe you're working with the SFF. It could be that if we follow your short hop toward the border we'll end up not reaching Pakistan at all."

"That's possible," Friday admitted. "So why didn't I cut you down back at the valley? That would have made certain I get things my way."

"Because then Nanda would have known she's a dead woman," Rodgers told him.

"Can you guarantee that won't happen if she crawls across a glacier with you?"

Rodgers did not answer. Friday had a sharp, surgical mind. Anything the general said would be sculpted to support Friday's point of view. Then it would be fired back at him. Rodgers did not want to do anything that might fuel doubts in Nanda's mind.

"Think about this," Friday continued. "We're following the directions of Washington bureaucrats without knowing where we're going or why. We've been running across the mountains for hours without food or rest. We may not even reach the target, especially if we carry each other around. Have you considered the possibility that's the plan?"

"Mr. Friday, if you want to cross the line of control you go ahead," Rodgers told him.

"I do," Friday said. He leaned in front of Rodgers. He looked at Nanda. "If she goes with me, I'll get her to Pakistan and safety."

"I'm staying with my grandfather," the woman said.

"You were ready to leave him before," Friday reminded her.

"That was before," she said.

"What changed your mind?"

"You," she replied. "When my grandfather was kneeling and you walked over to him."

"I was going to help him," Friday said.

"I don't think so," she said. "You were angry."

"How do you know?" he asked. "You couldn't see me—"

"I could hear your footsteps on the ice," she said.

"My footsteps?" Friday said disdainfully.

"We used to sit in the bedroom and listen to the Pakistanis on the other side of the door," Nanda told him. "We couldn't hear what they were saying but I always knew what they were feeling by how they walked across the wooden floor. Slow, fast, light, heavy, stop and start. Every pattern told us something about each individual's mood."

"I was going to help him," Friday repeated.

"You wanted to hurt my grandfather," Nanda said. "I know that."

"I don't believe this," Friday said. "Never mind your grandfather. Millions of people may go to hell because of something you did and we're talking about footsteps."

Mike Rodgers did not want to become involved in the debate. But he did not want it to escalate. He also was not sure, at this point, whether he even wanted Ron Friday to stay. Rodgers had worked with dozens of intelligence operatives during his career. They were lone wolves by nature but they rarely if ever disregarded instructions from superiors. And never as flagrantly as this. One of the reasons they became field operatives was the challenge of executing orders in the face of tremendous odds.

Ron Friday was more than just a loner. He was distracted. Rodgers suspected that he was driven by a different agenda. Like it or not, that might be something he would have to try to figure out.

"We're going to save Nanda's grandfather as well as those millions of people you're concerned about," Rodgers said firmly. "We'll do that by going northeast from here."

"Damn it, you're blind!" Friday shouted. "I've been in this thing from the start. I was in the square when it blew up. I had a feeling about the dual bombers, about the involvement of the SFF, about the double-dealing of this woman." He gestured angrily at Nanda. "It's the people who pull the strings you should doubt, not a guy who's been at ground zero from the start."

Friday was losing it. Rodgers did not want to waste the energy to try to stop him. He also wanted to see where the rant would lead. Angry men often said too much.

Friday fired up his torch again. Rodgers squinted in the light. He slowed as Friday got in front of them and faced them.

"So that's it, then?" Friday said.

"Get out of the way," Rodgers ordered.

"Bob Herbert barks, Mike Rodgers obeys, and Op-Center takes over the mission," Friday said.

"Is that what this is about?" Rodgers asked. "Your résumé?"

"I'm not talking about credit," Friday said. "I'm talking about what we do for a living. We collect and use information."

"You do," Rodgers said.

"Fine, yes. I do," Friday agreed. "I put myself in places where I can learn things, where I can meet people. But we, our nation, need allies in Pakistan, in the Muslim world. If we stay on this glacier we are still behind Indian lines. That buys us nothing."

"You don't know that," Rodgers said.

"Correct," Friday said. "But I do know that if we go to Islamabad, as Americans who saved Pakistan from nuclear annihilation, we create new avenues of intelligence and co-operation in that world."

"Mr. Friday, that's a political issue, not a tactical military concern," Rodgers said. "If we're successful then Washington can make some of those inroads you mention."

With Apu still clinging to him, Rodgers started moving around Friday. The NSA operative put out a hand and stopped him.

"Washington is helpless," Friday said. "Politicians live on the surface. They are actors. They engage in public squabbles and posturing where the populace can watch and boo or cheer. We are the people who matter. We burrow inside. We make the tunnels. We control the conduits."

"Mr. Friday, move," Rodgers said.

This was about personal power. Rodgers had no time for that.

"I will move," Friday said. "With Nanda, to the line of control. Two people can make it across."

Rodgers was about to push past him when he felt something. A faint, rapid vibration in the bottoms of his feet. A moment later it grew more pronounced. He felt it crawl up his ankles.

"Give me the torch!" he said suddenly.

"What?" Friday said.

Rodgers leaned around Friday. "Samouel—don't turn on the light!"

"I won't," he said. "I feel it!"

"Feel what?" Nanda said.

"Shit," Friday said suddenly. He obviously felt it too and knew what it meant. "Shit."

Rodgers pulled the torch from Friday. The NSA agent was surprised and did not struggle to keep it. Rodgers held the torch above his head and cast the light around him. There was a mountain of ice to the right, about four hundred yards away. It stretched for miles in both directions. The top of the formation was lost in the darkness.

Rodgers handed the torch to Nanda.

"Go to that peak," he said. "Samouel! Follow Nanda!"

Samouel was already running toward them. "I will!" he shouted.

"My grandfather—!" Nanda said.

"I'll take him," Rodgers assured her. He looked at Friday. "You wanted power? You've got it. Protect her, you son of a bitch."

Friday turned and half-ran, half-skated across the ice after Nanda.

Rodgers leaned close to Apu's ear. "We're going to have to move as fast as possible," he said. "Hold tight."

"I will," Apu replied.

The men began shuffling as quickly as possible toward the peak. The vibrations were now strong enough to shake Rodgers's entire body. A moment later, the beat of the rotors was audible as the Indian helicopter rolled in low over the horizon.

FIFTY-THREE

The Siachin Glacier
Friday, 12:53 A.M.

The powerful Russian-made Mikoyan Mi-35 helicopter soared swift and low over the glacier. Its two-airman crew kept a careful watch on the ice one hundred and fifty feet beneath them. They were flying at low light so the chopper could not be easily seen and targeted from the ground. Radar would keep them from plowing into the towers of ice. Helmets with night-vision goggles as well as the low altitude would allow them to search for their quarry.

The Mi-35 is the leading attack helicopter of the Indian air force. Equipped with under-nose, four-barrel large-caliber machine guns and six antitank missiles, it is tasked with stopping all surface force operations, from full-scale attacks to infiltration.

The aircrew was pushing the chopper to move as quickly as possible. The men did not want to stay out any longer than necessary. Even at this relatively low level the cold on the glacier was severe. Strong, sudden winds whipping from the mountains could hasten the freezing of hoses and equipment. Ground forces were able to stop and thaw clogged lines or icy gears. Helicopter pilots did not have that luxury. They tended to find out about a problem when it was too late, when either the main or the tail rotor suddenly stopped turning.

Fortunately, the crew was able to spot "the likely target" just seventy minutes after taking off. The copilot reported the find to Major Puri.

"There are five persons running across the ice," the airman said.

"Running?" Major Puri said.

"Yes," reported the airman. "They do not appear to be locals. One of them is wearing a high-altitude jump outfit."

"White?" Puri asked.

"Yes."

"That's one of the American paratroopers," Puri said. "Can you tell who is with him?"

"He is helping someone across the ice," the airman said. "That person is wearing a parka. There are three people ahead. One is in a parka, two are wearing mountaineering gear. I can't tell the color because of the night-vision lenses. But it appears dark."

"The terrorist who was killed in the mountain cave was wearing a dark blue outfit," Puri said. "I have to know the color."

"Hold on," the airman replied.

The crew member reached for the exterior light controls on the panel between the seats. He told the pilot to shut down his night-vision glasses for a moment. Otherwise the light would blind him. The pilot and copilot disengaged their goggles and raised them. The copilot turned the light on. The windshield was filled with a blinding white glow reflected from the ice. The airman retrieved his binoculars from a storage compartment in the door. His eyes shrunk to slits as he picked out one of the figures and looked at his clothing.

It was dark blue. The airman reported the information to Major Puri.

"That's one of the terrorists," the major said. "Neutralize them all and report back."

"Repeat, sir?" the airman said.

"You have found the terrorist cell," Major Puri said. "You are ordered to use lethal force to neutralize them—"

"Major," the pilot interrupted. "Will there be a confirming order from base headquarters?"

"I am transmitting an emergency command Gamma-Zero-Red-Eight," Puri said. "That is your authorization."

The pilot glanced at his heads-up display while the copilot input the code on a keyboard located on the control panel. The onboard computer took a moment to process the data.

Gamma-Zero-Red-Eight was the authorization code of Defense Minister John Kabir.

"Acknowledge Gamma-Zero-Red-Eight authorization," the pilot replied. "We are proceeding with the mission."

A moment later the pilot slid his goggles back into place. The copilot switched the exterior lights off and replaced his own night-vision optics. Then he descended through one hundred feet to an altitude of fifty feet. He flipped the helmet-attached gunsights over his night-vision glasses, slipped his left hand onto the joystick that controlled the machine gun, and bore down on the fleeing figures.

FIFTY-FOUR

The Siachin Glacier
Friday, 12:55 A.M.

Mike Rodgers's arm was hooked tightly around Apu's back as he looked out on terrain that was lit by the glow of the helicopter's light. The American watched helplessly as Nanda fell, slid, and then struggled to get up.

"Keep moving!" Rodgers yelled. "Even if you have to crawl, just get closer to the peaks!"

That was probably the last thing Rodgers would get to say to Nanda. The rotor of the approaching chopper was getting louder every instant. The heavy drone drummed from behind and also bounced back at them from the deeply curved slope of ice ahead.

Ron Friday was several paces ahead of Nanda and Samouel was in front of him. Before the lights from the helicopter were turned off, Rodgers saw both men look back then turn and help the young woman. Friday was probably helping her to further his own cause of intelligence control or whatever he had been raving about. Right now, however, Mike Rodgers did not care what Ron Friday's reasons were. At least the man was helping her.

Friday was wearing treaded boots that gave him somewhat better footing than Nanda. As the lights went out, Friday scooped the woman up, tugged her to her feet, and pulled her toward the peak.

Though the ice was dark again Rodgers knew they were not invisible. The aircrew was certainly equipped with infrared equipment. That meant the nose gun would be coming to life very soon. Rodgers had one hope to keep them alive. The plan required them to keep going.

An instant later the nose gun began to hammer. The air seemed to become a solid mass as the sound closed in on all sides. Rodgers felt the first bullets strike the ice behind him. He pulled Apu down and they began to roll and slide down the incline, parallel to the icy wall.

Hard chips of ice were dislodged by bullets hitting the ice. Rodgers heard the "chick" of the strikes then felt hot pain as the small, sharp shards stung his face and neck. Time slowed as it always did in combat. Rodgers was aware of everything. The cold air in his nose and on the nape of his neck. The warm perspiration along the back of his thermal T-shirt. The smell and texture of Apu's wool parka as Rodgers gripped him tightly, pulling him along. The fine mist of surface ice kicked up as he and Apu rolled over it. That was to be the means of their salvation. Perhaps it would still help Nanda and Ron Friday. Rodgers stepped out of himself to savor all the sensations of his eyes, his ears, his flesh. For in these drawn-out moments the general had a sense that they would be his last.

The two men hit a flat section of ice and stopped skidding. The fusillade stopped.

"On your knees!" Rodgers shouted.

The men were going to have to crawl in another direction. It would take the gunner an instant to resight the weapon. Rodgers pulled Apu onto his knees. The two men had to be somewhere else when fire resumed.

The men were crouching and facing one another in the dark. Apu was kneeling and half-leaning against Rodgers's chest. Suddenly the farmer clutched the general's shoulders. He pushed forward. With nothing behind him, Rodgers fell back with Apu on top of him.

"Save Nanda," Apu implored.

The gunning restarted. It chewed up the ice and then drilled into the back of the farmer. Apu hugged Rodgers as the bullets dug into the older man's flesh. The wounds sent damp splashes onto Rodgers's face. He could feel the thud of each bullet right through the man's body. Rodgers reflexively tucked his chin into his chest, bringing his head under

Apu's face. He could hear the man grunt as the bullets struck. They were not cries of pain but the forced exhalation of air as his lungs were punctured from behind. Apu was already beyond pain.

Rodgers brought in his knees slightly and kept himself buried beneath Apu's body. He was thinking now and not simply reacting. And Rodgers realized that this was what Apu had wanted. The farmer had sacrificed himself so Rodgers could stay alive and protect Nanda. The devotion and trust inherent in that gesture made them as pure as anything Rodgers had ever experienced.

Rodgers heard several bullets whistle by his head. He felt a burning in his right shoulder. One of the shots must have grazed him. His arm and back warmed as blood covered his cold flesh.

Rodgers lay still. Their flight and Apu's sacrifice had kept the helicopter occupied for a short time. Hopefully, it had been long enough for Nanda, Friday, and Samouel to reach the peak.

The gunfire stopped. After a few moments the sound of the helicopter moved over Rodgers's head. The chopper was heading toward the icy slopes. It was time for Rodgers to move.

Apu was still holding him. Rodgers grasped the elbows of the man's parka and gently pulled them away. Then he slid to the right, out from under the dead man. Blood from Apu's neck trickled onto Rodgers's left cheek. It left a streak, like warpaint. The elderly man had not given his life in vain.

Rodgers got to his feet. He paused to remove the dead man's parka then ran toward the slope. The helicopter was moving slowly and the American paced it. He stayed behind the cockpit and out of view. He was waiting for the Mi-35 to get a little closer. That was when things should start to happen.

The nose gun began to spit fire again. The red-yellow flashes lit the slope like tiny strobes. Rodgers could see Nanda and the two men running along the curving base, away from the aircraft. The gentle turn in the slope kept the chopper from having a clear shot.

The chopper slowed as it moved closer to the slope. The guns fell silent as the chopper tracked its prey. Flying this close the pilots had to consider rotor clearance, winds, and propwash. Rodgers hoped those were the only things the pilots were worried about. That would be their undoing.

Rodgers reached the base of the ragged slope. He felt his way along. The winds from the tail rotor were savage, like waves of ice water. Rodgers shielded his eyes as best he could. He would be able to see as soon as the guns resumed firing. He was going to have to move quickly when they did.

The chopper continued to creep along the glacier. The throaty sound from the rotors knocked loose powder from the crags. Rodgers could feel it hitting his bare cheeks.

That was good. The plan might work.

A few moments later the guns came to life. Rodgers saw the cliff light up and started running toward the others. As he expected, this close to the slope, the sound of the guns and the rotor shook particles of ice from the wall. The area around the helicopter quickly became a sheet of white. And the flakes did not fall. The winds kept them whipping around in the air, adding layer upon layer. Within moments visibility had diminished to zero.

The guns shut down just as Rodgers raced around the front of the helicopter. Even with their night-vision goggles, the crew would not be able to see him or their quarry.

Rodgers had judged the distance between himself and the others. He guided himself toward them by running a hand along the slope. Though his legs were cramping he refused to stop.

"We've got to move!" Rodgers shouted as he neared the spot where he had seen the group.

"What's happening?" Nanda cried.

"Keep going!" Rodgers yelled.

"Is my grandfather all right?" she demanded.

From the sound of her voice Rodgers judged the woman to be about thirty yards away. He continued running hard. A few seconds later he bumped up against one of the refugees. Judging from the height of the individual it was Friday. They had stopped. Rodgers made his way around him. The general reached for Nanda, who was next in the line. The woman was facing him.

"Grandfather?" Nanda shouted.

"Everyone move!" Rodgers screamed.

In a crisis situation, an individual's fight-or-flight mechanisms are in conflict. When that happens, the shout of an authority figure typically shuts down the combative side. A harsh command usually closes it just enough to let the survival instinct prevail by following the order. In this case, however, Rodgers's cry killed Nanda's flight response. Friday stopped moving altogether as Nanda became as combative as Rodgers.

"Where is he?" the woman screamed.

"Your grandfather didn't make it," Rodgers said.

She screamed for the old man again and started to go back. Rodgers stuffed Apu's parka under his arm then grabbed Nanda's shoulders. He held them tight and wrestled her in the opposite direction.

"I won't leave him!" she cried.

"Nanda, he shielded me with his body!" Rodgers shouted. "He begged me to save you!"

The young woman still grappled with him as she attempted to go back. Rodgers did not have time to reason with her. He literally hoisted Nanda off her feet, turned her around, and pulled her forward. She fought to keep her feet beneath her, but at least those struggles kept her from fighting with him.

Rodgers half-carried, half-dragged the woman as he ran forward. She managed to get her balance back and Rodgers took her hand. He continued to pull her ahead. She went with him, though Rodgers heard her sobbing under the drone of the oncoming chopper. That was fine, as long as she kept moving.

The slope circled sharply toward the northeast. Samouel was still in the lead as they rushed to stay out of the helicopter's line of sight. But without the added drumming of the guns to dislodge fresh ice particles, the pilot would soon be able to see them. Rodgers was going to have to do something about that.

"Samouel, take Nanda's hand and keep going!" Rodgers said.

"Yes, sir," Samouel said.

The American held the woman's arm straight ahead as the Pakistani reached behind him. He found Nanda's hand and Rodgers released her. The two continued ahead. Rodgers stopped and Friday ran into him.

"What are you doing?" Friday asked.

"Give me the torches and the matches. Then go with them," Rodgers said as he took Apu's parka from under his arm.

The NSA operative did as he was instructed. When Friday was gone, Rodgers took one of the torches, lit it, and jammed it into a small crack in the slope. Then he hung Apu's coat on a crag just behind it. Removing his gun from his equipment vest, Rodgers moved away from the ice wall. He got down on one knee, laid the torch across his boot to keep it dry, then pointed his automatic up at a sixty-degree angle. That would put his fire about sixty feet up the cliff. He could not see anything above twenty feet or so but he did not have to.

Not yet.

Within moments the helicopter crept around the curve in the glacier. The pilots stopped to kill their night-vision goggles. Otherwise, the fire would have blinded them. They switched on their exterior light, illuminating the side of the cliff. As soon as the chopper opened fire on what they thought was one of the terrorists, Rodgers also began to shoot. His target were bulges of ice nearest the top of the chopper. The nose gun ripped up the torch, dousing the flame. The roar also tore away more surface ice. At the same time Rodgers's barrage sent larger ice chips flying into the rotor. The blades sliced the ice into a runny sleet that rained down on the cockpit. The slush landed on the windshield and froze instantly.

The chopper stopped firing.

So did Rodgers.

While the chopper still had its lights on, Rodgers briefly considered taking a shot at the cockpit. However, since Afghanistan and Chechnya, the Russians had equipped many of the newer Mikoyan assault choppers with bullet-proof glass to protect them from snipers. Rodgers did not want the flashes from his muzzle to reveal his position.

The general crouched in the open, waiting to see what the helicopter would do. He calculated that it had been in the air at least ninety minutes. The pilot had to allow for at least another ninety minutes of flying time to return to base. That would strain the Mi-35's fuel supply. It would also put extreme stress on the chopper's thermal tolerance, especially if the crew had to fight an ice storm each time they fired their nose gun. Even though the windshield would defrost in a minute or two, the ice would chill the external rotor casing.

Rodgers watched as the chopper hovered. His heart was thumping double-time due to anticipation and cold. Except for being a hell of a lot warmer, Rodgers wondered if the young shepherd David felt the same after letting his small pebble fly against the Philistine champion Goliath. If successful, David's gamble could result in victory for his people. If it failed, the boy faced an ugly, obscure death in the dusty Vale of Elah.

The chopper's exterior lights snapped off. The glacier was once again in darkness. All Rodgers could do now was wait and listen. It took exactly fifteen heartbeats for him to hear what he had been waiting for. With a sudden surge of power, the Mi-35 turned and swung back along the glacier. The beat of the rotor retreated quickly behind the wall of ice.

Rodgers waited to make certain that the helicopter was really gone. After another minute or so the glacier was silent. Slipping his gun into his vest, he took the matches from his jacket pocket and lit the torch. He held it ahead of him. The flame cast a flickering orange teardrop across the ice. It dimly illuminated the ice wall. And with it, the fallen torch and the shredded parka.

"Thank you, Apu, for saving me a second time," Rodgers said. Throwing off a small salute, he turned and followed the others to the northeast.

FIFTY-FIVE

Washington, D.C.
Thursday, 4:30 P.M.

Paul Hood watched the clock turn on his computer. "Make the call, Bob," he said.

Bob Herbert and Lowell Coffey III were both in the office with Hood. The door was closed and Bugs Benet had been told not to interrupt the men unless the president or Senator Fox was calling. Herbert picked up the wheelchair phone to call Brett August. Coffey was seated beside Herbert in a leather armchair. The attorney would be present for the remainder of the mission. His job was to counsel Hood regarding international legal matters that might come up. Coffey had already strongly informed Hood that he was very unhappy with the idea on the table. That an American military officer was leading a team consisting of a Pakistani terrorist, an NSA agent, and what amounted to two Indian hostages. And he was taking them into what was apparently a Pakistani nuclear missile site that had been erected in disputed territory. The idea that this constituted an ad hoc United Nations security council team still wasn't working for him.

Hood agreed that Ambassador Simathna's plan was not a great idea. Unfortunately, it was the only idea. Bob Herbert and Ron Plummer both backed Hood up on that.

The TAC-SAT number Herbert had to input included not just the number of the unit but a code to access the satellite. This made it extremely difficult for someone to reach the TAC-SAT or use it if they found it. Hood waited while Herbert finished punching in the lengthy number.

As Hood had expected, he had not heard from the president and the members of the Congressional Intelligence

Oversight Committee. Over ninety minutes ago, Hood had e-mailed them a summary of the Pakistani plan. According to executive assistants to both President Lawrence and Senator Fox, they were still "studying" Op-Center's proposal. After a short, angry debate with Coffey, Hood decided not to tell the president or Fox what kind of Pakistani military facility Rodgers was visiting. He did not want the CIA crawling all over sources in the region to try to find out what was out there. Coffey argued that with events moving beyond their direct control, Hood had a responsibility to give the president all the facts and hearsay at his disposal. And then it was up to the president, not Hood, to decide whether to call in the CIA. Hood disagreed. He had only Simathna's say-so that there was a nuclear site out there. Hood did not want to legitimize a possible Pakistani ploy by routing it through the White House and thus making it seem valid. Moreover, news of a possible nuclear silo might trigger an Indian strike while Rodgers was out there. That, too, could serve Pakistani purposes by forcing the United States into a confrontation with India.

Even with the edited report he had presented, Hood did not expect to hear from the president or Fox before H-hour. If the operation failed, they would say that Hood had been acting on his own. It would be Oliver North redux. If the Striker mission succeeded they would quickly jump onboard, like the Soviets declaring war on Japan in the waning hours of the Second World War.

After all that Paul Hood had done to help President Lawrence, he would have liked more support. Then again, when Hood saved the administration from a coup attempt he was doing his job. Now the president was performing his own duties. He was stalling. President Lawrence was using the delay to create a buffer of plausible deniability. That would protect the United States from possible international backlash if the Kashmir situation exploded. The abandonment was not personal. It only felt that way.

Hood did not have the luxury of time. He had told Mike Rodgers that he would hear from Brett August in two hours. Two hours had passed. It was time to place the call.

Op-Center's director had rarely felt this isolated. There were usually other field personnel or international organizations backing them up, whether it was Interpol or the Russian Op-Center. Even when he was dealing with the terrorists at the United Nations, Hood had the backing of the State Department. Except for the nominal support of the new head of the NSA, and the help of Stephen Viens at the NRO, they were alone. Alone and trying to stop a nuclear war, a world away, with a cell phone. Even the National Reconnaissance Office was not able to help much now. The towering peaks of the glacier blocked the satellite's view of much of the "playing field," as intelligence experts called any active region. Ice storms blocked the rest. Viens had not even been able to verify there was anything but ice at the coordinates the Pakistani ambassador had provided.

Herbert and August had not spoken for nearly an hour. Herbert had not wanted to distract him. Hood hoped there was someone at the other end of the TAC-SAT to take the call.

Colonel August answered quickly. Herbert put the conversation on the speakerphone. Except for the shrieking winds behind him, the colonel's voice was strong and clear.

Ron Plummer and the Pakistani ambassador were still on Hood's line. As Hood had promised, he left that speakerphone on as well.

"Colonel, I'm with Paul and Lowell Coffey," Herbert told him. "We also have the Pakistani ambassador and Ron Plummer on the other line. You are all on speaker."

"I copy that," August said.

August would know, now, not to say anything that might compromise American security objectives or operations.

"What's been happening there?" Herbert asked.

"Apparently, nothing," August said.

"Nothing at all?" Herbert asked.

"We can't see much now because of the ice storm and darkness," August told him. "But the Indians turn on lights occasionally and as far as we can tell there are still roughly two hundred soldiers at the foot of the plateau. We saw them making preparations for an ascent and then they just stopped about ninety minutes ago. They seem to be waiting."

"For backup?" Herbert asked.

"Possibly, sir," August said. "The delay could also be weather related. We've got a nasty ice storm kicking around us. It would not be a fun climb. Sharab says the winds usually subside just after dawn. The Indians could be waiting for that. With diminished winds they could also bring in low-altitude air support. Or the Indians could just be waiting for us to freeze."

"You feel you're in no immediate danger?" Hood asked.

"No, sir, we don't appear to be," August informed him. "Except for the cold we're all right."

"Hopefully, we'll be able to move you out before too long," Herbert said. "Colonel, we'd like you to raise Mike and his team. If they've arrived at the coordinates, and only if they are at the coordinates, tell them that they have reached an underground Pakistani nuclear missile site. The site is unmanned and operated remotely. Tell them to stand by and then call me back. The ambassador will provide us with passwords that will enable the team to enter the silo. Once inside they will receive instructions on how to access video equipment that the Pakistani military uses to monitor the facility."

"I understand," August said. "I'll contact General Rodgers now."

"Let us know if he has not reached the coordinates and also report back on the condition of his team," Herbert added.

August said he would, then signed off.

Hood did not know whether anything Ambassador Simathna had said to this point was true. But after Herbert hung up, the Pakistani said something on which they both agreed.

"The colonel," Simathna said, "is a courageous man."

FIFTY-SIX

The Siachin Glacier
Friday, 2:07 A.M.

Exhausted and freezing, Rodgers and his team reached the coordinates Brett August had provided.

Rodgers had half-expected to find a field with a temporary Pakistani outpost. Perhaps a few mobile missile launchers, landing lights for helicopters, and a camouflaged shed or two. He was wrong. They found some of the most inhospitable terrain they had yet encountered. Rodgers felt as though he had stepped into some Ice Age environment.

A circle of surrounding peaks enclosed an area of about ten acres. The team had walked through a large, circular, apparently artificial tunnel to get through the wall. Starting very close to the ground, the slopes jutted out at steep angles. At some time in the past slabs of ice must have broken from the facades and covered the ground. Or perhaps this was an ice cave and the roof had simply collapsed. The field itself was extremely rough and uneven, covered with rough-edged lumps of ice and slashed with narrow, jagged fissures. The harshness of the terrain suggested it did not get much sun. There did not appear to be the kind of smoothness that came with melting and refreezing. They were also at a much higher altitude than they were at the mouth of the valley. He doubted that temperatures here got much above zero degrees Fahrenheit.

Samouel and Friday were still relatively alert but Nanda was numb. Shortly after the Mi-35 turned and left, the woman had fallen quiet. Her muscles and expression had relaxed and she seemed almost in a trance. She moved along as he tugged her hand. But she had a rubbery, unfocused gait. Rodgers had seen this kind of emotional shutdown in

Vietnam. It usually occurred after a GI had lost a good buddy in combat. Clinically speaking, Rodgers did not know how long the effects lasted. But he did know that he could not count on afflicted soldiers for days thereafter. After everything that had happened, it would be tragic if they could not even get Nanda to tell her story.

Samouel and Friday had been walking a few paces ahead of Rodgers and Nanda. After the men had a chance to light their torches and flashlights and shine them along the walls and ground, they walked over to the general. Friday handed Rodgers the cell phone.

"Here we are," Friday said angrily. "Now the question is where the hell are we?"

Rodgers released Nanda's hand. She stared into the darkness as Rodgers went to check the time on the cell phone. The cold was so intense that the liquid crystal screen cracked. The digital numbers vanished instantly.

"Well done," Friday said.

Rodgers did not respond. He was angry at himself too. The cell phone was their only link to the outside world. He should have foreseen what the intense cold would do. He closed the phone and put it in his pocket, where it would be relatively warm. Then he turned to Nanda. He warmed her exposed cheeks with his breath and was heartened when she looked at him.

"Look around, try and find out why we've been sent here," Rodgers said to the men.

"Probably to die," Friday said. "I don't trust any of these bastards, not the Indians or the Pakistanis."

"Or even your own government," Samouel said.

"Oh, you heard?" Friday said. "Well, you're right. I don't trust the politicians in Washington either. They're all using us for something."

"For peace," Samouel insisted.

"Is that what you were doing in Kashmir?" Friday demanded.

"We were trying to weaken an enemy that has oppressed us for centuries," Samouel told him. "The stronger we are the greater our capacity to maintain the peace."

"Fighting for peace, the great oxymoron," Friday said. "What a crock. You want power just like everyone else."

Rodgers had let the discussion go on because anger generated body heat. Now it was time to stop. He moved between the men.

"I need you to check the perimeter," Rodgers said. "Now."

"For what?" Friday asked. "A secret, open sesame passage? Superman's Fortress of Solitude?"

"Mr. Friday, you're pushing me," Rodgers said.

"We're in a big, cold shooting gallery thanks to the bureaucrats but I'm pushing you?" Friday said. "This is a freakin' joke!"

The cell phone buzzed in Rodgers's pocket. The general was grateful for the interruption. He had been getting ready to end the conversation by knocking Friday on his ass. It was not a logical Hegelian solution but it would have worked for Rodgers. Big time.

The general pulled the phone out and shielded it with his high collar.

"Rodgers here!"

"Mike, it's Brett," August said. "Have you reached the coordinates?"

"Just got here," he said. "Are you okay?"

"So far," August replied. "You?"

"Surviving."

"Stay warm," August replied.

"Thanks," Rodgers said.

The general closed up the phone and put it back in his left pocket. His fingers were numb and he kept his hand there. Friday and Samouel had stuck the torches in a narrow fissure and were warming themselves around it. Both men looked up when the phone call ended.

"That was short," Friday said.

"Op-Center needed to confirm that we're here," Rodgers said. "We'll get the rest of the plan ASAP."

"Does Op-Center already have the plan or are they getting it from somewhere in Pakistan?" Friday asked.

"I don't know," Rodgers admitted.

"We're being set up," Friday said. "I can feel it."

"Talk to me about it," Rodgers said. The man might not be likable but that did not mean he was wrong.

"Jack Fenwick used to have a word for operatives who accepted partial codes or portions of maps," Friday said. "The word was 'dead.' If you can't control your own time, your own movements, it means that someone else is."

"In this case there's a reason for that," Rodgers reminded him. "Security issues."

"That reason serves Islamabad and Washington, not us," Friday said. "Fenwick would never have cut this kind of deal with a hostile government."

All covert operatives were cautious. But there was something about this man that seemed paranoid. Maybe the strain of the trek had worn them both thin. Or maybe Rodgers's earlier impression was right. The son of a bitch was distracted. Maybe his distrust of Washington went further than he had admitted.

Fenwick was like that too.

"Did you have a lot of contact with Director Fenwick?" Rodgers asked.

The question seemed to surprise Friday. It took him a moment to answer.

"I didn't work closely with Jack Fenwick, no," Friday said. "He was the director of the NSA. I'm a field operator. There is not a lot of overlap in our job descriptions."

"But you obviously had some contact with him," Rodgers said. "You were stationed in Azerbaijan. That was where he worked his last operation. He had some personal, hands-on involvement with that."

"We talked a few times," Friday acknowledged. "He asked for intelligence, I got it for him. There was nothing unusual about that. Why do you ask?"

"You put a lot of faith in your instincts," Rodgers said. "We all do when we're in the field. I was just wondering if your instincts ever told you that Fenwick was a traitor."

"No," Friday said.

"So they were wrong," Rodgers pressed.

Friday made a strange face, as though he were repulsed by the thought of having been wrong.

Or maybe Friday was disturbed by something else, Rodgers thought suddenly. Maybe the man could not admit his instincts were wrong because they had not been wrong. Maybe Friday had known that Jack Fenwick was attempting to overthrow the government of the United States. Yet Friday certainly could not admit he knew that either.

The implications of Ron Friday's silence were disturbing. One of the keys to Fenwick's plan had been starting an oil war between Azerbaijan, Iran, and Russia. To help that along, CIA operatives based in the U.S. embassy had to be murdered. The killer of one of those agents was never found.

The phone beeped again. Rodgers and Friday continued to look at one another. Friday's hands were still warming over the fire. Rodgers had his right hand in his pocket. As they stood there they shared a subtle alpha male exchange. Friday started to withdraw his right hand from the fire. He apparently wanted to put it in the pocket where he kept his gun. Rodgers poked his right hand further into his own pocket so it bulged. Friday did not know where the general kept his weapon. It happened to be in his equipment vest but Friday apparently did not realize that. Friday's right hand remained exposed.

In the meantime, Rodgers answered the phone. "Yes?"

"Mike, are you in a clearing hedged by ice?" August asked.

"Yes," Rodgers replied.

"All right," August said. "Look to the northwest side of the clearing. At the base of one of the slopes you should see a perfectly flat, white slab of ice about two yards by two yards."

Rodgers told Friday to pick up one of the torches. Then he told Samouel to sit with Nanda. Together, Rodgers and Friday walked toward the northwest side of the clearing.

"We're on our way over," Rodgers said. "Brett, any idea what the shape is of the chunk we're looking for?"

"Bob didn't say," August replied. "I guess 'slab' means flat."

The men continued walking across the uneven terrain. It was difficult to keep their footing because of all the small pits, cracks, and occasional patches of smooth ice. Rodgers remained several steps behind Friday. Even if Rodgers did not stumble, a man with a lit torch could be a formidable opponent.

Suddenly, Rodgers saw a piece of ice that fit the dimensions August provided. They walked toward it.

"I think we have it!" Rodgers said.

"Good," August told him. "You're going to have to move that and then wait for me to call back."

"For what?" Rodgers asked.

"For the code that will open the hatch underneath," August said.

"A hatch to what?" Rodgers asked.

"To an unmanned Pakistani nuclear missile facility," August told him. "Apparently the Pakistanis use a video setup to monitor the place. You're going to use that equipment to make your broadcast."

"I see," Rodgers said. "Hold on."

Mike Rodgers felt a chill from inside. The setting no longer appeared prehistoric. It suddenly seemed calculated, like a theme park attraction. The ice was real but it had probably been arranged to look uninviting and confusing, to discourage ground traffic or overhead surveillance. Pakistani soldiers must have camped here in camouflage tents for months, possibly years, working on the silo and the setting. The Pakistani air force would have flown in parts and supplies, probably solo excursions at night to lessen the chance of discovery. If they were telling the truth, it was an impressive achievement.

Rodgers kicked the edge of the slab with his toe. It was heavy. They were going to need help. The general turned. He motioned for Samouel to bring Nanda and join them.

Just then, Rodgers noticed movement along the dimly lit wall behind Samouel. Shadows were shifting on the ice near the northeast slope. The movement was being caused by the torchlight. But the shadows were not being cast by the mounds of ice. The shadows of the ice piled near the walls were moving up and down. These shadows were creeping from side to side.

Right beside the entrance to the enclosure.

"Friday," Rodgers said quietly but firmly, "kill the light and move away from me fast."

The urgency in Mike Rodgers's voice must have impressed Ron Friday. The NSA operative shoved the torch into a fissure headfirst and jumped to his left, away from Rodgers.

"Samouel, get behind something!" Rodgers shouted.

The general's voice was still echoing through the enclosure as he ran forward. Rodgers was afraid the phone would fall from his pocket so he tucked it into his equipment vest. A moment later he tripped on a small pit and banged his left shoulder on a chunk of ice. Instead of getting up again he moved ahead on all fours, crablike. It was the only way to negotiate the uneven terrain without falling. He kept moving toward where he had last seen Samouel and Nanda. He did not feel pain. The only thing that mattered was getting to Nanda. And hoping that he was wrong about what he saw.

He was not.

A moment later the fire of automatic weapons sent deep pops and dull sparks bouncing from the icy walls.

FIFTY-SEVEN

Washington, D.C.
Thursday, 5:00 P.M.

Hood's office was supernaturally silent when Herbert's phone beeped. His heart had begun to race just moments before, as though he knew the call was coming. Or maybe he was just getting more anxious as the minutes crept by. Even if nothing was happening, Herbert did not like being out of touch.

The intelligence chief jabbed the audio button. Wind screamed from the tiny speaker. It seemed to draw Herbert into the Himalayas. Or maybe he was feeling something else. A sense of exposure. The sound was being sucked from Herbert's armrest to the speakerphone on Hood's desk. The intelligence officer was unaccustomed to working with an audience. He did not like it.

"Go ahead," Herbert shouted.

"Bob, I think something just happened at the missile site," Colonel August informed him.

Herbert fired a glance at Hood's phone. Then he looked at Hood. Herbert wanted his boss to mute the damn thing.

"Mike's ass is on the line," Herbert said through his teeth.

"The damage is already done," Hood said softly as he nodded toward the speakerphone on his desk where the Pakistani ambassador was still on the line. He raised his voice. "Colonel, what's the situation?" Hood asked.

"I'm not certain, sir," August said. "I heard gunfire and shouting. Then there was nothing. I hung on for a few minutes before deciding to call. I thought I could use the downtime to get the codes in case Mike came back on."

"Colonel, was there any indication who might be firing at who?" Herbert asked.

"No," August replied. "Before it started, all I heard was someone shouting for the others to duck and take cover. I assume it was General Rodgers."

"Are you still secure?" Herbert asked.

"Nothing has changed here," August replied.

"All right," Herbert said. "Hold on."

Hood turned to the speakerphone. "Mr. Ambassador, did you hear the colonel's report?"

"Every word," Ambassador Simathna replied. "It does not sound like a happy situation."

"We don't know enough to say what the situation is exactly," Hood pointed out. "I do agree with Colonel August about having the codes ready to give to Mike Rodgers. Perhaps if he can get inside the silo—"

"I cannot agree," Simathna interrupted.

"Why is that, sir?" Hood asked.

"Almost certainly those are Indian troops attacking the general's group," Simathna said.

"How do we know they aren't Pakistani troops protecting the site?" Herbert asked.

"Because the mountain troops that monitor the glacier have remained on our side of the line of control," Simathna informed him. "They were told of your incursion."

" 'Our' incursion," Herbert said. He did not even attempt to conceal his disgust. "There's a Pakistani on the team."

"He is under the command of an American military officer," Simathna reminded him.

"How do we know your mountain troops obeyed their instructions?" Herbert pressed.

"I am telling you they have," Simathna replied.

Hood scowled and dragged the back of his thumb across his throat. He was telling Herbert to kill the discussion he had opened. Herbert would rather kill the ambassador. They were trying to save this man's country from vaporization and he would not do a thing to help Mike Rodgers.

"Mr. Ambassador," Hood said, "we have to assume that General Rodgers and his people will prevail. When they do they'll need to get into the silo as quickly as possible. It would be prudent to give Colonel August the codes."

"Again, I cannot allow that," Simathna replied. "It is unfortunate enough that our enemies may learn of this strategic site. But at least the safeguards are still in place."

"What safeguards?" Hood asked.

"Removing the ice block on top of the silo will trigger a timed explosive within the hatch," the ambassador told him. "Unless the proper code is entered within sixty minutes the bomb will detonate. It will trigger a series of conventional explosions that will destroy the surface area."

"Killing the enemy but leaving the silo intact," Herbert said.

"That is correct," the ambassador told him.

"Mr. Ambassador, we are still facing a nuclear attack on Pakistan," Hood pressed.

"We understand that, which is why we must protect our silos from discovery," Simathna told him.

That remark got Herbert's attention. It got Hood's attention, too, judging from his expression. The ambassador had just revealed that there were other silos, probably in other remote areas. That was not an accident. He had wanted Op-Center to know that, and to know it now.

Herbert knew it would be pointless to ask how many silos there were or where they were located. The question was whether revealing that information to New Delhi would trigger an immediate nuclear strike against the region or whether it would force India to stand down. Probably the latter. If Indian intelligence did not already know about the silos they would not know where to strike. Perhaps that was why Simathna had mentioned it. The information would sound more authentic if it were leaked to New Delhi from a branch of U.S. intelligence.

Of course, as with everything else Simathna told them, Herbert had no way of knowing if this were true. For all they knew, there was only the one silo. And there was no way of knowing if there were even a missile inside. Perhaps it was still in the process of being built.

"Ambassador Simathna, I'm going to ask Colonel August to free up his telephone line now," Hood said. "He'll let us know as soon as he hears from General Rodgers."

Hood looked at Herbert. Herbert nodded and told August to sign off until he had reestablished communication with Rodgers. Then Herbert punched off the telephone and sat back.

"Thank you," Simathna said. "Please try to understand our position."

"I do," Hood insisted.

So did Herbert. He understood that Rodgers and August were risking their lives for people who weren't going to do anything to help. He had been in this business long enough to know that covert operatives were considered expendable. They were at the front line of disposable assets.

Except when you knew them.

When they had names and faces and lives that touched yours every day.

Like Rodgers and August.

Like Striker.

The room was silent again, and still.

Except for the desperate racing of Herbert's heart.

FIFTY-EIGHT

The Siachin Glacier
Friday, 2:35 A.M.

White and red flares exploded in the skies above the clearing. Rodgers could now see the soldiers who were firing at them. They were a handful of Indian regulars, probably out from the line of control. The four or five men took up positions behind ice formations near the entrance.

Rodgers immediately dropped to his belly and began wriggling through the broken terrain. Friday was behind the slab at the entrance to the missile silo. He was firing at the Indians to keep them down. Rodgers watched the entrance for signs of additional troops. There were none.

The flares also enabled Rodgers to see Samouel and Nanda. The two were about thirty feet away. They were lying on their sides behind a thick chunk of ice. The barricade was roughly three feet tall and fifteen feet wide. The Pakistani was stretched out behind the woman. He was pushing her face-first against the ice, his arm around her, protecting her on all sides. Rodgers did not have the time to contemplate it, but the irony of a Pakistani terrorist protecting an Indian civilian operative did not escape him.

Bullets pinged furiously from the top of the formation. The onslaught showered the two with ice. As the barrier was whittled down Samouel looked around. Mike Rodgers was behind and slightly to the right of the two. The Pakistani did not appear to notice him.

"Samouel!" Rodgers yelled.

The Pakistani looked over. Rodgers sidled to his right, behind a boulder-shaped formation. He wanted Nanda as close as possible, in case they managed to get inside the silo.

"Come back here!" Rodgers shouted. "I'll cover you!"

"Very good," Rodgers said. "Now tell me more about the ledge. Was there any way to get to the dish? Ledges, projections, handholds."

"I don't think so," Samouel told him. "It looked like a straight climb up a smooth wall."

"I see," Rodgers said.

The general had become slightly disoriented in the dash to save Nanda. He needed to get his bearings again. He turned himself completely around so he was facing what he believed was the back of the enclosure. He crouched on the balls of his feet.

"Friday, are you still at the slab?" Rodgers yelled.

Friday was silent.

"Say something!" Rodgers screamed.

"I'm here!" Friday said.

Rodgers pinpointed Friday's voice. He kept his eyes on the dark spot. At the same time, he reached into his vest and removed the cell phone. He gave the unit to Samouel.

"If Colonel August calls, tell him to keep the line open," Rodgers told Samouel.

"What are you going to do?" the Pakistani asked.

"Try and get to that dish," Rodgers replied. "How are you set for ammunition?"

"I have a few rounds and one extra clip," Samouel told him.

"Use them sparingly," Rodgers said. "I may need the cover when I start up the slope."

"I will be very careful," Samouel promised.

Mike Rodgers flexed his cold, gloved fingers then put his hands on the ground. He was anxious. A lot was riding on what he knew to be a long shot. He was also concerned about Ron Friday, about something the NSA operative had said earlier. Even if they got through this impasse Rodgers wondered if a deadlier one lay ahead. But that was not something he could afford to worry about now. One battle at a time.

After pausing to take a long, calming breath, the general once again began moving crablike across the rugged terrain.

FIFTY-NINE

The Siachin Glacier
Friday, 2:42 A.M.

Ron Friday listened as someone approached. He assumed it was either Rodgers or Samouel.

Probably Rodgers, the NSA operative decided. The go-get-'em warrior. The general would have a plan to salvage this mission. Which was fine with Friday. No one wanted a nuclear war. But barring such a plan, Friday also cared about getting the hell off this glacier and into Pakistan. And then from Pakistan to somewhere else. Anywhere that was upwind from the fallout that would blanket the Indian subcontinent.

Friday wanted out of here not because he was afraid to die. What scared him was dying stupidly. Not for a trophy or a jewel but because of a screwup. And right now they were in the middle of a massive screwup. A side trip that should never have happened. All because they had trusted the bureaucrats in Washington and Islamabad.

Friday waited behind the slab. The Indians must have heard the movement too because fresh gunfire pinged around the perimeter. There was not a lot of it. They were obviously conserving ammunition. They fired just enough to keep the person low and on the move.

Friday peered out at the blackness. His own weapon was drawn. His nostrils and lungs hurt from the knife-edged cold. His toes and fingertips were numb, despite the heavy boots and gloves. If he were shot, he wondered how long it would take the blood to freeze.

But most of all Friday was angry. It would not take much for him to point the gun at Rodgers and pull the trigger. The NSA operative was trying to figure out if anything could be gained by surrendering to the Indians. Assuming the Indians would not shoot the group out of hand, they might appreciate the American bringing them one of the terrorists who had attacked the marketplace. Surrender might well trigger the feared Indian nuclear strike against Pakistan. It might also save him from dying here.

The figure arrived. It was Rodgers. He crawled behind the slab and knelt beside Friday.

"What's going on?" Friday asked.

"There might be a way to get Nanda's confession on the air without entering the silo," Rodgers said.

"A silo. Is that what this place is?" Friday asked.

Rodgers ignored the question. "Samouel thinks he saw a satellite dish about ten feet up the slope," Rodgers continued.

"That would make sense," Friday replied.

"Explain," Rodgers said.

"When the flares came on I got a good look at the wall over the entrance," Friday said. "From about ten feet up on this side they'd have a clear shot across the opposite slope."

"That's what I was hoping," Rodgers said. "If there is a dish there, and we can get to the satellite cable, Samouel might be able to splice a connection to the cell phone."

The men heard movement from the other side of the clearing. Friday did not think the Indians would move against them. They would wait for the helicopter to return. But they might try to position themselves to set up a cross fire. If the Indians got Nanda the game was over. So were their own lives.

"We're going to have to get a good look at the dish before we do anything," Friday said.

"Why?" Rodgers asked.

"We need to see where the power source is," Friday said. "This is a good spot for a battery-driven dish. Oil companies use them in icy areas. The power source doubles as a heater to keep the gears from freezing. If that's the case, we don't have to go up to the ledge. We can expose the line anywhere and know it's the communications cable."

"But if the power source is inside the silo we have to get to the dish and figure out which cable it is," Rodgers said.

"Bingo," said Friday.

"I'll tell you what," Rodgers said. "You stay down and keep your eyes on the ledge."

"What are you going to do?"

Rodgers replied, "Get you some light."

SIXTY

The Siachin Glacier
Friday, 2:51 A.M.

Mike 'Rodgers moved to the far end of the clearing. He stopped when he reached the slope. Crouching and moving as quietly as possible he made his way along the wall. He wanted to be far enough from the slab so that Friday was protected. He did not need to be protected from what Rodgers was planning but from how the Indians might respond.

Rodgers hoped that Friday got a good look at the dish. Chances were good that Rodgers himself would not be seeing much. He would be busy looking for a place to hide.

The general stopped about twenty yards from Friday. That was a safe distance. He opened his jacket and removed one of the two flash-bang grenades he carried. The weapon was about the size and configuration of a can of shaving cream. He removed his gloves and held them in his teeth. Then he put his right hand across the safety spoon and slipped his left index finger through the pull-ring. He placed the canister on the ground and squatted beside it. Rodgers moved his right foot along the ground to make sure where the ice cliff was. He would need that to guide him. Then he pulled the ring, released the spoon, and rose. He turned and put his bare left hand against the slope. He felt his way around the thick bulges and barren stretches. He wanted to move quickly. But if he fell over something he might be exposed when the grenade went off.

Rodgers counted as he moved. When the general reached ten, the nonlethal grenade went off.

The nonlethal flash-bang grenade was designed to roll in a confined area, distracting and disorienting the occupants with a series of magnesium-bright explosions and deafening bangs. In this case, Rodgers was hoping the grenade would brighten the perimeter just enough for two things. For Friday to see the dish and Rodgers to find a place to duck.

There was a series of round-topped ice formations three feet ahead. They were about waist high and as thick as a highway pylon. They had probably once been much taller but looked as if they melted and refroze daily, gaining in girth what they lost in height. Rodgers did not run for them. He dove.

Rodgers hit the ground hard. He lost his breath, his gloves fell from his teeth, and he did not quite reach the barricade. But he got close enough so that he was able to scramble across the ice in a heartbeat. Fortunately, the heartbeat was still a measure of time he could use as bullets from Indian rifles chewed up the ice where he had been standing. As soon as he was down and safe he looked over at Ron Friday. Crouched behind the slab, the operative gave him a thumbs-up. Rodgers glanced at the ledge. There was a large black casing behind the base of the dish. Rodgers was glad Friday knew what it was. He himself would have had to go up and pry the cover off to try to read the cables.

As the light of the grenade died Rodgers looked over at Samouel and Nanda. The Pakistani was still lying down. But he had turned to look back at the other men. Rodgers needed to get him over with Nanda and the cell phone. This was probably the best time to do it.

Rodgers took out his weapon and indicated to Friday to do the same. Then he moved to the far side of the ice barricade. That gave him the clearest line of sight to Samouel. He held up three fingers. The Pakistani understood. He was to move out on a count of three. Rodgers gave the man a moment to prepare.

Samouel moved Nanda away from the boulder where they were lying. The Pakistani helped her to her knees and then to a crouching position. She seemed to be cooperating, aware of what she must do. Samouel looked toward Rodgers. The general quickly extended his fingers one at a time. At three, Samouel got up and pulled Nanda with him. She was in front, the Pakistani shielding her with his body. As the two ran forward, Rodgers and Friday immediately stood and began firing toward the Indians. The infantrymen were out of range but obviously did not know that. They ducked down immediately, giving Samouel time to cover most of the distance to the silo entrance.

As darkness enveloped the clearing a few more shots were fired from the Indian side.

"Don't return fire!" Rodgers shouted to Friday.

The general was afraid of hitting Samouel and Nanda in the dark.

The men listened to the crunch of the approaching boots. The gait was near but uneven. That was due, possibly, to the icy, unknown terrain. The sound skewed toward Rodgers's right, away from the silo. He crept to that side of his position and waited.

A few seconds later someone dropped beside Rodgers. The general reached out to pull whoever it was to safety. It was Nanda. Still on his knees, Rodgers wrapped his arms around her. He literally hauled her in and around him. Then Rodgers turned back to his right. He heard grunting a few feet away. The general crept over. He found Samouel near the front of the barricade. The Pakistani was on his belly. Rodgers grabbed the man under his arms. His bare right hand felt a thick dampness. The general pulled Samouel back behind the stumps of ice.

"Samouel, can you hear me?" Rodgers said.

"Yes," the Pakistani replied.

Rodgers felt around the man's left side. The dampness was spreading. It was definitely blood.

"Samouel, you're wounded," Rodgers said.

"I know," Samouel said, "General, I've 'screwed up.' "

"No," Rodgers said. "You did fine. We'll fix this—"

"I don't mean that," Samouel said. "I . . . lost the telephone."

The words hit Rodgers like a bullet.

Suddenly, gunfire erupted from the left. The short burst had come from Ron Friday.

"Our buddies are on the move again!" Friday said.

"Get down!" the general shouted.

Rodgers had no time for them. He reached into his vest and removed one of the two cylindrical "eight ball" grenades he carried. Those were the ones no one wanted to find themselves behind, the shrapnel-producing grenades. Without hesitation the general yanked the pin, let the no-snag cap pop off, and stiff-armed the explosive across the clearing. He did not want to kill the Indians but he could not afford to waste time. Not with Samouel injured.

Rodgers ducked and pulled Nanda down. Several seconds later the eight ball exploded, echoing off the walls and shaking the ground. Even before the reverberations stopped, Rodgers had pulled the nine-inch knife from his equipment vest. He had immediately begun prioritizing. Stop the Indians. Stop Samouel's bleeding. Then he would worry about the phone.

"Don't bother with me," Samouel said. "I'm all right."

"You're hit," Rodgers said.

The general cut into the man's coat. He put his right hand through the opening. He felt for a wound.

Rodgers found it. A bullet hole just below the left shoulder blade. He reached out to the right and felt for his gloves. He found them, cut out the soft interior linings, and placed them on the wound. He pressed down hard. He could not think of anything else to do.

The clearing was silent as the reverberation of the grenade subsided. There were no moans from the other side, no shouting. There was just deadly silence as time and options slipped away. Without the cell phone they could not communicate with August or hook up to the dish. Finding the unit in the dark would be time consuming, if it was even possible. Going out with a torch was suicide. And if they lost Samouel, none of it even mattered.

It had been a good plan. Ironically, they would have been better off following the instincts of a man who might well be a traitor.

Mike Rodgers crouched there, his arms held low. He continued to press on the makeshift bandage, hoping the blood on the underside would freeze. When that happened he would have to try to recover the phone, even if it cost him his life.

As Rodgers waited, his right elbow knocked into something in his belt.

He realized at once what it was.

Possible salvation.

SIXTY-ONE

Siachin Base 3, Kashmir
Friday, 3:22 A.M.

The Mikoyan Mi-35 helicopter set down on its small, dark pad. The square landing area was composed of a layer of asphalt covered with cotton and then another layer of asphalt. The fabric helped keep the ice from the lower layer from reaching the upper layer.

No sooner had the pilot cut the twin rotors than he received a message over his headset.

"Captain, we just received a message from Major Puri," the base communications director informed him. "You're to refuel, deice, and go back out."

The captain exchanged a disgruntled look with the copilot. The cockpit was poorly heated and they were both tired from the difficult flight. They did not feel like undertaking a new mission.

As the pilot looked over, he glanced past his companion. Through the starboard window of the cockpit he could already see ground crews approaching. There were two trucks crossing the landing area. One was a fuel tank, the other a truck loaded with high-volume hoses and drums of a solution of sodium chloride–ferric ferrocyanide.

"What is the objective?" the captain asked.

"The cell you were tracking before," the BCD replied. "One of Major Puri's units has them cornered. The unit estimates that there are four individuals but they do not know how heavily armed they are."

The captain felt a flush of satisfaction at the news. Although he had admired the way one man, armed with a pistol, had driven them back, he did not like being outsmarted.

"Where are they?" the captain asked. At the same time he punched up the topographical map on the computer.

"The Upper Chittisin Plateau," the officer replied, and provided the coordinates.

The pilot entered the figures. The criminals had simply followed the mountain. It was a particularly high, cold, inhospitable section of the glacier. He wondered if they had gone there intentionally or ended up there by accident. If intentionally, he could not imagine what was there. Perhaps a safe house of some kind, or a weapons cache.

Whatever it was, he could take the chopper around the glacier on the southwest side and be there in forty-five minutes.

"When we find them, what are our orders?" the captain asked.

"You are to retrieve Major Puri's team and then complete your previous mission," the BCD informed him.

The captain acknowledged the order.

Ten minutes later he was in the air heading toward the target. This time, he would not fail to exterminate the terrorists.

SIXTY-TWO

The Siachin Glacier
Friday, 3:23 A.M.

Samouel's blood was beginning to freeze. Rodgers felt it in his fingertips. They were the only part of his hands that had stayed warm.

As soon as that happened he picked up his knife and leaned close to Nanda. "I want you to come with me," he said.

"All right," she replied.

Together, they crept across the area between the ice barricade and the entrance to the silo.

"I'm coming in with Nanda," Rodgers said in a loud whisper. He did not want Friday thinking it was the Indians circling around.

"Is everything all right?" Friday asked.

"Samouel's been hit," Rodgers told him.

"How bad?"

"Bad," Rodgers said.

"You dumb bastard," Friday said. "And I'm even dumber for following you assholes."

"I guess so," Rodgers replied. He sidled next to Friday and handed him the knife. "If we're through with your debriefing, I'm going back to get Samouel. Meantime, I need you to start digging me a hole in the ice along the side of the silo entrance."

"That's how you're planning to get to the cable?" Friday asked.

"That's how," Rodgers admitted.

"It could be ten feet down!" Friday exclaimed.

"It won't be," Rodgers said. "The ice melts and refreezes out here. The conduit probably cracks a lot. They would not put it so far down that they couldn't reach it for repairs."

"Maybe," Friday said. "Even so, digging through three or four feet of ice is going to take—"

"Just do it," Rodgers told him.

"Up yours," Friday replied. "If Sammy boy croaks we're dead anyway. I think I'm going to have a talk with our Indian neighbors. See if we can't work something out."

Rodgers heard the knife clunk on the ice.

A moment later he heard the blade scrape the ice.

"I'll do it," Nanda said as she began chopping.

That caught Rodgers by surprise. Her voice sounded strong. It was the first indication he had that she was "back." It was their first bit of luck and the timing could not have been better.

Rodgers could not see Friday but he could hear his harsh breathing. The general had his right hand in his coat pocket. He was prepared to shoot Friday if he had to. Not for leaving them. He had that right. But he was afraid of what a cold, tired, and hungry man might say about their situation.

Ron Friday's breathing stayed in the same place. Nanda's action must have shamed him. Or maybe Friday had been testing Rodgers. Sometimes, what a man did not say in response to a threat said more, and was more dangerous, than a saber-rattling reply.

"I'll be right back with Samouel," Rodgers said evenly.

The general turned and recrossed the small area between the two positions. The Indians maintained their silence. Rodgers was now thinking they had been advance scouts for another party. Their orders were obviously to keep the enemy pinned until backup could arrive. Hopefully, that would not be for another half hour or so. If everything else went right in his improvisation, that was all the time Rodgers would need.

Samouel was breathing rapidly when Rodgers reached him. The general was not a doctor. He did not know whether that was a good thing or a bad thing. Under the circumstances, breathing at all was good.

"How're you doing?" Rodgers asked.

"Not very well," Samouel said. He was wheezing. It sounded as if there were blood in his throat.

"You're just disoriented by the trauma," Rodgers lied. "We'll fix you up as soon as we're done here."

"What can we do without the cell phone?" Samouel asked.

Rodgers slipped his arms under the Pakistani. "We still have my point-to-point radio," the general told him. "Will that work?"

"It should," Samouel replied. "The wiring is basically the same."

"That's what I thought," Rodgers said. "I'm going to get us to the cable and pry the back from the radio. Then you're going to tell me how to hook it to the satellite dish."

"Wait," Samouel said.

Rodgers hesitated before lifting him.

"Listen," Samouel said. "Look for the red line underground. Red is always the audio. Inside the radio, find the largest chip. There will be two lines attached. One leads to the microphone. The other to the antenna. Cut the wire leading to the antenna. Splice the red wire from the dish to that one."

"All right," Rodgers replied.

"You understand all that?" Samouel asked.

"I do," Rodgers assured him.

"Then go," Samouel said.

The Pakistani's voice had become weaker as he spoke. Rodgers did not argue with him. Pausing only long enough to squeeze Samouel's hand, Rodgers turned and hurried back to the slab.

SIXTY-THREE

The Siachin Glacier
Friday, 3:25 A.M.

Nanda did not remember much of what had happened since the helicopter had attacked them. She knew that her grandfather had died. But it seemed as if after that her mind had drifted. She was awake but her spirit had been elsewhere. The shock of her grandfather's death must have dulled her kundalini, her life force. That forced the Shakti to take over. Those were the female deities that protected true believers in times of strife. Using their own secret mantras and mandalas, the mystical words and diagrams, the Shakti had guarded her life force until Nanda's own depleted natural energies could revive it.

The shock of the latest explosions and the rattling gunfire had accelerated the process. General Rodgers's high-intensity activities of the last few minutes had finished it. Whatever alertness Nanda had always felt when she was dealing with the SFF had come back to her. And she was glad it had. The young woman's return seemed to have defused whatever tensions had been building between Rodgers and his fellow American.

Nanda continued to chisel, hack, and pry at the ice. She worked from left to right, cutting new inroads with her right hand while scooping out ice chips with her left. At the same time she felt for anything that might be a cable or a conduit. With their luck they would find one and it would be made of steel or some compound they could not break through.

Whatever the outcome, the activity of chopping the hard ice felt good for the moment. It helped keep her blood flowing and kept her torso and arms relatively warm.

Rodgers had only been gone a minute or two before returning. He came back alone.

"Where's your boy?" Friday asked.

"He's not doing too well," Rodgers admitted. "But he told me what to do." The general moved close to Nanda. "Hold on a second," he said. "I want to check the dig."

Nanda stopped. She could hear General Rodgers feeling along the perimeter of the slab.

"This is good," he said. "Thanks. Now I need you both to move back, over by the slope. Lie there with your feet to your chin, arms tucked in, hands over your ears. Leave as little of yourself exposed as possible."

"What are you going to do?" Nanda asked.

"I have one more of those flash-bang grenades I used earlier," Rodgers said. "I'm going to put it in here. Enough of the force will go downward. The heat of the explosion should melt the ice for several feet in all directions."

"Did our terrorist friend tell you what to do if the cable is inside two-inch-thick piping?" Friday asked.

"In that case we bury the hand grenade I have," Rodgers said. "That should put a good-sized dent in any casing. Now go back," he went on. "I'm ready to let this go."

Her hands stretched in front of her, Nanda knee-walked toward the slope. The ground was sharp and lumpy and it hurt. But she was glad to feel the pain. Years before, a potter, an artisan of the menial Sudra caste in Srinagar, had told her that it is better to feel something, even if it is hunger, than to feel nothing at all. Thinking of her own suffering and her dead grandfather, Nanda finally understood what the man had meant.

When she reached the wall, Nanda curled up on the ice the way Rodgers had instructed.

It did not escape Nanda's notice that the American had taken a moment to thank her for the work she had done. In the midst of all the turmoil and doubt, the horror of what had been and what might lie ahead, his word smelled like a single, beautiful rose.

That was the pretty image in the young woman's mind as the ground heaved and her back grew hot beneath her clothes and the roar blew through her hands, ringing her skull from back to jaw.

SIXTY-FOUR

The Siachin Glacier
Friday, 3:27 A.M.

Rodgers did not go as far from ground zero as the others. He knew that the explosion would not hurt him, though it would be hot. But he was counting on that. His exposed fingers were numb and he was going to need them warmed to work. He went as far as the edge of the slab and sat there with his knees upraised and his face buried between them. He used the insides of his knees to cover his ears. His arms were folded across his knees. He was braced for quite a bump when the grenade went off.

Rodgers made certain that the knife was back in his equipment vest and the radio was secure in his belt before he sat down. And he leaned to his left side as much as possible. Hopefully, if the blast knocked Rodgers over, he would not fall on the radio.

The in-ground explosion was even more potent than Rodgers had imagined. The ice beneath him rolled but did not knock Rodgers over. But the blast did take an edge of the slab off. Rodgers could hear the chunk as it whistled upward. The sound was shrill enough to cut through the surf-loud roar of the detonation itself. It came down somewhere to the left. Rodgers imagined the Indians initially thinking they had been attacked by a mortar shell. After a moment they would probably realize that the enemy had detonated another flash-bang grenade.

There were a series of lesser flashes and whiplike cracks as the grenade continued to fire. Before they died, Rodgers made his way over to the site. The explosion had cut a hole in the ice roughly four feet by four feet. Melted ice filled the excavation. Near the center was a severed cable.

While the last embers of the grenade still burned on the edge of the hole, Rodgers flopped on his belly and grabbed the dish-side end of cable. There were three wires bundled together inside a half-inch-thick plastic cover. One of the wires was red, another was yellow, and the third was blue. Rodgers removed his knife and pried the red one from the others. He cut the wet edge off and quickly scored the rubber sides of the wire with the tip of the knife. As he was finishing, the light from the last embers was fading.

"Friday, matches!" he said.

There was no answer.

"Friday!" he repeated.

"He's not here!" Nanda said.

Rodgers looked back. It was too dark to see that far. Either the NSA operative was hiding until he saw which way this went or, anticipating failure, he was making his way to the Indian side of the clearing. Whichever it was, Rodgers could not afford to worry about him. He laid the cable down so the exposed end was out of the melted ice. Then, moving quickly but economically, with a level of anxiety he had never before felt, Rodgers removed the map from his vest pocket. He unfolded the sheet away from the dying ember so it did not create a local breeze. Then he held his breath, leaned forward, and touched the edge of the map to the barely glowing thread of magnesium. He was afraid that if he touched the ember too hard it would be extinguished. Too light and the map would not feel it.

The fate of two nations had been reduced to this. One man's handling of the first and most primitive form of technology human beings had embraced. It put forty thousand years of human development into perspective. We were still territorial carnivores huddling in dark caves.

The paper smoked and then reddened around the edges. A moment later a small orange flame jumped triumphantly across the printed image of Kashmir. That seemed fitting.

"Nanda, come here!" Rodgers said.

The woman hurried over. Assuming the Indians did not move on them, the duo was safe for now. The remaining section of slab would afford them enough protection as long as they did not move from here.

Rodgers handed Nanda the paper when she arrived. He removed his coat, set it on the ice beside the hole, and told Nanda to put the map on it. He said the coat would not burn but he needed to find something else that would.

"Very quickly," he added.

"Hold on," Nanda said.

The young woman reached into her coat pocket and removed the small volume of Upanishads she always carried. She also removed the documents she was supposed to plant on the terrorists to help implicate them when they were captured.

"These devotionals will save more souls than the Brahmans ever imagined," she said.

Obviously, Nanda was experiencing some of the same spiritual and atavistic feelings Rodgers was. Or maybe they were both just exhausted.

As the papers burned, the general withdrew the radio from the belt loop and laid it on the coat. He bent low over it.

The radio was made of one vacuum-formed casing. Rodgers knew he would not be able to break that without risk of damaging the components he needed. Instead, he stuck the knife into the area around the recessed mouthpiece. Rodgers carefully pried that loose. The wire behind it, and the chip to which it was attached, were what he needed to access.

Still listening for activity from across the clearing, Rodgers used the knife to fish out the chip that was attached to the mouthpiece. He could not afford to sever the chip from the unit. If he did that, the chip itself would have no power source. That power came from the battery in the radio, not from the battery behind the satellite dish. He had to make sure he cut the right one to splice. He pulled the mouthpiece out as far as it could go and tilted the opening toward the light. Twenty years ago, this would have been a hopeless task. Radios then were crammed with transistors and wires that were impossible to read. The inside of this radio was relatively clean and open, just a few chips and wires.

Rodgers saw the battery and the wire that hooked the microchip and mouthpiece to it. The other wire, the one that led to the radio antenna, was the one he needed to cut.

Carefully placing the radio back on the coat, Rodgers used the knife to slice that wire as close to the radio antenna as possible. That would give him about two inches of wire to work with.

Crouching and using the tip of his boot as a cutting surface, Rodgers scored and stripped that remaining piece of wire. Then he picked up the scored cable from the satellite dish. He used his fingernails to chip the plastic casing away. When a half inch of wire was exposed, he twisted the two pieces of copper together and turned the unit on. Then he backed away from the radio and gently urged Nanda toward it.

It was the unlikeliest, most Frankenstein monster–looking, jury-rigged device that Mike Rodgers had seen in all his years of service. But that did not matter. Only one thing did.

That it worked.

SIXTY-FIVE

Washington, D.C.
Thursday, 6:21 P.M.

It was something Ron Plummer had never experienced. A moment of profound euphoria followed by a moment so sickening that the drop was physically disorienting.

When the call came from Islamabad, Ambassador Simathna listened for a moment then smiled broadly. Plummer did not have to wait for the call to be put on speakerphone to know what it was.

Mike Rodgers had succeeded. Somehow, the general had gotten the message to the Pakistani base that monitored the silo. They had forwarded the message to the Pakistani Ministry of Defense. From there, the tape was given to CNN and sent out to the world.

"My name is Nanda Kumar," said the high, scratchy voice on the recording. "I am an Indian citizen of Kashmir and a civilian network operative. For several months I have worked with India's Special Frontier Force to undermine a group of Pakistani terrorists. The Special Frontier Force told me that my actions would result in the arrest of the terrorists. Instead, the intelligence I provided allowed the Special Frontier Force to frame the Pakistanis. The terrorists have been responsible for many terrible acts. But they were not responsible for Wednesday's bomb attack on the pilgrim bus and Hindu temple in the Srinagar market. That was the work of the Special Frontier Force."

Ambassador Simathna was still beaming as he shut the phone off and leaned toward a second speakerphone. This was the open line to Paul Hood's office at Op-Center.

"Director Hood, did you hear that?" the ambassador asked.

"I did," Hood replied. "It's also running on CNN now."

"That is very gratifying," Simathna said. "I congratulate you and your General Rodgers. I do not know how he got the woman's message through but it is quite impressive."

"General Rodgers is a very impressive man," Hood agreed. "We'd like to know how he got the message through ourselves. Bob Herbert tells me that Colonel August is unable to raise him. The cell phone must have died."

"As long as it is just the cell phone," Simathna joked. "Of course, the Indians will certainly claim that Ms. Kumar was brainwashed by the Pakistanis. But General Rodgers will help to dispel that propaganda."

"General Rodgers will tell the truth, whatever that turns out to be," Hood said diplomatically.

As Hood was speaking the other phone beeped. Simathna excused himself and answered it.

The ambassador's smile trembled a moment before collapsing. His thin face lost most of its color. Ron Plummer did not dare imagine what the ambassador had just been told. Thoughts of a Pakistani nuclear strike flashed through his desperate mind.

Simathna said nothing. He just listened. After several seconds he hung up the phone and regarded Plummer. The sadness in his eyes was profound.

"Mr. Hood, I'm afraid I have bad news for you," the ambassador said.

"What kind of bad news?" Hood asked.

"Apparently, the slab on top of the silo was removed or significantly damaged during General Rodgers's actions," Simathna said.

"Don't say it," Hood warned. "Don't you frigging say it."

Simathna did not have to. They all knew what that meant.

The defensive explosives around the silo had been automatically activated. Without someone inside the silo to countermand them, they would detonate in just a few minutes.

SIXTY-SIX

Washington, D.C.
Thursday, 6:24 P.M.

Paul Hood could not believe that Mike Rodgers had gone
this far, worked whatever miracle he had conceived, only to
be blown up for something that could be prevented. But to
prevent it they would have to reach him. Though Hood, Herbert, and Coffey sat in silence, frustration under the surface
was intense. Despite the technology at their disposal, the men
were as helpless as if they were living in the Stone Age.

Hood was slumped in his leather seat. He was looking
down, humbled by this uncharacteristic sense of helplessness.
In the past there had always been another play in the book.
Someone they could call for assistance, time to move resources into position, at the very least a means of communication. Not now. And he suspected that Mike or Nanda or
the others had used up their guardian spirit quota stopping a
nuclear war. Hood did not think it would help to pray for
their salvation now. Maybe their lives and the lives of the
Strikers were the price they had to pay. Still, Hood did ask
quietly that whatever Christian, Hindu, or Muslim entities
had gotten them this far would see them a little further. Paul
Hood was not ready to lose Mike Rodgers. Not yet.

"Maybe Mike and the girl did their business and left the
area," Coffey suggested.

"It's possible," Herbert said. "Knowing Mike, though, he
would continue to broadcast for a while. They may have no
way of knowing that their message got through."

Coffey scowled.

"Even if they did leave, I'm not sure they would have gone
far enough," Herbert went on.

"What do you mean?" Coffey asked.

"It's dark, dead-of-night where they are," Herbert said. "My guess is that after all they've been through, Mike would have wanted to find a place to bunk down until well after sunrise. Let the area warm a little. If anyone was wounded, in whatever went on out there, Mike might have wanted to take time to perform first aid. The bug in the juice is we don't know exactly how much time is left before the blast. Obviously, Mike accessed the silo somehow to make the transmission. The explosives were armed when he moved the slab. That means we're well into the countdown."

"I can't believe those bastards in Pakistan can't shut the process down," Coffey said.

"I do," Herbert replied. "And I'll tell you what's happening right now. I've been thinking about this. I'll bet they put together a network of underground silos out there, all linked by tunnel. Right now the missile is automatically shifting to another site."

"You mean like an underground Scud," Coffey said.

"Exactly like that," Herbert replied. "As soon as it's out of range the silo and whoever found it go kablooey. No evidence of a missile is found among the residue. They can claim it was some kind of shelter for scientists studying the glacier, or soldiers patrolling the region, or whatever they like."

"None of which helps us get Mike out of there," Coffey said gravely.

The phone beeped as Herbert was talking. Hood picked it up. It was Stephen Viens at the National Reconnaissance Office.

"Paul, if Mike is still out in the Chittisin Plateau, we've got something on the wide-range camera he should know about," Viens said.

Hood punched on the speakerphone and sat up. "Talk to me, Stephen," he said.

"A couple of minutes ago we saw a blip moving back into the area," Viens said. "We believe it's an Indian Mi-35, possibly the same one they tangled with before. Refueled and back for another round."

While Viens had been speaking, Hood and Herbert swapped quick, hopeful looks. The men did not have to say anything. There was suddenly an option. The question was whether there was time to use it.

"Stephen, stay on the line," Hood said. "And thank you. Thank you very much."

Moving with barely controlled urgency, Herbert scooped up his wheelchair phone and speed-dialed his Indian military liaison.

Hood also did something. Inside, in private.

He speed-dialed a silent word of thanks to whoever was looking after Mike.

SIXTY-SEVEN

The Siachin Glacier
Friday, 4:00 A.M.

Rodgers was crouched behind the slab, his gun drawn as
he looked across the clearing. He had allowed the fire to die
while Nanda continued to make her broadcast. Although the
Indians had not moved on them, he did not want to give
them a target if they changed their minds. He could think of
several reasons they might.

If Nanda's message had gotten through, the soldiers certainly would have let Rodgers know by now. The Indians
would not want to risk being shot any more than he did.
Their silence seemed to indicate that either the Indians were
waiting for Rodgers to slip up or for reinforcements to arrive.
Possibly they were waiting for dawn to attack. They had the
longer-range weapons. All they needed was light to climb
the slopes and spot the targets. It could also be that the Indians were already moving on them, slowly and cautiously.
Ron Friday may have gone over to rat out their position in
exchange for sanctuary. That would not surprise Rodgers at
all. The man had given himself away when he registered no
surprise about why Fenwick had resigned. Only Hood, the
president, the vice president, the First Lady, and Fenwick's
assistant had known he was a traitor.

But Friday knew. Friday knew because he may have been
the son of a bitch's point man in Baku, Azerbaijan. For all
Rodgers knew, Friday may have had a hand in the attacks
on the CIA operatives who had been stationed there. One
way or another, Ron Friday would answer for that. Either
he'd hunt him down here or end their broadcast with a message for Hood.

With the fire gone, however, Mike Rodgers had another

concern. He had sacrificed his gloves and jacket for the cause. His hands were numb and his chest and arms were freezing. If he did not do something about that soon he would perish from hypothermia.

He took a moment to make sure that Nanda was protected from gunfire by what remained of the slab. Then he crept back to where he had left Samouel behind the ice barricade.

The Pakistani was dead.

That did not surprise Rodgers. What did surprise him was the sadness he felt upon finding the lifeless body.

There was something about Samouel that did not fit the template of an objective-blinded terrorist. In the Pakistani's final moments, while he should have been praying for Allah to accept his soul, Samouel was telling Rodgers how to splice the dish to his radio. Along with Samouel's dogged trek alongside two historic enemies, that had touched Rodgers.

Now, in death, Samouel was even responsible for saving Rodgers's life. The general felt grateful as he removed the dead man's coat and gloves. Stripping the bodies of enemies had always been a part of warfare. But soldiers did not typically take even things they needed from fallen allies. Somehow, though, this felt like a gift rather than looting.

Rodgers knelt beside the body as he dressed. As the general finished, his knees began to tickle. At first he thought it was a result of the cold. Then he realized that the ground was vibrating slightly. A moment later he heard a low, low roar.

It felt and sounded like the beginnings of an avalanche. He wondered if the explosions had weakened the slopes and they were coming down on them. If that were the case the safest place would not be at the foot of the slopes.

Rising, Rodgers ran back toward Nanda. As he did, he felt a rumbling in his gut. He had felt it before. He recognized it.

It was not an avalanche. It was worse. It was the reason the Indians had been waiting to attack.

A moment later the tops of the surrounding ice peaks were silhouetted by light rising from the north. The rumbling and roar were now distinctive beats as the Indian helicopter neared. He should have expected this. The soldiers had radioed their position to the Mi-35 that had tried to kill them earlier.

Rodgers slid to Nanda's side and knelt facing her. He felt for her cheeks in the dark and held them in his hands. He used them to guide his mouth close to her ear, so she could hear over the roar.

"I want you to try and get to the entrance while I keep the helicopter busy," Rodgers said. "It's not going to be easy getting past the soldiers but it may be your only hope."

"How do we know they'll kill us?" she asked.

"We don't," Rodgers admitted. "But let's find out by trying to escape instead of by surrendering."

"I like that," Nanda replied.

Rodgers could hear the smile in her voice.

"Start making your way around the wall behind me," he said. "With luck, the chopper will cause an avalanche on their side."

"I hope not," she replied. "They're my people."

Touché, Rodgers thought.

"But thank you," she added. "Thank you for making this fight your fight. Good luck."

The general patted her cheek and she left. He continued to watch as the chopper descended. Suddenly, the Russian bird stopped moving. It hovered above the center of the clearing, equidistant to Rodgers and the Indians. Maybe twenty seconds passed and then the chopper suddenly swept upward and to the south. It disappeared behind one of the peaks near the entrance. The glow of its lights poured through the narrow cavern.

Rodgers peeked over the slab. The chopper had landed. Maybe they were worried about causing an avalanche and had decided to deploy ground troops. That would make getting through the entrance virtually impossible. He immediately got up and ran after Nanda. He would have to pull her back, think of another strategy. Maybe negotiate something with these people to get her out. As she had said, they were her people.

But as Rodgers ran he saw something that surprised him.

Up ahead. Three of the Indian soldiers were rushing from the clearing. They were not going to attack. They were being evacuated.

What happened next surprised him even more.

"General Rodgers!" someone shouted.

Rodgers looked to the west of the entrance. Someone was standing there, half-hidden by an ice formation.

All right, Rodgers thought. He'd bite. "Yes?" the general shouted back.

"Your message got through!" said the Indian. "We must leave this place at once!"

Everything from Rodgers's legs to his spirit to his brain felt as though they had been given a shot of adrenaline. He kept running, leaping cracks and dodging mounds of ice. Either Ron Friday had gotten to him with a hell of a sell job or the man was telling the truth. Whichever it was, Rodgers was going with it. There did not seem to be another option.

Looking ahead, Rodgers watched as Nanda reached the entrance. She continued on toward the light. Rodgers arrived several moments later. The Indian soldier, a sergeant, got there at the same time he did. His rifle was slung over his back. There were no weapons in his gloved hands.

"We must hurry," the Indian said as they ran into the entrance. "This area is a Pakistani time bomb. An arsenal of some kind. You triggered the defenses somehow."

Possibly by tinkering with the uplink, Rodgers thought. Or more likely, the Pakistani military wanted to destroy them all to keep the secret of their nuclear missile silo.

"I can't believe there were just two of you," the sergeant said as they raced through the narrow tunnel. "We thought there were more."

"There were," Rodgers said. He looked at the chopper ahead. He watched as soldiers helped Nanda inside and he realized Friday had deserted them. "They're dead now."

The men left the entrance and ran the last twenty-five yards to the chopper. Rodgers and the sergeant jumped into the open door of the Mi-35. The aircraft rose quickly, simultaneously angling from the hot Pakistani base.

As the helicopter door was slid shut behind him, Rodgers

staggered toward the side of the crowded cargo compartment. There were no seats, just the outlines of cold, tired bodies. The general felt the adrenaline kick leave as his legs gave out and he dropped to the floor. He was not surprised to find Nanda already there, slumped against an ammunition crate. Rodgers slid toward her as the helicopter leveled out and sped to the north. He took her hand and snuggled beside her, the two of them propping each other up. The Indians sat around them, lighting cigarettes and blowing warmth on their hands.

The cabin temperature inside the helicopter was little higher than freezing, but the relative warmth felt blissful. Rodgers's skin crackled warmly. His eyelids shut. He could not help it. His mind started to shut down as well.

Before it did, the American felt a flash of satisfaction that Samouel had died on something that was nominally his homeland. Silo, arsenal, whatever Islamabad called it, at least it was built by Pakistanis.

As for Friday, Rodgers was also glad. Glad that the man was about to die on the opposite side of the world from the country he had betrayed.

Joy for a terrorist. Hate for an American.

Rodgers was happy to leave those thoughts for another time.

SIXTY-EIGHT

The Siachin Glacier
Friday, 4:07 A.M.

Ron Friday had been confused, at first, when he saw the chopper leave the clearing.

His plan had been simple. If Eagle Scout Rodgers had managed to come out on top of this, Friday would have told him that he had gone off to the side to watch for an Indian assault. If the Indians had won, as Friday expected, he would have said he had been trying to reach them to help end the standoff.

Friday had not expected both sides to reach some kind of sudden détente and leave together. He did not expect to be stranded on the far side of the clearing where the drumming of the chopper drowned out his shouts to the men. He did not expect to be stranded here.

But as Ron Friday watched the chopper depart he did not feel cheated or angry. He felt alone, but that was nothing new. His immediate concern was getting rest and surviving what remained of the cold night. Having done both, he could make his way back to the line of control the next day.

Where he had wanted to go in the first place.

Accomplishing that, Friday would find a way to work this to his advantage. He had still been a key participant in an operation that had prevented a nuclear incident over Kashmir. Along the way he had learned things that would be valuable to both sides.

Friday was slightly northeast of the center of the clearing when the light of the rising chopper disappeared behind the peaks. He had only seen two people join the Indians. That meant one of them, probably Samouel, was dead near the entrance to the silo. The Pakistani would no longer need his clothing. If Friday could find a little niche somewhere, he could use the clothes to set up a flap to keep out the cold. And he still had the matches. Maybe he could find something to make a little campfire. As long as life remained, there was always hope.

A moment later, in a chaotic upheaval of ice and fire, hope ended for Ron Friday.

SIXTY-NINE

The Himachal Peaks
Friday, 4:12 A.M.

Crouched against the boulders on the edge of the plateau, Brett August and William Musicant were able to see and then hear a distant explosion. It shook the ledge and threw a deep red flush against the peaks and sky to the northeast. The light reminded August of the kind of glow that emerged from a barbecue pit when you stirred the dying coals with a stick. It was a wispy, blood-colored light that was the same intensity on all sides.

August watched to see if a contrail rose from the fires. He did not see one. That meant it was not a missile being launched. The blast came from the direction in which Mike Rodgers had been headed. August hoped his old friend was behind whatever it was rather than a victim of it.

The inferno remained for a few moments and then rapidly subsided. August did not imagine that there was a great deal of combustible material out there on the glacier. He turned his stinging, tired eyes back to the valley below. Down there were the men who had killed his soldiers. Shot them from the sky without their even drawing their weapons. As much as the colonel did not want the situation to escalate, part of him wanted the Indians to charge up the peak. He ached for the chance to avenge his team.

The ice storm had stopped, though not the winds. It would take the heat of the sun to warm and divert them. The wind still swept down with punishing cold and force and a terrible sameness. The relentless whistling was the worst of it. August wondered if it were winds that inspired the legends of the Sirens. In some tales, the song of the sea nymphs drove sailors mad. August understood now how that could happen.

The colonel's hearing was so badly impaired that he did not even hear the TAC-SAT when it beeped. Fortunately, August noticed the red light flashing. He unbuttoned the collar that covered his face to the bridge of his nose. Then he turned up the volume on the TAC-SAT before answering. He would need every bit of it to hear Bob Herbert.

"Yes?" August shouted into the mouthpiece.

"Colonel, it's over," Herbert said.

"Repeat, please?" August yelled. The colonel thought he heard Herbert say this was over.

"Mike got the message through," Herbert said, louder and more articulately. "The Indian LOC troops are being recalled. You will be picked up by chopper at sunrise."

"I copy that," August said. "We saw an explosion to the northeast a minute ago. Did Mike do that?"

"In a manner of speaking," Herbert said. "We'll brief you after you've been airlifted."

"What about the Strikers?" August asked.

"We'll have to work on that," Herbert said.

"I'm not leaving without them," August said.

"Colonel, this is Paul," Hood said. "We have to determine whose jurisdiction the valley—"

"I'm not leaving without them," August repeated.

There was a long silence. "I understand," Hood replied.

"Brett, can you hold out there until around midmorning?" Herbert asked.

"I will do whatever it takes," August said.

"All right," Herbert told him. "The chopper can pick up Corporal Musicant. I promise we'll have the situation worked as quickly as possible."

"Thank you, sir," August said. "What are my orders regarding the three Pakistanis?"

"You know me," Herbert said. "Now that they've served their purpose I'd just as soon you put a bullet in each of their murderous little heads. I'm sure my wife has the road upstairs covered. She'll make sure the bus to Paradise gets turned back."

"Morality aside, there are legal and political considerations as well as the possibility of armed resistance," Hood cut in.

"Op-Center has no jurisdiction over the FKM, and India has made no official inquiries regarding the rest of the cell. They are free to do whatever they want. If the Pakistanis wish to surrender, I'm sure they will be arrested and tried by the Indians. If they turn on you, you must respond however you see fit."

"Paul's right," Herbert said. "The most important thing is to get you and Corporal Musicant home safely."

August said he understood. He told Hood and Herbert that he would accept whatever food and water the chopper brought. After that, he said he would make his way to the Mangala Valley to find the rest of the Strikers.

Hanging up the TAC-SAT, August rose slowly on cold-stiffened legs. He switched on his flashlight and made his way across the ice-covered ledge to where Musicant was stationed. August gave the medic the good news then went back to where Sharab and her two associates were huddled. Unlike the Strikers, they had not undergone cold-weather training. Nor were they dressed as warmly as August and Musicant.

August squatted beside them. They winced as the light struck them. They reminded the colonel of lepers cowering from the sun. Sharab was trembling. Her eyes were red and glazed. There was ice in her hair and eyebrows. Her lips were broken and her cheeks were bright red. August could not help but feel sorry for her. Her two comrades looked even worse. Their noses were raw and bleeding and they would probably lose their ears to frostbite. Their gloves were so thick with ice that August did not even think they could move their fingers.

Looking at them, the colonel realized that Sharab and her countrymen were not going to fight them or run anywhere. August leaned close to them.

"General Rodgers and Nanda completed their mission," August said.

Sharab was staring ahead. Her red eyes began to tear. Her exposed mouth moved silently. In prayer, August suspected. The other men hugged her arms weakly and also spoke silent words.

"An Indian helicopter will arrive at sunup," August went on. "Corporal Musicant will be leaving on it. I'm going to make my way back to the valley to find the rest of my team. What do you want to do?"

Sharab turned her tearing eyes toward August. There was deep despair in her gaze. Her voice was gravelly and tremulous when she spoke. "Will America . . . help us . . . to make the case . . . for a Pakistani Kashmir?" she asked.

"I think things will change because of what happened over the last few days," August admitted. "But I don't know what my nation will say or do."

Sharab laid an icy glove on August's forearm. "Will . . . you help us?" she pressed. "They . . . killed . . . your team."

"The madness between your countries killed my team," August said.

"No," she said. She gestured violently toward the edge of the plateau. "The men . . . down there . . . killed them. They are godless . . . evil."

This was not a discussion August wanted to have. Not with someone who blew up public buildings and peace officers for a living.

"Sharab, I've worked with you to this point," August said. "I can't do any more. There will be a trial and hearings. If you surrender, you will have the opportunity to make a strong case for your people."

"That will not . . . help," she insisted.

"It will be a start," August countered.

"And if . . . we go back . . . down the mountain?" the woman asked. "What will you do?"

"I guess I'll say good-bye," he replied.

"You won't try . . . to stop us?" Sharab pressed.

"No," August assured her. "Excuse me, now. I'm going back to join the rest of my unit."

August looked at the defiant Pakistani for a moment longer. The woman's hate and rage were burning through the cold and physical exhaustion. He had seen determined fighters during his life. The Vietcong. Kurdish resistance fighters. People who were fighting for their homes and families. But this furnace was a terrifying thing to witness.

Colonel August turned and walked back across the slippery, windswept ridge. Tribunals would be a good start. But it would take more than that to eradicate what existed between the Indians and the Pakistanis. It would take a war like the one they had barely managed to avoid. Or it would take an unparalleled and sustained international effort lasting generations.

For a sad, transient moment August shared something with Sharab.

A profound sense of despair.

SEVENTY

Washington, D.C.
Tuesday, 7:10 A.M.

Paul Hood sat alone in his office. He was looking at his computer, reviewing the comments he planned to make at the ten A.M. Striker memorial.

As promised, Herbert had persuaded the Indians to bring choppers from the line of control to collect the bodies of the Strikers. The leverage he used was simple. The Pakistanis agreed to stay out of the region, even though they claimed the valley for their own. Herbert convinced New Delhi that it would be a bad idea for Pakistanis to collect the bodies of Americans who had been killed by Indians. It would have made a political statement that neither India nor the United States wished to make.

Colonel August was in the valley to meet the two Mi-35s when they arrived late Friday afternoon. The bodies had already been collected and lined up beneath their canopies. August stayed with the bodies until they had been flown back to Quantico on Sunday. Then and only then did the colonel agree to go to a hospital. Mike Rodgers was there to meet him.

Hood and Rodgers had performed too many of these services since Op-Center had first been chartered. Mike Rodgers inevitably spoke eloquently of duty and soldiering. Heroism and tradition. Hood always tried to find a perspective in which to place the sacrifice. The salvation of a country, the saving of lives, or the prevention of war. The men invariably left the mourners feeling hope instead of futility, pride to temper the sense of loss.

But this was different. More than the lives of the Strikers was being memorialized today.

New Delhi had publicly thanked Op-Center for uncovering a Pakistani cell. The bodies of three terrorists had been found at the foot of the Himachal Peaks in the Himalayas. They appeared to have slipped from a ledge and plummeted to their deaths. They were identified by records on file at the offices of the Special Frontier Force.

Islamabad had also publicly thanked Op-Center for helping deter a nuclear strike against Pakistan. Though Indian Defense Minister John Kabir had been named by Major Dev Puri and others as the man behind the plot, Kabir denied the allegations. He vowed to fight any indictments the government might consider handing down. Hood suspected that the minister and others would resign, and that would be the end of it. New Delhi would rather bury the reality of any wrongdoing than give Pakistan a more credible voice in the court of world opinion.

Hood even got a thank-you call from Nanda Kumar. The young woman called from New Delhi to say that General Rodgers had been a hero and a gentleman. Although he had not been able to save her grandfather, she realized that Rodgers had done everything he could to make the trek easier for him. She said she hoped to visit Hood and Rodgers in Washington when she got out of the hospital. Even though she was technically an Indian intelligence operative, Hood had no doubt that she would get a visa. Nanda's broadcast had made her an international celebrity. She would spend the rest of her life speaking and writing about her experience. Hood hoped that the twenty-two-year-old was wise beyond her years. He hoped she would use the media access to promote tolerance and peace in Kashmir, and not the agendas of India or Nanda Kumar.

The praise from abroad was unique. Even when Op-Center succeeded in averting disaster, Hood and his team were typically slammed for their involvement in the internal affairs of another nation—Spain or the Koreas or the Middle East or anywhere else they handled a crisis.

Despite the praise coming from abroad, Op-Center took several unprecedented hits on the home front. Most of those came from Hank Lewis and the Congressional Intelligence

Oversight Committee. They wanted to know why General Rodgers had left the Siachin Glacier without Ron Friday. Why Striker had jumped into a military hot zone during the day instead of at night. Why the NRO was involved in the operation but not the CIA or the full resources of the NSA, which had an operative on-site. Hood and Rodgers had gone over to Capitol Hill to explain everything to Lewis and to Fox and her fellow CIOC members.

They might just as well have been speaking Urdu. The CIOC had already decided that in addition to the previously discussed downsizing, Op-Center would no longer be maintaining a military wing. Striker would be officially disbanded. Colonel August and Corporal Musicant would be reassigned and General Rodgers's role would be "reevaluated."

Hood was also informed that he would be filing daily rather than semiweekly reports with CIOC. They wanted to know everything that the agency was involved with, from situation analyses to photographic reconnaissance.

Hood suspected the only thing that protected Op-Center at all was the loyalty of the president of the United States. President Lawrence and United Nations Secretary-General Mala Chatterjee had issued a joint statement congratulating Paul Hood for his group's nonpartisan efforts on behalf of humanitarianism and world peace. It was not a document the CIOC could ignore, especially after Chatterjee's bitter denunciation of the way Hood had handled the Security Council crisis. Hood could not imagine the kind of pressure Lawrence must have applied to get that statement. He also wondered how Chatterjee really felt. She was a pacifistic Indian whose nation had tried to start a nuclear war against its neighbor. Unless she was steeped in denial, that had to be difficult for her to reconcile. Hood would not be surprised to hear that she was resigning her post to run for political office at home. That would certainly be a good step toward peace in the region.

All of which served to make this a very different time, a very different memorial service. It was the last time Paul Hood and the original Op-Center would do anything as teammates. The rest of them would not know that yet.

But Paul Hood would. He wanted to say something that addressed a new loss they would all soon be feeling.

He reread the opening line of his testimonial.

"This is the second family I have lost in as many months . . ."

He deleted it. The statement was too much about him. Too much about his loss.

But it did start him thinking. Although he was no longer living with Sharon and the kids, he still felt as though they were together in some way. If not physically then spiritually.

And then it came to him. Hood knew the line was right because it caught in his throat as he tried to say it.

Hood typed with two trembling index fingers as he tried to see the computer monitor. It was blurry because he was blinking out tears over what was supposed to be just a job.

"This I have learned," he wrote with confidence. "Wherever fate takes any of us, we will always be family. . . ."

Samouel nodded. The Pakistani pulled Nanda away from the ice and bundled her in his arms. Crouching as low as possible, Samouel ran toward Rodgers. The general rose and fired several rounds at the Indians. But as the light of the flares began to fade, and the last streaming embers fell to earth, the soldiers stopped shooting. Obviously, they wanted to conserve both their flares and their ammunition. Though Rodgers kept his automatic trained on the entrance there was no further exchange of gunfire. The ice walls kept even the wind outside. An eerie stillness settled on the enclosure. There was only the crunch of Samouel's boots on the ice and a deep, deep freeze that caused the exposed flesh around Rodgers's eyes to burn.

Samouel and Nanda reached the ice boulder. The Pakistani slid to his knees beside Rodgers. He was breathing heavily as he sat Nanda with her back to the ice. The young woman was no longer in the near-catatonic state she had been in earlier. Her eyes were red and tearing, though Rodgers did not know whether it was from sadness or the cold. Still, they were moving from side to side and she seemed to be registering some awareness of her surroundings.

Samouel moved toward Rodgers. "General, I saw something when the flares went off," Samouel panted.

"What did you see?" Rodgers asked.

"It was directly behind the place where you and Mr. Friday were," the Pakistani said. "On one of the lower ledges of the slopes, about nine or ten feet up. It looked like a satellite dish."

An uplink, Rodgers thought. Of course.

"Maybe that has something to do with why we were sent to this place," Samouel continued.

"I'm pretty sure it does," Rodgers said. "Was the dish out in the open?"

"Not really," Samouel said. "It was set back, in a little cave. About five or six feet it seemed." The Pakistani shook his head. He sighed. "I can't say for sure that it was a dish. There was white lattice, but it could have been icicles and a trick of the light."

"Would the site have been visible from the air?" Rodgers asked.

"Not from directly overhead," Samouel told him.

Rodgers glanced back. It was too dark to see the ice wall now. But what Samouel just said made sense. If there were a video setup somewhere inside the Pakistani missile silo, then there had to be an uplink somewhere on the outside. The dish or antenna did not have to be on the top of a peak. All the dish needed was an unobstructed view of one area in the sky. A single spot where a communications satellite, possibly Russian or Chinese built-and-launched, was in geosynchronous orbit. The cables connecting the relay to the silo would probably be relatively deep inside the ice wall. Whoever designed an uplink for this area would not want the wiring too close to the surface. Melting ice might expose the cables to wind, sleet, or other corrosive forces, not to mention leaving it visible to passing recon aircraft.

"Tell me something, Samouel," Rodgers said. "You wired some of the bombs and remote detonators for Sharab, didn't you?"

"Yes," Samouel said softly.

"Do you have experience with radios?" Rodgers asked.

"I have worked with all kinds of electronics," the Pakistani told him. "I did repair work for the Islamabad militia and—"

"On handsets too?" Rodgers interrupted.

"Walkie-talkies?" Samouel asked.

"Not just walkie-talkies," Rodgers said. He stopped for a moment to gather his thoughts. His questions and plans were racing ahead of the answers. "What I mean is this. If there is a satellite dish on the ledge would you be able to hook a cell phone to it?"

"I see," Samouel replied. "Is it a government cell phone with safeguards of any kind?"

"I don't think so," Rodgers said.

"Then I can probably rig something as long as you can expose the satellite cable," Samouel told him.

"What kind of tools would you need?" Rodgers asked.

"Not more than my pocket knife, I would imagine," Samouel said.